D0209635

HOUSE OF STONE

HOUSE OF STONE

A NOVEL

NOVUYO ROSA TSHUMA

W. W. Norton & Company
Independent Publishers Since 1923
New York • London

House of Stone is a work of fiction. With the exception of some well-known historical and public figures, all of the characters are products of the author's imagination and are not to be construed as real. Where actual historical or pubic figures appear, the situations, incidents, and dialogues concerning those persons have been invented by the author. In all other respects, any resemblance to persons living or dead is entirely coincidental.

First American Edition 2019

Printed in the United States of America

For information about permission to reproduce selections from this book, write to Permissions, W. W. Norton & Company, Inc., 500 Fifth Avenue, New York, NY 10110

For information about special discounts for bulk purchases, please contact W. W. Norton Special Sales at specialsales@wwnorton.com or 800-233-4830

Manufacturing by LSC Communications, Harrisonburg

ISBN 978-0-393-63542-3

W. W. Norton & Company, Inc.
500 Fifth Avenue, New York, N.Y. 10110
www.wwnorton.com

W. W. Norton & Company Ltd.
15 Carlisle Street, London W1D 3BS

1 2 3 4 5 6 7 8 9 0

For T. D.

CONTENTS

PROLOGUE

I am a man on a mission. A vocation, call it, to remake the past, and a wish to fashion all that has been into being and becoming. It all started when my surrogate father, Abednego Mlambo, sought me out in my lodgings two days ago with a bottle of Bell's in one hand and two crystal glasses pressed to his chest. He was dressed in a pair of his faded, beige don't-touch-my-ankles trousers that give him the look of a civil servant, complete with a matching shirt.

He held the crystal glasses in place with his chin, one balanced atop the other, the bottom glass clasped between the thumb and forefinger of the hand clutching the Bell's, the top glass muzzling his mouth, so that his voice reached me as though a daydream, as he said, raising his free hand and slapping my back, that he appreciated how I had taken his son Bukhosi under my wing, playing big brother, and that I was like a son to him and he would, from then on, call me his surrogate son.

It would have been perfect, and may even have made me cry, for no man ever claimed me as his son, had Abednego not beaten me to it, his sagging yellow face suddenly mugged by sadness as he began to shed tears for that Bukhosi, like he has been doing ever since the boy went missing. If only he knew how the boy once made the eerie confession that he wished it was I who was his father and not he, Abednego, never mind that I'm only twenty-four and Bukhosi had just turned seventeen.

He's been missing for over a week, since the beginning of October. Yes, I must say it again to believe it, it's already beginning to feel to me as though the boy never existed at all: *Bukhosi is missing.* BUKHOSI IS MISSING. Bukhosi is missing. Abednego sat down heavily on my little put-me-up bed, still clutching the whisky and the glasses, and snottily apologized for crying. I watched his tears drip-dripping into the crystal glass, like our taps on the days when the municipal doesn't cut off the water supply, and tried to cluck sympathetically. He confessed that it pained him to say the boy's name out loud, to look up as though at any moment he would hear his heavy steps thudding on Mama Agnes's polished cement floor and see his plump, walnut face peeping around the living room door.

I wanted to reach out and hold him, but we had never shared such moments, him and I. I had seen him lean into Mama Agnes's embraces, inhaling the scent of her perfumed bosom as she hugged him in greeting when he arrived home from those long hours at the Butnam Rubber Factory. I had also caught him and Bukhosi once, locked in an uncomfortable grip, something almost like a hug, but not quite, for their faces were held apart even as they squeezed each other's shoulders.

'We'll find him,' I said, relieving him of the glasses but not the whisky, which he clutched possessively. 'I'm here for you.'

'Bukhosi,' he muttered again, wincing as he said it, speaking it out loud in the same way God bespake Adam into existence, croaking *Bukhosi* and therefore he was; except he wasn't. And me, I winced because I suspected he may never be found, for I was there with him when he disappeared – we were chanting side by side at the rally held by the Mthwakazi Secessionist Movement only nine days ago, on Sunday 7 October, in Stanley Square. The flame-lilies were raging, the sunflowers sashaying and our secessionist leader Dumo spraying us with his saliva as he frothed up a call to arms, to secession, to revolution, to freedom!

'Secede from the country Zimbabwe,' he cried. 'Secede!'

'Secede!' echoed our fevered chorus.

'For our brothers killed in the '80s in the Gukurahundi Genocide!' he cried. 'Secede!'

'Secede!' we echoed.

'Secede from tyranny!'

'Secede!'

While we were thrusting peaceful fists of revolt in the air, the riot police thrust themselves on our gathering, gathering those of us who could not run fast enough into the backs of their police vans. And that was the last time I saw Bukhosi and that's when he went missing.

What would Dumo say to me now? *Speak Truth to Death or Live a Dead Lie!* I never understood half of what Dumo said, but he had an uncanny knack of somehow hitting your heart, regardless. Dumo, who tried to be my mentor and, more importantly, nursed my grief after my Uncle Fani's death, a grief that turned me delirious for a time; Dumo who, even so, never tired of lambasting me, telling me I was useless as a revolutionary protégé, lacking the kind of recklessness necessary to resurrect insurrection.

But what does it matter what he would say to me now? I'm the one who's survived and he's the one who's disappeared, thanks to those mad man antics of his. Poof! Like a spoko. He too was gobbled up by one of those police vans the day of the Mthwakazi rally, and has not been regurgitated since.

Like Bukhosi, I doubt I'll ever see Dumo again. It was he who taught me that a man could remake himself by remaking his past. So, when Abednego said I was like a son to him and that he would, from then on, call me his surrogate son, I felt a swell of pride and the prick of opportunity. Perhaps, as my surrogate father's son, I can be blessed with some familial affection and, in this way, finally powder away the horrors of my own murky hi-story bequeathed to me by parents I never knew.

I have begun calling him, jokingly but in all seriousness, surrogate father. And let this surrogacy business fool no one, I intend to be as close to the Mlambos as any real son would be, bound, happily, by the Bantu philosophy of ubuntu, that communal pedigree. And even though I'm just a lodger in the pygmy room they have squeezed into their backyard so as to rent out in these trying times, only the narrow corridor of a dirt path separates me from their back door; even though I'm just their lodger, we already have a shared history, the Mlambos and I, for though they don't know it, I grew up in this house, it belonged to my dearly departed Uncle Fani.

Perhaps, despite his incessant worrying over Bukhosi, Abednego really is beginning to think of me, too, as his son. Why else did he then wipe his eyes, set his shoulders and proceed to pour us both generous portions of Bell's in the crystal glasses? And why, in spite of the fact that I knew that he's a recovering alcoholic who's been sober for five years straight, since 2002, and even has a five year AA Bronze Medallion to prove it, did I indulge him and drink the Bell's? Perhaps it was because of my eagerness to consolidate this new claim to sonhood. He quaffed his Bell's much faster than I mine, topping himself up often and liberally, until he was drunk blind and chatty proper, and then began chittering at length about his past. I did, then, what I understood he was asking me to do; I began to chronicle the family hi-story he was entrusting me with, like any good son would.

Our conversations, which started two days ago, are more in the way of one-sided confessions and always in the pleasant company of whisky – which I've started supplying since, without it, my surrogate father is rendered a grumpy mute – and take place in between our community searches for Bukhosi. We sit more often than not in Mama Agnes's living room, just he and I, he slumped in his sofa, I administering the Bell's. It takes him a while to get to the meat of the matter – he does have a tendency to go on and on about the boy. Mama Agnes, thankfully, is always away during the day and, sadly, late into the night, these days, either at work on the other side of town in the leafy Suburbs at Grahams Girls' High where she teaches English, or at her church Blessed Anointings where she goes every day to beg, bully and bootlick the Holy Ghost into revealing the whereabouts of her Bukhosi, so far to no avail. My surrogate father has given himself indefinite leave from his work at the Butnam Rubber Factory, until his son is found, he says.

These intimacies that my surrogate father has begun sharing with me are what Bukhosi always wanted from him. The boy badgered our father about the family hi-story. 'Baba,' he would ask, at first timidly, for he anticipated the rage such questions caused Abednego, who was never stingy with the belt. 'Baba,' although not even the prospect of the belt deterred him. 'I want to know, Baba,' so strong was this desire, so brilliantly did it flicker in his emerald eyes. 'How did you grow up…?' Shimmering like a thing hungry and searing and lost. 'Where were you during… what was…' Growing ever more defiant after I introduced him to Dumo, who took him under his wing, like he had tried to do for me, feeding the boy's hunger to know the past. 'I *need* to know, you *have* to tell me…' His seventeen-year-old voice booming with a dangerous bass, suddenly mature in its insolence, different from his usual brattishness. 'I demand to know what happened during Gukurahundi!'

What anguish this caused our father! I noticed how his hands trembled, how it wasn't anger that made his mouth froth and sputter but something more substantial, making the sweat break out across his forehead. And though he beat the boy, it wasn't really the boy he wanted to beat, but, it seemed to me, himself…

The boy didn't know when and how to push, didn't know how to cultivate the kind of rapport a son needs to have with his father. But I've been watching, I've been paying attention, and I know how to be around a man when he's down. There's a certain silence that's soothing, and the way to do it, I've discovered, is to act as though what has just happened, the flimsy beating and ineffectual yelling and the tremors, is nothing. To change neither tone nor body language. And I did this well; if I was reading the paper when a beating happened, I would continue to read the paper. I only sort of interfered when Mama Agnes was home, for she would rush to the scene, yelling for Abednego to stoppit as she tried to leap between him and the boy. Here, I would jump up and dither behind them, as though I were doing something useful. And afterwards, I would make Mama Agnes a cup of Tanganda tea, steeped for five minutes in boiling water, with a dash of lemon, just the way she likes it.

The only thing I ever ventured to say to Abednego, just once after one of his altercations with the boy, was, 'Were I your son, I would never speak to you like that.' I made sure not to look at him as I said this, to keep my eyes glued to the TV, which I had been watching when the whole thing happened, so that it was as if what I was saying was really nothing. And right afterwards, I turned up the volume and laughed along to whatever show was on, though I don't remember much about it now, I wasn't paying attention. I could feel Abednego's eyes on me, and my heart was loud in my chest. I feared I had pushed too hard, that I shouldn't have said anything, and that by speaking about it, I had angered him where I meant to soothe. But he didn't rebuke me; he didn't say a thing. Instead, that evening, after the electricity had abruptly cut out, as it usually does nowadays, he invited me to sit with him around the fire in the backyard, where Mama Agnes was making supper, and play a game of draughts.

To hear him call me 'son', even if 'surrogate son', when he sought me out two days ago in my lodgings, was the sweet fruit of a long labour. But never would I have thought my surrogate father would not only call me 'son', but bring me into the intimacies a father shares with his son – the family hi-story. Perhaps, had my surrogate brother Bukhosi understood our father and known how to talk to him, he, too, would have been brought into the intimacies of our family hi-story, and gained the solid footing he so desperately needed, but because of the lack of which he became lost, and because of the possession of which I am now found. Lost and found! *Lost and found.*

BOOK ONE

OF FATHERS AND GRANDFATHERS

A man of consciousness, gifted with a mind and a blank screen and a keyboard such as I have, makes his own hi-story proper. There is no better way of gaining possession of yourself than chewing the bones of the mind over the question, *Who am I?* And who you are starts with a robust family lineage in which to cultivate your roots. A man has to be able to trace the details of his family hi-story at least two lineages down, to his grandfather. Otherwise, he can't really claim to be standing on solid ground. You have to be able to point to a man and say, 'That's my grandfather.' Or make do with a sepia-tinted photo, at least, chewed at the edges by the affectionate teeth of time.

As my surrogate father has neither glossy photo nor the confidence to point and say, 'That's my grandfather,' I have been left with the task of resolving the matter of our family lineage. And it hasn't been easy, this. For, one moment, while ensconced in the toasty Bell's, Abednego claims that his father was the man he grew up calling 'Baba', husband to my surrogate grandma, that treacherously demure woman who was in her heyday such a blot-out-sun, so blinding was her beauty. And then, the next moment, having become much too heated from the Scotch whisky, he makes rather dubious assertions that his real father is a certain James Thornton, once-upon-a-time owner of that Thornton Farm whose lush harvests salivated many a tongue in the adjoining Tribal Trust Lands where young Abednego grew up, relegated to live there by the state during the time of racial segregation, back when Zimbabwe was still Rhodesia.

When he blubbered this in my lodgings two days ago, I wrinkled my nose and raised an eyebrow. Frowning, he pulled up his shirt sleeve and thrust his arm in my face, prodding the flesh. His inner forearm, which doesn't get much sun, is closer to cream than yellow, and the hairs are a pale gold rather than a deep brown.

As though sensing still my scepticism, he launched into a dramatic monologue of the day the farmer attempted to lay claim to what, by blood and sperm, was allegedly his. Baba was sitting outside his hut in the shade of the mopane tree on the morning in question, cleaning his FAL rifle and decked in his full Rhodesian African Rifles army apparel – a bush-green shirt tucked into pleated shorts, woollen hose tops, black stick boots and a slouch hat – busy bobbing his head solemnly to my (surrogate) Uncle Zacchaeus as he read verses from the bible, in an English that the old man understood and extolled but did not himself know how to read, when Farmer Thornton came wheezing over the hill of the north-east, from the direction of his farm, telephone cord in trembling hand, dust simmering about his sandalled feet. My surrogate father Abednego, who had been crouching behind the kraals some hundred paces from the mopane tree, listening to Zacchaeus read and trying rather unsuccessfully to mimic his brother's fanciful pronunciations, straightened up and gawked at the farmer.

'Give me the boy!' cried Farmer Thornton, gesticulating towards Abednego and lambasting Baba for not looking after him right, for sending the little munt Zacchaeus to school and not my surrogate father.

My surrogate father began to squirm, his yellow face ripening at the farmer's outburst. He'd never thought, in all his nineteen years, that *he* could go to school. Zacchaeus was the special one, the younger son and yet the cimbi of Baba's heart, and although something bilic used to brew inside him during those first days when he would watch his younger brother being shaken awake every morning to go to the sole school for Africans in the district some thirteen kilometres away, this bile had since settled in its rightful place in his gallbladder.

The farmer's outburst made him feel all funny inside. He knew and had always taken secret delight in the fact that the farmer had always had a thing for him. Everybody knew, Baba, mama and even Zacchaeus whose buttocks the farmer always thrashed with a telephone cord whenever he caught them stealing crops in his fields. But this impassioned outburst, now, that was another thing altogether, bound to find the ears of the wind and be carried for an entire jealous village to hear. And so he squirmed, my surrogate father, and scowled and made all sorts of ugly faces, all the while secretly savouring the farmer's words.

Baba raised his rifle until it was trained on Farmer Thornton. 'Get away from here, mani, you fucking civvy!'

'You dare to shoot me? You dare to shoot me, you munt, you dare to shoot a Rhodie?'

'A Rhodie? You want to prattle to me about being a *Rhodie*? I was a Second Lieutenant in the Royal Rhodesian African Rifles, damm*it*, I served under Colonel J. F. Clayton and His Majesty Colonel-in-Chief King George VI, I fought alongside your *superiors* in Burma, the well-tempered Brits, bless their hearts, I killed men worthier of life than you, you *Rhodie*, and I will shoot you right here right now for nuisance behaviour in the presence of army personnel!'

Out of the corner of his eye, to his right, my surrogate father caught sight of his mama thrusting her head out of the kitchen hut, and then, upon seeing Baba and Farmer Thornton and the gun, she snatched it back in.

'Step back, civilian! I'm warning you!' yelled Baba.

'Just give me the boy!'

Baba spat and cocked his rifle.

Off ran Farmer Thornton, back to his farm that flanked the Tribal Trust Lands, his red dungarees stopping just short of his ankles, making him look like a ragamuffin fleeing the scene of a crime.

Later that night in my pygmy room, I clickety-clacked on my MacBook and Googled this James Thornton. I found his blog, RHODESIANS NEVER DIE, which, along with a host of memories, patriotic ballads and tchotchkes of days gone by, plus the key words 'Rhodesia', 'Prime Minister Ian Smith', 'platoon', 'munts', 'gooks', 'G. A. Henry' and 'terrs', sports sixteen thousand email subscribers and an average of fifty thousand unique visitors each month.

I was surprised to see that my surrogate father and the farmer share a distinctive pair of wide, flared nostrils shaped like inverted teardrops, which seems to rather settle the question of fatherhood, even though immediately after recounting the Battle of the Fathers, Abednego had suddenly and vehemently declared to me that he was no son of a settler, that the old farmer was senile, that he had received his yellow skin from his mama's side, passed down through the genes by an Indo-Caucasian great-great-great-great-grandma.

He's going to have to come to terms with it all, sooner or later. Patrilineage is, after all, the well from which a man's identity springs; we are our fathers' sons, inheriting traits, mannerisms, talents and penchants. What delight to know your roots! To be firmly rooted. To look into a face and see in it something of your own. To notice a familiar tic. To come into knowing of your father's fathers and their fathers before them.

What would his life have been like had he known, from the very beginning, his true ancestry? I wonder what my life would have been like, had I grown up knowing my father. There are terrible rumours, but no, this man who my Uncle Fani named, five years ago on his deathbed, has so much darkness in him, and me, haven't I always leaned towards radiance? Besides, he was delirious, Uncle Fani; who is to trust the piffle of a dying man? But what would it have been like, to grow up knowing my forebears? What would it have been like for my surrogate father, had he grown up knowing his forebears? Would he have grown up roaming not the gecko-studded mud huts of his Baba's compound but the dapperwood halls of that two-storey Thornton Farmhouse, his yellow skin made prickly by the disapproving glares from the framed photographs of his forefathers – the farmer's temerarious grandpapa William Thornton Senior, slayer of natives and founding father of the Colony of Southern Rhodesia, and his equally valiant papa Captain William Thornton Junior, slayer of both natives and Germans in World War One under the flag of His then Majesty King George V – God Save the King!

These lives of our ancestors are chronicled on Farmer Thornton's blog, which, given the farmer's declared ambitions of attracting a large enough following to turn his Life and Times into a TV series, offers an embarrassingly uncensored hi-story of our patrilineage, the Thorntons.

This blood and sperm business started when the farmer lost his young Sonny Boy, killed in March of '74 when those bantu terrorists puppeteered by World Communist Elements ambushed his regiment's truck near the Rhodesian army camp at Fort Hare – the farmer's words as per his blog, not mine! He was twenty-two and the only heir to the Thornton dynasty. Or maybe not. Though there aren't outright confessions of Abednego as the bastard son from the farmer on his blog, I did find, amidst raunchy recollections of gyrating to the rhythm of cocoa-coloured hips in his younger days, a hangdog confession of 'an ebony belle whose tsako made his heart lollop'. Can it just be coincidence that the pictures I've seen of my surrogate grandmother show a woman whose broad grin is split with a perfect gap between her two front teeth?

Said belle was the cause of his fall-out with his Ennis (Mrs Thornton) who threatened to leave him, foul-mouthed with fury, using words she never used, like *Fassyhole* and *Quashie*, until the farmer asked her if she'd been hanging around a Mrs Willoughby again. Ennis's threats must have won the day, because there is little much else said about this ebony belle in the pages of his blog. Instead, these amorous accounts give way to the farmer's rants against Her Majesty's government for betraying his beloved Rhodesia.

These rants are very lengthy, at times talking about Rhodesia as though the past were present, cursing the 'Mother Country and her cronies for selling the whites down the river', at other times devolving into fantasies of a twenty-first-century Rhodesia that has been reinstated to its former glory... 'Make Rhodesia Great Again!' These diatribes bring him a surprising number of views for each of his posts, but none so much as the one that went viral about how he found his Ennis lying on the floor one day in the '80s, during the time of the Gukurahundi Genocide, having been raped and strangled by the dissidents. I cried when I read about Mrs Thornton's brutal murder. She would have been my step-grandma, my surrogate-surrogate grandma. Reading the farmer's reminiscences, I felt that I'd lost my very own flesh and blood – my very own grandma!

Yesterday, Abednego asked me, for the umpteenth time, where it is I think 'he' could have gone.

I could feel something hot and crusty rising in my chest. 'Who?'

His shoulders fell. 'No, wena. Don't do that. You know who.'

I leaned over and tipped the bottle of Bell's into his glass. I needed him to stay focused. I wanted to find out what happened after Farmer Thornton had tried to claim him as his son. 'You were telling me about being sent to Bulawayo, after your Baba sent the farmer packing?'

He just sat there, blinking at the damn glass. 'I was going to take him to watch soccer that Sunday, you know. Highlanders was playing at Barbourfields Stadium. I had thought… He was behaving strangely, did you notice?'

'What was it that made Baba suddenly decide to send you and not Zacchaeus to—'

'The other day, he raised his voice to his mother. It was like a fist, the force of it, and I saw how she flinched—'

'—why did Baba send you to Bulawayo?'

'Maybe he spoke to you, did he tell you anything? About where he was going?'

I sighed.

'Did he tell you anything?'

'He didn't.'

'You don't have even one idea, nje, where he might have gone?'

'... hmm hmm.'

'What?'

'I said, I have no idea where he went.'

'But you'll come with me tomorrow morning to look, isn't it?'

'OK.'

'He liked you... Likes. He *likes* you... I always tried to be a good father. He knew that, didn't he? Knows. He *knows*.'

How creased his yellow face became! It flitted between an inward, mustard despair and a jaundiced hope that radiated outward, towards me, enveloping me, filling the room, filtering between the burglar bars of the living room windows and out into the Monday afternoon. I was suddenly overwhelmed by the urge to lean over and squeeze his arm. Instead, I fisted my hands and tucked them beneath my armpits. 'Yes, of course, he knew you loved him.' I could have told him what the boy had really thought of him; but is there a point in crushing a man with the truth? 'He always told me how he loved you.'

A light glinted in his eyes.

'Don't worry!' I said. 'We'll find him!'

He seemed to consider this. 'You think so?'

'Certain hundred per cent!'

I am, of course, certain of nothing. But what does it hurt to give a man a little hope? He is, like me, floating, my surrogate father. He, like me, never managed to get close to his Baba. Like him and Bukhosi, him and his Baba had a rather tenuous relationship. He and Uncle Zacchaeus were born after their Baba's abrupt return from his service in the Second World War, where he had fought on behalf of the Mother Country under the Rhodesian African Rifles, serving for four and a half years. For four and a half years, Abednego's mama was a fresh, young, supple bride without her husband to cultivate her. No wonder she and that Farmer Thornton… And then, he returned to her an old-young man, my surrogate-surrogate grandfather, with voices in his head. This version of the old man, with his voices, is all my surrogate father knew of him, although he remembers his mama relating wistfully another Baba only she had known, a charming young man with wild ambitions of one day acquiring enough education to become someone important, like a teacher or even a lawyer, forced by the times to work as a labourer in the Tsholotsho Mines, a job that began to kill his dreams piece by piece… And then, like most young men at the time, he had, taken over by the querulous passions of youth, run off after the romance of war, that unbearably seductive mistress who promises the kind of ecstasy young men dream of in their sleep, wetting them with excitement.

His discharge papers, according to Uncle Zacchaeus, who'd started snooping around the souvenirs decorating the old man's hut ever since he'd learned how to read, said, *Reason for Discharge: Severe Stress Response Syndrome. Recommendation: No longer fit for service.*

Abednego was nineteen when his Baba sent him off to Bulawayo, in April '74, just a month after the death of Farmer Thornton's Sonny Boy and, I'm guessing, about the same time that the farmer would have visited the Mlambo homestead.

I tried one more time to get him to speak. 'Come on. Let's talk about other things. Tell me, why did Baba send you to the city?' I already knew, of course. I can imagine how angry Baba would have been when Farmer Thornton marched in demanding his progeny back. It's easy to pretend that some things aren't true until some loudmouth speaks them into being and makes them concrete. And once out of the mouth, a secret cannot be taken back. It hovers in the air and becomes pregnant from all that potent silence, birthing, inevitably, a new course for a life.

Abednego turned the tumbler of whisky and then drained it. As if the alcohol oiled his voicebox, he settled back into his chair, and finally resumed his story.

'Atte-nnn-*tion*!'

He had been summoned to the old man's hut. He raised his hand in a reflexive salute.

'Right, soldier, get on the floor and give me fifty!'

'Sir, yessir!' he said, and lowered himself to the dung-and-mud floor, where he began to huff and puff out fifty press-ups. Baba began pacing the length of the hut, his boots making muffled thumps that Abednego could feel vibrating through his palms.

'The enemy is upon us, soldier,' Abednego heard him say, his voice rising and falling with his pacing. 'I'd say we attack, but a tactical retreat would be the wiser thing to do, for now.'

'Whatever you think is best, sir!'

'Don't interrupt your Lieutenant, soldier, I'm doing some thinking.'

'Sorrysir!'

'I'd say we withdraw further south. Tsholotsho's probably too close, and too small, hardly a hamlet, they'll find us there. Hmmm, what to do…'

'… twenty-two, twenty-three, twenty-four…'

'… I'd say Bulawayo's the place.'

Abednego stumbled and flopped. 'Did you say Bulawayo, Baba?'

He could scarcely believe what Baba seemed to be saying – he, and not Zacchaeus, was going to experience big-city living!

Zacchaeus whose eye, at sixteen, had already taken on the sheen of arrogance as it cast itself across the rocky, scraggly Tribal Trust Lands to see not sand and scrub but faraway places, big-city living in Bulawayo.

'I shall forage towns and cities, brother, and even whole countries, for worldly wisdom,' his younger brother had taken to declaring of late during such moments of haughty-eye-roving. 'I shall fashion myself into a Great Colonizer, a Cecil John Rhodes, a David Livingstone, a Christopher Columbus. I'm destined for great things! Everyone sees it in me. Say, what do they say about you, brother?'

And so there he was, my surrogate father, having been in the city of Bulawayo for four days, failing still to name one auspicious thing anyone in his village had ever said about him. He was standing outside the Rhodesia Railway Station, carrying an application for the position of train driver, which he'd happened upon in the classifieds of the *Bantu Terrorists: Rhodesia's Communist Threat* newspaper sheet he had in hand, ogling the station's red-brick facade and its tusk-coloured entablatures, and squinting horribly, so as to better see, through the mist of his humble roving eye, the blurry visions of the towns cities and countries he intended to forage, and the foggy self-fashioning into a Great Colonizer a Cecil John Rhodes a David Livingstone a Christopher Columbus, when he saw, flickering past, neither flash nor vision, but Thandi, a distraction he would otherwise have ignored were it not for the fact that his manhood reared to attention, like a flag suddenly thrust at full mast.

'Thandi?' I asked, desperately intrigued.

'Shut up, mani, I'm talking,' he barked back.

Thandi. She was walking down Customs Avenue, glistering umber limbs swaying one-two one-two, as though to a song, breasts bounce-bouncing and buttocks jounce-jouncing to the same tempo.

All at once, the railway was forgotten; the city could be foraged for wisdom another day; said manhood was busy conducting public misdemeanor; and before he knew what he was doing, he was following her.

THANDI

It felt good to accompany Abednego and the neighbourhood committee in search of the boy today. Honestly, I didn't want to go, but the way Abednego warmed up to me after I offered to print out posters of Bukhosi's blunt face to plaster all over our Luveve Township made it all worth it. He slapped me on my back, and said, 'Yebo yes, boy!' His hand lingered there, warm and solid, and I leaned into him slightly; I could smell Bukhosi's Lifebuoy soap on him.

After the community search, which consisted of going door to door asking after the boy, and pasting up his posters, my surrogate father invited me to share a beer with him at the shebeen. My heart lolloped at the thought that it would be just us two, but then he also invited the other men from the township who had accompanied us on our search. And though I sat next to him, and tried to laugh louder than the other men at his jokes, which weren't all that funny, he didn't once look my way. It was as if I wasn't there. I can't stand him when he gets like that. Eventually, I slipped away, and took a khombi into town; I just couldn't stand feeling as though I was back to just being his lodger again.

I found myself retracing the steps across the city my surrogate father took when he followed the young woman, Thandi, from the railway station all those years ago.

Yes, he followed her. What else could he do but follow her?

(I felt strange, having to look up the old, colonial names of the streets back in Thandi's time when Zimbabwe was still Rhodesia. It was like I had been transported to another Bulawayo on another Earth in another multiverse. I found myself pussyfooting on those colonial streets of the past, as I'm sure my surrogate father had, too.)

She hurried down Customs Avenue, took a left onto Prospect then another quick left onto Jameson; a right onto Fourteenth Avenue; crossing the wide thoroughfares with incredible speed, past Fort, past Main, continuing across Abercorn, across Fife, across Rhodes; and then a left onto Grey Street, where she slowed down and walked with her hands tucked in the front pockets of her sapphire frock, straining her neck as she ambled past the Royal Cinema to glimpse the white teenagers standing in line.

She crossed the street and entered Downing's Bakery, redolent with the aroma of freshly baked bread, which my surrogate father could smell all the way out on the pavement where he stood looking sheepish waiting for her to emerge, too afraid to follow her in. She appeared a few minutes later with a steaming chicken pie and a Fanta, which made his stomach rumble, and turned left onto Selbourne Avenue, moving at a leisurely pace, munching on her pie and pausing every so often to tilt the Fanta to her lips. Down Selbourne she sauntered, across Rhodes Street he followed her, where he paused, gaping at the off-white building of the Bulawayo City Hall with its Tuscan columns and the tower clock chiming every quarter hour. She crossed Fife Street and was now strolling across Abercorn, then Main, where all of a sudden he dropped to the ground, startled before the Gatling Gun, which stood threatening him outside Asbestos House, its muzzle trained on him and Selbourne Avenue behind. But the gun was just a monumental relic, rusty and out of use, without a gun master. Embarrassed, looking furtively about to make sure no one had seen him, he stumbled after her, on Selbourne Avenue still, across Fort and then Jameson, and then a right onto Lobengula Street. Here the crowds became darker of skin and also more compact, the thoroughfare still impressively wide. Her shapely rump beckoned him, flitting seductively in and out of the throngs, until she swung quite suddenly into Ticki-Tai Convenience Store at the corner of Lobengula and Third Avenue.

Ticki-Tai Convenience Store, where the young woman Thandi worked, on Lobengula Street, is now a phone-and-internet shop. I stood on the pavement staring at it for a long time, much in the same way my surrogate father said he stood waiting for Thandi in April '74. I even leaned against the broken parking meter outside the phone-and-internet shop, much like he said he had leaned against a parking meter all those years ago outside Ticki-Tai, in a pose of affected nonchalance. There he remained, sweating in an afternoon sun that seared the Bulawayo skyline, until the shadows began to spread across the pavement and cast a soothing shade where he stood. When his legs began to burn and still Thandi had not appeared, he shuffled back to the entrance, counted *one, two, three*, and ducked inside.

The interior was stuffy, suffused with the sweet scent of strange spices and the earthy smell of chickenfeed, with one aisle leading from the entrance along which he had to sidle, his chest rubbing against sacks of produce, and also television sets, radios, gramophones, bags of mealie-meal and sugar, piping, taps, sinks and steel rods.

'Hello? Yes? May I help you?' she said in English. Her voice was tantalizing, like a glob of honey on the tongue.

She was sitting on a high stool behind the counter. A book was perched on her lap, dipping into the col between her thighs.

'Eh... halloo,' he said. He found he could not look her in the eye.

'Yes? How can I help you? Are you looking for anything in particular?'

'Actually, ehm...' He rubbed his palms on the back of his trousers. 'It is you I am looking for.'

Her face shadowed. 'What do you want?' And then, her eyes falling on the *Bantu Terrorists: Rhodesia's Communist Threat* newspaper sheet that he still clutched in his hand: 'Who sent you?'

He was both taken aback and thrilled by the directness of her manner. No shy giggling, flits of the lids or shrug of the shoulders like the girls in his village.

'Ahem... let me, let me introduce myself. I am Abednego Mlambo, the Mlambos of Lupane, near St Luke's Mission Hospital, do you know where it is? I, I saw you walking and ehm... you are so beautiful...'

She threw back her head and laughed, bringing into profile the striking length and curve of her neck. Her breasts jiggled beneath her exquisite little collarbone. He wondered if they were soft and mushy like the inside of an over-ripe pawpaw, or lumpy like the inside of a granadilla.

He smiled and scratched the back of his head.

'I love you,' he said finally.

Laughing still, she shook her head.

'But I do!'

'Th-andi? Vat is it? Remember, you is at vork. No visitors during vork hours.'

He turned around, to find a large Indian woman in a silver lehenga standing by the 'staff only' entrance at the back, frowning not at her, but at him. She pronounced the 'Tha' part of her name as the English 'Th-a', with her tongue between her teeth, instead of the soft Ndebele 'Ta' in which the tongue tapped the palate.

'Sorry, baas,' she said, in a voice that, he thought, was not without mockery. 'You have to go,' she said to him.

Gone were his ambitions of finding work as a train driver for the Rhodesia Railways, gone Abednego the Great Colonizer, the Cecil John Rhodes, the Christopher Columbus. He had begun to imbibe his brother's dream; square and bold, black and white, clear lens; but now, Thandi smogged his vision. He spent his days lying on his camp bed in Emakhandeni hostels, which he shared with his Uncle Lungile and Cousin Solomon, huffing in reverie; or otherwise prancing about on the narrow cement corridors outside, giving dramatic little damoiseau-en-détresse sighs in response to his uncle's increasingly exasperated requests that he come in to the Sun Hotel to apply for the position of dish washer, where he could work his way up to the position of a kitchen manager, just like he, Uncle Lungile, had and Solomon one day would.

He began hounding poor Thandi, for as far as he was concerned, it was she who hounded him. He was indefatigable in his pursuit, making him reckless with the wad of cash his Baba had packed him off to Bulawayo with – a rare gesture of love that had made him kneel before the old man's feet. He came each day to Ticki-Tai and stuffed Thandi with chicken pies, showering her with countless bottles of Fanta, until she proclaimed an aversion to pastries and fizzy drinks. He chased after her as one pursues conquest. No, he did not want to forage towns, cities and countries. It was the soft hills of her breasts he longed to scale, the mountains of her buttocks he longed to conquer. He longed to tour the umbra landscape of her body, to discover crevices and fault lines hitherto unknown even to her, to be the first to clamber between the plateaus of her thighs and slide his flag into her summit, naming it like a god, just like Da Gama or Columbus or Livingstone or Rhodes; his own Wonderland.

'Yes,' she said, finally, to seeing him outside of the stifling confines of Ticki-Tai – where they were chaperoned by the glares of the Indian woman – though I imagine her eyes must have fluttered from weariness rather than delight.

How to explain to her that he, too, was fatigued? Tired of obsession, drained by mania, enamoured of revolt? Never mind that her surrender was without enthusiasm, a victory still demanded a victory dance; so that later, alone in the communal bathroom of the hostel, he would bend his bony legs, click his fingers and bob-bob-bob to the floor.

'There is a soccer field, down the road, just around the corner from here, on Second Avenue. Meet me there tomorrow, during your lunch break?'

She checked that there weren't any customers lurking in the aisles before she replied, 'Listen. Listen, I'm not one of your makhaya girls, OK, your rural girls you just see and profess love to, and then take into the bush to fuck. OK?'

She said *fuck* in English. He gaped at her. Such a vulgar woman! Were hers really the ranges he wanted to colonize?

'You makhaya boys need to learn some manners,' she continued. 'I'm not some piece of meat you just happen upon and just prod prod to your liking. I'm an Angela Davis and you'll respect my feminality. OK?'

He wanted to ask, *Who is Angela Davis? Is she your mother? Is your mother Angela Davis? Why does she have a white person's name?* She looked pissed off, though, so he just nodded.

She regarded him out of the corners of her eyes. 'You ask a cultured girl out for lunch. And afterwards, a play.'

'Hmmm.' He pretended to be considering this, though his heart was in his throat. He had no idea where to take her, what she expected out of lunch and *play*. What sort of *play* was this? Did she mean playing under the covers? Was she propositioning him?

'I can get us some nice food from the Sun Hotel,' he said finally. 'And afterwards we can... *play*.'

Her eyes lit up. 'The Sun Hotel... yes, that's actually a brilliant idea.'

'No no, I didn't mean *take* you there, I mean, you know no muntus are allowed there, right? What I meant was that my uncle, I mean I could get us food from the kitchens and then we could go somewhere nice like maybe Centenary Park and sit under the trees with a blanket...'

'Don't be ridiculous,' she said. 'That sort of thing is for people who have nowhere proper to go, and then they end up trying to grope one another behind the bushes. Meet me outside Ticki-Tai on Saturday after my shift. Two p.m. sharp. And don't keep a girl waiting.'

The days leading up to Saturday were long, and unnecessarily hot and sticky. He sweated a lot. Cousin Solomon stole a tin of homemade relaxer from Uncle Lungile's room that smelled strongly of raw eggs. Abednego watched tentatively through a piece of broken mirror as Solomon smeared it all over his kinky hair.

'Are you sure it won't fry my scalp or burn my hair or anything?'

'Promise always, cousin! I'm just gonna let it sit for a few minutes, then wash it off, and then, trust me, when your girl sees you, she won't be able to take her eyes off you!'

His scalp itched after Solomon washed off the mixture, and it began to tingle when his cousin greased his hair with sticky gel and then combed it back so it would lie flat; but the relaxer hadn't set properly, so his hair rose in a curvy bump, sweeping up and away from his face.

'Are you sure I look OK, cousin?' he said, tilting his head from side to side, appraising the shiny do. 'Isn't my hair supposed to lie flat? What's this bump?'

'Ah, no, cousin, this is the pompadour conk! You look like a black Elvis Presley!'

'Who's this Elvis Presley and why must I look like him?'

'Never mind, you look like an American rocking and rolling star, that's all. We've washed the rural off you, cousin. You've become the kind of man city girls love. Your girl's eyes are gonna drop when she sees you!'

Saturday arrived, and my surrogate father found himself standing outside Ticki-Tai at the appointed hour, two p.m. sharp, an arm wrapped around the parking meter, the other cocked on his hip, the pompadour conk flourishing up and away from his face. Indeed, at first, when Thandi emerged, dressed in a long, backless floral sundress and in the company of not one, but two young men, one of them white, she almost didn't recognize him. She stood there appraising him, and then, just as a smile began to spread across his face, she threw back her head and laughed.

It turned out he didn't look like a rocking and rolling star and, what was worse, the date was between him and Thandi... and the two young men – Frankie, whose face ripened under his glare, and Mvelaphi who, sniggering, kept calling him 'merry andrew'.

Abednego wanted to grab Thandi as they piled into Frankie's sky-blue Ford Anglia and shout, *What kind of date is this? Who are these people? Is it because I don't have a car?* But he just got in, Thandi settling in the front seat with Frankie, leaving him to squash up against Mvelaphi in the back.

In this way, they drove to the Sun Hotel, my surrogate father scowling ineffectually. When they pulled up in front of the grand entrance doors, out they bounded, he trailing behind, up the steps and across the lobby, ignoring the hushed whispers of the white guests as they hastened into the hotel restaurant, where Frankie, who kept clasping and unclasping his hands, cleared his throat and announced to the brunette hostess that they had a reservation. The hostess paused, looked from Frankie to Thandi to Mvelaphi – her eyes resolved into tiny slits when they settled on my surrogate father – and back again.

'I'm sorry, sir, but I… we don't allow natives in this establishment…'

Abednego looked about him sheepishly. Balding and permed heads had risen from the restaurant bowls to stare at them. But the other three seemed neither surprised nor flustered.

'Why?' said Thandi. 'Why are you sorry? What, exactly, are you sorry for?'

The hostess stumbled back as though she'd been slapped. 'If you don't leave, I'm afraid I'll have to call security…'

As though triggered, Thandi, Frankie and Mvelaphi strode past the hostess into the restaurant, and began manoeuvring from table to table, grabbing food from the guests' plates. The diners began to yell and shriek, some attempting to shimmy off their chairs, while others flung napkins at the disrupters.

'Citizens against the Colour Bar!' the three yelled, before stuffing Beef Stroganoff and Peach Melba, Salisbury Steak and Eggs Benedict, Chicken Marengo and Waldorf Salad into their mouths.

'Say yes to black!'

'Citizens against the Colour Bar!'

'Say yes to black!'

Outside, sirens could be heard in the distance. Upon hearing the wheew-wheewing, the three Citizens against the Colour Bar made a dash for the exit. Thandi shoved Abednego, who had been standing by the restaurant entrance all along, and tugged at his sleeve.

'Run!'

He raised his head just then, and glimpsed, peeping through the double doors at the other end of the restaurant, the mortified face of his Uncle Lungile, and his astonished Cousin Solomon next to him. He flinched, turned and fled.

I haven't heard my surrogate father guffaw like that in a long time! I have been replaying our scene this afternoon in Mama Agnes's living room, where I found him when I got back from town; the way he threw back his head and roared when I reminded him, as I handed him a glass of Bell's, which he quickly downed, what he told me yesterday about his first date with Thandi. It was a loud, startling sound, so full and wild and free.

I found myself laughing too, like a fool, even after the man treated me like shit under his boot this morning at the shebeen, even after all I had done for him, shuwa, printing posters of the boy's face and accompanying him on his community search. But I couldn't help it, it pleased me to see him like that; I've only heard him laugh like that with Bukhosi. And now there he was actually laughing like that with me!

'So, what happened between you and Thandi?' I asked, chuckling. 'Where is she now? How come you ended up with Mama Agnes?'

The man changed, just like that, nje. The laughter died in his throat. He suddenly remembered that it was Tuesday, and he was supposed to pick up some cooking oil for Mama Agnes from a friend who works at Buscod Supermarket in town. He stood up, with great effort, for he'd been drinking heavily, first the beer at the shebeen, and now my faithful dose of whisky. I rose with him, and we just stood there, in the tiny space between the sofas, he adjusting the waist of his trousers, staring at the floor, me biting my lip, watching him. He looked suddenly so weary I wanted to reach out and clap him on the shoulder, and to apologize, for I felt somehow responsible for his sudden despondency. But I dared not touch him. I don't know if I could take his rejection.

I still can't believe what he told me yesterday, though; to actually think Mvelaphi, that black chap, the Citizen against the Colour Bar, is none other than our Minister of Mines, the Hon. M. Mpofu. It's hard to imagine the man as some sort of young, impassioned anarchist; he's now as conservative as can be, a government yes-boy with the rolls of fat clinching his abdomen like a tyre, and the requisite eighteen-bedroom mansion, private jet and three mines, not forgetting his very own soccer team – all paid for, of course, by his modest public servant's salary… If only Thandi could see him now! He's nowhere near that Citizen against the Colour Bar who accompanied her and my surrogate father on some seditious business at the Sun Hotel.

After Frankie had dropped the three of them off at a shabby building on Customs Avenue, my surrogate father, still overwhelmed by the protest he had inadvertently taken part in, was disappointed to discover that Thandi didn't want to play after all. Not play *play*. Instead, she took him to what she called *a play*.

The room was cloaked in gloom. My surrogate father remembers a pair of tiny windows hugging the ceiling, but he had to struggle to make out the faces around him. He couldn't look for too long because the stares he received back were hostile.

'What you looking at, yellow face?'

'You like what you see, heh?'

'Who sent you?'

Yellow face! No wonder Frankie had dropped them off in his car but refused to come in. My surrogate father studied the floor and followed Thandi's feet. She was busy exchanging hugs with these strange people, laughing and talking in hushed tones, and he, he had to follow her like her puppy dog. Worse, she seemed to have forgotten him, and was instead busy standing in the crook of Mvelaphi's arm with her elbow resting on his shoulder. At one point, she tugged at Mvelaphi's waistcoat, playful like, in a way that my surrogate father longed for her to tug at his chest hair.

A hush descended, heralding the start of the *play*. There was nowhere to sit but on the floor, and my surrogate father was surprised to find Thandi next to him, warm in the pack of bodies. She caught his eye, smiled and clasped his hand. Mvelaphi, who had remained standing, noticed and stared long and hard.

'Viva to the struggle!' yelled Mvelaphi suddenly, his eyes twitching, making Abednego jump.

'*Viva!*' the crowd roared back.

'Majority Rule Now!'

'*Viva!*'

'Down with Smith and the Colonizers!'

'Down!'

'Viva the Book of Life!'

'*Viva!*'

'Down with Sithole and the Sell Outs!'

Abednego's eyes widened as it dawned on him—

'*Down down down!*'

—that he was in fact in a terrorist group meeting. Ohmygad!

His heart hammered his chest. He needed to get out of there pronto, whatwashappening, all he'd ever wanted was to drive a train, now look where this Eva had led him. Everyone knew what they did to terrorists here, who hadn't heard the stories? He bit back his panic, however. He would have eaten any fruit for his Eva, braved any serpent, plunged into any terrorist sinfulness, if it meant being with her... Oh, he felt so hot! Her hand in his felt hot, the room was hot, everything, his heaving chest, the sweat-beaded nook between her breasts, her face sparkling like a river stone—

'This week, we are going to rehash a scene from Césaire's play *Et les chiens se taisaient*,' said Mvelaphi, breaking my surrogate father out of his reverie, and though he was talking to the whole room, his eyes never left the pair. 'I had the fortune of touching the great man's garment during a trip to Paris last year, where I was part of a delegate of activists lobbying for black majority rule in Rhodesia.' He snapped the lapels of his waistcoat against his bony frame. 'And I have found there is nothing, rien *rien*, that I, humble man of words, can say that Monsieur Césaire has not dit in so beaux les words. I was so inspired, I said to myself, I must share l'inspiration in my homeland avec the brave men and women of the struggle! So, j'introduis an excerpt from the Aimé Césaire play *Et les chiens se taisaient*!'

Still tugging at his waistcoat, he positioned himself on one side of the room, while, to my surrogate father's dismay, Thandi got up and abandoned him for the pseudo-stage, where she stood next to Mvelaphi and brought his face to her heaving bosom. Thandi's posture became weary, and Mvelaphi's boyish. And now, they were one, and the play was to begin.

▪

I found a copy of Césaire's play online. I can see how it would have been enticing to the young revolutionaires. It entices me also! It has become, since its production, a minor success, one of Césaire's crowning achievements, and has toured the world.

My toes tingle even as I read it now; I can feel my body morphing into its rhythms, contorting itself into the repose of The Rebel, as Mvelaphi must have done playing the lead role in that back room, carried away by the play's lyricism.

I can see him, that once-Rebel, lean and sinewy on that pseudo-stage, bristling with Rebel Rage. And here I am, bristling in my pygmy room with its low roof, my head bent onto an imaginary chest, Thandi's chest, The Rebel's Mother, my Mother; I can feel it heaving with urgency, I can feel her full breasts against my cheek, her arm around me, her tears falling warm and rapid on my face. And there we are, on the pseudo-stage, Mother and I:

THE REBEL: My name – an offence; my Christian name – humiliation; my status – a rebel; my age – the stone age.

THE MOTHER: My race – the human race. My religion – brotherhood.

THE REBEL: My race: that of the fallen. My religion... but it's not you who will show it to me with your disarmament! 'Tis I, myself, with my rebellion and my poor fists clenched and my woolly head. I remember one November day; it was hardly six months ago. The master came into the cabin in a cloud of smoke like an April moon. He was flexing his muscular arms – he was a very good master – and he was rubbing his little dimpled face with his fat fingers. His blue eyes were smiling and he couldn't get the honeyed words out of his mouth quick enough. *The kid will be a decent fellow,* he said, looking at me, and he said other pleasant things too, the master – that you had to start very early, twenty years was not too much to make a good Christian and a good slave, a steady, devoted boy, a good commander's chain-gang captain, sharp-eyed and strong-armed. And all that man saw of my son's cradle was that it was the cradle of a chain-gang captain. We crept with knife in hand…

THE MOTHER: Alas, you'll die for it!

THE REBEL: Killed… I killed him with my own hands… Yes, 'twas a fruitful death, a copious death… It was night. We crept among the sugar canes. The knives sang to the stars, but we did not heed the stars. The sugar canes scarred our faces with streams of green blades.

THE MOTHER: And I dreamed of a son to close his mother's eyes.

THE REBEL: But I chose to open my son's eyes upon another sun.

THE MOTHER: O my son, son of evil and unlucky death—

THE REBEL: Mother of living and splendid death,

THE MOTHER: Because he has hated too much,

THE REBEL: Because he has too much loved.

Oh, see now, what you have done to me, Césaire; my face is wet!

My surrogate father managed to find a bit of alone time with Thandi after the play; Mvelaphi, who had something no doubt revolutionary to attend to, had to leave them, begrudgingly, I imagine. They took what my surrogate father claims was a lovers' stroll in the city. (Lovers' stroll? The man is making things up now. But he was hopeful, at least; that's good.)

'Are you a terrorist?' he asked her.

She laughed – eish, what was it with her and all this laughing, laughing at him all the time?

'Not a terrorist. A freedom fighter.'

'They say you are terrorists on TV. That you are crippling the country. Bombing roads, destroying infrastructure, killing innocents while they sleep in their farms at night.'

'But the play, was it not beautiful?'

'Indeed, it was.' (I imagine like me, it must have brought tears to his eyes!)

She laughed – again! – and fished out of her handbag a folded picture that she shielded from the wind with her body and beckoned him to look. He could smell her city-girl scent, something sweet that made his head spin, that reminded him of the taste of a queen-cake.

He recognized the man in the photo immediately. Who did not know Joshua Mqabuko kaNyongolo Nkomo, co-founding leader of ZAPU, the Zimbabwe African People's Union, agitator against all that was holy and sacred to the nation of Rhodesia, hated terrorist, prisoner of the state, dangerous communist, calculating Marxist? Devout Methodist, Teacher and Husband?

He could tell, from the many creases on the photo, that she'd spent hours staring at the man; the small, laughing eyes, the measured smile, the chubby, handsome, contemplative face.

'When you look into his eyes, what do you see?' she asked.

This was an important-sounding question, and so he groped around for an important-sounding answer. 'The future?'

(The past, surrogate father, the past! How can a man see the future if he can't understand the past? Always, you must be looking back over your shoulder, to see what history is busy plotting for your future.)

My surrogate father says he remembers very little of what Thandi said to him, only that it was a long monologue and that he was dizzy from the intoxication of being so close to her. He nodded vehemently to her impassioned stories, for her fervour was infectious. He was empty and in need of filling, and she, she was overfull.

'I see the fate of my father in those eyes, Abed,' he remembers her saying to him as she stared wistfully at Joshua Mqabuko's photo. 'My father, he died, two years ago in the mines in Tsholotsho.'

'My father too used to work at the mines in Tsholotsho before he became a soldier,' he said, glad to offer something useful to their intimate-bonding-over-photo.

'And that is terrible. Have you heard of the conditions there? The government gave my father a piece of land where nothing could grow, and so he was forced to go and toil in the mines, like somebody's mule. My grandfather, he was a soldier in King Lobengula's personal ibutho. He was rich. Lots of land, lots of cattle, and primed to have many wives. But my father ended up dying in the mines, with neither his family nor his dignity. So. There is no other way but to fight for freedom. Me, I want to be free. Don't you want to be free?'

For the first time, my surrogate father saw his surrogate father not as the fearsome bull of the Mlambo clan, uMlambo kaMdlongwa, whose voice boomed into the night making it shudder, whose thoughts sprinkled the land with light. Suddenly, Baba was shrivelled; a hoary carapace lolling all day beneath the mopane tree in an RAR uniform, cradling a rifle and prattling to the ghosts of a tenebrous past.

He clutched Thandi, more to prevent himself from falling than anything else, for he was assaulted by a terrifying vertigo. But now, he was as close to her as he'd ever been. Being the opportunist that he was, he kissed her. (We have these opportuntistic tendencies in common. A man with ambitions always has to be on the ready! You need an instinct for these things.) And that kiss, from the mischievous sparkle in my surrogate father's eyes as he told me, was, no doubt, the beginning of propitious things. It was a gesture without thought, and he flinched, waiting for Thandi's reprimand. But when he opened one eye, he saw that she was smiling.

'I'm going to fight in the war,' she said, her voice husky.

'You, a woman?'

'Why not? There are many women in the struggle, birthing the struggle, feeding the struggle, carrying the struggle, nursing and wiping the buttocks of the struggle. I can't stand living like this any more.'

He paused. At that moment, the mist that had fogged his mind since coming to Bulawayo cleared, to reveal the rays of his destiny pricking an azure sky, the Mount Nyangani of his future ploughing through the clouds of his existence. 'I'm going to fight in the war, too. With you. Together.'

A BUDDING ROMANCE

He was afraid to go home that night, the memory of his uncle and his cousin gaping at him from behind the kitchen doors of the Sun Hotel restaurant still fresh, so he lingered about the city centre well past nine, the designated curfew for Africans, and moseyed down King's Avenue, quite unperturbed by the prospect of being stopped by the po-pos. He cut across Makokoba Township, where the kwela music boomed even at that witching hour, and where fires could be seen flickering outside the asbestos-slat houses huddled together as though for comfort, and arrived at the Emakhandeni hostels near to midnight. His Uncle Lungile was awake still, seated on the edge of his mattress with its sagging centre, and seated next to him was Cousin Solomon, regarding him with eyes opened wide, whether from surprise or awe or perhaps just the effort of staying awake he did not know.

Did he know, demanded the old man, that what he had participated in that afternoon amounted to criminal activity, could even be considered, in these delicate times, *terrorrrrist* activity – Lungile shuddered – and earn him a good fifteen to twenty years in jail? Was he trying to give his poor father all the way back in Lupane a heart attack, heh?

'Not a terrorist,' Abednego said, trying to look solemn. 'A freedom fighter.'

'A freedom what? Mfana... wena... you haven't been here even three months, and already... instead of looking for a job you... now they'll never hire you at my kitchen, in fact, if they ever see you there again, they will most likely call the police! You certainly made yourself memorable what with that outfit looking like a Goli guluva... do you know you could have got me fired?'

Here he stared at the floor, while his uncle raged on. He could hear Cousin Solomon's stifled giggles, followed by some riotous throat-clearing. He wanted to look up and wink at his cousin, but he dared not risk meeting his uncle's glare.

'... hooliganism... city swallowing you... write to your father...'

He immediately sobered. 'Uncle, please don't tell Baba, I won't do it again, I promise.'

Having convinced his uncle not to write to Baba on the promise he'd find work, he got a night job as a security guard at the Bulawayo Drive-In, where he patrolled the rows of cars with a sjambok in hand, dressed in starchy black fatigues and a brand-new pair of boots that made him walk stiffly, solemnly, nodding at the white movie-goers and trying not to stare too hard at the steamy goings-on inside their cars. Instead, he tried to concentrate on the movies, fascinated to observe that the white people of Rhodesia, too, lived vicariously through white people from elsewhere, their lives over there in London and New York displayed on the big screen. He longed to share these wonders with the people back home in Lupane and he attempted to relate them to an amused Thandi, whom he spent his free time during the day trying to distract at Ticki-Tai while avoiding being thrown out by her boss. He noticed how she was more indulgent of him, though when she laughed – and she still did that a lot – he was unsure whether she was laughing *with* him or *at* him, although he was nevertheless pleased to be the source of her mirth.

It's hard to imagine quite what she saw in my surrogate father. He would, no doubt, attribute it to some sort of imagined, irresistible charm on his part, but dare I say he had nothing to offer the girl? He himself admits to having been intimidated by her rambunctious nature; the haughtiness of her Angela Davis and her feminality which demanded to be respected; the way her footsteps claimed the street; the way she always looked him straight in the eye, as though searching there for a deeper truth... deeper truth to what? He felt there was nothing mysterious or hidden in him; he was a makhaya boy as transparent as a rural boy could be, painfully aware of how gauche he was next to Mvelaphi and of course Frankie and of how little he understood the world, the city, her.

Why would Thandi – popular, beautiful and intelligent, and clearly possessing an adoring posse – end up choosing my surrogate father, a rural boy with nothing to offer her, neither in sophistication nor upward mobility? Perhaps, for a mutinous blot-out-sun such as she, who thrived, as the diners of the Sun Hotel would no doubt attest, on the shock of going against the status quo, she meant the choosing of a man who was so far below her league as a declaration of her freewill. She strikes me as one of those females who wish it were a woman's world, and resent those men like Mvelaphi who attempt to court smart women with an aggressive intellectualism, always preaching or correcting (with a condescending haughtiness) where they would do better to listen and learn. And so, here was my surrogate father, a young man enamoured of her and who listened to her rather than preached – and never seemed to correct her, only drinking in her every word like it was uluju – a man who, by compelling her to fill in the gaps left by his sometimes-awkward silences, pushed her to express herself to the fullest.

Whereas in reality, we know that my surrogate father's silences were not borne of any deliberate interest in listening to Thandi or delighting in her speech, which he found both intimidating and fascinating, but were because he truly did not know what to say to her, and many times had no idea what she was talking about.

It would have been a Saturday, he tells me, when the shop was quiet and her boss away, that she asked him, rather shyly, if he would like to see where she stayed. And though he was overjoyed, hopeful that this was perhaps the opportunity for real *play*, he nodded calmly, in an approximation of nonchalance. And so, it was on a rather nippy afternoon in May that she led him down the dusty township streets of Njube, named after one of the Ndebele King Lobengula's sons, where she seemed, once again, to attract greetings and laughter from passers-by like inhlwa to bulb light.

I can picture that house better than my surrogate father described it, a semi-detached in a row of small semi-detacheds, hedged in by a dense shrub – something basil-coloured, like a Pittosporum – cut low to about waist-height, with two huge boulders placed like goal posts at each corner of an ungated entrance, most likely painted white to make them look pretty – for Thandi strikes me as the kind of young woman who would have taken pride in appearances. The house seemed to my surrogate father incredibly small for a belle as dazzling and zesty as she. He was secretly pleased, though, to see how humble her accommodation was, as this boosted his confidence; why, his father's homestead in Lupane was much, much bigger than this, sprawling over almost half an acre, with five huts and a kraal and grazing lands nearby! He stood in the front entrance, taking in the sitting room; the window to his right as I see it now, facing out onto the street, shaded from prying eyes by a curtain – something pretty like one of Mama Agnes's window hangings – white lace crocheted in diamond shapes, undulating with the late afternoon breeze, little diamond-patterned suns speckling a peacock-print sofa below; to the left, placed midway along the width of the room, a television set looking like a radio (I remember how Uncle Fani refused to do away with our old-fashioned TV and its tiny screen, and I couldn't see a damn thing, but he held on to it, Uncle Fani, he would hug it when he cried, and he began saying, after watching *Back to the Future*, that it was a time-machine to the past, where all the people he loved were trapped). Beneath the TV, serving as a stand, a wide, bruised, solid shelf of alternating light-wenge and grey-beech with a compartment below for a turntable and a box of dials, and beneath this, pleated layers hemming in a cupboard – and though he never owned this, Uncle Fani, he dreamed of it plenty, his eyes foggy as he showed me the pictures in the TV Sales & Home newsletter. I imagine this would have been the kind of appliance in Thandi's home, it would have been so befitting for her, its grandeur making my surrogate father catch his breath as he pointed and asked, 'What's that?'

'Oh, that's a gramophone,' Thandi said, and she fluttered over and began to fiddle with the dials. 'A Blue Spot, we, mama – mama got it from her baas as a Christmas gift last year.'

'What does it do?'

She laughed, but softly this time, and he realized that she was, in fact, self-conscious. 'It plays records. Shall I play something? What would you like?'

She placed a record on the turntable, and a peculiar strumming of guitars filled the room. She began to twirl and sway her hips, in a manner that he thought was suggestive but could not be sure, and so he just stood there, by the front door, and watched her. When she spun around and found him standing stiff and solemn, she ended her movements abruptly, switching off the gramophone, and the silence, or lack of harmonious sound, seemed to make her unusually shy.

'Would you like to sit down?' she asked, motioning to the sofa.

He nodded, and made his way stiffly to the sofa, where he lowered himself slowly, his hands stretched out below him to feel for the seat, finally settling his buttocks on the very edge, refusing to succumb to the sofa's cosy incline. She sat down next to him, nervous as he appraised the room. Opposite the sofa was a shelf proper, with a slew of books, and above this, black and white photos stuck to the wall, one of a younger Thandi, baring a gap-toothed smile at the camera, with her cheeks plump and her long neck scrawny – he smiled – and next to this were pictures of other people he didn't know, but one who he guessed was her mama, so strong was the resemblance of the striking neck, the penetrating gaze, the defined angles of the face, the nose small and wide, the cupid's bow defined. And above these were wall hangings, the first one copper-plated, with what he recognized as Psalm 23 engraved, then another bible verse he couldn't recognize in a clay plate, and next to this a green and white crochet of Mary holding a haloed, blond baby Jesus.

'Oh, I didn't know you were a Christian,' he said to her, although what he no doubt meant to say was, *You don't strike me as a Christianly woman.*

'Oh, that, that's my mama's. I mean, I am a Christian yes but, those hangings belong to my mama.'

It dawned on him then that this was in fact not her house but her mother's, and how absurd it had been to assume she would own a house; she was, what, eighteen, nineteen like him? Where would she have got a house from? And although this realization placed her more firmly in the realm of ordinary beings, the thought that her mother might walk in at any moment made him jump up.

'Oh no, she's away,' Thandi said, as though reading his mind. She squeezed his hand. 'You can relax. She works in Bradfield and only comes home at the end of each month.'

'Ah, phew. Well, not that I... What does she do, your mother?'

Her hand dropped his. 'She's a maid. She works in the suburbs. For Sir Bartholomew Pearce.'

'Pearce? Isn't that Frankie's surname?'

'Yes. Sir Bartholomew is Frankie's father.'

'And is Frankie your boyfriend?'

'And what if he is?' she snapped, face flushing. 'What business of yours is it? You think I couldn't date him?'

He was taken aback by her sudden anger. 'I'm sorry,' he tried, although he had no idea what he was sorry for.

She softened a little, and he attempted a change of subject. 'And what's that book for?' he asked, pointing at a peculiar volume with a camel-skin cover on the shelf.

Here he'd done well, for her face bloomed to its usual animated radiance. 'Ah, *this*.' She got up and picked up the book. 'Is my most prized possession, which I share only with those I consider trusted friends.' She winked at him.

'Eh? And what is it?'

'It's my special project,' she said, resuming her seat next to him. She flipped open the cover, to show him not a printed book, but some sort of journal, with the A3 pages unlined, and curlicue script scribbled across in black ink.

'I'm working on retracing the history of my family. Remember

I told you my grandfather was a soldier in King Lobengula's personal regiment?'

'You? You wrote this?'

'Yes, it's a script I'm writing. For a play. Frankie's helping me with it. And some drawings I've been doing, to help me visualize the costumes for my cast.'

'You're writing a play,' he said, dumbfounded.

'Perhaps you may feature in it…' Again she winked at him. 'Come, let's act out a scene. This is in 1889, after King Lobengula has realized that that liar Rhodes tricked him into signing away half his kingdom in the Rudd Concession, and here he's confronting that snake-in-missionary-clothing Charles Helm, who he'd thought was his friend and who'd advised him to sign the concession. Here, you read here, you can be King Lobengula and I'll be Helm.' She cleared her throat.

He wanted to say, *I don't know how to read*, but the very thought of how this would widen and possibly make irresolvable the gap between them made his heart beat faster. He squinted at the pages, blinking rapidly, and then looked up at her.

She stared back. 'Well? You start, read from right here.'

'Why don't you read out loud for me?' he said. 'I would love to just listen to you read.'

'You don't want to be in my play?'

'No… I mean, of course I would love that, if I can act, that is, but… we can try another time. Right now, read for me, please. I just want to hear you read.'

'All right.' She smiled at him shyly, but it was fleeting, for the next moment she was en poise, her face taking on irony, her voice suddenly gruff, the syllables flat, filling the whole room and, he was sure, spilling out into the street.

Of course, my surrogate father barely listened to a word, and so the true content of that camel-skin prized possession is lost to posterity. But he supplied the names to me and so I'll do the rest – any self-respecting man such as I who sets out on the redemptive task of redescription has to be familiar with the stories of the so-called great men who have deemed themselves the makers of history. I know our King Lobengula's story well enough; I know Cecil Rhodes's story too well. I imagine a sapient soul such as Thandi would have been familiar with these histories, too. No doubt she would have begun with that famous lamentation our King Lobengula is said to have caterwauled after discovering Rhodes *et al.*'s duplicity:

'Did you ever see a chameleon catch a fly? The chameleon gets behind the fly and remains motionless for some time, then he advances very slowly and gently, first putting forward one leg and then the other. At last, when well within reach, he darts his tongue and the fly disappears. England is the chameleon and I am that fly.'

I imagine her voice becoming lyrical as she mimicked an imaginary Charles Helm, with the intonations proceeding as though from her nostrils: *'I doubt there can be peace without your honouring your end of things, Your Kingship. As I have already said, all has been in good faith, and Her Majesty, the Queen Victoria, was very pleased to hear of the progress we have made in coming to an affable agreement.'*

Gruff and flat again: *'Away with your child's tales, Charles! Tell me, would mineral rights of a similar expanse of land in England go for this very same sum?'*

Acquiring a nasal haughtiness: *'Well… I wouldn't be in a position to comment on that, Your Kingship. However, your mark of approval sits on the document, and I'd say that makes it binding…'*

Gravelly and angry: *'Be done with your evil scheming, Charles! What is this piece of paper to me? I shall send an envoy to your Queen, only with whom I can speak of such adult matters as an equal. I shall tell her I've been overrun by greedy men from her country who harangue me every day with demands for concessions this concessions that. She must come here and see me herself, so we may settle matters as equals.'*

'I'm afraid it's not up to Her Majesty, Your Kingship. It is up to our courts and Parliament…'

'Oh, you and your folly, Charles! Why do you enjoy tormenting me with your child's tales? First, you make me put my mark on papers that tell lies, now you tell me of a queen who has no power… what kind of foolishness is that?'

This is where she would have paused, and looked up at him, becoming bashful again. 'Well? What do you think?'

'More! More!' he said, clapping rah-rah.

He visited her many times thereafter, and begged her to tell him her family hi-story. And in this way, he learned about her grandfather, the mettlesome Impikade Hadebe, cousin to Queen Lozikeyi Dlodlo, King Lobengula's senior wife, and who had served as part of the king's personal regiment. He had been a valiant warrior, she told him dreamily, defending the Nation of Mthwakazi at the Battle of Galade in 1893 when it was attacked by somebody called Doctor Jim and his troops under instruction from that colonizer Rhodes.

Here, Thandi flipped through the pages of her camel-skin-bound book, to show my surrogate father the drawings she'd done of her grandfather. They were, he attests, very good; pencil and watercolour sketches of a copper-hued warrior in a shimmering ostrich feather headdress and a knee-length leopard kilt, with purfles made from oxtail hide adorning his arms and calves, and also gold and beaded bracelets tinkling around his wrists and ankles. His poses were athletic; kneeling amidst the khaki-coloured veld grass in one, his slim face peeping between his oxhide shield and assegai; leaping in the air in another, wielding a stout stick, the slits in his earlobes caught by a brilliant splash of sunlight sparkling off the upper left corner of the page; and in another still, sliding his assegai into the chest of a settler, whose blue shirt was stained with blood, his arms flung backwards, as though to curb a fall, his astonished grey eyes staring into the face of Impikade.

They were sorely defeated at the Battle of Galade, Thandi told him, thoroughly walloped by men who made claims to civility and yet found pleasure in the killing of the bantu men, women and children.

'More exhilarating than partridge hunting,' they said.

'Humanitarianism,' they called it.

It seemed to my surrogate father that it was this, the narrative of war rather than war itself, which incensed Thandi.

The impis, with their assegais and their Martini-Henry rifles, hadn't stood a chance against the English Maxim and Gatling guns, their cannon and their rifles. This counted as the darkest period in the Kingdom, for the royal town Bulawayo was burned to the ground, as was custom, and the king fled, never to be seen or heard from again, his valiant spirit kept alive only through rumours of being spotted here and there, and ephemeral promises of his imminent return. And what were a people without a king? They were a people with a queen. In the absence of King Lobengula, protocol decreed that Queen Lozikeyi take over; she had shared not only his bed but also his secrets, and was therefore as powerful as any man.

(My once-mentor Dumo was an admirer of our Queen Lozikeyi. Mother of Mthwakazi! UMpangazitha! Materfamilias... Our Virgin Mary? No, that can't be right. I become so awestruck I forget the totems! Eish, this always made Dumo mad. I must look them up; I have them saved on my Mac somewhere.)

Here, Thandi showed my surrogate father a watercolour drawing of our Queen, who looked stout, her small face pretty, a multicoloured cloth draped around her shoulders and covering also her loins. A beaded apron hung from her waist, and brass and iron encircled her arms and legs; from her head fluttered the azure feathers of a jaybird. She stood still and unsmiling, her hands clasped across her bosom, and behind her were visible the beginnings of a beehive dwelling.

Thandi's grandfather was with the Queen when, in 1896, right under the unwary eyes of those haughty Europeans, who really ought to have known better, she led her people in a second battle, the War of the Red Axe. But even though this war was bloody and long, forcing Rhodes and his cohorts from imperial England into negotiations with the Queen, it, too, was ultimately lost. The State of Mthwakazi was toppled, and left to die in the dust of the very land that had been stolen from it.

And so, Thandi concluded, Rhodes and his settlers had driven the bantu peoples out of their fertile land, upsetting the whole of the culture and its way of life, making out of young men farm labourers and mine workers. Impikade, who by then had two wives and five children, four of them sons, refused to do menial work – as far as he was concerned, he was a warrior and a servant of the Ndebele royal family. As a result, his home was burned down, his daughter raped and killed and his sons taken to work in the mines. One of these sons, Mzilethi, was Thandi's father, whom she saw only occasionally growing up, for he spent most of his life shambling about in the darkness of the Tsholotsho mines, searching for and yet unable to find the light.

'And now, the valour of our people and the glory of the Mthwakazi Nation lives not in any history book, or in any official account, where we are nothing but savages without culture, without history or glory or anything worth mentioning and passing on, but in here,' she said, pressing her hand to her chest. 'I heard the stories from my father, passed down to him by his father, my grandfather, and which I shall one day pass down to my children.'

'My father never told me any stories,' my surrogate father said. 'By the time I was born, he'd come back from the Second World War, and all he could remember was fighting *for* England, not against it. Nothing before it. I used to think it was funny.'

'So, you see, Abed, why we must fight in the war, and prepare for the time when our leader Joshua Nkomo assumes power, and we can restore the dignity of our people.'

'Prepare for this time how?'

'You know, we shall burn all of this to the ground when we win the war, like all conquerors of any land. They shall all go up in flames, the Royal Cinema, Asbestos House, that City Hall, everything, that maniac Rhodes's statue and the Gatling Gun relic, nothing shall be left standing. We shall burn down the lie that the English have made of us!'

'You want to destroy these sturdy buildings? And then what shall replace them, huts?'

'Don't be silly. We'll buy materials from the Chinese and the Soviets, state of the art stuff, and build a royal city fashioned after Ndebele architecture, worthy of King Lobengula himself.'

This kind of thinking would be very appealing to Dumo. A modern city that narrates Mthwakazi history through its architecture! A reinterpretation of the Expressionist era; domes upon domes, semi-circular structures out of whose radii flourish other semi-circular structures, creating secret rooms and semi-rooms and rooms on top of rooms; rooms of flight, of fancy.

Of (im)possibility.

▪

Usually, after telling him these hi-stories, she had the urge to go out dancing. It was as though reimagining the past had welled up in her excess energy that demanded to be expended, for she would dance for hours on end, oblivious to the June cold or the late hour, at the Njube Community Hall where many of the dhindindis were held, disco and soul music blaring from a gramophone placed at one end of the hall. She would sway down to the floor and undulate her hips as she slowly rose back up, flitting her eyes at him, running her hands down his back while he stood there looking stiff. At times, the community hall projected films from a bioscope, and charged an entry fee, but during these she was always too restless, the excess energy making her shuffle in her seat, and clasp and unclasp her hands. He preferred these to the plays she attended in the room on Customs Avenue, however, and which she liked to drag him to, the possible penalty of whose terrorist activity terrified him. But she brushed this concern aside, saying there were more important things at stake than jail; for she and Mvelaphi had been precociously developing the Césaire play *Et les chiens*, and were making plans to tour the whole country to showcase the two-person production.

It was after one of these bioscopes at the community hall that she let him into her mother's house – she never let him in after the dancing or the films, although he walked her home every single time, ever hopeful – where she pressed him onto his back across the peacock-print sofa, and lay atop him. Her mouth was hungry, searching his lips, his face, her tongue flickering in and out, making him hungry too; before he knew what was happening, she'd unclothed him and was astride him and he was inside her. He clung to her, she flinging back her head and pumping her hips and hurling throaty moans at the roof, her full breasts beaded with sweat from the exertion of it, he stunned and delighted and warm inside her, taking all of this in, how it was she who was doing the doing and he the one who was being done when, before he knew it, she was shuddering and he was shuddering with her, deep inside her, and then she was rising, and he felt himself slipping out of her luscious warmth, the heat of her flesh leaving him, exposing him to a cold draught.

One day, in September, during one of his visits, some two months after the beginning of their sexual encounters, about which they never spoke but which continued in that fashion, she sat down next to him with a paper and a pencil, and a slim, yellow book with the five vowels, a e i o u, dancing across the cover. She took his big, tough hand in her dainty one, moulded it around the pencil, opened the yellow book and pointed at the letters.

'We'll start with teaching you how to write,' she said. 'Then learning how to read should be easier.'

He stared at her. 'How did you…?'

'This is how you write your name,' she continued, moving his hand with hers, slowly, painstakingly, until letters began taking form across the page.

'See? You've just written your name.'

He stared at the crooked letters, saw that indeed he had, and tried not to cry.

THE MBIRA

Even in his absence, Bukhosi is here, tucked in every worry line etched on our father's face, in the hunched posture of Mama Agnes's back each morning as she heads out to Blessed Anointings. Some days I don't even see her; she arrives home late from her prayer sessions with her Reverend Pastor, and leaves for work in the morning before I'm awake. I miss spending time with my surrogate mama!

I decided to stay up last night so I could see her. I waited with my surrogate father in the gloom of the sitting room; the electricity had gone again. My surrogate father has been sullen since running off the other day to pick up Mama Agnes's cooking oil, clamping up whenever I ask about Thandi, and refusing, despite my best efforts, even one drop of Bell's. We spent the whole of yesterday seated in the sitting room, in a battle of wills, me trying to get him to take just one sip of the whisky, he pursing his lips, glaring at the wall, willing Bukhosi to reappear, declaring himself mute unless the boy popped up abracadabra before his eyes, and snapping at me to shurrup when I pleaded with him to continue with his story.

I have been trying to figure out how to get him to open up; I think I may need stronger medicine for that obstinate heart of his. I understand that he's worried about the boy. I miss him too, sometimes. But I'm here for our father, aren't I? I'm here, I can be the son who will never leave, who won't disappoint, who is eager to learn from him and who will always show him affection. Why can't he see that?

When Mama Agnes finally walked through the front door, I quickly slipped the bottle of Bell's I had been trying to feed Abednego beneath my shirt, but she must have caught the glint of the bottle in the moonlight spilling through the window, or heard the swirl of the liquor as I hid the bottle, for her head snapped in my direction.

'What's that?'

'It's nothing,' I said.

'You've been drinking? Zamani? You're letting him drink when you know—'

'Leave us alone, mani,' snapped Abednego. 'We do what we like. This is my house, mani. You hear? My house!'

'You know how you get when you drink—'

'Hayi shuttup, mani, you are not the boss of me.'

She sighed, then, my surrogate mama, a long sigh that made me slump my shoulders. And then, the next moment, she clapped her hands; I jumped. They had had a breakthrough with the Holy Ghost! Thanks to the Reverend Pastor's ceaseless prayers, she had finally seen a vision of her Bukhosi walking down a street somewhere. Bless the Reverend Pastor! He had done so much for them, shuwa. If it hadn't been for him and his faith... From the noise of the street in her vision, and the hooting khombis, it looked like somewhere in Johannesburg... Maybe the boy had run off there! The Reverend Pastor certainly thought so. But most important was that her nanaza was all right. Their prayers were paying off. They just had to keep praying, and all would be revealed soon. How faithful was the Holy Spirit!

I congratulated her, saying this was, indeed, something to rejoice in, although my heart beat wildly as I stood up to hug her. The boy can't be in Johannesburg, can he? I saw him with my own eyes, being thrown into that police van at the Mthwakazi rally. Could he have escaped? But then why would he go to South Africa instead of coming home? How powerful, exactly, is this Holy Ghost? Does it really have the powers to reveal all, and if so, what, exactly, does it intend to reveal, how does it intend to reveal it and when?

Mama Agnes met my embrace with open arms. I inhaled her soothing, fruity fragrance. I never got to hug my own mama and smell her; I imagine this is what she would smell like.

When she finally pulled away (I released her reluctantly), I followed her into the kitchen, where she lit a candle, took her supper from the fridge and began to eat it cold.

'I want you to know, Ma,' I said, whispering so Abednego wouldn't hear us. 'About what you saw… I've been trying to get Father to stop drinking. You notice how drunk he is, every night?'

She sighed again. 'I've been trying to get him to come to church with me. The Reverend Pastor can deliver him from the drink demon that has taken over him. I don't know what to do. Sometimes, when his drinking gets so bad, he becomes…' She shuddered.

'He just needs a gentle hand,' I said, helpfully. 'Because we don't want him to start hiding the bottles from us. But don't worry, Ma, I'll look out for him.'

She smiled. 'That's exactly what Bukhosi would have done.'

The boy would have done no such thing! He was a little

weakling, and yet others found him easy to love. Even Dumo, who always praised his zeal for the Mthwakazi Secessionist Movement, anointing him a real maverick, a soul made of the fine stuff, possessing the recklessness of a true revolutionaire. In this praise, which he seemed to heap upon Bukhosi more and more aggressively, was the screaming indictment of my own failures, for I was given to asking questions rather than accepting answers. Like an old toy, I was quickly tossed aside, and the boy, the new favourite, won over Dumo's affections, which had previously been reserved for me. They even began to see each other outside of our tri-party meetings. It's not my fault that the boy went missing! Not really, when you think about it! He wouldn't have even been there at the Mthwakazi rally were it not for Dumo, so he's more to blame than me!

'Yes,' she continued, unwitting of how much it hurt me to hear her praise the boy. 'He was good for Abednego. He grounded him, you know? Without him, he's just become a mess. He probably needs to keep busy, that's why he keeps going out every day to look for our nanaza. I pray our Bukhosi comes back to us, so everything can go back to being all right.'

I slinked off to my lodgings before she could hear my sobs.

I long to show my surrogate father what I've written, to show him the beginning of his – our! – hi-story on the page; to win his fatherly approval. But would he indulge me, what with him looking so terrible this Friday afternoon? Yesterday's abstinence proved short-lived, the man has been drinking the cheap beer from the shebeen all morning, ever since Mama Agnes left for her prayers with the Reverend Pastor. He's terribly drunk, slumped in his chair, his elegiac insobriety casting its shadow across the

Mlambo sitting room. Even though the sun punches through the little star-shaped holes in the lace curtain, the sitting room is still shrouded in gloom, a gloom not only caused, I have surmised, by my surrogate brother's vanishing, but also by too much clutter. The sitting room was never this cramped when Uncle Fani and I lived here. We didn't have these plump sofas that lull you to sleep; we didn't have my surrogate father's armchair; and we certainly didn't have the armchair Bukhosi used to occupy.

That empty chair is maybe the loudest indictment.

On the wall, beneath a photo of our parents in wedding garb with the inscription *August 1987*, is a bigger, framed portrait of the enlarged face of baby Bukhosi at one year old, cupped in a bonnet strung around his chubby chin. He assesses me with frightened, emerald eyes. It's telling, isn't it, that although there is, in this family living room, a photo of mother and father and then a photo of son, there isn't a photo of mother, father and son? I see not the unity of the holy trinity.

Below the photos, rammed against the wall next to Bukhosi's armchair, is a peeling bookcase holding a very precious book, the boy's Tiffany-blue baby album, chronicling his crucial formation years. Beneath the album is a dusty shelf of peculiar books that often supplements my own reading, otherwise no doubt unread and almost entirely for show: *Das Kapital*, *The Color Purple*, *Qilindini*, *I Speak of Freedom*, *The Art of War*, *uSethi eBukhweni Bakhe*, *Love in the Time of Cholera*, *Quotations from Chairman Mao Tse-tung*, *Without a Name*, *Nabokov's Butterflies* and also some poetry, Wordsworth's 'Laodamia', Chitepo's *Soko Risina Musoro*, and a tattered edition of *The Complete Poetical Works and Letters of John Keats*.

There's also a television on a glass TV stand – which my drunk surrogate father is watching intently – and a Newegg CD shuffle radio and a kitchen table whose cobalt is in an embittered battle for attention with the maroon of the sofas. There is no space for four-sitter kitchen tables in the kitchens of Luveve, and so the kitchen table must impose itself upon the living room. I see in the battle between the kitchen table and the sofas Mama Agnes's struggle for middle class relevance. But no matter! I am sure whenever she looks at her possessions cluttering the living room, she is comforted by the illusion of plentitude. I understand it; growing up we were poor, thanks to Uncle Fani's drinking sprees, and I yearned, whenever his weeping would bounce off the walls and reverberate in our sparsely furnished house, for the comfort of a plush sofa to cushion the sound. I get how empty spaces can creep like a draught into the heart and fill it, too, with lonely emptiness.

Speaking of emptiness, I'm ashamed to confess that last night I dreamed about Thandi... She was astride me, pumping her hips and hurling throaty moans at my pygmy roof, her pawpaw breasts calling out to me, and in my dream, I licked them, those gorgeous pawpaws, I licked them and sucked them and nibbled on them, and oh, they tasted so good. Yes, I know it's obvious that I've never been with a woman. I've never experienced that most transcendent of human pleasures, as natural as breathing or eating or laughing, akin to gobbling copious amounts of chocolate or a teensy snort of ubuvimbo. I admit, female feathers make me shy. I see, in all of them, my mama, whom I never knew but know of, bless her spirit, though she rests not in peace. But not in Thandi! And now, no matter how hard I try, I can't get her out of my mind. I yearn for more of her. But he deprives me, my surrogate father. I can't stand him when he's so glum and sullen-lipped, like this.

But wait – here comes a familiar tinkle from the TV that sets my surrogate dada alight; it's a ruling party jingle, a bewitching symphony of drum and guitar, mbira and hosho. Before I know what the hell is happening, my foot is going tap-tap-tappity-tap.

I wasn't born yet during the liberation struggle, but even I, falling prey to the strumming and the drumming, feel my blood roiling with the guerilla morale of the '70s; my pitter-pattering heart yearns for a little fracas, my hands fumble about for a weapon, and my throat itches with a warring cry. O what juju tricks are these that history is playing?

It wafted in the gunpowder-smog like braaied carabeef, the stench of our charred soldiers, croons the raspy voice of the Minister of Agriculture and Lands from the television. He, or some other ruling party songster, is always serenading the TV and radio air waves with these jingles, interrupting, indiscriminately, our family viewing to educate us on our patriotic history, in their version of which the ruling party is the country's sole superhero, every other sucker be damned. They are very catchy, these ruling party jingles; I have often heard children carolling them, their voices chorusing from the street into my pygmy room.

My surrogate father has begun to sway softly in front of the television, like a snake in front of a pungi. Peasants, in the accompaniment of their lead singer, the Minister of Agriculture and Lands, fill the screen, decked in the most elaborately woven suits made from African print, on which feature the faces of His Most Excellent Excellency our Comrade President Robert Gabriel Mugabe, in various states of anime, from benevolence, to humility, to bliss. They are busy shaking their booties, the peasants and their lead singer the Minister of Agriculture and Lands, busy getting down real hard and proper. Jingle-jingle they go to the liberation struggle, nimble fingers plucking furiously at the mbira, that revered thumb piano that has the power to evoke the ancestors; it summons the body, flails the limbs, discombobulates the soul and casts the spell of togetherness – together we live, together we suffer, together some live better than others and others suffer more than some – so that, like a puppetry of Pinocchios, we boogie to the beat of our Geppetto.

Toolooloo, wails the mbira.

Remember the slushy rain? croons the Minister of Agriculture and Lands' raspy voice. *Remember the slippery hearts? Oh, our brothers!*

'I remember slushy rain and slippery hearts,' croaks my surrogate father. 'And Skinny Zacchaeus in an oversize helmet and glasses that looked like a handy man's goggles, wailing like a woman at a funeral.'

My heart starts thumping. He speaks! I slip my hand beneath my shirt, pull out the sloshing Bell's, twist the bottle-top – 'Hmm, and what happened next, surrogate father?' – lean over, and fill his waiting glass.

'He kept asking me if we were going to die, going to die, oh *fuck*, are we going to die, Abeddie?

'Will you *shoosh*, I said. Are you trying to get us killed?

'Best we surrender and negotiate, yes? he replied, the little mouse! He said, you know I was the first President of the Debating team at school, I can lobby on our behalf—

'And I cut him off and yelled, just shutt*up*, please!'

(He seems to waver, whether caught in the moment of the memory or waking out of it I can't tell. I lean over, pick up his glass and proffer it to his lips. He gulps down a mouthful, like a baby on a teat.)

'He wouldn't stop, the little nincompoop, so scared, I swear he wet himself. Why didn't we just take Muzorewa's deal and form a coalition government with the whites? he cried. Why didn't we just deal with this like civilized human beings, heh? I don't blame them for thinking us savages. What is this, heh? This *gorilla* warfare. Like we're still wearing animal skins in the bhundu? Heh?

We'd better give ourselves up, me I can't die here, I've a degree from Oxford, destined for great things, I'm not a violent man me, I—

'I swear if you don't shut that trap I'm going to put a bullet in that dwala head of yours!

'Finally, he shuttupped, the little mouse! Busy sniffling as I held my dying men. My comrades, bo! We served together in Joshua Nkomo's ZIPRA military wing, yoh, and every day I remembered him from my Thandi's photo and I thought how proud of me she would be! But nothing can ever prepare you for watching your men die.'

Something clinches my chest as he speaks, something that makes it difficult to breathe, a born-free type of guilt. Yes, I am a born-free, birthed in 1983, after the war for liberation, after our independence in 1980. I fold myself humbly on Mama Agnes's sofa and try to grunt comfortingly, to no effect, as my surrogate father stifles a sob.

Everywhere, the smell of death, oh, death everywhere! croons the raspy male voice from the TV.

Toolooloo, wails the bewitching mbira. *Toolooloo toolooloo toolooloo!*

'I smelled death everywhere!' cries my surrogate father. 'Everywhere death!'

MaBorn-free, where are your SAFN-49s? croons the raspy male voice. *Where were you during the struggle, maBorn-free?*

I sink lower into the sofa.

Toolooloo!

'I clung to my SAFN-49 rifle,' says my surrogate father. 'And when the landmines began exploding, I almost shat myself! I could no longer see Zacchaeus—'

Do you remember Camp Pyonyang?

'—and I remembered my time in Camp Pyonyang—'

Toolooloo!

Do you remember China?

'—I remember China—'

Toolooloo! Toolooloo!

Do you remember the wise words of Chairman Mao?

'—Chairman Mao asked us, what is it that we always strive at? And we chorused, dialectics: the art of arriving at the truth through the logical deduction of logical arguments!

'Very good! said Chairman Mao, kind grandfatherly Chairman Mao who had offered his services to our nationalist leaders, donating his time and knowledge of the evil machinations of capitalism. Tell me, he said, what is it that I said capitalism aims to do?

'And we chorused, to provide an anti-synthesis, Chairman Mao, to rule through the logical deduction of illogical arguments!

'And he beamed, Chairman Mao, our Messiah in Holy Trinity with Marx and Stalin, he beamed and said, come, follow me, and I will make you fishers of men!

'We cried, make us fishers of men, Chairman Mao!

'And he replied, what is it, my little black disciples, that we fight against?

'Here we cried, the forcing of the peasant off his land, his only real power, into slavery so he may sell his labour!

'And I wept for my father, the bull of the Mlambo clan. Our ancestors were kicked off the land when the settlers came, to make way for Thornton Farm. Crammed into the Tribal Trust Lands where not even the thorn tree dared flourish! My Baba, strong and proud with the gait of an ox, his spirit was broken in the Tsholotsho mines. And then – crook! – he was carted off, just like that, to fight their wars over there in Europe, of all places.

'Very good! said Chairman Mao. And what is it that we are aiming to do?

'Communism is a hammer that we use to crush the enemy! we chorused.

'A seraphic grin spread across Chairman Mao's divine countenance.

'What is our ultimate goal? he asked, testing us one more time.

'The people, and the people alone, are the motive force in the making of world history! we cried.

'He winked at us then, Chairman Mao, and we felt the glow of certain victory warming our bellies.'

What of our brothers who died for this our Zimbabwe? Oh, let them not die in vain! MaBorn-free, let them not die in vain!

Toolooloo! Toolooloo toolooloo toolooloo!

'I stumbled through the smoke yelling for Zacchaeus,' says my surrogate father, slumping in his chair, looking suddenly frail, so frail and so old. 'I found him trembling beneath bloodied limbs, covered in the stench of burnt human flesh. He was alive! Bruised but unharmed. I clung to him. I clung to the little mouse. I cried.'

He wipes his tears on his shirt sleeve and turns away from me to face Bukhosi's sofa.

SPEAR-THE-BLOOD

Dumo warned me about this, about how the state apparatus hijacks our hi-stories, appropriates them, rewrites them, edits out the wrinkles and then feeds back to us some real sweet-tasting shit. This shit tastes so good that sometimes we're even tempted to swallow! Tsk-tsk!

Dumo's eyes glittered whenever he talked about the machinations and cover-ups of power, what he called reading the ink beneath the ink, a skill he burnished by quoting widely from his eclectic library. For, to be any kind of respectable vanguard, he liked to say, a man had to rid himself of the stifling confines of education, that top-down programme enacted by a state to produce conservative men and women in thrall to its doctrines, be they tyrannical and unruly, and instead invest in an intimate relationship with *knowledge*. During those days, when I was still an infant in this revolutionary business, still suckling on Mother Knowledge's bounteous titty – before Bukhosi usurped me as his heir apparent – when Dumo's extensive book collection was my first foray into vast worlds, hi-stories, dreams and ideas spanning from as far back as Valmiki's *Ramayana* to Plato's *Timaeus* to the Solomonic *Kebra Nagast* to Equiano's *The Life of Olaudah Equiano* to Goethe's *The Pied Piper* to Ekra-Agiman's *Ethiopia Unbound*, all I could offer in response to my mentor was a tentative nod, and an attempt at my own premature theorizing.

'What we need,' I said to Dumo, my head still going bop bop bop with foggy wisdom, 'is to expose the truth.'

He threw back his symmetrical head and guffawed. 'What is truth?'

'Well, the truth is—'

'There's no such thing as truth, mfana! Truth is optics. And there are so many options out there, these days it's all about choosing your flavour. You like your truth blackberry-cherry or you like it lemon-lime? There's even a zero-calorie truth!'

'But the truth of Gukurahundi isn't optics!' I cried. 'What happened to my mama isn't optics.'

'You're going to have to be smarter than that, if you're going to survive in this world,' Dumo snapped. 'What we are trying to do is to seek justice for our people and what they experienced under the Gukurahundi Genocide at the hands of the state apparatus. To say, look, I'm a human being, and what happens to me matters! Everyone out there in the world is holding a megaphone, mfana, and it's the most dazzling one that gains audience. And audience is power. Audience is freedom! We are aiming to latch onto a loud megaphone. To add some flavour to our truth, to attract some moths, you understand. We're trying to *own* the truth…'

To *own* the truth? Dumo could often sound perilously like the very people he was denouncing – although there was something seductive in the idea of owning the truth, I admit. Achilles, Napoleon, Shaka, all men who have shaped their own truths until hi-story has believed it and accorded them greatness! Still, I do not aspire to greatness; I simply aspire to make sure my surrogate father doesn't swallow shit, sweetened, zero-caloried or otherwise.

The glazed-over, painstakingly edited, jingled half-truths trumpeted by the peasants in the accompaniment of their lead singer the Minister of Agriculture and Lands don't fool me. This is not how things happened. My poor surrogate father is remembering not his own, but the state's memories, shoved down our throats every single day for the past several years so that they are beginning to replace our own memories. He has never been to China. As far as I know, surrogate Uncle Zacchaeus never even fought in the war, let alone sheltered in a tangle of bloody limbs. The only limbs he sheltered in were the warm, open legs of Lady America! No, my surrogate father is eating some shit! I don't blame him. In these days of food shortages, what with the supermarket shelves gaping empty, shit tastes so good. Look, even me, I was beginning to shimmy left and shimmy right on Mama Agnes's sofa, yearning to shake my booty and slip into the nostalgia of guerilla warfare. And I wasn't even born yet during the liberation war! What the man needs is another strong dose of that truth serum, Bell's. When I hand him a glass of the syrupy liquid, he downs it in one, making him cough violently, though when our eyes meet, he grins. Reminiscing about the war has fired up his belly and fired up his loins, and I know, as his eyes glaze over and that silly love-struck smile topples his scowl, that we're getting back to the things that matter, that matter to him and therefore to me.

The year was 1975, the summer at its wettest, the month December, the day dusk, the air rain-plump, the crickets cricking, the cicadas cicadaring and the sky leaking marigold and tangerine and ginger. The loamy Lupane soils were waterlogged, making my surrogate father and our beloved Thandi slip and slosh through mud. They'd been walking for almost five hours, from the stop where the Shu Shine bus had dropped them off, a distance that my surrogate father could easily cover in two and a half hours, but then they'd had to make regular stops along the way on account of Thandi and her pregnancy, asking for water and respite from several homesteads. (So, Thandi was pregnant! Ha, but why am I surprised? With all that marathon humping on her mother's peacock sofa, what did they expect?) So that, by the time they reached my surrogate-surrogate grandfather's residence, word had already reached the bull of the Mlambo clan that they were on their way, and a motley crowd of nosy villagers had made itself available to witness their arrival.

There! The nosy villagers thrust their nosy fingers at the couple appearing over the hill of the north-east, their nosy bodies trembling with barely concealed excitement as the two silhouettes tromped through the mire, he leading the way, she shambling behind, their shadows stretching with the sinking sun. To their left was the Thornton Farm, with the dapperwood, double-storey farmhouse lying on the brae, flanked by a pair of baobab trees, its windows reflecting the last teary streaks of light. Next to the farmhouse, outbuildings slanted into the valley below, gloomy where the light could no longer reach. Abednego paused, squinted, and shaded his eyes; he could make out, lined up along the incline, the bulkier shapes of soldier trucks, their veld-green tarpaulins flapping in the breeze. Next to him stood Thandi, huffing and puffing. He appraised her, her hand on her hip, barrelling his five-month-old pregnancy, and smiled. She scowled. On they trudged.

He found Baba sitting in his same spot in the shade of the mopane tree, though he'd never seen him in such strange garb before; the old man was wearing a white robe, like a dress, with a green sash across, and leather sandals. A green, plastic rosary swung to-fro from his neck.

'Baba!' he cried, spreading his arms wide as he strode towards the old man. 'Mlambo kaMdlongwa!'

The old man neither responded nor looked up. Instead, it was my surrogate grandma who unplastered herself from the crowd and flung herself into his embrace. She felt smaller, frailer. The village, too, which had once been for my surrogate father a source of wonderment, seemed to him to have shrunk, and to carry about it a provincial fragility. It wasn't disdain he felt for his village, no, not in the way Frankie and Mvelaphi and perhaps even Thandi had once had disdain for him, but something altogether more intimate, an anxiety for its rustic nature, which he felt could not withstand the inevitable assault of the metropolis. He wasn't the only one who felt this change, which he took to be a change in the village, but which was really a change in *him*; he could see it, in the way his mama stepped back and regarded him, in the gawking of the nosy villagers, and especially in the way Zacchaeus studied him from a distance, goggle-eyed at the sight of his cerulean seersucker suit, now creased and the hem of the trousers muddy, and taking in also his matching tie now loosened and his pink shirt with the top buttons undone. It was his only suit, the only smart pair of clothes he owned, but it had been important for him to arrive in his village with a metropolitan bearing, a decision he now felt unsure of, for he hadn't thought it would separate him so harshly from his past and the people and things he loved.

'Ma, Baba,' he said. 'Meet your makoti.' With that, he nudged Thandi, who'd been standing in his shadow, into the limelight.

'Ah, welcome, makoti,' cried my surrogate grandma. 'Oh, my son, look how beautiful she is!'

I can imagine those nosy necks turning giraffe-like from that motley crowd, everyone straining-for-a-look-see; some shuffling and some shoving, and then nosy lips murmuring:

'... But see how she grips her mother-in-law's hand, firmly like that, for shame shuwa, no shyness, she doesn't even look away...'

'... Not even a curtsey...'

'... Isn't she supposed to go to the father and kneel...'

'... Ah, hear how loud she laughs, what kind of makoti...'

'... Pregnant already, when did they do the bride price negotiations, me I don't remember...'

Out of the corner of his eye, Abednego saw Baba getting up and, without looking his way, threading through the crowd to his hut. He hesitated and then, smiling blindly into the twilight, followed the old man.

'... Ah, did you see...'

'... Not even one look from the father...'

'... Not even a greeting, nje...'

Baba sat in the dark, away from the entrance. Atop one of the mud walls, leaning against the thatch roof, angled to catch a ray of sun or a glint of moon squeezing through the tiny window in the wall opposite, was a framed painting of the Liberation Hero Jesus Christ. He wore his thorn crown with majestic forbearance, Comrade Jesus, dangling from his cross in the martyr spirit, dazzling, saintly eyes painted in the commonplace blue staring back at a staring Abednego. My surrogate father frowned – he did not remember having seen the Liberation Hero dangling there before.

'May my poor ears be protected from the sin of blasphemy!' launched my surrogate-surrogate grandfather. 'To hear from the blessed lips of my own brother that my son has turned away from the glorious path to slither into bed with the slimy terrorists!'

My surrogate father stood wordless in front of his surrogate father, seething from his Uncle Lungile's betrayal and also struggling to understand why-the-hell Baba was speaking to him as if from a pulpit.

'Curse you, boy, curse you! I hope, for your sake, that you have not been entrapped forever by the fowler's snare!'

'I don't understand, Baba.'

'You don't understand? *You don't understand?* Of course you don't understand, boy, what man floundering about in the dark was ever able to pinpoint a thing? Repent, boy, repent! Repent from the terrorists and accept Jesus Christ as your lord and saviour!'

'Eh…'

'Eh? Is that all you can do, eh? Grunt like a pig, while Satan squeezes the very life out of you, leading you away from the path of righteousness to the dark alley of death? And who is this heathen girl you bring here with her swollen belly? Is the belly yours?'

'Yes, Baba. I… you are going to be a khulu.'

'Don't call me father, I'm no father to no fornicating infidel! Why do you lie with a woman without the blessing of the Lord? Do we know this Delilah? Were we ever introduced to her family? Where is she from? Do you know? Does anybody know from whence this Delilah came?'

'Her name is Th-Thandi and she's, she's an Angela Davis…'

'Heh? You picked up a stray city girl who has no roots to speak of, is that it?'

'No, no no, she comes from Hwali, near Gwanda, I… we—'

'Shut your mouth, boy! You shall speak not of your sinning in my house!' With this, the old man produced a bible, which Abednego recognized as belonging to Zacchaeus. 'Kneel before me and accept Jesus Christ as your lord and saviour! We shall scrub you clean, and that Delilah of yours with you, and I shall speak to Father Dlodlo at the church to arrange a wedding as soon as possible. Meanwhile, you shan't lie with that heathen in my home, is that clear?'

He stared at his feet. In his head, he heard Thandi's protests just before they'd left Bulawayo for Lupane: 'I'm not a rural girl me, I can't live in the village!'

And his entreaties, which he'd actually almost believed: 'You'll have a good time, my cream-pie, you wait and see, my father has many cows, and Lupane is not even like a village, we have the St Luke's Mission Hospital just nearby, there is no work that you shall do, no pail on your head that you shall carry, you'll live like a queen, it's only for a little while…'

His heart sat stone-like in his chest. In the city, the impending baby had quickly overtaken the passions of the liberation struggle; with a dictatorial spirit it took over the weekend bioscopes and the night dancing and the intoxicating inculcations of Frankie and Mvelaphi; at one of the secret meetings, a quivering Thandi playing The Mother in Césaire's *Et les chiens* staggered midway through the play and barfed on the Rebel himself; their friends who were watching, mistaking this for a part of the performance, flung themselves into the stuffy air in effervescent applause, seeing the metaphor of their existence so earnestly enacted. Thandi was forced to abandon her revered role and attend to maternal duties and, what was worse, the play took off shortly thereafter, touring the towns and cities of the country and even foraging into neighbouring Zambia and then Mozambique, where it caught the wandering eye of a French-British director who, with his obsession for all things L'Afrique and African women especially, demanded to be allowed to turn it into a movie, in which would feature not only Mother and Rebel Son but also many pointless scenes of ebony belles writhing half-naked to ancestral drums, leaving behind a livid Thandi who would for the years to come lament this missed opportunity at stardom. Before the young lovers knew what was happening, the practicalities of love had colonized the carefree pitter-patter of romance. Where to stay with woman and baby? Abednego could not very well ask to continue sharing lodgings with his Uncle Lungile, who, after the Sun Hotel incident, did not hold Thandi in very high regard. And anyway, no women were allowed in the hostels. Even now, he was harbouring Abednego illegally, and if the police found out… When was he planning to move out, anyway?

'How about you continue staying with your mother while I sort things out?' Abednego had suggested to Thandi.

'Stay with my mother, do you think she'll allow me to stay in her house pregnant and without you even coming forward to pay damages? She'll kick me out and tell me to go and live with the man who has made me into a woman!'

And indeed, her mother had.

'OK, how about you go to your rural home in Gwanda for a while…' Abednego had then dared to suggest.

To which she broke into a terrifying fit, scratching and clawing at his face. 'Go back like this, with this big belly and no man and no freedom fighting to show for it? I am never going back to that bhundu unless I am dragging not a baby belly in front of me, but the carcass of the liberation struggle behind me. I'm a freedom fighter, you hear? A fighter. I shall give birth to the struggle—'

'Yes, my love, I hear you, but first you must give birth to a baby, and we must make preparations.'

'This is all your fault! You did this on purpose! You wanted this to happen!'

'Never, my love, never never never! But now that it has happened, I shall never leave your side. I shall look after you and my baby.'

'I'm not going to live in the bhundu.'

'We have to go, only for a little while.'

'You'll have to drag me kicking and screaming.'

'We have nowhere to stay here.'

'Perhaps you are not hearing me.'

'You'll love it.'

'There's nothing to love in that cesspool of backwardness.'

'We'll go just for a few months. Until after you give birth and you are strong enough to return. My mama is good with babies, I promise.'

'It won't be more than six months? Promise me. I can't stand that backward bhundu living and all those terrible rules women must follow. Angela Davis would never stand for this.'

'Six months, I promise.'

On the fourth day of my surrogate father's return, he found himself labouring on a wall for the hut he intended to share with his beloved, my beloved Thandi, who had since usurped a glum Baba from his throne beneath the mopane tree, where she now sat, and could be found sitting always, cradling her belly, moaning theatrically about the heat, the flies, a glass of iced water, please thank you.

As he stood to wipe sweat from his forehead, he saw two figures wandering into the Mlambo homestead. He recognized Father Dlodlo immediately, with his eyes bulging like a dragonfly's, making him look perpetually frightened. The other was a lanky fellow whom he had never seen before, dressed in tattered jeans and a flimsy, black-netted vest. Zacchaeus appeared suddenly beside Father Dlodlo and began fawning over his robes. The priest patted his head.

'Look at how big he is!' Father Dlodlo exclaimed at my surrogate father, his dragonfly eyes almost going *pop*! 'My, my, the boy has filled out, he's practically a man now, yoh! Come, Spear-the-Blood, meet a boy who has been to the city.'

The lanky fellow just stared at him, long and hard, his thumbs tucked into his jean pockets, his left shoulder slouching as though he were leaning against a doorpost. Abednego half-raised a hand, nodding at the fellow, who made a point of not nodding back. Smiling hesitantly, he turned back to the priest. 'And how are you, Father?'

'Oh, I'm excellent, very excellent! Your brother here has been doing excellent things, he took all the subject prizes in his year at the school, just excellent!' Dlodlo grinned at a half-scowling Abednego. 'We pray that he follows in your footsteps and goes to make something of himself in the city.' Here it was my surrogate father's turn to beam. 'Eh... boy,' the Father ventured, rubbing the back of his head. 'Your father came to see me about wedding preparations and eh... atonement...' He inclined his head towards Thandi, who was sitting in her usual place beneath the mopane tree, her swollen belly squatting sinfully between her legs.

Abednego lowered his eyes. 'Oh... we weren't thinking, hadn't thought about a wedding yet, I'd have to ask Thandi, city girls are different, you see, you can't just—'

'What is there to be asking?'

It was Spear-the-Blood who had spoken, his voice raspy, and when Abednego looked up, he was met with the fellow's mocking gaze.

'Is she not your woman? Is the belly not yours? So? Stop nuisancing and let the Faader do his job.'

'Spear-the-Blood here is a friend,' Father Dlodlo said quickly. 'Eh, forgive his manners. But he's been doing important work here in the area, him and the comrades.'

'Very important work. In fact, why not be coming and seeing

for yourself? We're having a pungwe at the school in a few days,' Spear-the-Blood clucked, clearly pleased to be finally the centre of attention.

My surrogate father shrugged, motioned to his muddy hands, and resumed plastering the half-erected wall. 'As you can see.'

'Everybody else will be there,' said Spear-the-Blood. 'If people see you are not going, they too might think it's OK not to be going, and I don't want you to be setting a bad example, you see. Or you're traitoring like your old man, fighting for the white man?'

'Don't call my father a traitor.'

Father Dlodlo shot Spear-the-Blood a warning look.

'All right, so he's a little bit loosing in the head. OK, I am understanding that. Anyone living in this godforsaken country and all the supremacist bullshit we are having would be getting a little crazing sometimes. OK, I am understanding. But you, you are not crazing. You are very sober boy from the towns, and the other people, especially the young boys, they are looking up to you. So, you will be setting good example and you will be coming to the meeting.'

'I don't think so.'

'This is not a requesting.'

Abednego narrowed his eyes. Through the netted vest, he could see the fellow's oversize nipples glinting in the morning sun like a pair of polished buttons. 'What type of meetings are these, anyway? Why are they held at night, and why are they compulsory?'

Spear-the-Blood moved closer, putting his arm around my surrogate father's shoulder. The fellow smelled of dagga and sweat. 'Look over to the white man's farm. Can you see it?'

Thornton Farm looked little different to Abednego than usual, except for the line of tarpaulined trucks in the driveway he'd first noticed on his trek to his father's homestead four days before. He hadn't paid them any mind then, but now, he could see clusters of men busying themselves behind what looked like a barricade.

'A scout post,' Spear-the-Blood continued. 'A whole platoon down there. As you are knowing, there is a war going on, comrade. We, the guerillas, are trying to be taking back this country from the whites. But we can't do it alone, can we? We are needing everyone to be participating. We are needing food, clothes and supplies. We are needing young, able men like yourself to be joining the fight, and young able women like your pretty wife over there,' he nodded towards Thandi, 'to be cooking for us, bringing us water, helping us out, things like that.' He took a step back, grinning, but the smile did not reach his eyes. 'Now, anyone who is reluctant to be playing his part in this very important mission may be mistaking for a spy, for traitoring. And you don't want to be knowing what we are doing to traitors, comrade. Are you understanding what I'm saying?'

Abednego nodded, reluctantly.

'So, I will be expecting to see you at the pungwe in a few days, comrade.'

They had flitted in and out of the community like spectres for the past several months, Spear-the-Blood & Co., having conducted, first, secret meetings with the dragonfly-eyed Father Dlodlo, and then having summoned the whole village to their pungwes, their night gatherings, before recruiting young boys to go and fight as guerillas in the war, which was quickly escalating, against the rogue Republic of Rhodesia.

On the night of the next pungwe, Thandi was, to my surrogate father's dismay, excited. Of course, she would have been excited! This doesn't surprise me at all; this was everything that she had wanted, all along; to be at the frontline of the revolution. I imagine Spear-the-Blood's visit to the Mlambo homestead energized her and pulled her back to her activism. I can see the old, charming Thandi resurfacing here, and her idealism propelling her out from under Baba's mopane tree.

They gathered at the school, Thandi jibber-jabbering about how jealous Mvelaphi and Frankie would be when she told them that she was fighting side by side with the rebels. My surrogate father, on the other hand, was fearful for both his life and Thandi's. He was alarmed to have plopped himself in the middle of this dangerous struggle when he'd mostly been faking his interest in the rebellion in the city so as to impress Thandi.

Spear-the-Blood began by hauling a teacher and a well-known elder to the front of the ragtag gathering of subdued villagers, where he proceeded to pummel them with the butt of a rifle, repeatedly on their heads and backs and any exposed body parts.

'Nobody is above the struggle!' he declared. 'Nobody! Nobody is too big for the struggle! When we are coming here needing your help, nobody is too big to be busy complaining behind our backs. You are thinking you are having too much education, heh? You are thinking you are having too many years, that you are better than everybody, heh? Nobody is above anyone else in the struggle!'

My poor Thandi! I can see her mouth dropping.

'The struggle is for freedom for all of us! Are you understanding what I'm saying?'

'My father, he was a chief before the whites came and scrambled up everything,' came a timid murmur from among the subdued villagers. 'He was a chief above Dingwayo here, who is busy lying to everyone claiming a chiefly lineage. Will you restore me to my rightful position of chief after the war?'

The most vulgar words were mortared from the relations of Chief Dingwayo, shelling the speaker into silence.

'And me, just last month the District Administrator came and took a third of my fields and relocated them to a new family which is moving into the Tribal Trust Lands,' came another complaint. 'Now, my plot was already smaller than everybody else's, and to be having even more land taken away from me is just not right. I know the District Administrator has it in for me because I refused to marry that ugly niece of his—'

'You are the ugly bastard, you Jepheth, with a face like your mother's pussy!'

There rose a cacophony of other requests, complaints and demands, which it took several minutes for Spear-the-Blood to quell. 'All of these matters are of no consequence,' he said, provoking another racket. 'We are needing to, we are needing to band together and and and to be *freeing* ourselves, the whites, they are our enemy—'

'But it is you who comes and takes food we don't have from us. Our children are starving because we give all we have to you. First the whites spat on our being and made us live like slaves in our own lands, now you have taken our sons and made us seedless. You are busying scaring the Faaders at the church also, turning the House of God into heathen business. And just last week, you bombed the local clinic, now we must travel how many kilometres for treatment—'

'Be stopping that traitorous talk!' yelled Spear-the-Blood, pinching the space between his eyes. 'The clinic was an institute of the white man. We are having our own local healers here. What is there to be missing? Do you want me to be going and reporting back to our leaders of the nationalist movement what type of spineless swines are roaming this part of the land?! We have been working so hard trying to free all of you cockroaches from white bondage; our leaders have been jailed too many times, and now, they've had to be going into hiding, over there in the USSR and over here in Zambia. And now it's the eleventh hour and you want to be backing out of the struggle? Do you know what they shall be doing to traitors when we win the war, heh? To those who refuse to be lending a hand to the struggle...?'

It was here that my Thandi learned just how bourgeois her form of idealism really was! No one in the village was exempt from the demands of food and clothing from the guerillas, not even the Mlambo family and the urgent needs of their pregnant new makoti. Abednego watched, dismayed, as the fat shed itself from beneath Thandi's skin, making her reel from the weight of her baby load. Even she, what with her visions of dragging home the carcass of the liberation struggle, was frightened by this brand of Spear-the-Blood & Co.'s justice. Every day she cried, every day she pined after big-city living and cursed the day she met my surrogate father, and not even his romantic, manly gesture of building them a hut all by himself could kindle her. She became a pariah, what with her haughty-city-girl airs and her refusal to help with the cooking or any other womanly chores, screaming to anyone who cared to listen how she was an Angela Davis who demanded that her feminality be respected. And hadn't Abednego promised that she'd live like a queen? Not even my surrogate grandma, with her inclination towards agreeability, could put up with such eccentricities. It was, to my surrogate father's dismay, my Uncle Zacchaeus with whom she became close friends, Zacchaeus with whom she seemed to have in common that haughty-roving-eye, with whom she could dress up Marxian rhetoric in fancy English words.

'Stay away from her, brother. She's mine.'

'Whatever did she see in you, brother? I could never see you landing such a girl.'

'Well, I did. And you didn't. I've been to the city. And you haven't. So, I'm warning you.'

'Yes, you've been to the city, and yet you have come back more or less the same buffoon that left. I can see through you, and your fancy city clothes with their ridiculous feminine colours—'

'It's the fashion of the day! Something you wouldn't know anything about.'

'Yes, but I've been to school, I know things you will never know. I shall forage towns and cities, and even whole countries, for worldly wisdom, I shall fashion myself into a Great Colonizer—'

'Oh, shurrup, you've been singing that song for as long as anyone can remember, and yet here you are still, stuck in the bhundu.'

In spite of what my surrogate father says now, I imagine he got a little satisfaction from witnessing his brother wince, and walk away, for once with nothing to say.

That inevitable day when Spear-the-Blood came on behalf of the liberation struggle to collect a son from the Mlambo family – his eye cast upon Zacchaeus, having mistaken his passionate intellectual posturing on behalf of the war for eager brawn – was also the tragic day of Baba's death.

And this, the story of how my surrogate-surrogate grandfather died, is the type of tale you'll never read verbatim in any official history book, for, as Dumo would say, those who know it are the kind of inerudite folk who, aside from being asked to pose for Red Cross and WHO newsletter photos, aren't thought to possess that much-needed epistemological savoir faire. It's also the kind of scandalous scuttlebutt that any self-respecting son would be loath to remember, let alone share, and which not even Bell's has been strong enough to coax free. Believe me, I have tried. But it turns out that stronger medicines of more stellar quality have been required. Such as a 750ml bottle of Johnnie Walker Blue. And so, putting my faith in the distillation prowess of the Scots, I have paid Johnnie a tithe, and Hallelujah! Plied with the tongue-loosening flavours of cocoa and cedar, entranced by the potent whiff of leather and spice, palating the meditative notes of moss and peat, my surrogate father has begun to avow. He has declared, he's confessed, he's proclaimed! And thus, the story of how my surrogate-surrogate grandfather met with Death, that intimate companion he'd first encountered in '44 on the battlefield at Scraggy Hill, Shenam, Burma, and whose ballsy exploits had since overawed his mind, goes like so:

When the old man saw that terrorist picaroon Spear-the-Blood swaggering into his homestead as though into the backyard of some pagan commoner, having added as part of his renegade attire a candy-coloured bandana which he'd wrapped around his kooky-shaped head – covering, fashionably, one eye – and flaunting also some rusty-looking firearm which the fool was holding the wrong way round, he, Ziphozonke Majahamane Mlambo, recently born again and faithful to the causes of both Christ and Country, hastened to his hut to don the patriotic raiment of the Rhodesian African Rifles, more commonly known under the acronym RAR, which, when pronounced properly, sounds like a ferocious roar, *RRRAARRR!*

He intended to shoot the picaroon dead. He especially intended to shoot him dead when he heard him bullying first my surrogate father and then more forcefully my Uncle Zacchaeus into partaking in his traitorous activities no doubt decreed and blessed by the odious hand of Lucifer. But as he stood checking and then cocking his FAL – polished, clean, not a spot of rust anywhere – he heard the terr conferring on his boys the details of an imminent ambush upon the House of Thornton, the abode of that bigoted noncombatant he cared nothing for but in whose residence a division of the nation's army currently resided.

He stepped out of his hut and faced the boy fair and square, raining upon him all of the curses of the bible which he'd thus far learned by heart and then demanding that he come with him to hand himself in. Naturally, the bhantinti declined. There was a moment of confusion, and panic even, as the scoundrel raised his firearm – the right way round – and pulled the trigger. Luckily, thanks to the candy-coloured bandana, the scoundrel had forsaken vision for fashion, and the shot whizzed past my surrogate-surrogate grandfather to lodge itself in his darling mopane tree.

For this alone, he would have shot the little satan.

Instead, he decided to rally the troops, so he turned and ran – yes, ran, to the hasty jeers of Spear-the-Blood – out his gate and across the hill of the north-east, headed for my surrogate grandpa's farm. His teeth rattled in his mouth, his flesh undulated in the wind, and in his heart he felt a thrill such as he hadn't felt in a long time.

There was a young private holding sentry at the bottom of the brae where the soldier trucks were stationed and several tents had been pitched. When my surrogate-surrogate grandfather saw the private, he raised the hand holding the FAL and waved frantically.

'The Major General!' he wheezed. 'Get me your Major General!'

The young private gaped in astonishment at the munt bearing down upon him shouting some incoherent native war cry clad in combat gear and brandishing a firing weapon.

A skinny lad fresh out of teenhood, having just turned twenty, this was his first conscription. He was still wet behind the ears and a little jittery and missed very much his mama's peanut butter and jam sandwiches and the Snake Park and the Bulawayo fast life riding shotgun with his brother who was part of the Grey Street Cowboys, but he missed especially the boobs of the girl of his dreams, Miriam Hibbert, which he described three hundred and twenty-one times in the long, explicit letters he wrote her but never sent – which were found among his things after his death in a terr ambush and were published years later as part of his farmer father Matthew Robert Borris's best-selling memoirs, during that millennial year 2000 when the white farmers of Zimbabwe were kicked off the land and settler literature became en vogue – detailing how he wished to give it to her long and hard. He, like me, was yet to copulate with any woman. He was yet to have even his first kiss.

Upon seeing the enemy bearing down upon him, primed for assault, the young private raised his FN FAL rifle, aimed and fired. He was shaking and this was his first combat and he couldn't keep his hands steady and the target wouldn't stop moving and so he just kept on firing and firing and firing and firing…

The first bullet struck my surrogate-surrogate grandfather in the belly, lifting his feet a little off the ground, as though propelled into weightlessness by some supernatural force. He felt nothing at first, only euphoria, and then a keen burning sensation in his gut such as he had never known. He screamed. He screamed to Christ and Country, he screamed, The Lord is my shepherd I shall not want, Rise O voices of Rhodesia, He maketh me lie down in green pastures, Bringing her your proud acclaim, He leadeth me beside the still waters, Grandly echoing through the mountains, He restoreth my soul, Rolling o'er the far flung plain, He leadeth me in the path of righteousness, Joining in one grand refrain, Yea though I walk through the valley of the shadow of death, Ascending to the sunlit heavens, I fear no evil, Telling of her honoured name, For thou art with me, Rise O voices of Rhodesia!

His scream carried across the brae, across the valley, and through the Mlambo stead; those who heard it said it was like a barn owl screeching, those who saw him claimed he seemed to flutter like a bundle of green clothing flapping in the wind. All who were present, guerillas and army alike, branded him in their unofficial hi-stories as a traitor. For, he had been to one side a fucking RAR and to the other a batshit munt and thus he had worked for the enemy.

It was here, as he lay on the ground trying to plug the hole in his belly, as the world around him gradually dimmed, that my surrogate-surrogate grandfather finally understood, sparkling clear, the gift that military life had unwittingly given him; the gift of seeing not black men die – for he'd witnessed this plenty of times throughout his life and had always known just how cheap in this world a black man's life was – rather, he'd been granted the gift of seeing white men die, die like flies, die in the most wretched ways, ways unmentionable which kept him up at night and which were unfit for men to die; he'd witnessed this and come into an awakening, finally, which neither his life of toil in the Tsholotsho mines nor that of patriarch in his home could have proffered him. He had come into the knowing, from the time he saw his Colonel J. F. Clayton blasted to fokol at Scraggy Hill, Shenam, Burma, that the white man was no god; the white man was no god, Holy Hallelujah, the white man was no god, and although God was a white man, *the white man was no god!* He'd gripped this knowing and clung to it and trembled with elation and come out of it feeling fully like a man standing not beneath any other man and thus relieved of the yoke of humiliation that had burdened him all his life, first as a nigglet beneath the boot of the settler in the Tribal Trust Lands, and later as a kaffir beneath his whip in the mines.

Too late, too late, this knowing… it crept upon him and gave his muddled mind clarity and he proclaimed one last fervent cry of thanks to Christ and Country – Rise O voices of Rhodesia, Thy rod and thy staff they comfort me – before he choked on his last breath and died.

FATHERS

The recounting of my surrogate-surrogate grandfather's death has deteriorated my poor surrogate father to a stuttering mess. Oh, Johnnie! Johnnie, what have you done! His nostrils, wet and drippy, and now the colour of strawberries, keep inflating to alarming proportions and then deflating back again to their already generous size. He looks too much like my Uncle Fani now, like he may drag me onto his lap and cling to me and cry into my chest like I'm his mama.

I, too, am not without grief for my surrogate-surrogate grandfather's passing. But I can't afford to break down while my surrogate dada is in this state. It's as though you passed only yesterday, grand-dada! May you be resting in peace, wherever you are, whether it's with the fucking RARs or the batshit munts.

(As I channelled you last night in my pygmy room, rendering your last moments on this earth as imaginatively as my gifts of redescription allow, I almost felt your hand on my shoulder and your voice in my ear. We were as one!)

I feel as though I've always known you! That man you raised as your own even as the sting of adultery made you cruel, he weeps for you, grand-dada. He loved you! It is not for a son to collapse before his collapsing father. The best I can do is to clasp my surrogate dada's clammy hand, that's the best I can do, and clear my throat as I grasp for something meaningful to say. Ahem…

'… Father—'

'Bukhosi?' he says. 'Bukhosi, is that you?'

I sigh loudly, and side-eye him. He's staring at me intently, and I see hope inflaming those puffy eyes. 'It's Zamani.'

'Come here, Bukhosi!'

He dives, yes, like he's our very own Glen Walshaw at the Swimming Olympics plunging into the deep end, stretching out his arms towards me as he springs from his sofa. I happily catch him, for it's into my arms and not Bukhosi's that he's diving, dammit, whether he knows it or not. I grip him by the armpits and drag him back onto his sofa and perch my little tush on his armrest. I begin to rub his back.

'There's nothing to be ashamed of,' I say.

'He was a traitor!'

'Hush, now, Father, ssshh…'

'And b-b-because of him *we* were called traitors, the people of our village remember him as a tr-tr-trai*tor*, history—'

'Sshh… What is this hi-story business?' I put on my best Wittgenstein impression. 'Our real selves lie buried deep in the stupor of a murky present, in which the act of living is ahistorical, and all that matters is breathing, waking *now*, now eating, now shitting, now bathing, now walking. And above all, feeling. What the hell is hi-story? Things that didn't belong to anyone and belonged to everyone being claimed by someone, demarcations, lineages and hi-stories being created abracadabra and made real in the mind, and then consolidated through tales told and then revised to suit not only the mood of the day but also the vision for the future, memory aided and ab*ated*, yes, by delusion, constantly recreating and justifying, and thus no truth ever mattered except that which was believed to be true.' I pause emphatically, as I'm sure Herr Wittgenstein would. 'So, your Baba, Father, my beloved surrogate-surrogate grandfather, carried no shame except that which is common to all of man. How is the value of a life to be measured? So he fought on behalf of Rhodesia in the Second World War. So he was part of the Rhodesian African Rifles. So he pledged himself to serve country, to the honour and duty demanded by soldierhood. What are honour and duty and country except the trinity of a live, moving hearse into which we throw conquest's history-riddled bodies? What do you suppose those soldiers of the Schutzstaffel told themselves as they flung in the name of honour and duty and country Jewish bodies, warm and breathing still, into the furnaces at Treblinka? What do you suppose the founders of the US of A were thinking as they wiped out whole Native American populations? And those soldiers of our own Mugabe's 5 Brigade, what do you suppose ran through their minds as they hacked and hacked our people to death in Matabeleland during Gukurahundi? I imagine they all saw themselves as ordinary men, just men and even boys who had mothers and lovers waiting somewhere with rose-scented memories bosomed in their chests.'

At the mention of the 5 Brigade and Gukurahundi, my surrogate father begins to convulse. He blinks at me wildly, and tries to push me away, squirming at the feel of my hand on his back. I bend over and grab Johnnie from the floor and shove it to his lips, feeding him straight from the bottle. I grip him by the neck, but I can feel him trying to push me away, his body struggling away from the sofa, away from me. My grip on his neck tightens, and I pull him close, until his head is resting against my chest. I'm pouring Johnnie straight into his mouth. He swallows, sputters, begins to cough. I lift the drained bottle from his lips and place it on the floor.

I imagine his throat must be burning and that's why tears are streaming from his eyes and down the sides of his face.

'Are you trying to say something, Father? Hmmm?'

His eyes, glistening red with the tiny veins visible in the sclera, are trained on me.

'There, there, Father, everything is going to be OK.'

We sit like that, me cradling him, for a long time, until his head lolls on my chest, and his body becomes limp. I gently push him back on the sofa, until he is sitting slumped with his back against its incline.

'Father?'

He groans.

'Father, can you hear me?'

His eyes flutter.

'Do you see me, Father? It's Zamani. Say, "Zamani." Say, "Zamani, my son."'

He just groans. No matter! I slide my slim torso next to him, on the sofa. I cup his yellow cheeks and bring his face close to mine.

'It's your son, Father. It's me, Zamani.'

He's comatose, now, I don't think he can hear me.

'I love you, Father.'

I stare at those closed eyes, imagining their penny hue; stare into those teardrop nostrils, at that moist, peeping thicket. I bring my blueberry lips close to his and kiss them. They are cold, his breath warm. It reeks of Johnnie.

My Father.

I sidle up against him. Take his hand and place it across my tummy, where it rests on my hip, limp. Take my Nokia N76 out of my trouser pocket. Angle it above us. Press my cheek against his.

Smile into the camera, and snap our selfie. I shove the phone back into my pocket and put my arms around him. Place my head on his chest.

'It's going to be all right, Father.'

Together, we watch the Saturday twilight through the sitting room window, creeping stealthily across the sky.

This morning, my surrogate father told me he thinks he should stop drinking. He was wearing his scotch jacket, a Gideons' pocket size bible fisted in his hand. I recognized it as belonging to Bukhosi.

'Oh?' I said. 'Is something the matter?'

He refused to meet my eyes, saying as it was a Sunday, he had decided to go to church with Mama Agnes and pray for the boy.

I had already planned our day; we were going to sit together in the sitting room like we always do, I would bring Johnnie, and he would tell me what happened with Thandi after Spear-the-Blood dampened her enthusiasm for revolution. (I dreamed about her again last night. Maybe my surrogate father could tell me where she is, and I can go and visit her! I would love to sit beside her and watch her talk. I bet she's still a blot-out-sun.)

My surrogate father never goes to church, and I couldn't help but be crestfallen at his announcement; I think I hid it well. I forced myself to sound chirpy as I said, 'Oh, great, wait, let me put on something decent, and I'll come with you.'

'No.'

We stood there by the back door, both startled by the force in his voice. And then, he said, 'We are going for a private prayer session with the Reverend Pastor. It's family only. You can pray for us here, if you like.'

I smiled. 'Of course. And if there's anything else you need me to do?'

He nodded vaguely, and then turned around and walked back into the house. He didn't even say goodbye, like Mama Agnes did, as they left in his red Peugeot 405, even though I waved at him. I spent the morning pacing up and down the dirt path that separates my pygmy room from the main house. Then, I went inside the house, and stood by the boy's sofa, appraising his baby portrait hanging on the wall above it. His frightened baby eyes were now frightening. I sneered at that portrait, I glared at it, I even tried to stare it down; but the feeling of fear did not leave me. I sat down on the boy's sofa, but I could not sit still. A dreadful discomfort overtook me, and I found I could not bear to sit on it, *his* sofa, so I got up and began pacing, again.

Finally, I decided to visit Old Ntombazi. The traditional healer lives far away, Makokoba certainly isn't just a stone's throw away on foot, but the walk calmed me. I used to take this very route to Old Ntombazi with Uncle Fani, in his last years, when he discovered the magic of ubuvimbo root powder. I needed some ubuvimbo, and Old Ntombazi is the only one in the city purported to have it. I know a strong opiate like this will do my surrogate father good; it will lighten his mood, just as it used to do for Uncle Fani, and maybe get him talking to me again. Then he won't look at me the way he looked at me this morning – I couldn't stand that look, like I was a stranger, or something worse. *It's family only.*

The old witch charged me a whole arm and practically both of my legs, but I came away with what I needed, and I knew Abednego wouldn't be able to last the whole day at Mama Agnes's church. Marathon prayer requires an endurance and a faith he doesn't have. I found him at home when I returned from Old Ntombazi, and immediately made him some tea. Ha! That surprised look on his face when I offered it to him was priceless; I bet he expected I was going to offer him some Johnnie.

Still, he declined the tea.

'It will help you get over your hangover,' I said. 'You look really terrible.'

'I'm fine.'

'No, you're not.'

'Kanti, what's your problem?'

He was glaring at me. I decided to stand my ground, and said, 'You are a grown man,' I even tried to flatter him, 'a strong-willed man. I understand how difficult it has been, with my brother missing, and—'

'Will you stop it.'

'What?'

He sighed, as though talking to a small child. 'I'm tired of you always coming here—'

'If you don't want the tea, just say so.'

'I already said I don't want the tea. Can you just leave me alone, I want to be alone, nje, for once. Whenever I look up, here you are, hovering like a fly. Kanti, what do you want?'

'I want to help—'

'Can you go away. Can you just get out of here. Fuseki, bye bye!'

I cupped my ubuvimbo-laced tea and crawled away, back to the stifling confines of my pygmy room. I wept as I looked at our selfie on my Nokia, before stuffing it under my pillow. I don't know what to do; I've been trembling all afternoon; I feel... lost.

I shouldn't have drunk the tea. It made me feel vulnerable, and I ended up doing what I promised myself, from the day Abednego called me his surrogate son, I would stop doing. I opened my

Red Album, and indulged myself with pictures of that man… my father… *purportedly* my father. Where is the proof? And yet I admit I have, ever since Uncle Fani's deathbed confessions in 2002, searched for the man in newspapers and in history books. I have cut him out from the dailies, I have ruined many a library book tearing out certain pages, and I have pasted it all into my Red Album. I have tried to trace, like a story, the man's life. I have even watched him, followed him, stalked him, and dreamed of lining him up in the crosshairs of a rifle scope – but why do I torment myself with these thoughts? I have studied with expert concentration that face the colour of black feldspar – can't a man tame his obsessions? – I have caressed those lips in the shape of a flat-bellied heart; I have traced with my thumb those cheeks that curve elegantly from either side of the columella in the distinguished silhouettes of smoking pipes – dammit, the man does have a fine bone structure!

And then, always, after this inspection, my hand rises involuntarily to stroke my own face, which is the colour of black feldspar. And if I take a piece of paper and cut it into the shape of a heart and then clip off the bottom, I have the shape of my lips exactly. Also, I have the most aesthetic cheeks, whose bone structure is profiled by shaded slopes on either side of my nose.

Could it be that his darkness is in me? But I love Abednego. I wish to know my surrogate father far better than this man who is my father, who cannot be my father; eish, but why, Uncle Fani! Why did he have to confess his secrets to me? Why did he tell—Ah, what is the use of torturing myself with these memories? I'm a man on a new path, after all. By the end of these chronicles of our family hi-story, I shall be born again, into a Mlambo son. I shall have succeeded in escaping the dreadful past bequeathed me by my uncle on his deathbed.

And yet, I can still smell the cough-drop smell of which my uncle always reeked his whole life, the smell of a hi-story which had burst many-a-time, over the years, from his eyes in long, dreary, inexplicable squalls, in response to which I, first as a scrawny kid, would thrust my finger at his glistening face and burst, 'Look, Uncle Fani is crying! Like a gal!' This seemed to amuse him, and at times he even managed to smile through his tears. And then, as a pimpled teen pockmarked by pubescent shame, I began to lend him my bony chest, reluctantly I admit, for what the hell was a grown man crying for, on which to lay his head and mewl. And then I could bear it no more, and sought refuge in my tattered volume of *Lord of the Flies*, in the pages where Simon speaks to the pig's head, which I'd read out loud, shouting at the top of my voice as though at a recital in a big hall, so as to drown out those horrible, deep-throated, grown-man sobs.

It was always me and Uncle Fani; just us two. The story of how my mama – and apparently my father – died in a mysterious fire when I was a baby was told and retold in our house until it began to take on the texture of lore.

'But no aunts…?'

He shook his head.

'No cousins…?'

No cousins.

'No—'

'It's just me and you, mfana, OK?'

How could it just be me and him? Where were the intertwining branches of our family tree, those boughs that should have hung heavy with the fruit of grandparents, aunts, uncles, cousins, nephews and nieces? Where was our rural home?

'Why do you bother me with all these nonsense questions? Am I not mother and father enough to you?'

His walnut eyes taking on a sad hue as they took in my searching, hungry face; I his nephew who had been like a son to him, and at times even tried to be a mummy; this man who had been like a father to me, albeit not a very good one, and who had on occasion tried to be both father and mother.

It was just us two.

Did I feel the dark seeds of the man who fathered me swirling in me even then? Have I inherited his traits? His mannerisms? His dark talents? His penchants?

Am I my father's son?

ǂKHOĀ

I knew he wouldn't be able to stay away from the drink. Just one day, and by the end of yesterday he was already sweating. Only one day after his professed sobering up, and already he was thirsting after Johnnie like nothing else could ever quench him. I understand his thirst; the Red Album has been haunting me since I made the mistake of opening it, and I have been thirsting after our family hi-story to fill these holes I feel echoing like hollow chambers.

I could hear him pacing outside my pygmy room while I stayed locked inside, still sore from his sharp words and still woozy from the ubuvimbo. His agitated fluttering has alarmed Mama Agnes, though. He's going to get us caught! She came to see me yesterday evening in my pygmy room, saying she was worried about him, he'd been acting strange, going to church with her and then coming back home in a funk, and now outright possessed by some evil spirits. I was pleased that she sought counsel from me, and pretended to spend some minutes pondering this.

'Should I call the Reverend Pastor to come and do some prayers? First my son and now my husband...'

'No no, leave him to me, Ma. He talks to me, I'll get to the bottom of this.'

'Are you sure?'

'Hundred per cent.'

'Let me call the Reverend Pastor…'

I sighed, and tried to smile. 'Just wait, Ma. I know what I'm doing. I can help him.'

I didn't think he would hold out through the night. I feared he would invade my lodgings. But he didn't! He waited until Mama Agnes had left for work this morning. I applaud him! He respects my Mama Agnes that much, at least. We were supposed to go on another community search for Bukhosi today, and increase our radius, but he cancelled even that, telling our neighbours he would call them later, he just needed to follow up a lead or some such. I heard one of the neighbours saying that they would press on without him; he promised to catch up with them later and then he barged into my lodgings. The way he was sweating! The way his hands were trembling. The way his penny eyes glinted as they scouted my room for Johnnie.

I didn't want to give him any, lest his conscience decides to come back again and he wants to blame me for his drinking. I offered him some tea, instead, with a pinch of ubuvimbo. He looked at the tea like I was trying to insult his tongue, his facial muscles twitching as he said he just wanted something to relax him, some little thing, nje, just one drink, what would tea do for him?

'So tomorrow you can call me a fly?' I said, inclining my head to one side.

'Just one glass! OK, you are not a fly, half a glass, ke, just a little bit – give it to me!'

'See, you are shouting now,' I said sulkily.

'I'm not shouting—'

'—but you are.'

'I'm just stressed, bantu, I, I just need a sip, please…'

I had to promise him a glass of Johnnie for him to try out the tea. He gulped it down impatiently, burning the roof of his mouth in the process, but I could see a sparkle in his eyes when he was finished. It was such a delight to see him looking so euphoric for a change, instead of the dull stupor that booze has been getting him into of late, where he can't even talk, he just sits and weeps about Bukhosi or Baba, depriving me of the whereabouts of my Thandi.

And now, here we are, back in Mama Agnes's sitting room where we belong; our hi-story room. His tongue has gone totally loose, my surrogate father, busy hooking me with roundabout yarns of Zacchaeus and Thandi and something about a war and a son, which I must now, with all the skill of arti-farce I can muster, put into proper order.

Following the death of his surrogate father at the hands of a wet-behind-the-ears private, and the stories circulating thereafter from all quarters about the old man's perfidious nature, which many theorized was a hereditary trait carried in the Y-genome – which in village speak was a curse passed down from the ancestors for some wrong done by a forebear, thus manufacturing from their vitriol a lineage of traitorous Mlambo males who had been selling out everybody since time immemorial – my surrogate father had no choice but to flee for his life. Under night cover, he bolted into the bush, not to the war, no, but into hiding, hunkered down by my beloved Thandi who refused to be left behind.

As a result of the unpatriotic actions of both father and brother, my Uncle Zacchaeus, too, had to flee, for a Mlambo son Spear-the-Blood intended to conscript, whether older yellow face or younger parrot mouth he did not care. Under night cover, with the assistance of Father Dlodlo, who understood very clearly that his star pupil was destined not for the brawn of the bush but the brains of bureaucracy, where all the real decisions were made, my Uncle Zacchaeus fled the village for his first taste of big-city living, and, true to the vision of his haughty-roving-eye – but especially the influence of that great political body the Catholic Church – he tumbled across towns, cities and countries until he found himself at Oxford University, Oxford, England. Here he began studies in law but, taken over by the flourishes of the great English poets, that Wordsworth and that Keats – and also unsaintly visions of a naked Thandi gyrating before him with her swollen baby belly, to which he pumped his manhood repeatedly every night, ejaculating prosodies in her honour – he abandoned the law for a wispy BA in English Literature.

He graduated in '79. That great political body the Catholic Church had had great civic ambitions for him but, having discovered in him not concrete precepts of the law but rather eccentric flights of linguistic fancy, they nevertheless put him to good use in the vaulted rooms where men of political intention gathered. He was even invited, the same year as his graduation, to Lancaster House in London where that new, sparkling babe Zimbabwe was conceived through some rather clumsy coitus. He bowed demurely before the men of political intention – those Britons who were led by Lord Carrington on one side, and on the other side the Patriotic Fronters led jointly by Robert Mugabe and Joshua Nkomo – he bowed and trembled, felt the power of the politicos quivering through his body, felt it shivering down his spine and then shivering back up; he twitched as it crept into his soul; it tickled his tongue, it warmed his larynx, it summoned Keats, who laughed boisterously and declared, *To Hope, my dear Sir*

Zacchaeus, an ode To Hope! and out tumbled the eccentric flights of linguistic fancy, and though none of the politicos could understand the effervescent young man's libretto-like speech, they all agreed that he had outdone himself, and it was thanks to this stellar performance that he was later invited to wax lyrical at Zimbabwe's first Independence Day celebrations at the Rufaro Stadium on 18 April 1980.

A young sage! declared the politicos. An old soul! Indeed, indeed, the young man would go far.

The young man would indeed go far, much farther and in more dangerous ways than any of the politicos, in their prophetic proclamations, had intended. He, after all, hadn't the capacity for irony, my Uncle Zacchaeus. Hadn't a satirist's bone in him. If he had, he may have escaped the fate that befell him. For, it was at Oxford, where he returned after independence in 1980 to do his Masters and then PhD, that he cultivated the intellectual umbrage that ferried him to infamy in the late '80s and '90s, not only in Zimbabwe but also in New York where, fleeing state persecution for his writings about the Gukurahundi Genocide, he spent fourteen years of his adult life.

What I cannot forgive him for, though, and what was most likely the cause of the irreparable fall-out with my surrogate father, are his incestuous writings about my beloved Thandi, scribbled during his Oxford University days in his leather-bound diaries which, under the euphoric urgings of the ubuvimbo-laced tea, my surrogate father has retrieved from their hiding place atop his wardrobe and proceeded to show me. To covet your own brother's woman! Who is with child! To not only covet her, but to indulge the most graphic of sexual fantasies, and to record them with maiesiophilic zeal! That, now, is the crime of crimes! The man – otherwise a genius – even plagiarized Wordsworth's

'Laodamia', all in the name of Thandi. Laodamia, wife of Protesilaus, that great leader of the Phylaceans and the oracular hero of the Trojan War of Greek mythology, appeared in Uncle Zacchaeus's dreams with the likeness of Thandi. He imbued her, the Laodamia of his dreams, with umber skin and the most sybaritic curves, falling during many an afternoon into a haze in which he heard Thandi's voice lilting, *Celestial pity, I again implore; – Restore him to my sight – great Jove, restore!* While he, the intrepid Protesilaus, martyr and saviour of the idyllic kingdom Phylace, came up from the Greek underworld Hades to comfort and chide her, and at times French kiss her before laying down with her, and in one diarized fantasy even returning with her back to the underworld.

His is the type of family hi-story that deserves to be written out of the history books! In fact, the man deserves to be written out of our family hi-story altogether for his vices! I shall conclude by saying: my Uncle Zacchaeus, otherwise a very affable fellow, was a lecherous libertine who deserves to fry in the fieriest of furnaces for lusting after my Thandi.

What is it about my beloved that has us men banging our heads against each other so? If only my surrogate father would get to the part where he tells me what became of her, if only he'd tell me where she is now, I'd go and pledge my love to her this very day! I imagine she has aged well, my inamorata, that her lovely umber skin has only matured handsomely with time.

Is she as spirited now as she was back then, in January '76, when, still brimming with passion and a penchant for theatrics, she fled with Abednego who at that moment she hated for having brought her to the cesspool of backwardness that was Lupane? What else was she to do? She was with child and, besides, she certainly hadn't signed up for the kind of hardcore militancy

Spear-the-Blood & Co. demanded. No, this bhundu living with my surrogate father's family had sobered her proper, especially having to witness the way Smith's army had gunned down her nutso father-in-law in broad daylight and then had had the gall to go around claiming he'd been a loopy gook trying to blast them all to kingdom come.

No, my Thandi just couldn't handle this crude rural warfare business, this running off into the mountains and what-not, gun-toting men on every side of her. She was a city girl through and through, and her true calling, she realized, lay in disrupting the ritzy eating rooms of the likes of the Sun Hotel and also prancing about on a stage wooing tears from an audience, whether sympathetic or hostile, for at the bottom of it all the essence of all (wo)mankind was feeling – sweet poignant, heady feeling – feeling which, with her pregnancy, was now terrorizing her and making her dizzy and weepy so that Abednego could do nothing but stare at her feeling helpless while she slapped him with all the feeling she could muster.

'It's all your fault, all your fault, all your fault...' was all she could say, thrice like that, although secretly she must have been grateful: his bringing her here had forced her to see first-hand what would have been in store for her had they managed to enlist with the comrades and gone to Zambia.

'I'm sorry,' was all my surrogate father could say, though for what, he was not entirely sure.

Off they fled from the homestead of my grand-dada, the jingoistic Ziphozonke Majahamane Mlambo, renegade for Christ and also Second Lieutenant of the Rhodesian African Rifles, who'd been presented with his colours by the Mother Queen herself, Her Majesty Queen Elizabeth Alexandra Mary, back in those days in '53 when her skin was still taut and chiffon-coloured and her hair had about it the spry hue of pecan-sangria. Off they scuttled, nipped at the heels by the gun-toting Spear-the-Blood, and also the venom-spouting raconteurs of the crimes of my grand-dada, that two-timer said to have been two-ing the RARs and timing the munts.

Off they went over the mild hills of Lupane, across the scraggly bush, headed south on foot, walking along the Bulawayo–Victoria Falls road, hitching a ride in the Morris Minor of a compulsive smoker with a Red Cross armband and a thick Swiss accent, who was not headed, as they had hoped, to Bulawayo, which lay further to the south-east, but who took instead the road that shot off like a forefinger from the thumb that is the A8, past Bayi-Bayi and Pondo and Tsholotsho, making a final stop in Plumtree, that bland, dull border town south-west of glamorous Bulawayo, where nothing ever happens, but which they found uncharacteristically ahive with activity. For war was on its way, and Spear-the-Bloods had sprouted everywhere, intending to make martyrs out of young men. And so, from here, too, they had to flee, tumbling across rivers, fences and towns until they found themselves at Dukwe Refugee Camp, Dukwe, Botswana.

The campsite, my surrogate father says, struck a terrible dread in my inamorata. It stretched over some fifteen square kilometres of unfenced scrubland, the entrance demarcated by a cluster of buildings that housed the Aid Orgs and the church groups, and next to this a gathering of large tents where a Sister Bhictoria of the World Health Organization – nunned up in blistering and biting weather alike – administered, on behalf of all the charities, the food and clothes rationing, her wimpled face a perpetually severe glare. Separated from these by a patch of Kalahari soil, red and fine and on windy days billowy, and where the refugee children liked to play, were rows of tents, their tarpaulins fastened to the outer edges of low mud walls that had been built to prevent the rain from leaking in. Thandi took on the pastime of decorating the mud walls using a blend of soil and spit, sometimes crushing leaves into the mixture to variate the colours.

She was angry at being separated from my surrogate father and allocated a women's tent, in which they had to squeeze up against each other in groups of up to twenty. She didn't understand what the hell was happening, the whole of her life just turned upside down like so, in a matter of months! From script-writing revolutionary-acting Citizen against the Colour Bar to preggas refugee in the middle of nowhere in a foreign land fleeing war from her beloved home!

And war is exactly what it was. By 1976, it was raging in earnest throughout the whole country. I looked up the statistics at our National Archives. More than twenty thousand lost their lives, tens of thousands more, like my Thandi and my surrogate father, ruthlessly displaced. The ruckus between the colonists and the nationalists lit up the whole country – a fight over Anglo-Saxon values that was bitter to the end – spilling over into neighbouring Mozambique and Zambia. Meanwhile, a fratricide was going on between the nationalist parties themselves, a battle for the people's souls.

All around Dukwe Refugee Camp was nothing but the red soils of the Kalahari, scattered with clusters of shrubs and the more resilient acacia trees and the occasional kopje; in short, a dry and unimpressive landscape graced by the hunchbacked kudu or the sprier springbok, which must have made my inamorata's breath catch in her throat as it sautéed over three metres in the air or leapt across the plains in a nimble allegro, its tan and beige coat a rippling muscular sheen. They heard that lions roamed the area but had never seen one, but they glimpsed, occasionally, the Khoi San, who lived in the bush around the camp but who hardly ever made themselves visible, not until my Thandi joined the young women who ventured into the bush to pick mpulunyane, which they sold to the Khoi San, who then fermented it until it became a most potent brew, skittling even the most seasoned drunkard.

I imagine whenever she appraised this landscape and saw the drought-endued, cosmopolitan-deprived terrain that had become her life, my poor inamorata could not help but weep. My surrogate father watched her, helpless, for she was inconsolable. He had to be careful to keep his distance, for she could no longer stand the sight of him, in the same way that the smell of raw eggs or the taste of peanut butter made her nauseous. Not even his building them a hut in an area separate from the tents that was designated for the married, a lie they told Sister Bhictoria so they could live together and shored up by Thandi's oversize belly, could mollify her.

I can see them, on that fateful day in April of '76 in the bush where the baby was born. My poor inamorata must have felt the vibrations that travelled across the underbrush running through her feet and up her spine and into her pregnant belly. The ground trembled, and then somewhere, whether far away or nearby my surrogate father could not say, rumbled a rumble that swelled into a roar. And out of nowhere appeared a lion, out of that scraggly bush, a real, live, roaring lion, its mane shuddering, a delicious gold springing from the sides of its face and darkening to a handsome hickory as it travelled all the way down to its belly, its nostrils flaring as it dropped its chin and pulled back its lips to display moist, black gums and sharp, yellow canines.

My inamorata dropped her jaw and her basket of mpulunyane. The next moment, my surrogate father was in front of her, crouching with his hands spread wide, startling the beast, which roared and swiped at the air with its huge paw.

'Run,' he hissed at her.

But she couldn't run, poor Thandi, she couldn't run and instead her trembling legs gave way. It was then, as my surrogate father stared into Death's ochre eyes, that my inamorata's water broke and trickled down her thighs, that a Khoi San woman leapt out of the scraggly bush, out of nowhere she leapt thrusting herself between the lovers and the lion, my surrogate father tried to scream but couldn't find his voice, my inamorata found her voice and screamed, the woman bared her teeth and barked, the beast bared its gums and snarled, the baby was coming, the Khoi San woman was hissing, Thandi was groaning, the lion was growling, she spread her legs, it licked its nose, she fisted her hands, it shook its mane, she began to cry, and off it sauntered.

This is the story of his son's birth as told to me by my surrogate father. I admit, the ubuvimbo had done him a number, but this is what I got.

So. Baby Bukhosi was eased into the world by the hands of ǂkhoā of the Khoi San, ǂkhoā The Lion Whisperer. He announced himself to the world with a ferocious wail, a squirming mega-baby alarmingly oversize not only for the meagre diet on which my inamorata had subsisted for the previous months, but by any ordinary-world standards.

It was Thandi who named him Bukhosi, Princehood, for he had been born in the bush under the kingly roar of a lion and was thus a royal, lucky little neonate.

I must interject here, to clear any confusion, and state outright that this Bukhosi, this mega-baby who had his wrinkled little forehead smeared with a thumb of spit by ǂkhoā of the Khoi San, this princeling who received from ǂkhoā The Lion Whisperer a blessing recited in a click-click onomatopoeic tongue, whether in the language of the lions or in her own Khoekhoe dialect we shall never know, is not our Bukhosi, my poor surrogate brother who has been missing for two weeks now. I don't know what happened to this *other* Bukhosi, where he is and why my surrogate father has not spoken of him until now. I worry that maybe he's up to his fibbing again; perhaps he's confusing things; perhaps, caught in the euphoric clutches of ubuvimbo, he's given way to fantasy. But he seems now to be adamant about this Bukhosi, who he claims was born not on 18 April 1990, the birth date of our Bukhosi, but on 18 April 1976, a full fourteen years prior.

And so, cradling that chubby load, beholding in that tiny face the agreement of my surrogate father's teardrop nostrils with her own sepia eyes, stroking skin so buttery and honey like the father's but which would, in the coming months, darken handsomely to her own burnished umber, my Thandi began to cry. When she lifted her tearful gaze, my surrogate father's eyes, too, began to moisten.

The birth of Bukhosi, according to my surrogate father, seemed to mellow my inamorata, so that all inclinations of impregnating herself with the liberation struggle went out the proverbial window, and instead motherhood colonized her.

Their baby felt to my surrogate father like a focus, so welcome in the never-ending monotony of the camp: lining up outside the USAID tent for food, lining up outside the Red Cross tent for hand-me-downs, attending the abstinence lessons outside the WHO tent, lying under the cluster of acacia trees near the camp entrance… It had begun to seem to him that waiting had become his whole life.

But, each time Thandi clasped his hand or leaned her head against his chest – he taking this moment to bury his face in her mfushwa hair, which sprung from her head like a tropical forest – he was overcome by a lightness of spirit. These memories of her give me a lightness of spirit!

This Shangri-La was destined not to last, however, for one day in May the following year, just a month after little Bukhosi turned one, a truck arrived without warning at Dukwe Camp to take the men of Rhodesia away to a separate camp at Chifombo base in Zambia, that country which is shaped like a Fattail scorpion and rests its portly abdomen atop teapot-shaped Zimbabwe, née Rhodesia.

This request to separate the sexes had been put forward by Sister Bhictoria. She had tired, she wrote in a redacted report to the WHO, which I found gathering dust in our National Archives, of waging a losing war against the STD epidemic ravaging the camp, and having to deal with the refugee babies who popped out almost on a daily basis, and was fast losing faith altogether in the possibility of un-lusting these fugitive infidels of Aafricah.

As they dragged him on that fateful day in May to the idling truck, my surrogate father grabbed hold of Thandi's hand and tried to hug his son for what could be the last time. Sister Bhictoria stood pursing her lips and waving her rosary, murmuring how everything was going to be all right, no need for all this crying now, abstinence for Jesus, blessed be the celibates.

My surrogate father thought of Thandi and his son every single day in Chifombo, which turned out not to be another refugee camp, as had been promised, but a clustering of a different kind; he found himself in a training base for the guerillas, where every day he ran combat drills, during which they learned the Art of War as strategized by the great Master Sun Tzu, and where every day my surrogate father saw young men being loaded into vans and driven back into the charnel house from where they had just fled.

There were whiffs in that base of rebellions-within-the-rebellion, fantastical rumours of coups and assassinations, and the most ferocious power struggles going on at the very heart of the Zimbabwe African National Union (ZANU (PF)), which had broken away from my Thandi's hero, Joshua Mqabuko kaNyongolo Nkomo's Zimbabwe African People's Union ((PF) ZAPU). Something about some eager beaver with a serious face and oversize glasses named Robert or Gabriel or some such said to be playing some sick chess moves in this breakaway party and managing to manoeuvre to the top seat of the High Command. But more matter-of-fact and thus maddening was the buzz about the High Command having already betrayed the lunchpail principles as expressed by Chairman Mao, for they could be seen busy gorging themselves on hotel food and first class flying to that Britain and that America, and preferring to secure spots for their offspring brats in that Harvard and that Oxford, instead of maybe Shanghai Jiao Tong University or People's Friendship University.

Meanwhile, as the leaders of the revolution pigged out on first class living, the guerillas languished on weevil-infested rice in bases such as Chifombo. My surrogate father did not care much for this power grabbing business by this Robert nerd-boy or angel Gabriel whatever and his breakaway ZANU what-what party; he cared neither who was gorging on what in which hotel nor whose beloved among the guerillas was sleeping wherever without whatever; he concentrated instead on trying to remember the smell of Thandi's hair, on rendering her smile, on recalling Bukhosi's face, day after day, polishing their memories in his mind until they began to fog, to his horror, from all that rubbing, a day becoming a month becoming a year becoming three, and he spit-shining the same memories still as though to shield himself from this useless progression of time that seemed to be hustling him further and further from his beloveds.

During the day, he often imagined what kind of father he would be to the boy, while at night, in that damp room in the guerilla base, he would think of his own childhood. More often than not, his mind would turn to Farmer Thornton, who had once tried to claim him as his own, and who had always shown him a disturbing amount of kindness while treating Zacchaeus – that libertine who is now dead to me and shall henceforth be referred to only as that brother, for I intend to deny the letch the honour of recognition in my chronicles – with the contempt he deserved.

When my surrogate father was thirteen, he cut holes in the fence of the Thornton Farm with that brother, who was ten at the time. They slithered across Farmer Thornton's fields, stealing sugar-cane and green-squash and maize-cobs that were not quite ripe, which they'd roast over the glowering embers of the evening fire, in the camouflage of night so their mama wouldn't see. He'd never been caught, Abednego, but Farmer Thornton had happened upon that brother many-a-time, and proceeded to swat him with the cord of a telephone plug; Baba on the other hand had never walloped him, but thrashed Abednego constantly, sometimes without reason.

They were squatting in Farmer Thornton's fields, that brother cradling their loot, when they heard, coming from the direction of the farmhouse, the barking and howling of the farmer's Tibetan Mastiffs. They fled back to the high fence, but couldn't locate the holes. They were trapped.

'If you give me a leg up over the fence, I'll teach you how to read,' said that lecherous-then-treacherous brother to Abednego.

Abednego hesitated; he also didn't want to be beaten up by the farmer! But, oh, how he yearned to learn how to read! How many times had he begged that brother to teach him?

'All right,' he said finally. He put the huge watermelon he had stolen to one side and laced his fingers together, letting that brother of his step into his hands and scramble over the top of the fence.

No sooner had that brother disappeared from view, not even sparing a backwards glance, than a hand grabbed him from behind; he felt his shirt tightening around his chest. When he looked up, it was into the terrifying eyes of Farmer Thornton. He yelped, even though he'd promised himself he'd be brave.

'Now, what have we here? So, *you* are the other little thief.'

He had seen blue eyes before, those of the missionaries who came door to door, proselytizing and patronizing; he had even seen russet eyes, but never eyes as green as Farmer Thornton's. He had never been so close to a white face before, so close he could feel the tobacco breath hot on his skin, and follow the strange mesh of capillaries, like tribal marks across the white skin, glowing red in the sun.

The farmer dragged him all the way to the farmhouse. There, he dropped him on the floor by the kitchen entrance, where Sonny Boy, who had just turned sixteen, was busy fiddling with wire and sticks to make a bird trap he intended to set by the banks of the Bubi River. Farmer Thornton disappeared into the house. Abednego was too scared to move.

He could hear Mrs Thornton rattling around in the kitchen. He smelled an aroma that made his stomach fart. Were they going to cook him? Was that it? Chop him up and stew him for those ferocious Mastiffs of theirs? They looked like they could eat a human whole, those dogs. A boy, especially.

Sonny Boy studiously ignored him, still fiddling with his trap. There was a time when they had been cordial to one another, even played together, but the tensions between their families, and between the farmers and the kinsfolk living on the Tribal Trust Lands, had been thick in the air ever since the state of Rhodesia had declared itself independent two years before, in '65 – a furious response to the Mother Country's betrayal of her promise to grant the self-governing colony independence under minority rule (and in return for which she had received the colony's best armies during the Second World War) and not majority rule as she was now trying to do.

When my surrogate father heard the wooden floors groaning beneath the weight of the farmer's boots, he tensed his pelvic muscles. He stared at those boots, afraid to raise his eyes. They were tan and faded and wrinkled like an old man's cheeks. They were *huge*. Farmer Thornton must have had the biggest feet he had ever seen. The big boots got bigger and bigger, until they came to a halt by the kitchen entrance, right beneath his face. They made his nose crinkle; they smelled of Kiwi polish and paraffin.

Finally, he looked up. The farmer was carrying a plate in one hand, a knife in the other.

When Abednego saw the knife, he began to cry.

'What's wrong, little fella? Here you go.'

Farmer Thornton placed the plate next to him. There was a wedge of watermelon, which the farmer began to slice. He handed Abednego a piece. Abednego was too scared to refuse. The watermelon was cold; a sharp pain cut across his teeth.

'Tastes good?' Farmer Thornton asked.

Abednego nodded, wiping the juice dribbling from his lips.

'When you want, you ask, OK? No more stealing. You're lucky you're not hurt; I've put traps all over my fields, ever since my produce started going missing.'

That was the last time he ever slinked into the Thornton fields. And although that lecherous-then-treacherous brother did not keep his promise of teaching him how to read, he became a little legend among the village boys as he told of his ordeal:

'He lifted you up, with just one hand, high up in the air?'

'Yes, and he had eyes like a green mamba…'

'Yo, yo yo yo, yo!'

'And as he lifted me his eyes turned red…'

'Red!'

'And then blue…'

'And then blue!'

'Yes, and he took out a big hunting knife, and said he would skin me alive and paste me on his wall, like the heads of the antelope hanging in his living room…'

'Yoh, yoh yoh yoh, yoh!'

'But I fought him, and wrestled the knife from his hands…'

'Ah, ah ah ah, ah!'

'Then he said I was so brave, and that I have such nice skin, and I shall marry his niece when I grow up…'

'Wo, wo wo wo, wo! White girl, mfana! You are going to be a big man!'

'Yes, and he said he will take me to go and see his great big god who lives in the sky, who gives them green eyes and red eyes and blue eyes, and his god will give me green eyes like he has, and pale glowing skin…'

I glance at my surrogate father's eyes to check their colour, and am disappointed to see that they are still brown, and furthermore, that they are getting moist once again. 'Dukwe was a terrible time for my chicken-pie and my boy, and they didn't have me there to protect them!' He fumbles about for a tissue – ah, but where will he find some Alibaba Facial Wipes these days? He lands, instead, on yesterday's *Chronicle*, crumples the face of His Most Excellent Excellency, looking solemn at some inauguration or other, brings it to his nose, and blows. 'We'd left home without really thinking it through, you see, had had no choice, uprooted from our home and all we knew just like that. Oh, the trauma of it!'

Oh, the trauma of it! For little Bukhosi, the camp at Dukwe was all he knew, it *was* his home. The other refugees – people I'm sure my Thandi wouldn't have otherwise associated with had it not been for their being cooped up together in that camp under the grind of time, day after day, month after month, year after year, until one year became two became three, all feeling the same as the one before – had become their family.

Thandi remembered the refugees well, and would often tell my surrogate father about them, when they reunited after the war. There was Ndali, whom she described as a grown man who was skinny like a boy, always lying beneath the acacia tree outside one of the men's tents, sniffling and dipping his head every now and then to smear his tears against his SWAPO tee-shirt, declaring loudly that the world was a motherfucking Gehenna. There were the Mbilu twin sisters, who could be found entangled in one another in the sand outside their tent, busy disentangling each other's hair, which sprang from their heads with a delicious lushness, squishing lice eggs between thumb and forefinger, making little Bukhosi squeal as they made a 'cc cc' sound. There was Sister Bhictoria and her Bread of Life, given to Bukhosi by the Sister's wrinkly hands, made from her great-great-Nanna's special recipe, as she always told the plump little boy and his mother, stuffing the oily bread into his mouth, pausing every now and then to appraise him, to lift his legs and arms, press her hand against his belly, and peer into his mouth, admonishing him not to go out and play with the savages, they'd give him ringworms, that's what.

Little Bukhosi would nod but, after receiving the Bread of Life, one morsel at a time, he'd slip away and scamper off to the edge of the camp, where ǂkhoā of the Khoi San, ǂkhoā The Lion Whisperer squatted, just outside the camp demarcation, but within viewing distance. ǂkhoā in whom Thandi had entrusted her son's well-being, much to Sister Bhictoria's chagrin, Sister Bhictoria who never tired of the opportunity to wave her King James bible in the direction of the wilding woman.

Bukhosi would sit on ǂkhoā's lap and bring his little umber forehead to her big peanut butter one; he'd stare into her slanting, laughing eyes, dazzled by the glimmer there, the glimmer of the sun, she called it; he'd tap-tap a chubby little finger against ǂkhoā's petite, triangulated nose and watch with glee as it crinkled, the nostrils flaring in playful annoyance; and then, he'd break into giggles, quenched by the knockabout laughter that gurgled deep and full from ǂkhoā's small, fleshy lips.

And just like I used to bellow to Uncle Fani as a child, 'Tell me again, Fani, the story of how the world began!', I can hear little Bukhosi screeching, 'Tell me again, ǂkhoā, the story of how the world began!'

'All right…' ǂkhoā ever patient, unlike my Uncle Fani, never tiring of telling the boy his favourite story, never yelling at him to go away, but taking instead his hand and leading him into the bush, where she proceeded to frown thoughtfully at the shrubs. 'One day Kaang, the San god, created the world. But he was lonely, and so he decided to change into an eland, so he could run across the plains. But, again, he got tired, so he decided to make himself into a praying mantis, so he could jump from tree leaf to tree leaf. In this way, he created every animal living in our world. But then, one day…'

'What happened one day, ǂkhoā?'

And she, plucking the roots of a shrub and slipping it into her leather bag: 'One day, the animals that Kaang had created turned against him, and so, heartbroken, he decided to go and live up in the sky, away from all that he had created...'

'And what did he do to the moon!'

Sinking her teeth into a bulbous root, which at once began to sputter with an onion-coloured juice, which she squeezed out into a calabash: 'Well, it was dark and lonely up there, and his wife Coti had stayed behind here on earth, so Kaang made himself a light, a great big round light, which he called the moon...'

'And he made the moon cry!'

'Here, drink this, it will protect you from the diseases of the white man – so whenever the people of the earth need water, they do a rain dance and plead with Kaang, who is still angry at them for attacking him, so angry that their rain dances make him cry, and thus his tears fall from the sky and rejuvenate the earth.'

And he, little Bukhosi, trying to make a brave face as he gulped the bitter juice, just like the brave face I tried to make at Uncle Fani's rebuffals: 'Tell me the story of the beast Ga-Gorib!'

'All right. One day there was a beast called Ga-Gorib...'

I can imagine Thandi watching them from a distance, her Bukhosi and his ǂkhoā, fascinated by the ease with which the boy had picked up the Khoi San woman's click-click language, with how he laughed so easily in her presence. I imagine this intimacy between ǂkhoā and little Bukhosi sometimes made my inamorata envious, as it would any mother upon seeing her son mothered by another woman, much like how Abednego's continued snubs of my affection while he pines after the boy, who didn't even appreciate him like I do, hurt me.

It was thanks to ǂkhoā and her strange herbs and roots, Thandi told my surrogate father, that she and little Bukhosi never suffered, in that refugee camp, from any disease, despite the poor diet and, during one month, a vicious cholera epidemic. ǂkhoā who – at once impenetrable and penetrating, distant and contemplative as she watched the goings-on of the camp with curiosity and yet without the slightest envy, cackling in response to Sister Bhictoria's ape-like gestures beckoning her with the King James bible towards the light of the Lord – had made Thandi see just how big the world was, how it existed on many plains at once.

It would crumble, this world in which Bukhosi spent his formative years, on that historic day in March 1980, when they heard a terrifying drone coming from somewhere up above. Three aeroplanes descended upon the camp, whipping up a terrific dust storm. The camp unravelled as everyone flung themselves to the ground – they looked like fighter jets for sure. But it wasn't bullets that sprayed the cowering refugees, just flyers; sheaves upon sheaves rained down upon the camp and its surrounding areas like the dead quail and frosty manna for the Israelites in the Desert of Sin. Thandi stood up from where she had flung herself beneath a scraggly bush, her eyes moving wildly, her chest fluttering, until she caught sight of her son in ǂkhoā's grip by the entrance of the camp. She sighed, grinned and began to make her way towards them, the flyers crinkling under her bare feet. She bent and picked up a leaflet.

'RHODESIANS COME HOME,' she read. 'WE ARE ZIMBABWE NOW. MUGABE HAS WON! COME HOME. ZIMBABWE WELCOMES YOU.'

A NEW COUNTRY

He never got the honour of experiencing combat up close, my surrogate father. He was never deployed to the front, but stayed cooped up in his damp bunker thinking of that Farmer Thornton and talking to the apparitions of Thandi and his boy, right up until the end when, on that fateful day of 28 December 1979, just several days after that Lancaster House Agreement – where a young, polished Zacchaeus had launched his career – word reached the Chifombo base that they'd done it, the guerillas had walloped Prime Minister Smith's army so bad the wretches had finally begged for surrender. The war was won! He had been handed his discharge papers; and just like that, history found him anew and declared him a war hero, redeeming, if only briefly, my grand-dada's traitorous legacy, and like all war heroes, my surrogate father was eligible for a lifelong pension plus benefits plus eternal thanks.

On an unruffled March morn in 1980, he finally beheld his Thandi again, stepping off the train from Francistown, no longer fleshy but dainty as she placed carefully first one sandalled foot and then the other onto the platform, her floral dress whipped about her thin legs by a gust of wind blowing from the tracks. She had a doek wrapped around her head, covering that mfushwa hair he loved so much, bringing attention to the steep curve of her jaw and also elongating her striking neck, all the more defined now that she was thinner. A fresh mint, she was! She hadn't yet seen him, for she still had her head angled inside the train; she tensed her muscles, pursed her lips and lifted something; and then there he was, his boy, being placed heftily onto the platform, beautifully burnished and impressively plump. And there, his mother's eyes, light-hued on his tiny face, and my surrogate father's own replica nose so wonderfully proportioned!

She appraised the boy's face, frowned, smeared a lick of spit on her thumb and rubbed his cheek. He squirmed and yanked his face away. That was when she looked up and saw Abednego. He smiled, but her gaze remained pensive. He began to make his way towards them, threading through the passengers who had alighted from the Francistown train, walking briskly across that wide platform that was so nippy in that early morning air, taking steady strides that belied his pitter-patter-pittering heart. She waited for him, not moving, just watching. And then he was standing before her and drowning in the smell of her and it was as though he were back in that store Ticki-Tai all those years ago watching her jiggling breasts and giddied by her scent. He flung his arms around her waist. She clung to him and began to cry. She smelled of sweaty mustiness and something altogether more vast: the Kalahari. It was a long time before they separated. He looked down to find his boy studying him with open curiosity. He pulled the boy towards him, bent down and clutched him like that day three years ago when the truck had come for him at Dukwe.

'Say hello to your father,' said Thandi.

The boy mumbled a greeting and smiled shyly.

Thandi, though dainty, was formidable. They strode down Customs Avenue and turned into Abercorn and then Prospect, in that country now named in the interim Zimbabwe-Rhodesia, in which they could now walk into the Sun Hotel cool as they pleased without having to be accosted by the 'whites only' sign or the watchdog staff, this Bulawayo in which things had changed but which still retained about it a 1950s English aura. My Thandi expressed bewilderment in this their new leader Robert Gabriel Somebody, wondering out loud how it was that her own charismatic Joshua Nkomo had failed to hold the sway of the masses, but glad nevertheless that they were free, *they were free*, unbelievable. My surrogate father tried to grunt helpfully, looping his twinkie finger around hers. He felt, suddenly, brittle. It was as though he would break or could break and her delicate formidability was the thing that now kept him intact, that had always kept him and would always keep him.

Those first months back together in that new country, a country they could now claim freely as theirs, during which they lodged in the sitting room of a one-bedroomed semi-detached in Makokoba Township belonging to Uncle Lungile – who lamented every day the loss of Cousin Solomon, who had left in '76 with a training battalion for Cuba but was said to have walked out of the barracks one day and disappeared into the bustling streets of Old Havana, never to be seen or heard from again – were a strange and strained performance in which he was trying to find his way back to her and hoped that she was learning to love him proper. For, he had no illusions about the fact that during their time in the city he'd been to her just a rural boy whose affections had amused, if not flattered her, and it was the pregnancy that had brought them together and their Bukhosi who now bound them. But he loved her. I love her!

She preferred to spend her time in sombre silence, her eyes flitting about, interested no longer in her camel sketchbook nor in locating her old buddies Frankie and Mvelaphi, and although he yearned to know what had happened in that camp in his absence, he also feared to know, and so he took gratefully only the morsels she fed him, moistened and bite-sized and thus sliding easily down his throat, of Sister Bhictoria and her increasingly feverish sermons and the magnificent ǂkhoā and her healing herbs and the Mbilu twin sisters and skinny Ndali. It was his boy who worried him especially, for he seemed perpetually disoriented, and often slipped into an incomprehensible click-click tongue. When my surrogate father tried to hold him, he would kick and punch and cower in the sitting room corner, refusing to be consoled.

'I think it's best I take him to your village, so he can be with his people,' said Thandi. 'Ease him into the rhythm of things slowly.'

He was surprised to hear this, as was I when he told me: Thandi wanting to go to the cesspool of backwardness! He acquiesced, wishing he could accompany her but having to stay behind and await army demobilization. I was even more surprised to learn that while in Lupane, my inamorata pioneered a groundbreaking school named 'The Angela Davis ǂkhoā Learning Centre' that insisted on an avant-garde, holistic approach to learning, incorporating both the knowledge of the missionaries and that of the nosy villagers, who gawked at this bizarre city woman who once scorned them but was now telling them that they possessed as much knowledge, if not more, than the Faaders – possessing more knowledge than the Faaders! – and that they could harness it to do groundbreaking things.

('And how, exactly, would you like us to break this ground?' I can imagine them asking, stomping their feet against the hard and clearly unbreakable ground.

'By grounding yourselves in what you already know,' my Thandi would have responded, ever solemn.)

But they were together at Rufaro Stadium on the fêted eve of the birth of the new nation, Thursday, 17 April 1980; it was also the eve of Bukhosi's birthday, which is also, incidentally, the eve of *our* Bukhosi's birthday. Thus, the day felt extra special, as though all those crowds cavorting at Rufaro Stadium had congregated to pay homage to their boy, and thus, their boy was a metaphor for the nation and they, his parents, were its most intimate founders, its closest ancestors. How I wish I had been there at those Independence Celebrations, staggering in that staggering crowd with my surrogate father and especially Thandi! My Thandi who had walked the streets of Salisbury agape, with cautious abandon, for although the most brutal acts of the war between the Rhodesian and guerilla forces had taken place in the bush, where the bantu peoples, victims of chemical and biological weapons wielded by the Selous Scouts, had died hellish deaths from poisoned water and anthraxed meat, soft insides burning, black skin blistering, the city, too, bristled from its war scars: the bombing by the guerillas of the Woolworths store on First Street that had shrilly made the front page news, shaking the city out of its metropolitan reverie; the devastating rocket-blast of the fuel depot in Southerton just two years before the war ended, shocking the whole country and, despite Prime Minister Smith's assurances, crippling morale; the constant drone of helicopters patrolling the city amidst the Saturday luncheons and Sunday dinner parties; on-the-ground battalions prowling suburban streets to weed out from servants' quarters the terrs-in-hiding, who were now the liberation heroes. And now, on the eve of independence, the city was riotously loud, as my surrogate father says, where during the war it was said to have been spectral – as though all that post-war jiving in the jazz clubs and the beer gardens was a heady, if not defiant, release of breaths long held.

How rejuvenated Thandi must have been by those cavorting crowds at the Rufaro Stadium, in that backless sundress my surrogate father loved so much, her emaciated frame beginning to fill out after years of refugee living. Perched atop my surrogate father's shoulders was the birthday boy, their Bukhosi. His plump lips were set in a firm line, his hands wrapped around my surrogate father's head. My surrogate father caught Thandi wincing each time the guerillas paraded past in their fatigues. They must have brought back memories of her younger, feisty self, and her ambitions of giving birth to the liberation struggle, of carrying it, feeding it, nursing and wiping its buttocks. Perhaps, standing as an ineffectual civilian before these war heroes, a part of her regretted not having gone into the bush with the likes of Spear-the-Blood. She kept telling my surrogate father how she was proud of him, for he was in fatigues too, although he never left her side to join the comrades, probably because he was too ashamed of claiming the status of war hero when he hadn't spent even a single day on the battlefield.

The air was carnivalesque, merry with military bands and marching troops, chimurenga songs and church choirs, and celebrity songsters like Oliver Mtukudzi and Thomas Mapfumo, before whom the youth swooned, much to my surrogate father's amusement – he felt terribly awkward, he had been away for too long not just in years but in experience, and wasn't familiar with the flavours of the day.

How I wish I had been there! Holding Thandi's hand. Cupping her face, and maybe even bringing it close to mine and filling it with kisses.

This most joyous of days for our Zimbabwe was one of the

darkest of days for my surrogate grandpa's Rhodesia, so dark, in fact, that the memory of it haunts the pages of his blog. He recalls how the day in question found him slumped in his cavernous seat in his lounge, his gaze angled not at the fireplace but across his shoulder through the window at a rural dust storm that twirled and sashayed across his fields; a bad omen. On his lap sat five-year-old Sonny Boy (2.0), the glorious reincarnation of his Sonny Boy (First Generation) who had died what had been not only a premature but was now also clearly a useless death, seeing as Rhodesia, thanks to the treachery of the Mother Country, had suffered a most shameful defeat at the hands of those bantu terrorists puppeteered by World Communist Elements! Next to them on a coffee table was the picture of Sonny Boy First Generation standing proud and tall next to the Honourable Prime Minister of former Rhodesia, Ian Smith, in the uniform of Deputy Commander of the Independent Company Rhodesia Regiment, showing all of his teeth to the camera.

I imagine Mrs Thornton, like many of those dispirited Rhodies, felt compelled to flee the country; she looks, in her photos on the farmer's blog, with her fiery red hair and russet eyes, like she was a practical woman; she would have tried to talk sense into Farmer Thornton: 'We *must* leave. Please, James. Everybody's leaving, we can't stay here, the terrs have won, they are running things now, they're going to turn this place into a communist cesspit, with photos of Stalin and that dreadful man, what's his name, Marx, everywhere. We *can't* stay here, lord knows what they'll do to us if they find us.'

And that Farmer Thornton, no doubt patriotic then as he is now, would have clung stubbornly to the corpse of Rhodesia: 'And where shall we go? Where will we go? This is our home. We've worked so hard, too hard... damn those snooty Brits! Dammit!

But all this time Smith was making speeches on the radio to say we were winning the war?'

'I know, I know, James, but we can't stay. They'll probably ship us off to some gulag. Can you imagine, breaking stones in a labour camp under the command of some kaffir? And what will become of me? They'll have their way with me. Is that what you want? Please, we have to go, I heard the Fosters say they're going to try their luck in South Africa...'

'We don't have any money to buy a new farm in South Africa. And I'll be damned if I'll live in some stuffy block of flats like an abandoned geriatric.'

'But if they come...'

My surrogate grandpa stroked Sonny Boy 2.0's hair and cocked his rifle. 'Let the bastards come. I'll be ready.'

It would turn out, among many other surprises, that there was nothing to get ready for; that chap, Robert Whatshisname, agitator against all that had been holy and sacred to the nation of Rhodesia, hated terrorist, former prisoner of the state, dangerous Maoist, calculating Marxist, devout Catholic, Husband, Teacher, Autodidact, and now Prime Minister, would turn out to be quite the magnanimous gentleman, extending the arm of peace and reconciliation to the refugees of former Rhodesia.

But on the eve of 18 April 1980, the future seemed bleak to a thoroughly depressed Mrs Thornton and my surrogate grandpa whose conviction, care, hope and doubt had been rekindled by the reincarnation of Sonny Boy.

What of the dead? Could they still see the future they had died for?

O peasant tongues frothy with provincialist rhetoric! O rural hearts pitter-pattering to the vision of dozens of little Dazhai villages culled from the white agricultural scape! O men and women who, having nothing already, and therefore with nothing to lose, clung so gullibly to the utopic postulations of your intellectual leaders!

How drunk you were with ambition!

How voluble were your chants! – *For the people by the people.*

But, of course, in order to reach your Promised Land, first you had to die.

O Thursday night giddy with swaying crowds and freedom curdled like sweetened amasi and heady scents of flowers mingling in the heat! At around ten p.m., Bob Marley clambered up onto the stage at Rufaro Stadium with the Wailers, and shouted into the mic, 'Viva Zimbabwe!'

The crowds outside, high on the opium of independence, began to press against the gates, trying to get in. Those inside, propelled by this force, moved towards the stage. Abednego felt Thandi's moist hand slipping from his. He fired her name into the surge, lifting his boy from his shoulders and pressing him to his chest. But her face was lost in the wave of euphoria that tided the masses towards Bob Marley.

The police, overcome by fear, slipped into animated violence like a second skin; they began thwacking the people with their batons, and the people wailed, so that their independence brimmed over into the night into a collective howl.

The VIPs, penned in their elevated stand, were caught by the cameras in what was later proclaimed as joyous weeping, overwhelming emotions at this monu-mentous day, this emancipation of the black-and-brown peoples of the House of Stone… but, in fact, the overzealous policemen, in a state of frenzy, had flung tear gas cans whichever way, including at the cordoned-off stand, much to the Very Important People's pompous chagrin. And at first, uncomprehending, the wailing people below cupped their hands to receive the flying cans, welcoming yet another gift of their independence – was this free Coca-Cola? – and then, when this independence stung their eyes and threatened to make them blind, they cried even harder.

As the crush subsided and calm began to be restored, Abednego managed to catch sight of Thandi at the very back of the stadium, near the exit, where she stood bruised but otherwise unharmed.

'I thought… I thought…' he said when he reached her, pressing her head to his shoulder so she wouldn't see the tears in his eyes, their Bukhosi snuggled between them.

She laughed. 'I'm a freedom fighter, remember?'

There was a cheer from one end of the stadium, near the cordoned-off stands. My surrogate father looked up just in time to see the guerillas entering the stadium, marching in their fatigues towards him, across the field, and parading next to them troops from the Rhodesian army. The crowd quelled in a momentary hush, then swelled as His Most Excellent Excellency Prime Minister Robert Mugabe appeared. Even Thandi, who had been disappointed that her Joshua Mqabuko hadn't won the inaugural elections, screamed. My surrogate father, too, waved a hand and ululated. The Prime Minister purred past them, in a white Mercedes, frilled by a heavy entourage of motorcycles. The Mercedes halted by the flag poles set on the field, where the independence ceremony was to take place.

O Prince Charles lowering the Union Flag!

O Rhodesia Rifle Corps melodizing *God Save the Queen*!

O fireworks bombing the night, O guitars tickling the air!

Abednego inhaled sharply as the Zimbabwe flag began to rise up its pole. A misty, blue light shone on the flag; somewhere behind them, gun shots cracked, twenty-one of them: a gun salute. The crowd went berserk. His Most Excellent Excellency stood solemnly by a lantern, beside the new flag. He was dressed just as primly then as he dresses now, in a chic, single breasted suit, with his signature toothbrush moustache, his oversize glasses sitting on his cheeks. He straightened his back. Lit the Independence Flame. The crowd rose to a fever-pitch, shouting, screaming and dancing, the pain of the thwacking and the tear gas of a moment ago now forgotten. When Abednego turned to Thandi, she was clutching Bukhosi, smiling at the Independence Flame, crying.

O drunken crowd, O seductress song!

His Most Excellent Excellency took his oath of office at around midnight, 18 April 1980. Even now, his Independence Speech stirs something in me! Although, I admit to feeling a little guilty at being moved by it, knowing what he later did... Oh, but isn't it beautiful? It's filled with so much hope, so much love!

My surrogate father has been going on and on about that brother of his, who was invited to perform at the Independence Celebrations. That's how they were reunited, after the war; my surrogate father saw him on the stage and shouted, 'That's my brother! Hey, hey, that poet is my brother! *Yes, I know him very personally, he's my brother!*'

I Googled this so-called seminal poem he performed; I found it on some obscure site. He was a darling boy of the nation for a while, after independence, getting invitations to every ambassador's party, gracing every important function, even making it to the State House once or twice. Then, after his protests against the Gukurahundi Massacres that tainted our country right after independence, forcing him to flee into exile to the USA, he was disappeared from the official records; most of his poetic achievements were wiped clean; it was as though he had never existed. His history was re-rewritten, briefly, heroically, some seven years ago, when he returned to the country in prodigal fashion, after fourteen years in New York. Ha! He'd spent fourteen years abroad in that New York, where he lectured, conducted research and penned numerous essays on his homeland Zimbabwe, which was gradually replaced by liberal references to that country Africa, written in a prose that verged on hyperbole in its lyricism and intensity, and published widely in journals, periodicals and books which were routinely lauded at conferences, not only securing him tenure at New York University but also gaining him fame and notoriety among the secret society of academia.

Each time his works were applauded, he became angry, writing long responses to this inappropriate applause, which were published in the *New York Times*, earning him more applause, which in turn incensed him even further.

He was a loveless, wifeless man, and instead dedicated his life to studying the foundations of colonialism, that Bergsonian concept of the native as animal, loveable in the way that a dog could be loveable, but not in the way that the human being (*sic*) the European was loveable.

His writings on Africa were more poetic than prosaic, and tended especially towards abstraction, slipping into florid metaphors that evoked a nostalgic purity, those grand African dynasties in which, he wrote dreamily, there had been no war, hunger or poverty, and where everyone had lived in Edenic peace, and man, having already transcended his destructive nature, had been well on his way to becoming a metahuman, that is, until the barbaric hand of colonialism clenched its fist, of course. He penned epic ode after epic ode to those medieval Sahelian kingdoms south of the Sahara, washed lily-white the Somali states on the Berber Coast, vivified idyllic visions of the Islamic sultanates of Sudan, evoked hazy scenes of the great African city Benin, and produced soppy praise poems in honour of that empire Great Zimbabwe, the rumoured capital of the grand Queen of Sheba. It was time to blind the darkness that had been named Africa with profuse light, he wrote.

The day, in the year 2000, when he learned about the farm invasions taking place in Zimbabwe, he declared, in a final state-side essay, the people of his home country 'The Niggers of Africa', praising them for reclaiming their dignity from undignifying white slavery, before packing his bags and returning home.

But he was dismayed to discover that home, upon what he'd dreamed would be a prodigal return, was still tinged with the sinister tones of the past, and his illusions about the Great Emancipation of The Niggers of Africa gave way to disillusions about our government, which further curdled into outright contempt, making him reckless in his disquisitions on the nation's leaders. Anyone could have foreseen that mysterious car accident in 2003 in which he met with Death.

They tried to obliterate him again from the nation's history, although it has been admittedly difficult this time, what with the internet and everything; traces of him linger everywhere, online and in archives, obstinately, like a virus.

The poem he performed at the Independence Celebrations isn't that bad; in fact, it could be said to be good. But I shan't give him the honour of granting him any more voice in my pages; he doesn't even deserve these paragraphs I have wasted on him.

It's my Thandi I wish to dedicate whole chapters to; my Thandi who comes to me now, her umber skin fuzzy in the residual tear gas in the stadium on that magic night of independence, shiny under the lights, like the seed that is found inside a chestnut fruit. Her full lips the fleshy texture of the husk.

He asked her to marry him that night, Abednego, in the most

unromantic way; he just stood there, without even a ring, and piped out something to the effect of: 'Eh, if it's OK with you, I'd like to make us formal. I'd like us to stand before the courts so I can make you my wife.'

Couldn't he at least go on bended knee, like they do in the movies?

THE MEN IN THE RED BERETS

I'm beginning to seriously worry about my surrogate father. I've never seen him in the state he's in, at times wet-eyed with sadness and at others wide-eyed with terror. It's as if he is living in his memories rather than the present day, so much so that it's even as if he is forgetting Bukhosi. I must record faithfully the calendar of what I see to be the beginning of his evident deterioration – the day is Wednesday, the year 2007, the month October, the date 31st. It is increasingly difficult to get him to respond to me; talking to him is like summoning him from a netherworld; when I asked him about Thandi yesterday, he pursed his lips, hugged himself and turned his back to me. He has told me many stories, most of them roundabout, but at this point I'm stuck, for there's a gap in his tales. He jumped from being with Thandi at the Rufaro Stadium on 18 April 1980 to being married to Mama Agnes in 1987. I yearn for us to be as we were the other day, Father and Son, when he let me snuggle up next to him on his sofa and we took a selfie.

His behaviour has even alarmed Mama Agnes; she brought the Reverend Pastor to pray for him yesterday evening. He arrived dressed in his signature three-piece Canali suit. Such a fine marvel of craftsmanship, a delicious white against the Reverend Pastor's sweltering baobab bark skin, with pearly buttons dotting the lapels of the waistcoat, and silver dove cufflinks cuffing the shirt. One glance at that suit, or, for an eye less discerning than mine, one brush against that soft blend of camel and angora, evoking in the body sensations akin to a (lover's) caress, confirms that the suit is the real thing, one hundred per cent Canali, no Chinese Fong-Kong. This can only mean one thing: the Reverend Pastor must have ordered it all the way from Italy, I suspect with the offerings from his congregation, probably paid for in full by the weathered purses of the likes of my Mama Agnes.

Watching the Reverend Pastor in action, I remembered Mama Agnes's proud story about how she stumbled across his Blessed Anointings church. She came across a poster of the Reverend Pastor five years ago, in 2002, on a City Council bin, advertising a revival at his Blessed Anointings church, and felt an inexplicable pull. And wasn't she glad she had followed the urgings of the Holy Ghost, because how else would she have known that the Catholic Church was not for her, and that her spiritual blessings were to be found at Blessed Anointings?

The Reverend Pastor prayed for Abednego all evening and into the early hours of this morning, and even broke into tongues, Mama Agnes muttering beside him, clapping her hands, her eyes shut tight. My surrogate father just sat on his sofa, licking his lips. I sat opposite him, my eyelids clenched, occasionally opening them to scout the room. Our eyes locked once, but I quickly shut mine; he hadn't wanted me there. He had said, once again, that this prayer session was private, a family thing, but my Mama Agnes had insisted that I be there, seeing as more prayers meant more weapons against the evil spirits that Satan has sent to afflict her home and her husband. And besides, she said, I lived in their yard, I was practically part of the family. I stood there beaming. I could have kissed her! So, there I was at the family prayer meeting, mumbling and occasionally yelling a loud, 'Hallelujah!', just like Mama Agnes. I saw her smiling at me at one point in the night, and began to yell with more verve.

The Reverend Pastor left some forty minutes ago, just after two a.m. Tjo! The man has marathon stamina. He prayed non-stop the whole time. He didn't have his Mercedes with him today, and asked Abednego to drive him home. When my surrogate father scowled, digging his rump a little deeper into his seat, Mama Agnes offered to drive him instead. Even I was surprised, because she doesn't like to drive, especially at night.

And now, though I've tried, gently and then more forcefully, to steer my surrogate father in the direction of my Thandi and his Bukhosi, he has remained sullen-lipped. I must get him talking about my inamorata again! I promise, this is the last time that I ply him with Johnnie. I've added a bit of ubuvimbo for a stronger effect, OK perhaps more than just a bit, but I need to get that heavy tongue of his wet proper!

He grudgingly takes my concoction. I watch him, to make sure he swallows the whole thing. He gulps it greedily, sticking his tongue out to lick the walls of the glass when he's finished. I get up and lock the front door, and then check the curtains to make sure Mama Agnes is still out. And then, satisfied, I resume my seat opposite Abednego. He has his head tilted back, his mouth open, shaking the glass for any last drop of Johnnie.

'So,' I say, leaning forward. 'Tell me what happened after the war. Where is Thandi? And this other Bukhosi, where is he?'

He's become a most trusted friend, that Johnnie Walker Blue! Trumpeting the blues better than Miles Davis! Seducing even the most reluctant raconteur. For isn't my surrogate father now working his vocal pipe harder than any piper?

The year was '81, the summer at its mildest, the month February, the day brill, the birds chittering, the children chattering and the sky blazing sapphire and arctic and alabaster. He paused to survey Entumbane Township, Abednego, and was pleased by what he saw. Everywhere, the flutter of activity; men in tattered vests and shirtless men in sinewy movement, pivoting up-down up-down to the *kong kong* of their hammers, smashing rocks, gasping under the weight of cement blocks, staggering, pausing to lean against half-erected walls, slab dabbing brick mortar brick, and up went houses in the newly built Entumbane, layer by layer, corner by corner, wall by wall, zinc sheet by zinc sheet. On the streets, mostly men, mostly soldiers from that Joshua Nkomo's ZIPRA army wing but some also from that Prime Minister Robert Mugabe's ZANLA army wing, many of them still awaiting demobilization, sauntering past or dragging the remains of landmined feet or otherwise just sitting with their legs dangling in the gullies outside complete or almost complete houses, lagers in hand, cigarette smoke whorling from brooding mouths to form rings around blank faces.

The air that summer was tense with the residue of war. My surrogate father trudged warily across Entumbane, clad in his ZIPRA uniform. There was a careful, almost coiled manner in the way the ZIPRA and ZANLA cadres spoke to one another – each searching the other's eye, appraising the other's posture, provoked by the slightest twitch of a smile, the tightening of a fist – ever since talk of hidden arms caches in Joshua Nkomo's ZIPRA military camp, of jealousies about the Prime Ministership and subsequently soldier mutiny, of some divisive elements from ZIPRA who had thus been downgraded from war heroes to warring terrorists. And what was to be done about those weaselly peoples of Matabeleland, who had betrayed the baby nation by voting not for Prime Minister Mugabe's ZANU (PF), the one true living party of the nation, but rather for that Joshua Nkomo's (PF) ZAPU, party of the traitors and the losers and the fatsos? Re-education! Extensive and thorough re-education of the cockroaches, so that they could learn a thing or two about patriotism!

He was glad, my surrogate father, that Thandi had taken Bukhosi to the village for a little while, and was not here for this. The tensions between his cadres and those of the ZANLA seemed to be escalating daily. He scurried through the streets of Entumbane, clutching his demobilization cheque, saluting and at times waving at his comrades-in-arms, who saluted and sometimes waved back, nodding at the women walking about stiffly in their fatigues, bowing demurely at their counterparts with the sucklings squirming on their backs, until he reached the half-erected house he was building for Thandi. He squinted up at the builder who was angled above him on a ladder busy fitting the last of the zinc sheets, and said, 'The house, it's going to look great, Jonas. It calls for a celebration. Plus. I got a job today. I'll be working the machines at Butnam Rubber Factory. Aren't I a lucky bastard, eh?'

Jonas chuckled, tipped his cap. 'Indeed, a bastard you are, Mr Abed. As for being lucky, well, I'd say it's your woman who is lucky, having you build this house for her, that's what.'

He chuckled. 'Is it safe to go inside?'

'Eh, it's up to you, but if something falls on your head...!'

He tucked his nose and mouth into his shirt collar as he manoeuvred beneath the ladder into the interior of the almost complete house. He was certain that Thandi would want to move back to the city once the tensions had eased and she saw the home he'd built for them. What was a year apart in a whole lifetime of metropolitan love? A blink and it was gone. Only joy lasted! Only love.

Drones of dust hovered in the air, sunlit sparkles of grey and silver, so that he beheld his house through a dreamy veil. Over there, to his left, beneath the naked window where rubble had piled up, was where they would place his TV and her gramophone and watch late-night feature films of *Dr. No* and *Goldfinger* and *From Russia with Love* and afterwards sway to Nina Simone's lilting staccato. In that corner, diagonally across from where he stood, they'd ram their sofa and spend many hours folded into one another. (How I wish to spend many hours folded into my inamorata, tucked in her mature bosom!) And then, shuffling ahead, through another doorway, ah, this would be the kitchen; there wasn't the present chalky smell of cement but instead the future aroma of Thandi's cooking, the scent of rosemary and oregano and simmering stew. And stepping in here, through another doorway to the right, this would be their love-nest; they'd push a double bed into that corner over there, beneath the window, where they'd spend many hours making babies (oh, spare me please, surrogate father!), a whole soccer team, yes, and then this next room here would be Bukhosi's and his unborn brother or sister. (For she was with child again, my Thandi! My surrogate father was not a man who wasted time. Jonas the builder was right – he *was* a lucky bastard!)

'She's going to love it,' he shouted to Jonas. 'Jonas?'

He rounded the house back to the front. 'Jonas?'

He found Jonas standing beside the pile of bricks for the house and a wheelbarrow, which he hadn't seen there before, circled by four men who, from their uniforms, he recognized as ZANLA cadets. One of them was holding Jonas by the scruff of his shirt. They turned to Abednego as he approached.

'Ah, look, another cockroach,' one of them said.

Abednego kept his stride steady as he approached them, although his heart was battering his chest. 'What do you gentlemen want?'

'"What do you *gentel-menn* want?"' one of them parodied. 'Who knew that cockroaches could speak?' The others laughed.

Abednego swallowed. 'Leave my property, right now.'

'"Leave my *properly* right now." What properly do you own, iwe? You mean this?' He pointed at the bricks. 'Why, these are mine!'

With that, two of the ZANLA cadets began grabbing bricks from the pile and placing them in the wheelbarrow.

'Hey, hey, wena, stoppit!' yelled my surrogate father. 'Hey! Fuseki!'

'Did the cockroach just say foetsek to me?'

'I said fuseki, leave my bricks alone.'

'What did you say?' asked the one who was clearly the leader. He retrieved a pistol from the small of his back, cocked it, and raised it to Abednego, aiming it between his eyes. 'What did you say to me?'

Abednego swallowed. 'I said, fuck your mother.'

'Heyi, iwe—!' The leader hit Abednego across the forehead with his pistol. Abednego staggered back but did not fall; out of the corner of his eye, he saw Jonas spitting into the face of the cadet who had him wrung by the collar. There was a scuffle, a shout, and then two men were on top of Jonas, punching him and kicking him and pummelling him with bricks. Abednego made as if to lunge at them. But before he knew what was happening, his feet had turned and were sprinting him out of there. Two ZANLA cadets yapped at his heels.

He was halfway down the street when he heard gunfire. He didn't dare slow down, even to turn and see if Jonas had been hurt.

He threw his limbs as he ran. The stench of summer clamped his nostrils. His fists thrust through the air, booted feet pumping down the streets of Entumbane, now deserted. The flesh of his arm tore against a jutting fence, oozing blood and maddening the hounds nipping at his heels.

He tackled a green door and burst into a room reeking of sex. Tripped over a pair of blanketed bodies. The flash of a sweaty breast, the nipple puckered; sweltering rolls of flesh. He raised an apologetic hand at the fellow with his buttocks firmly wedged between the thighs of motherfucking-sweet sovereignty, pumping to the new independence – 'Sorry!' – dashed through the kitchen with its clutter of mismatched chairs, down a short corridor and through the back door, into a rupture of light. Tumble tumble he went over more fences, across the cluttered meadows of township existence. The meaning of his own life flickered as in a bioscope: Thandi; Bukhosi, his nasberry son; and his unborn baby.

He ran until the sound of blood thumping in his temples drowned the batter of his assailants. Then, suddenly, out of nowhere, he heard a shout behind him. He tried to run faster. But his legs were beginning to feel like sorghum porridge, and he stumbled. A hand gripped his shoulder. The hounds had finally caught up with him! He spun around, swinging a fist, right into the jaw of a skinny fellow dressed in his own ZIPRA uniform.

'Hey!' yelled the fellow, punching him back. Abednego staggered and fell, blood sputtering from his mouth. 'Why did you do that?' said the fellow, helping Abednego to his feet. 'Yoh, you look like you've braved the crocodiles of the Limpopo, comdrade, and then?'

'... Must... run...' panted my surrogate father, pointing in the direction from which he had come.

'Run? Run from what, those morons? Is that why you're running?' He shook his head. 'Comrade! Kanti, where is your spine? Where are they? Where are the idiots? Show me, I will take care of them!'

'I don't know... they were behind me and I've been running and... I must have lost them...'

'Ha, comrade! Running? You want the idiots to think we are cowards, that we can't beat them? Come, let's go look for them!'

'No, no no no, I... tired...'

'Heh! What kind of soldier are you? All right, come this way...'

It was only when he followed the fellow through a cobweb of backstreets and into a lilting house that Abednego recognized him as none other than Spear-the-Blood. He seemed happy enough to see my surrogate father, although he never tired of teasing him about his propensity to flee – 'Ha, but, comrade! All this running, all the time? First you ran away from the war in your father's village, now this? Kanti, what kind of soldier are you?' – and even tried to get him to join him on his prowls in search of fighting, his voice husky with a lust for battle. But my surrogate father refused, using my Thandi and his Bukhosi as an excuse.

'What about us, your family, your comrades! Ah. Won't you fight for your place in this our new country?'

Instead of joining in the fight, Abednego refused to leave, and would spend the next few days hiding in the gloom of Spear-the-Blood's living room from the escalating fighting between the ZANLA and ZIPRA cadres action-packing the streets of Entumbane. The contagion of violence spread quickly, the township descending into chaos in only a matter of hours, and very soon, the two factions were engaged in all-out war, the battle stretching as far as neighbouring Essexvale, the army mobilizing once again.

Abednego, having stayed put, was assaulted by visions of Thandi and his boy dancing to the tune of gunfire before tumbling to the ground puppet-like. He thought of them constantly, as hours turned into days in Spear-the-Blood's bunker, trapped by the ongoing combat from leaving for Lupane, Spear-the-Blood coming and going from the battle, sometimes returning triumphant, other times forlorn, his face slicked with blood, and once brandishing the ear of an enemy.

And then a singsong voice ushered echo-like one afternoon from Spear-the-Blood's radio to announce in rote fashion that *they had a War of Wrath on their hands, repeat, a War of Wrath on their hands*; The Dark Lord intended to snuff out Comrade Nkomo's supporters, and had just released his latest hybrids – wargs and orcs of beastly proportions tilting on their heads red berets with sickle-spangled emblems busy executing in the village of Mbengwane by the Celane River near Lupane terrors unimaginable even to the most nefarious mind.

Upon hearing the name of his village mentioned in the same sentence as wargs and orcs, my surrogate father was finally stirred into action. He enlisted a final favour from his unlikely comrade and host, Spear-the-Blood, and had himself smuggled out of Entumbane beneath the canopy of a UN jeep. The jeep dropped him off at the city outskirts; from there he travelled for many days on foot, gypsy style along the Bulawayo–Victoria Falls road.

Here he let his imagination run away with him; he saw himself in his mind's eye arriving in his Baba's homestead to part burnt stalks of unharvested maize and sliding over sun-grilled boulders to behold outside the silo a bucket upturned, curdled goat milk foaming at the corners of the proverbial mouth, flies splashing about in milky pools, sun bathing their green fat bodies; outside the kitchen hut the hasty etchings of a broom, in the yard an accumulation of avocado leaves sticky with the blood of my surrogate grandma, my inamorata – my inamorata! – and Bukhosi, and right there beside their bodies over-ripe pawpaws that, too, had fallen to their squishy deaths. And then right here, outside my grand-dada's hut, sat the old man's black stick boots, side by side on the cansi outside the door as though at any moment the old man would appear with grinning whiskers brandishing his FAL rifle.

He's beginning to falter, my surrogate father. His lips have started to twitch; he's hugged himself again, lifting his knees to his chest, trying to crawl down the back of the armchair. I grab Johnnie from the floor and feed him straight from the bottle – 'Here, just a sip, you'll feel better.' Gulp goes his Adam's apple, that curse from the rib woman Eva that doth deepen the voice, loosening desire and lust and temptation, the amber balance of cocoa and cedar and leather and spice and moss and peat swirling to work once again its magic. But he doesn't seem to be getting better at all! He's started crying.

I would lend him my chest to cry on, like I used to do for Uncle Fani, but I need him to get back to telling me what happened. I retrieve my little plastic packet of ubuvimbo powder from my pocket, take just a pinch and shove it into his mouth with my finger. He looks at me, startled; but his eyes glint at that familiar taste, and he begins to suck, greedily. The feel of his warm mouth around my finger, the urgent suction it makes, is exhilarating. It feels delicious! I can be there for him in any way that he wants. Can't he see? I'm the son who is here, who will never leave!

It's with great effort, and a little reluctance, I admit, that I pull my finger away, savouring the tingling feeling where my surrogate father's mouth has been. 'And then what happened, was Thandi there when you got to the village? Was she all right? Tell me!'

He arrived in Lupane to find his Bukhosi and my inamorata and my surrogate grandma alive still and well, and before he could stop them like a broken tap the tears were gushing from his eyes. He flung himself at my inamorata who, angry at his infrequent visits no doubt brought upon by gyrations with prostitutes and God-knows-what-other-manner-of-riff-raff, turned her swollen baby belly away from him and continued with her English class under the mopane tree. She'd been doing wonderful things in the village, my Thandi; not only had she started both children's and adults' literacy classes in her Angela Davis ǂkhoā Learning Centre, as well as rallied together the women to form a Women's Committee, she had also written a petition to the new District Administrator, Jepheth, regarding inheritance laws and the plight of the widows of Matabeleland North.

Life seemed to be going on as normal, and my surrogate father was beginning to think that maybe the wargs and orcs were a bit of an exaggeration, figments drawn from a war-pummelled imagination and writ large by Stress Response Syndrome; he was beginning to relax a little and think, why not spend a few days at home basking in the warmth of family living, rubbing Thandi's feet and also pressing his ear to her belly, even taking his boy hog hunting and showing him a thing or two, and then maybe in a week or so he could scout the horizon and see what to do, maybe return with Thandi and Bukhosi to show them the surprise house in Entumbane.

He spent several peaceful afternoons siesta-ing in my granddada's hut, a room in the homestead his mama no longer wanted to enter. He enjoyed lying on the old man's mattress, one arm folded behind his head, looking up at the Liberation Hero Jesus

Christ, who'd remained steadfast atop the thatch roof, maintaining his loving gaze even as his comrades had since forsaken him to the vicissitudes of wear and tear, to the wind and the dust, and the spiders that entangled him in cobweb crucifixions. Battered but not beaten, was the Liberation Hero, fixing his imperial stare on Abednego lying in that now neglected room in which he could still smell his Baba, could still hear his voice booming, 'Get on the floor and give me fifty, soldier!'

He was beginning to relax and even dabble in a little nostalgia when, all at once, from the north-east, came the sound of trucks. He leapt up and rushed out to behold them lurching into the Mlambo homestead, a convoy of soldier trucks with flap-flapping tarpaulins. On this day, my surrogate grandma was away at the Ladies of St Luke's Church Choir practice, and it was the English class for the youngsters that my inamorata was conducting beneath the mopane tree; at the sight of the trucks, frightened feet began thudding on the ground as the children tried to flee. Out tumbled... Black Jesus and his men. (Black Jesus! What the fuck is he doing in this story? How has he jumped from my hi-story to—? What the?) With them was Jepheth, hunched behind Black Jesus, as though trying to hide, thrusting a finger at Abednego. Abednego scrambled through the commotion, away from them, in search of Thandi and his boy. There they were, over there, near the kitchen hut; they were being hauled into the low-walled enclosure leading to the kitchen entrance. He scrambled after them. They ran harder, the children, all around him, left right and centre everywhere, whipping up a dust storm, only to be caught by the jaws of wargs and orcs tilting on their heads red berets with sickle-spangled emblems that caught the eye of the sun.

He parted his arms, Black Jesus, bared his teeth and said, 'Let the little children come to me.'

The Men in the Red Berets – some of whom wore floppy, army-green hats with the bonnets tied around their chins like innocuous peasants – prodded the little children into his arms. He bent and hugged them, patted their heads, cupped their chubby cheeks and said, 'Do not hinder them, let them come hither, for Tophet belongs to such as these.'

The little children began to cry.

Thandi started screaming. Now the children, trembling in Black Jesus's embrace, began to scream too. He cooed to them and they quietened down, although many of them trembled still. Bukhosi began to cry. He tried to run to his father, but Black Jesus yanked him back. Abednego threw himself at his son, only to be met with a fist. It smashed his nose. He crumpled to the ground, whereupon the wargs and orcs leapt upon him and went to work. He clutched his head. Brought his knees to his chest. Di di pa pa gi gi *crunch.*

Somewhere Thandi was yelling, 'Mayibabo! Mayibabo mayibabo! Nkosi yami mayibabo!'

The fists and boots rained down. He thrashed at the air. Bit his tongue. Blood flooded his mouth. He gulped. Began to choke. A rusty taste burned his throat. He glimpsed, through eyes puffed up and wet, the Men in the Red Berets herding the children into the kitchen hut, the swirl of Thandi's pink skirt in their midst. She kicked and flailed, beating her captors with her fists and her elbows and her arms. She broke free. Rushed towards Black Jesus, towards the boy. Black Jesus gripped the boy with one hand. Raised the other. Slapped her across the face with the back of his hand. Punched her in the stomach. She doubled over. Hugged her belly. He grabbed a clump of her mfushwa hair. Yanked her back up. Slapped her. Spat. Raised his hand. In his hand was a scythe. The scythe sliced through the air. It sliced into her belly. Sliced her belly open. She staggered. Clutched her belly. Her belly was spilling. Spilling her intestines, her colon, her stomach. Spilling her spleen, her pancreas, her liver. Spilling her foetus.

Thandi lay in the dirt. Beside her spilt belly. Beside her intestines, her colon, her stomach. Beside her pancreas, her spleen, her liver. Beside her twitching foetus. Her abdomen was bloody. Her eyes rolled into the back of her head.

Bukhosi shrilled.

Abednego vomited.

The boy was yelling for ǂkhoā.

He ground his face into the dirt.

'Do you want to live?' said Black Jesus.

Somewhere, a shuffle.

Little feet pitter-pattering.

Pitter-pattering little feet.

A great whoosh. Something hot on his arms. He opened one eye. Squinted. Looked up. The kitchen hut was on fire. The hut was burning. Inside, the burning children were screaming. The screaming children were burning.

A screaming thing capered out of the burning hut. It was an apparition. A ball of flames. It skidded across the compound. He'd never heard the boy scream. Not like that. Black Jesus leaned forward. Picked the boy up. Flung him back into the burning hut.

He retched.

Something sweet. Dizzying. His head. It hurt.

He couldn't stop retching.

Grinned grotesquely.

'Do you want to live?'

Called for his Baba.

This man. Black Jesus. 'Baba? Your Baba can't help you now. Eh, eh! I'm the only one who can save you. Don't you know? I'm like

Jesus Christ. Your life is in my hands. I can heal. I can raise the dead. I can say whether you live or not. Do you want to live?'

He shook his head.

He was retching.

Jesus Christ!

Black Jesus. He cackled. 'Perhaps it's mercy I shall dispense on you today and not the justice that you deserve. What is your name? Heh? What? All right, Ahmed, what would you do if you were in my shoes, Ahmed, heh? If a stupid sonofabitch was trying to destroy your country, your family, all the things that you love? You stupid people of Matabeleland busy voting for that loser fatso's ZAPU party, instead of our Mugabe's ZANU (PF). Trying to weaken our new nation by voting for the losers, eh? You would, like me, fight to protect your country from such fuckers. I am Jesus Christ. He who followeth me drinketh from the well of Life. So again, I ask, do you want to live?'

He shook his head.

His throat hurt.

Jesus Christ!

'Yes. You may not see it now, but the truth is that you do not want to die. And me, I am a reasonable man. So, I will spare your life. Even your people, I can raise them from the dead, if I want. There is nothing that I cannot do. Nothing.'

Jesus Christ!

Chuckling. Shuffling. Whistling. Moving. Engine revving. Tyres braying. Fading stutter. Silence.

Everywhere hurt.

His eyes fluttered.

Thandi's abdomen was abuzz with flies.

The foetus had stopped twitching.

The children had stopped screaming.

The hut was still burning.

He wanted to get up. Get up and fling himself into the blaze.

He didn't move. Lay in the dirt. Sniffing. Sniffling.

Somewhere yonder. On the blistering horizon. Somewhere. A cock crowing.

UNCLE FANI

My Thandi!
My inamorata!
This cannot be.

That man! Black Jesus!
It can't be!

My Laodamia!
Thou meetest death at the hands of that most vile Trojan brute,
that Hector that hath slain your beloved Protesilaus—

Here I lie roasting in this divine hell, Hades!
While thou, my belovedest,
doth scamper across the meadow lilies up yonder in Elysium—

That man! Black Jesus! He killed – you died at the hands of – that man! He who smoulders like an ember in my own skull! How has he ended up in Abednego's—? Impossible! Why does he keep taking everything away from me? First my mother, then my past, my hi-story, my very essence, and now you, my inamorata!

Celestial pity, I again implore; – Restore her to my sight – great Jove, restore!

Celestial pity refuses to restore you to my sight. For the past two days, ever since my surrogate father's confessions about your death, ever since he broke down, breaking me in the process also, ever since learning about how you, too, like my dear mama, died a brutal death at the hands of Black Jesus, I have been cooped up in my pygmy room communing with the religious teachers. I have prostrated myself before the ancestors, before Buddha, before Zoroaster, before Confucius, before Krishna, before Mohammed, before Jesus! I have begged them each in turn to guarantee that were I to take my own life, they would be able to unite me with you, my inamorata, on the other side, whatever the other side may turn out to be. I swore to the ancestors to drink from the ancestral shrine, I oathed to Buddha to follow the Eightfold Path, I promised Zoroaster I'd convert to Zoroastrianism, I pledged to Confucius to take up the banner of Confucianism, I vowed to Krishna to adhere to the laws of Karma, I swore to Mohammed to pray to Mecca five times a day, and I guaranteed Jesus a most ardent disciple. Please don't think it is cowardice that has prevented me from going through with my Romeo-esque plans, my inamorata! I was only too prepared to drink from the poisoned chalice and declare, *thus with a kiss I die*. It is only that I've received no assurance of casting mine eyes upon your umber visage from any of these indomitable gods, and for fear of taking my life only to find no you waiting for me on the other side, or no other side in which to be waited for, I've decided it is best to suffer the rest of my days on this earth with the comfort of my surrogate father's memories of you in mine manly bosom!

I don't even know what the hell is going on. The very hi-story I am trying to run away from. The old me I am trying to purge. Memories I've been trying for so long to forget. About my Uncle Fani and the day he died. About my mama. I think Abednego broke me. I think I may have broken him also. We broke each other in the living room just as the morning outside broke the night sky, he crying for the family he had lost, and I crying for you my inamorata, crying, breaking, and falling into one another's arms. He clung to me. I to him. I cupped those wet, yellow cheeks and brought that face close to mine. I stared into those penny eyes. He let me bring my blueberry lips close to his. He did not pull away. I kissed him. He let me kiss him. His lips were moist and cool; his warm breath smelled of ubuvimbo and Johnnie.

'Uncle Fani!' I cried.

'Bukhosi!' he replied.

I never got to kiss Uncle Fani, never got to cup his cheeks. I just sat and watched as he lay dying at Mpilo Hospital in January of 2002, struck dumb. Even as I sat beside his hospital bed, I was still unable to understand his crying. There he lay, a man of fifty-seven who looked closer to seventy-seven, wrinkles slashing the whole of his tawny face, travelling the breadth of his wide forehead, right down the impasse leading to his smooth, droopy nose, converging towards his uni-lip, to disappear beneath a grey Balbo beard. There were hi-stories mapped all over that face, laid bare by every single one of those wrinkles; perhaps that's why, as he aged so prematurely, he became so unbearable to look at.

He lay on his hospital bed with my fingers in his cold bony grip and his other hand raised to the second-floor window, where he kept calling out a name, Zodwa, my mama's name, though I did not yet know it, Zodwa Zodwa he kept murmuring, oh Zodwa you have come for me, but there was nothing there, just the bare branches of a jacaranda tree. His rheumy walnut eyes were fixed not on me, his nephew who had been like a son to him, and at times even tried to be a mother, lending him my skinny chest to cry on, but rather on Nurse Clarence, who was fluttering over him and checking his drip and fluffing his pillows, all useless, for he was dying and no amount of fluttering or fluffing would change that. Meanwhile, her ample rump busied itself with beckoning me away from this man who had been almost like a father to me, Nurse Clarence's rump shaped like two voluptuous brackets that rolled in and strained against and threatened to burst out of her crisp uniform. It was as he lay dying and I sat mesmerized by Nurse Clarence's undulating buttocks that Uncle Fani finally coughed up the hi-story that had been gagging him his whole life.

'It was in '83 when they came,' he began.

'Who, Uncle? Who came?'

'Mina, I was herding the cattle back into their kraals, and Zodwa and Ntokozo were in the silo, I don't know where mama was but they found her, they found us all. Me, mama, Zodwa, Ntokozo, Jabu, Andile, Donsekhaya, Velempini and his wife Khathazile, their daughter Khohlwa, then our brother Celani, then Phephelaphi, Hluphekile and Skhubekiso. Is that it, how many is that…? Oh, yes, and Qedindaba. Baba was long dead by then, he'd died a hero in the war and had been buried at the Heroes' Acre in Phelandaba.

'They were just young men, nje, maybe five of them, but they had guns and they were wearing the red berets with these shiny scythe badges so, and so we knew who they were. They said there was a meeting at Tshipisane Secondary School, that an important man had come to the village and we had to be there. It was getting to be evening, I remember Velempini shook his head to them and said, it's late, mama needs to take her pills for her high-high and then she needs to sleep. But as he was turning to go into the hut, they shot him. In the head. He just fell down, just like that, di. Mama started screaming and Khathazile flung herself at his body and she's rolling and rolling and yelling mayibabo oh woe is me wangenza Thixo wami oh and now everyone is screaming and the killers are shouting shurrup shurrup wena mama shurrup all of you or-o you will be next but how can we stop we can't stop. They are speaking Shona and nobody can understand them, me I can hear them because I had spent some months in Mberengwa panning for gold but I was staring at them with my eyes wide open like I can't hear the swine. Then Celani is saying let's go better we go with them it will be all right but mama is not going nowhere she is pointing and shouting Velempini my son oh bo oh my son how can you survive the war only to die like this oh and Khathazile is screaming better they kill me now also oh bo oh bantu oh what about Khohlwa think about your child and she is getting up and we are going with the killers and these are just youth you understand me I could snap their skinny little necks if it wasn't for those guns.

'We are at Tshipisane and it's like the whole village is there, what is happening everyone is asking who is this person who is come is maybe it's the President somebody says but the killers tell us it's Jesus who is coming. Jesus? Yes they say don't you know you stupid fools that you have a Jesus?

'And then the man he comes he is wearing army uniform so, like combat gear and a beret but it's green so, he is black black so, like a polished stone and has these whitest eyes you have ever seen they put him on a stage and Celani says that is him that is the beast and we look at him because everybody knows Celani he's working with the dissidents for days he goes nobody knows where he is going and then he is coming with fancy things at home that don't belong to him. You know him I ask he nods says that's Black Jesus.

'Black Jesus is walking up and down up and down the stage he starts to talk to us he says with man nothing is possible but with me your Jesus everything is possible. He is speaking in Shona and one of the killers is translating for us to Ndebele. Where two or three are gathered I am there with them says Black Jesus and here we are all gathered in my name do you know why I'm here? He asks. Hmmm? Do you know? I'm here because my disciples here are not spreading my gospel. I have told them that we need bodies, we need bodies to sow here in this barren land, but what are they doing, they are just slapping you, just beating you, why are they not shedding your blood? Heh? Are they afraid of you? Heh? Are the women too beautiful? Heh? So I am here to help them do what needs to be done. You maNdebele all of you are busy hiding dissidents in your midst you are a useless good for nothing people and what has no use must perish. But we won't make it easy for you no no no, you are going to feel it, you will feel it, you will go hungry here there will be no food allowed here, we shall burn all your crops and you will starve until you start eating your dogs, then you will be eating the rats and even the cockroaches, and then you are going to start eating your children. Horayiti now sing! I can't hear you, mhani, I said, start singing!

'And we are trying to sing and many hours are passing by and mama faints, yoh, and we are trying to wake her but they beat us they say leave her Celani shouts mgodoyi fuseki and he is trying to pick her up and they shoot him and now he's dead.

'Now they are throwing us into these big trucks so and just like that they are driving and when I look back I see mama they have left her kneeling in the dust cupping her head and shake shake shaking it so like somebody who has lost everything. Nobody knows where we are going me I'm with Zodwa and little Khohlwa we can't see anybody else here after a long time the trucks stop later we find out we are at Bhalagwe camp and there is nobody around for kilometres to help us.

'They are beating us every day and taking the women as their wives Zodwa they take to Black Jesus. There is a white man who is coming there they call him Lakin I know him he has come before to our village during the war with Smith's army and taken us to the Protected Villages where they wire us with electricity and hang us upside down and they are shoving sticks up the women and saying we are good for nothing munts who should have gone extinct long ago. He's CIO first he was CIOing for Smith killing us in the war now he is CIOing for our President doing the same thing. He keeps directing the killers telling them what to do more force he keeps saying it's the only thing the kaffirs understand and he's laughing showing us clean shining teeth and the killers are laughing with him and beating us harder. CIO Lakin is taking me they take me to the holding shed he makes the killers wire my thing and tie a rubber around my balls and this man Black Jesus he is shouting me in Shona saying I'm a dissident me I'm screaming no no never then where are the dissidents he asks I tell him I don't know. Lakin is twisting the electricity and one of the killers he is coming for me with a truncheon—' He began to tremble, Uncle Fani, he began to tremble. I tried to stop him.

'Uncle,' I said. 'Uncle, stop. Nurse Clarence! Nurse!'

But he wouldn't stop. 'I never see Khohlwa again but Zodwa tells me that they took plastic and burned it until it was hot hot hot and then they made her spread—' He gulped. 'And then the next time I see Zodwa her tummy is growing and growing Black Jesus is punching her in the stomach and saying my little bitch my little whore when the cunt explodes I'm going to – he was going to kill you but your mother she loved you she makes me promise, promise to try to escape take the baby with you please look after my baby please and you were born in the night and we put you in a satchel and I took night cover and we managed to cross Zamanyone hill in the west and a headmaster there gave us a ride to the missionary hospital but I get home I find there is nobody. I am waiting and waiting for them; mama Andile Donsekhaya Ntokozo Skhubekiso Jabu Hluphekile Khathazile Qedindaba Phephelaphi. How many is that? Yes, ten. Out of ten zero come back and I am like to myself I must burn this place down and forget and go away and never come back otherwise I am going to die being here alone with all these memories it is going to kill me better to not remember. Your mama I made her a promise to look after you and I keep that promise.'

He exhaled, a long, seemingly infinite exhalation, I think with relief. Me, I couldn't think. I couldn't think and, for a long time, I didn't want to understand what he had said. How could he lay on my shoulders something like that? Wtf was I to do with it? He died that night, the relief of passing on the burden of knowledge enough to allow his spirit to finally soar to the heavens.

Isn't this the hi-story Bukhosi always wanted to know, before he went missing? For which he got a beating whenever he asked our father, 'Baba, what happened in the '80s, what was Gukurahundi?' *That* was Gukurahundi, Bukhosi. It was the lead rain of our new country, Zimbabwe, sent to wash away *us*, the chaff. It was the state-sponsored murder of twenty thousand of your kin. How was our father to tell you that? How was he to tell you that within that number were the only two people he ever really loved?

I saw how it hurt the boy. I saw how it was hurting my surrogate father. It hurt me also. That's why I took the boy to Dumo, to get answers. Dumo who never beat him or turned him away but answered all his questions earnestly, with an intoxicating passion, proclaiming, 'We must secede! We can never be free, until we are allowed to mourn our dead, to acknowledge that they died, and how they died, and to exhume their bones in the unmarked mass graves in which they lie with strangers and perform the proper burial rites!'

I'm not ready to perform any burial rites for my inamorata! It feels as though she died only yesterday! How can she be dead? Stolen from me by Black Jesus, just like he robbed me of my mama! Will I never be free of Black Jesus? Shan't I ever be able to cleanse my blood of him? My past of him? The beast! Destined in life to be the henchman of a President, plagiarizing, during that terrible time right after our independence from white rule, the most creative ways of torture: severe-beatings hut-burnings asphyxiation falanga abnormal-body-positions rape dry-submarine electric-shocks lack-of-sleep immobilization constant-noises screams stripping excrement-abuse sham-executions and special-contraptions-copied-from-Pol-Pot-Dacko-Amin-and-perhaps-some-unnameable-elements-of-the-CIA-with-speculated-but-unconfirmed-blessings-from-jolly-Uncle-Sam. His reputation preceded him in red carpet fashion all over the land of Mthwakazi, his shadow blotting out even the tiniest suns of children, who were deemed by his Christ-like powers to be guilty-by-association.

Proudly granted, in '87, after this most impressive exhibition in Matabeleland of ruthless ambition, a spot at the Royal College of Defence Studies in the Land of Her Majesty.

Proudly capped, in '91, Commander of the Air Force.

Six foot two and thin-shouldered.

Skin the colour of hematite.

Would she have been able to love my face, my mama? Would she not have looked into it and always seen... but no, she loved me, my mama, she loved me! She even had me smuggled out at birth to get me away from that Black Jesus.

BLACK JESUS

Every day for the past week, my surrogate father has left the house in the evening – to search for Bukhosi, he says, although nobody knows where he goes – only coming back at dawn. I've begged him to let me come with him, but always he glares at me, as though he blames me for the boy's disappearance – it's not my fault! – before huffing off. He has also made it a point to leave the room whenever I enter, and to be never home when I come knocking, or when he is, to pretend not to be there, even though I can sometimes glimpse him through the lace curtain staggering about drunk in the living room, even though I sometimes shout, 'Father, I see you!', to which he sometimes ducks behind a sofa. The other day he said the most hurtful thing; he yelled, 'I'm not your father! Leave me alone!'

I don't understand it. Didn't we just share a moment last week in Mama Agnes's sitting room? Didn't we share our grief? I thought it would bond us. He let me cup his face. He even let me kiss him, on the lips.

Eh. What more does he want?

Perhaps I've been wooing the wrong parent. It's a mother's

loving touch that I need, not this drunkard of a man who keeps rejecting me, despite my best efforts.

Mama Agnes appreciates me – didn't she invite me to join them for the prayer meeting last week? *He's like family.*

I wish I had Dumo's gift of the gab, so as to find the words with which to charm her, relate to her, coax out of her her own history. Dumo, that cold and calculating revolutionary, that manipulator of searing and super-sharp, Corning Gorilla Glass-coated, iOS upgradable, pixelated vision, who managed to innovate his Gukurahundi trauma into software for his fantastical ambitions.

But I'm no Dumo! My words seem to fall flat in Mama Agnes's ears; though I have tried, these past few days, to sprinkle in her cochlea questions about her past, her lips have remained sealed. It's her daily prayer sessions at Blessed Anointings with the Reverend Pastor, and also the sleepless nights worrying about Bukhosi, that preoccupy her.

Without my surrogate father's accounts, with Mama Agnes all clammed up, and with nothing to do but skulk around my pygmy room, Black Jesus is beginning to take over my life again. For a long time after my Uncle Fani's deathbed confessions, he haunted me. I thought of him day and night. I could not sleep. Even when I did manage to get some shut eye, he came to me, though I could not tell in my dreams whether he was beckoning me or mocking me. Whereas before, I had been perfectly content with Uncle Fani being my only family, a gaping hole now opened in my heart, a need for… love! A mother's love, a father's love, *my* mother's love, *my* father's love. I became obsessed with the idea of knowing Black Jesus.

What's it like, to be loved?

I bought the Red Album, and began hunting for him everywhere. It started in the newspapers; and then I began to loiter at the Bulawayo Public Library, where I razored him out of the history books. I even visited our National Archives in search of flyers bearing his likeness from our liberation war, photos, sketches, anything…

And now, I am back to that album again, studying every contour and shade of that face, his expressions, his physique. Here he is, on the first page of my album, hand on hip, a beret slanting fashionably over his left ear. His full figure has been shrunk into an envelope-sized photo. The corners of his mouth are caught in an upturn, hinting at a smile. His eyes, with the whites super-white and the pupils mahogany dark, hold the lens with a quizzical friendliness. He looks so small in that photo, so minuscule, so insignificant. I could fit him in the palm of my hand and squish him and he would cease to exist.

Soon, though, the album was no longer enough; I felt I had to see him in action. I wanted to study him, the way that Nabokov studied his butterflies. I wanted to examine the way he walked, talked, laughed; I wanted to pin him to a corkboard, the prize specimen of my collection. I Googled him, and began to watch all the propaganda the state bombards us with on TV, to catch whatever glimpses of him I could. I would see flashes of him, and play them over and over in my mind, appraising him and comparing myself to him. I even began to try to walk and talk like him. Slowly, I sloughed off Uncle Fani's grief-stricken modesty, a burden that had hunched my shoulders, as it had his. I began to prance about with my back straight, lengthening my height, my shoulders thrown back in the casual way of a man who is used to authority. When I laughed, I tried to do it nonchalantly, beginning with a spreading of my lips and a shaking of my shoulders, and then followed by a low bellow. It didn't come naturally to me, so used was I to Uncle Fani's lugubrious laughter.

But I gained great satisfaction from those rare moments of minor success at mimicry. Although the more I mimicked and the more successful I became, the crueller I felt! I bought a French beret and wore it over one eye. I would swagger about our Luveve streets feeling almost like a new man, for even osisi regarded me with a surprised, wary interest, they who had never considered me with any romantic notions but only a patronizing kindness, sometimes taking pity on me and feeding me, right through my teens when Uncle Fani squandered all his government pension on booze – so poorly, I think now, was my apologetic stature then.

Their new interest pleased me no end, yet, feeling myself a better man and thus above them, they who had never had any womanly time for me, I made sure to have no time for them now. Perhaps this is only what I told myself. Deep down, I was properly afraid of them, not knowing how to woo them, unclear as to what I would have done had they accepted my advances, as they seemed now ready to do, not schooled, as were many young men my age, in the art of fondling a breast or licking a nipple or tickling those mysterious lady-parts, which were said to be moist and excitable, and the proper teasing of which, with skilled finger or artistic tongue, was guaranteed to get a lady to let you into her Eden. What is worse, I was now assaulted by visions of my mama, she who I had never laid eyes on but whose face I now saw conjured in every female countenance.

Oh, but how intoxicating was the girls' interest in my bad-boy persona! I thoroughly enjoyed it, this sense of having influence over another person. I went back again and again to Black Jesus, trying on more of his mannerisms, talking to my Red Album, studying it, exhilarated by the sense of power it gave me. But then a viciousness began to grow in me, and this frightened me, and confused me, as I also was overcome by an insane joy. It was the joy of recognition! To see yourself in another human being; the parent root, ubaba, dada, the father who sprinkles his seed and produces spawns in his likeness. In this joy was disgust, and fear, and grief, disgust at myself for my happiness, fear of the man and the things he had done, grief for my dear mama! The malice grew and threatened to overwhelm me, I could feel it as a menacing, almost physical presence; I resolved to stop what I was doing, to forget the man and everything Uncle Fani had told me, and move on as though the past had never been.

But then, one day, I saw Black Jesus at a presidential event at Rufaro Stadium that was broadcast live on TV, squashed between His Most Excellent Excellency, whose chin was slumped on his chest, and The Crocodile, who kept flashing a crocodile smile at the cameras. It was the longest viewing of him I had seen, and I took him in hungrily. He had one leg slung over the other knee, his leather Ferragamo shoes shining for the cameras. He was dressed in a blue Air Marshal uniform. The navy blue jacket tapered from his epauletted shoulders. It clung to his taut body. It ruffled across his abdomen. Then it flared out on either side of his slim hips. From the epaulette on his right shoulder dangled a plait of gold braids, like curtain shades. They curved and fastened just below the top button of his jacket. He had on a sash across his jacket, in the colours of the country flag. Or the ruling party flag – the colours are the same. It is the same colours or it is the same flag. Po-*tae*-to Po-*tah*-to. His shoulders began to shake. He leaned towards The Crocodile and whispered something in his ear. The Crocodile's shoulders too began to shake. What were they saying? Why were they laughing? The peaked cap sitting low on his head shaded his face. I wanted to see his eyes. I wanted to look into them and see what was there. But instead, it was the Zimbabwe Air Force emblem on his cap that kept winking at me. The

African Fish Eagle emblem resting serene atop the soapstone kept winking at me. But Black Jesus, I couldn't see his eyes. I wanted to see his eyes. I wanted so badly for him to wink at me.

I began to dream of meeting him in the flesh. Where before I had desired to know him, I now felt that *he* had to know *me*. More than imitating him, I yearned to find out what parts of himself he saw in me. This tormented me. *Were* there parts of him in me? The ferocity I had felt electrocuting me ever since I had begun my Black Jesus mimes, was it an awakening of the seeds of the father in the son? How could I wish to be like him, after all the things he had done, to our people in Matabeleland, to my mama! And yet, if he were my father... I could imagine his contempt at my torment, he who had no regard for the human in 'human being'. Contempt! I wouldn't be able to bear it from him. I yearned for his respect, even if I could only get him to give it grudgingly. It would not be enough to tell him that I was his, even though one look at my features and there'd be no denying it. No, I would have to *show* him that I was his son. But how? I had no intention of murdering some poor innocent just to prove a point to the brute, I'm no monster! But if it was him I killed... *That* would be my experiment. *That* would be my proof. There would be no monstrosity there, only an Oedipus style justice.

I admit! My mind was racing; my thoughts tumbling together as if they were in a washing machine; I was unwell! But all I could think of was... how would I do it? How would I kill him? I could attend a political event where he was present, and get close enough to pull out his gun and shoot him. I would catch him as he fell, my arm around his shoulders to support his neck, my hand cupping his cheek, cradling him in my arms as he died; an act of love between father and son; for I yearned to cup that face and bring it close to mine; I yearned for the glint of recognition.

Would I be able to do that? How could I do that? Could I stare into that face and be faced with the truth of my own face? To have to stare into those mahogany pupils swimming in their super-white whites; to place my hands on those finely hued cheeks and trace with my thumb the wonder of their smoking-pipe silhouettes; to impress my flat-belly heart lips on those lips the shape of a flat-bellied heart; to feel the kiss of death hot and moist on my skin; it's more than I could bear!

When His Most Excellent Excellency came down to Bulawayo for a rally a few months later, I saw my chance to meet Black Jesus. I made sure to attend the rally at the Barbourfields Stadium, dressed in the requisite ruling party regalia with His Most Excellent Excellency's face emblazoned all over my shirt. It was a torrid day in September, nine months after my Uncle Fani's death. I was sweating profusely. My throat was parched. I was feeling nauseous; my head was throbbing, making my eyes sore, and there was a constant hum in the back of my mind, like a muttering voice. I had been telling it to shuttup all morning, but it wouldn't let me alone. But I was determined. I bullied my way through the crowds, until I was near the front by the cordoned-off red carpet down which the big-wigs marched solemnly from their vehicles to the VIP tent.

I peered impatiently over the bopping heads; the arrival of the big-wigs took a long time, almost a whole two hours. They dribbled in, all of them with His Most Excellent Excellency blazoned on their ruling party attire, busy waving and smiling regally at the screaming crowds as they marched down to their tent, where we could see them sipping from misted glasses. I stared at those glasses, at the cold beads running down their sides, their foggy interiors thick with ice cubes. I forced dry air down my throat with each gulp from those glasses.

Finally, he arrived! I saw him first by his shoe; a shiny, pointed leather Ferragamo stepping out of the limo that had come to a halt by the red carpet. And then, that Air Marshal cap emerged, and his face… I couldn't see it clearly beneath his cap, but I felt he was looking at me. My breath caught in my throat. And then His Most Excellent Excellency emerged from the limo, too, and Black Jesus turned to say something to him, and our moment was gone. But I kept my eyes on him; I strained my neck to see him, watch him, appraise him, my heart pummelling my chest now. Then, he removed his cap and tucked it beneath his arm, revealing a head of closely cropped hair. He was shorter than I had imagined; in my dreams he had taken on colossal proportions.

I hadn't realized I was clenching my fists until my palms began to throb from the force of my nails digging into my skin. I took a deep breath, exhaled. Relaxed my hands. My plan was to leap over the rope cordoning us povo from the VIPs, sprint across the red carpet, ducking the bodyguards who would no doubt try to stop me, and grab Black Jesus's gun from its holster. There would be no time for hesitation; I would point it between his eyes, yell 'Father!' and as the recognition, compounded by confusion, spread across his face, I would shoot him right between the eyes. I would live out the rest of my days with a clean conscience, for I would have cleansed myself and vindicated my mama, and would be happy in the knowledge that mine was the last face the bastard had seen before he died.

I elbowed my way through the people standing between me and the cordon. Black Jesus and His Most Excellent Excellency were walking slowly, as though taking a leisurely afternoon stroll, paying their screaming fans no mind. I gripped the rope and leaned forward, ready to jump over it; they were almost parallel to me.

'Hey!' It was one of the bodyguards, a white, muscular fellow with a big, bald head. He was striding towards me, his hand on the holster by his hip. I tensed, ready to spring.

It was the sight of the boy that saved me. He was waddling between Black Jesus and His Most Excellent Excellency, dressed, obscenely, in a mini replica Air Marshal uniform. He looked no more than six or seven.

Skin the same shade, the colour of the rich black clay that can be found along the Gwayi River floodplain.

My eyes swayed wildly from father to son to father. The boy had his face turned away from me, his head angled up, trying to mirror the father's movements, miming as though he, like Black Jesus, were speaking to His Most Excellent Excellency, shaking his head in tandem. His Most Excellent Excellency, laughing, pointed at him, and Black Jesus looked down at him. His flat-bellied heart lips broke into a smile. He pulled the boy towards him and hugged him. Bent and kissed the small, round head.

My coiled body loosened.

I raised my hand and touched my head.

'Hey!' The bodyguard had reached me now. He shoved me, right into a group of spectators behind me, who staggered and fell, I falling on top of them. 'Step back! No touching the ropes!'

I didn't even apologize as I got up, didn't return the rough shoves of the spectators, didn't take any notice of the bodyguard. My eyes were on Black Jesus and the boy. It was at that moment that I realized that I hadn't ever wanted to kill Black Jesus. No. What I yearned for, so very badly, was for him to kiss me on my round head, too.

He came in tonight, my surrogate father, back earlier than usual, having come from one of his mysterious solo searches for the boy. It was the first time in a week and a half that he sought me out – and he did it by crashing into my room without knocking, flinging open the door while I was tapping away at my MacBook. He was staggering, and at first I thought he was drunk, but when I clocked his drooping features, as though at any moment they would drip-drip away, I realized he was drunk with grief. I can understand; the double blow of first having to deal with Bukhosi's disappearance and then now having had to relive the deaths of my inamorata and his boy, would be enough to drive any man mad. His madness even zapped time, so that in his hi-story the fighting at Entumbane and Black Jesus happened together, and not two years apart, as in History. History does not know his pain. What is time, anyway? You can no more tell a man not to feel what happened eons ago if to him it's as though it happened just yesterday. Dumo would say that this is a good thing! The greatest sin is to forget! The bitter gulp of hi-story is a necessary penicillin against the myopia of the present!

Abednego glared at me with open hostility, and I wondered if he blamed me for having dredged up our family hi-story. 'Give me the thing,' he said, holding out his hand, palm-up.

'What?'

'The thing! You've been giving me something. I want it. Give it to me.'

I looked up at him innocently. 'What are you going on about?'

He blinked rapidly. 'The thing I tasted on your finger that day when – I tasted it in the drink you gave me, also. Give it to me!'

'I don't know what you are talking about.'

'Give me the thing! Where are you hiding it? Give it to me!'

With that, he began ransacking my lodgings, upsetting my little put-me-up bed, shoving my Mac to one side, emptying my satchel, rifling through my clothes. I would have given him some ubuvimbo, had he not looked at me with such coldness; after everything I had done for him! So, I just sat there, my arms folded across my chest, watching him smugly. His hands were trembling.

'Please,' he said, finally. 'Give it to me. What is it? Where did you get it? Please. I need just a little bit, I haven't been well and I—'

He stopped and glared at me. I thought he was going to attack me, but instead, he turned and shambled out of my pygmy room, and I heard him go into the house. I sat there for a long time, surveying the mess he had made of my belongings, dismayed. I had never before been so humiliated by him. Was he unaware of the power he had over me, of the power a father has over his son?

He shuns me, my surrogate dada, now when I need him more than ever. I, too, am hurting. I keep staring at our selfie from the other day, me nesting in the crook of his arm, busy smiling for the camera, his other hand resting on my hip, eyes closed. It hurts me to think of what we've become now, looking at that photo. I find myself seeking solace in the Red Album, thinking of Thandi, thinking of my mama, remembering Uncle Fani, and fending off the dark cloud that threatens to engulf me. I feel so alone! I've been forsaken by Abednego, who goes off alone each night, God knows where; Mama Agnes spends all her days working or on her knees in front of the pastor. What about me? I have been unable to leave my lodgings. What is worse, I'm frightened even to go to sleep! I'm afraid to shut even one eye, for she comes to me in my dreams, my inamorata, she mounts me still, only now my wet dreams have lost their sweetness, and no matter how hard I try, in these dreams which have become nightmares, to push her off me, to plead with her to dismount me, she gallops and pants until she has had her fill.

It feels as though Thandi died only yesterday! My inamorata!

I was just dozing off, after my altercation with my surrogate father, having put back to order my humble lodgings and crawled onto my little bed, and tried unsuccessfully to fend off sleep, for I could already hear her howling in my dreams, my succubus, when I heard screaming coming from the main house. I leapt at once from my mattress and out of my room, slamming against the back door with the full force of my weight – though it's never locked, it needs force to push open and squeaks horribly, for which I must utter a silent apology at night whenever I am pressed for the loo – and dashed into the house to find Mama Agnes cowering in the living room, between the bookcase and Bukhosi's sofa, my surrogate father standing over her, his fist raised. I looked down, took in the swollen rearrangement of Mama Agnes's face, looked back up at the man, grimaced, grabbed his arm and spun him around.

His eyes fell on me, wild. '*You*,' he hissed. 'What have you done to me? Give me the thing—'

I punched him. He staggered, blinking repeatedly. He looked about him, first turning that large head of his left, and then right, and then towards me, and then at Mama Agnes, his generous nostrils trembling, and then, without a word, he shoved past me and out of the house.

I gathered Mama Agnes in my arms and led her to her sofa. She was crying. I yearned to cup her face, to look into those eyes, to kiss her and hush her, but that otherwise beautiful scape had swelled to tender proportions, and it was all I could do not to cry. I offered her a cuppa, that's the best I could manage, Tanganda, with a dash of lemon, just the way she likes it. Then I sat down and watched patiently as she sipped it. This seemed to calm her, for she stopped crying, her sobs receding to sniffles.

I reached out and took her hand, nursing it as if it were a baby bird. 'I don't know what's got into him,' I soothed. 'It's so unlike him!'

She looked at me witheringly. Things had always been like this, she said. They had been like this from the very beginning, and even though she believed he had changed, he was back to his old ways again, back to his drinking and his beatings, and it was because Bukhosi was missing, she knew, it was the stress of their missing boy, and if only he'd come back to them, she knew everything would be all right again!

'I'm here, Mama Agnes, I can make everything all right!' I hissed, but it was as though she couldn't hear me.

I was glad that the electricity had gone as usual, glad for the darkness, for I know not what manner of guilt my face betrayed as I sat there trying to breathe lightly, not knowing where to burrow my shame. For, isn't it because of me that my surrogate father has become, once again, a wife beater? Isn't it I who encouraged him when he started drinking Bell's, despite the fact that he's a recovering alcoholic? Isn't it I who has been plying him non-stop with Johnnie? And if only I'd given him a bit of ubuvimbo earlier when he came begging… It's my fault that Mama Agnes's face is like puff pastry!

She leaned in to me, Mama Agnes, and placed her head on my chest. I tried to keep steady; the smell of her Ponds Lotion, the oily spray on her weave, were exhilarating. I imagined this is what my own mama would have smelled like. I imagine she would have found comfort in my arms, just like this. I carefully placed an arm around Mama Agnes's shoulders. She didn't shrug me off, like my surrogate father would have done. Instead, she snuggled up against me.

'I'm here for you, Mama Agnes,' I cooed gently. 'Everything is going to be OK. You deserve better than this.'

'I do, but it's what I've got, Zamani,' she replied. 'I have to play the cards that I've been dealt.'

And she's right, Mama Agnes. We've got to play the cards we've been dealt. I thought of my surrogate father, God knows where in the night. I thought of the cursor blinking on the screen of my MacBook, of my grand project. I thought of me and Mama Agnes, unwittingly brought together by Abednego's violence. I thought of being a true part of this family, of being a rooted man, a new creation who has broken free of the vicissitudes of the past and who can thus say of it, 'I am the one who willed the past' and not, 'It is the past, that tempestuous bastard, that has willed me.' We have to play the cards we have been dealt. And so, I turned to Mama Agnes and smiled encouragingly.

'How did it all begin?' I coaxed. 'Tell me all about it.'

BOOK TWO

AN ARRANGED MARRIAGE

What kind of family hi-story would it be, anyway, that chronicles the surrogate father without also ushering forth the voice of the surrogate mother? Though we can only suppose at fathers, deny our fathers, hate our fathers, renounce and denounce our fathers, even kill our fathers, we can only love our mothers and cling, with a force bordering on the primal, to the mother–child bond, in particular the mother–son bond, which is of the sacred kind and on which whole nations are to be built. Just look at that Helen of Troy! Look at that Mbuya Nehanda! Look at our Queen Lozikeyi! Look at the Queen of Sheba, whose mothering was so strong and whose bosom so bounteous that the Egyptians, the Jews, the Arabs and the Ethiopians fight over ownership of her legacy to this very day. Even the Brits are wise enough to realize the nurturing power of a mother, that's why they plead over and over with God to Save the Queen!

I wish Mama Agnes had known Abednego before Black Jesus turned him into the man she met. It was her father, of course, who made the choice, back in '87, of whom she was to marry, when she was but a lassie, barely sixteen, with only hillocks for breasts; he who negotiated the lobola with my surrogate father prior to the arranged meeting. She ought not to have been surprised by her father's instincts to marry her off, though. Hadn't he, after all, saved his homestead from annihilation during the past four years by steadfastly applying the formula of profit? When the Men in the Red Berets first came in '84 to Mama Agnes's village, Kezi, in Matabeleland South, having been armed and trained in Nyanga at the banks of the Nyangombe River for His Most Excellent Excellency Prime Minister Robert Mugabe by North Korea's great Kim Il-Sung – a case of the master teaching his prodigy – raping, looting, chopping willy-nilly, screaming *Are you a dissident? Are you a dissident?*, no answer good enough, hadn't he, her father, sworn allegiance to leader-and-country, and offered himself up as a spy? Had they not been spared the worst of the horror as a result, while those less practical of their neighbours faced massacres of whole clans? And hadn't her father done the same thing some six years before that, during the liberation war, when that colonizer Prime Minister Smith's Rhodesian army had come rat-a-tatting on village doors?

She hadn't wanted to marry my surrogate father, Mama Agnes. She'd been in love with another, a visiting apprentice priest from the Mashonaland North District named Father Reuben. He was slim, with skin the colour of matured baobab bark and an uncivilized afro, which he said regretfully he would have to trim, thanks to his civilizing vocation. And eyes that were too beautiful for a man, the burning colour of the winter bushveld. Everywhere he went, he wore a rosary and clutched a King James bible to his chest. Mama Agnes likened him to Jesus himself, a man of parables who left gemstones of (en)light(enment) wherever he walked. Now, here was a man who had the power to fill the craters gaping inside her with something more meaningful than the things her mama had said to bury and which she had so desperately tried to forget.

'Forget about Bhalagwe,' her mama had said. 'The leaders of the nation have ordered us to forget. To the future we must attend!'

But who could ever forget a concentration camp? Who could forget the day they took her and her sister Nto, and her brothers Trymore and Mwangi and Promise, how her mama, left behind in the village, had blackouts every single day until they returned, just she and Nto and Trymore, with neither Promise nor Mwangi, Trymore who now had only a stump where his arm had been? Memory loomed everywhere, like an accusation, in Trymore's eyes, in the eyes of the entire village, in the way they shuffled and the way they whispered and the way their bodies twitched like something was biting them and in the way the maize refused to grow. It ruffled the landscape and filled it with wraiths, so that even when there was nothing there, nothing tangible, Mama Agnes could not survey their compound, with its mud huts arranged like an L – the kitchen buttressing the corner, with her parents' hut on one side, and the boys' hut and girls' hut and the silo on the other side – without some chilli smarting in her chest, like one of her mama's big red Sahara Reapers. There would always be ghosts lingering there, wouldn't there always be ghosts? Lurking over there by the kraals at the bottom of the homestead, opposite the boys' hut, where the Men in the Red Berets had appeared, abracadabra just like that, floating in the evening mist like spectres. And her mama screaming *Run you children mani run do you want to die do you want to die run mani!*

But forget. That's what her mama had said, even though I imagine she could feel the memories of that time straining against the confines of her mind, Mama Agnes.

Her infatuation took root the day Father Reuben compared sitting on the fence of religion with being pregnant.

'You cannot be half pregnant,' he said, his gentle hand on her shoulder. 'You're either pregnant or you're not.'

That he chose pregnancy as the medium for his life-lesson danced in her head for the weeks to come. It could only mean one thing. He wanted to get pregnant with her. She entertained thoughts of cattle herded all the way from Mashonaland North District scrambling into the Ndiweni kraal. Her mama's warning about keeping her virginity sacred flew straight out of her head as she fantasized about the feel of Father Reuben inside her. She would not even play the shy, hesitant girl. She would say yes before he finished his proposal, and they would go to the stream…

She pulled away from me, Mama Agnes, and leaned forward, chuckling in the darkness. I could feel her blushing. I feared the spell my surrogate father had put us under was broken. I groped about desperately for something useful to say. Finally, I placed a tentative hand on her shoulder.

'I know what you're talking about,' I said, lowering my voice into a conspiratorial whisper, but with a dash of mirth in it. 'I, too, remember what it was like to be curious in my teens. Ach, I was so in love with my best friend's sister!'

I had no best friend as a child, and certainly wasn't in love with anyone's sister, but this seemed to land with her just the right way; Mama Agnes chuckled again, and I felt her shoulder slump as she leaned back on her sofa.

'I found every excuse possible to go to the Catholic church,' she confessed, though she had turned away from me now and was facing my surrogate father's empty sofa opposite us. 'I even signed up to be an Usher, and followed Father Reuben wherever he went.

"Father, what do you think of my flower arrangement?" I would ask. "Father, would you like to drink from my dish? The water is fresh from the stream. Father, Father, Father…"'

If Father Reuben noticed her infatuation, he ignored it. He was always cordial, treating her with the same respect that he treated everybody else, which made Mama Agnes feel like just another insignificant sheep in the flock under his patronage. She fell into a depression, eating little and barely concentrating in class. When her teachers asked her why her grades were dropping, for she was an excellent pupil with first rate grades, she shrugged and said the ten kilometres she had been walking to and from school for the past four years was becoming too much for her.

'You have a bright future ahead of you, Agnes,' her science teacher said. 'It's through education that you will be able to get out of this rural coop, and see the better world. There's a scholarship offer from the Catholic Church, for one to go and further their studies in a college in Massachusetts. We have put your name forward, but now it's up to you, to make sure your grades are up to par. Don't disappoint us. You can be absolutely anything you want, Agnes. Anything.'

Mama Agnes wanted to be Mrs Father Reuben. She didn't care if Massachusetts was part of the better world. Her ambitions stopped at the altar of a Catholic church somewhere in the Mashonaland District.

'Oh, I was so foolish then…!'

'No, no no, Mama A, don't be so unkind to yourself. You were in love. I, too, know what it is like to be in love.'

(Softly, softly, Zamani!)

One afternoon, after the Sunday service, she found herself strolling side by side with Father Reuben, listening attentively to one of his parabolic life-lessons, and daring to challenge his theories here and there. They were stumbling across one of the village's narrow, rutted paths flanked by maize fields that stood spare in November. The maize stalks were slowly browning, as though they were being turned over the embers of a fire.

'Is this all there is?' she wondered, scowling.

It was so hot that her lilac blouse, which usually hung loose on her frame, clung to her back and refused to let go. Father Reuben stopped and gazed down at her through eyes that squinted against the glaring sun.

'You're unusually bright, for a girl,' he commented.

Mama Agnes blushed. She had heard this many times before, but now, coming from Father Reuben's lips, it hit her with a sacred iridescence. She opened her mouth to say something, and the next moment Father Reuben's lips were on hers.

O sweet Virgin Mary, virgin that you are, virgin that young Mama Agnes is but virgin that she no longer wishes to be!

There she stood trembling with moist sweetness, with sweet moistness, for how moist was the sweetness, how sweet was the moistness, 'twas sweet, 'twas moist, the lips of holiness impressing themselves upon her. And the light, O, that overly bright light that made the landscape wriggle before her eyes like a siShikisha dancer, how it flooded her, how it wriggled, how it consumed! She swears, even to this very day, Mama Agnes, how that kiss ushered the moment when she looked up and saw the face of God.

Banished from her mind was Bhalagwe! To Father Reuben she concentrated her energies.

'See you at the next service,' said Father Reuben, pulling away.

That week was the longest week in Mama Agnes's young life. The days dragged by, accumulating into boring, painful hours whose only purpose seemed to be to torment her. Sunday arrived at last; she wore her best outfit, a shimmering dress that she usually reserved for weddings, but when she got to the church, Father Reuben was not there – he was attending a service in a neighbouring village. Rage and disappointment formed an unpleasant concoction that left a bitter taste in her mouth. It was Father Chipato, the rheumy-eyed priest, who conducted the service. He forged through the scripture in a loud, aggressive tone, thrashing the congregation to submission with his Shona. Each time he said 'Hallelujah!' the congregation groaned 'Hameni!', even though everyone from the village was Ndebele. His language paralysed them, and reminded them of the apparitions in the red berets. They, too, had spoken Shona, as they blessed the villagers with a horror such as they had never known possible. And so, there they stood, wailing 'Hameni!', but the louder Father Chipato preached, the more their bodies twitched, flinching against the memories of things they felt but had tried to forget.

When Mama Agnes saw Father Reuben the Sunday after Father Chipato's visit, she hissed, 'How could you keep me waiting last Sunday?'

To which he whispered, 'Meet me by the river, right before the spot where the boys swim, after lunchtime devotions.'

Mama Agnes was torn between anger and excitement. A part of her told her to skip the river rendezvous, just to spite Father Reuben. But the fear of putting him off for good tore at her thudding little heart, so that, promptly after the lunchtime devotions, she found herself sitting on one of the polished rocks that jutted out of the riverbank.

Father Reuben had chosen their meeting place well; large boulders rose one on top of the other on either side, converging to form a crevice where they could not be seen. Several uninterested livestock nibbled at the grass, their lolling bells going *nkende nkende* in the heat. A dog could be heard barking in the distance, from one of the homesteads sprawled intermittently across the terrain.

She dipped her feet in the water and kicked gently, so as not to make a big splash. This part of the river was shallow and clear. There were several such pockets along the Mpopoma River, where the water flowed with a gentle, almost imperceptible current. From where she sat, she could hear the boys splashing in another pocket of water around the bend. Further down the river was the girls' spot. Sometimes the boys planned mischievous invasions, during which they'd creep up on the girls and hide their clothes, then begin throwing stones and delight themselves with the sight of a dozen semi-naked, squealing females splashing about in the water.

The afternoon shadows began to lengthen. Mama Agnes was beginning to think that Father Reuben would not come when he appeared among the rocks, like Jesus by the Sea of Galilee.

She wanted to pout and say, 'You're late.'

Instead, she smiled shyly and berated herself for being so obvious. She did not know what type of courting game they were playing. He was not bold and abrupt, like the village boys who professed bottomless pools of love and beat you up if you tried to be cagey with them.

She receded, once again, into shyness. I understood perfectly; these were not the kind of intimacies a mother would share with her son. But she was in such a vulnerable, suggestible state, and I, I only wanted to connect with her!

'You remind me of myself, when I was young, Mama A,' I said encouragingly. 'The things I used to say to my best friend's sister! Why, I had no idea you used to be such a wildling in your youth.'

She laughed, and immediately winced; the swellings on her face were too fresh. 'I must go to bed,' she said, suddenly sombre.

I had pushed too hard. 'Oh? Are you sure?' I tried to sound casual. 'I really don't mind sitting here with you a little longer, if you like.'

'No, you've done enough for me as it is. It's late, and I'm so tired.'

She stood up and shuffled to the sitting room door, and then paused, waiting for me to leave.

'Zamani?'

I didn't want to go. I could feel my chest heaving. Something in there felt strangely tender.

'I'm not going,' I muttered defiantly. 'I'm not leaving you alone in this house. What if Father comes back and you need me? I'll sleep here, Mama Agnes,' I said, as I plumped the cushions of the sofa and lay down.

She seemed to consider this for a moment. 'All right,' she said, finally. 'You can sleep in Bukhosi's room. And Zamani? Please don't – he's not always this bad, and, I don't want the whole township gossiping—'

'I would never do such a thing, Mama Agnes,' I said, trying to hide my joy. And then, I dared to add, as casually as possible, 'After all, families protect one another and keep each other's… secrets.' I let that word, 'secret', slide deliciously off my tongue.

For the first time, I spent the night in the main house, in those sheets that still reek of the boy. The warmth of it took me by surprise; I remembered this room when it was still mine, when I lived here with Uncle Fani. It was different then, coldly bare, without the mother's touch that it now had, imprinting itself on the boy's ironed jeans and tee-shirts bulging out of the old wardrobe; in a teenage boy's impatient attempt to impose order, I imagined at a mother's admonishments, as could be seen in his pile of dirty clothes hidden behind the door, and the rubber slippers and Nike trackies shoved beneath the wardrobe. There was the boy's attempt at personality, too, in the glossy posters of Beyoncé and Kanye West caught in a beam of moonlight looming large on the wall to my right. And beside the bed where I had plomped myself, on an inverted crate that served as the dressing table, stood an empty bottle of Brut, and next to it a shaving stick, Lifebuoy soap, Axe roll on and an open tin of Ingram's Camphor Cream whose minty scent was fighting a losing battle with the boy's musky odour.

I imagined myself sleeping here every day, the room reeking of *me*. The wardrobe filled with my clothes, fresh with the scent of Mama Agnes's Sta-soft Lavender Fabric Softener, her sweet, motherly admonishments waking me up early on a Saturday morning to clean my room. I could feel my face breaking open, and I was so glad the electricity was still gone.

Mama Agnes was standing by the boy's door, and I imagined it must have been difficult for her to be there, without the boy. I smiled, imagining that my presence in the boy's room soothed her, that she saw, in me, Bukhosi. I tried to think of something to say, of what she may like to hear, of what the boy would say to her, but before I could say anything, she had mumbled a 'goodnight' and disappeared into her own room next door.

I didn't go to sleep but sat on the boy's bed, listening intently to her movements through the wall as she got ready for bed, trying to think up a ploy to get her talking again. I heard the creak of the mattress, and imagined she must have settled herself on her bed, and was now probably snuggling in her sheets. Soon, she would be asleep! I couldn't let her slip away.

I let out a loud sob, and then proceeded to weep theatrically.

'Zamani?'

She was back by the boy's door! I stifled a sob.

'Zamani! What is it? I'm coming in.'

I waited for her to take a few steps, and then turned my face away from her. 'I miss Bukhosi,' I said.

She sighed wistfully, as though catching a breath. 'Oh, mfanami, I miss him too!'

There, she had called me 'mfanami'! And though this is but a generic term of endearment used by motherly women for any agreeable young man, those who do helpful things like carry their groceries from the supermarket to their doorsteps, it thrilled me to hear it. I even imagined she meant it literally. 'My boy.' Her son!

'Being here, in his room with his things, it's brought back memories…' I said, keeping my voice soft still.

'I know!' said my Mama Agnes. 'But don't you worry, everything is going to be all right, OK? The Reverend Pastor still thinks he's in South Africa. The Holy Ghost is never wrong!'

'What was he thinking, running away like that?'

'I don't know, uyazi, I raised him in the church, not to be doing thug things, running away like a guluva…'

'But then, who knows what the impetuous young think? I, after all, tried to run away with my best friend's sister! And I'm sure you, too, Mama Agnes, could be impetuous in your youth. Couldn't you? Just look at what happened with Father Reuben! What… what did happen? What happened, Mama Agnes?'

Here she was quiet; she seemed far away. And then she began to chuckle. 'Well…'

And just like that, I found I had brought my Mama Agnes back to the conversation at hand! I can only surmise that she lay with Father Reuben. She spared me the embarrassing details of the act itself, only saying how, 'afterwards', he had left as soon as he could. And thus, it has been left to my own imagination, virgin that I am, to supply the details of what undoubtedly must have been, for a teenage girl, a clumsy, discomfiting experience of first-time coitus. Nothing pleasurable at all! What pleasure is to be found in a priestly finger prodding between virgin legs? What enjoyment is to be summoned by an ecclesiastical hand gripping a hillock breast? And what of coming face to face, for the first time, with that strange organ the phallus? What can a first-time glimpse of this body part, ebony and thick and erect, engender in the female mind except visions of unbecomingness? For, tool of pleasure that it is, even I know that the phallus is not a very pretty organ! It frightened even me the very first time I stroked myself with pubescent urgency and found it swelling and swelling until it became ramrod straight, demanding to be appeased! It does take some getting used to! So, imagine my poor Mama Agnes assaulted, for the first time, by this unruly body part, wondering how it will ever fit into her lady-parts, and confused also by the heat of her supple teenage body, when, before she knows what is happening, the feeling of something hard and sharp plunges into her, like the tip of a knife. What can she do but cry when she beholds the blood trickling down her thighs, what can she do but bury her sobs in the lapels of Father Reuben's jacket?

And what does that Father Reuben, fornicator after the priestly fashion, as has become so common over the years among the Catholic order, do?

'Agnes,' I can hear him saying. 'Agnes. It's getting late. I have to go.'

And off he hurries, without a backwards look, tripping over the underbrush, his eyes instead flitting about for any watchers-by.

This would have only made a confused Mama Agnes cry harder. She would have expected something of a love slap, would have wanted to hear Father Reuben say with that determination of men who are betrothed that he was coming to her home to speak with her father. But he didn't do any of these things, that Father, and that is perhaps why 'afterwards', when she had calmed down and washed the slick from between her legs, Mama Agnes walked to the Father's lodgings.

What kind of man was this Father, eh?

The priests' compound, Mama Agnes told me, was behind the Catholic church building. It was a brick block with asbestos roofing that ran the length of the yard and was subdivided into bedrooms, with the privilege of a diesel-engine generator to power the electricity.

She spotted Father Reuben seated on the stoep outside his room, a silhouette against the light spilling from his open door, his movements exaggerated by the shadows on the walls as he gesticulated to the other priests, who were clumped around a gas stove near the entrance of the compound. They looked strange to Mama Agnes without their priestly garb, so, so *ordinary*, so disappointingly *mortal*. But not Father Reuben, no. His hairy legs, protruding from a pair of faded shorts, were firm, the muscles of his calves well carved, the chunks of thigh disappearing into his shorts deliciously thick. When their eyes met, he did not make a move to get up. Instead he bent and scooped up a handful of roasted groundnuts from a dish on the ground.

'Ah, if it is not young Agnes. You know with your enthusiasm for the Church, you ought to become a nun.'

The other priests laughed softly.

Mama Agnes could not meet his gaze. 'I need to speak with you.'

'At this late hour? You should come tomorrow.'

'I need to speak with you now.'

Father Reuben got up, stretched and said something in Shona to one of the priests. There was a ripple of laughter. Finally, he turned to a squirming Mama Agnes, and, grabbing her arm, hastened her to the gate.

'What do you think you're doing?' he hissed. 'Go home! It's late and your family must be worried by now.'

'You have to speak with my father.'

'Speak with your father about what?'

'About my lobola, of course! This afternoon, you made me your wife.'

(I wanted to blurt out here, 'His wife, Mama A? But you know priests can't…' But I dared not interrupt.)

Father Reuben held her firmly by the shoulders. 'Agnes, listen to me. Go. Home. We will discuss this tomorrow. Now, go home, please.'

'No.'

'What?'

Mama Agnes folded her arms and eyed him defiantly. Tears were welling up in her eyes. 'Everybody will know what I've done.'

'No one will know what you've done unless you tell them! Now, go home. It's dark, no one will see anything, and first thing tomorrow morning, I will come to your father's homestead.'

'You are lying.'

'Agnes, please! Do you want your father to kill me? These things must be done properly. I cannot escort you at this late hour to discuss such an important matter with your father. Are you crazy, woman? Go home!'

'You promise to come tomorrow?'

'I have said I will come! Now go!'

She slinked into her father's homestead just as her mama was dishing supper. She looked up at Mama Agnes, who was hovering in the shadows, away from the light of the fire. 'Eh, what is it? You look like a ghost, has the hare finally been eaten by the lion?'

'Ah, nothing, Ma. Just evening prayers.'

'You need to stop with this church of yours, your father will not be happy. Here, take his food to him.'

'It's that priest she likes, Ma,' Nto blurted.

Mama Agnes whacked her sister on the head. 'Shut your dirty mouth! S'phukuphuku. It was just night prayers, Ma.'

'It had better be, because we have an important visitor coming at the end of the week.'

Mama Agnes didn't care about any important visitors. She begged a headache and retired to the hut she shared with Nto. She lay awake for a long time, staring into the dark, trying to imagine Father Reuben's impending arrival. She would make sure to stay well out of sight, until she was called to identify her visitor. She had witnessed the ritual several times before, most recently when it had been her cousin's turn when she was wedded to a Kalanga from Tsholotsho. All the young girls would be called to gather outside her father's hut.

They would be asked, 'Do you know any of these men?'

For the suitor would not travel alone. The girls, feigning surprise, would gasp riotously, and the cheekiest of the group would say, 'I think that one has been eyeing me from a distance.'

Mama Agnes would keep her eyes on the mud floor as she pointed at Father Reuben and acknowledged him as her suitor. Then the group of girls would be dispersed and the lobola negotiations would begin.

Her reverie was broken by Nto. She had not heard her sister come in.

'I saw you,' she whispered. 'By the river with that priest of yours. I saw you.'

Mama Agnes sat up. 'I don't know what you're talking about.'

'You had better not have done what I saw you doing, because

there's a suitor coming for you at the end of the week. A rich man who has a house in the city.'

'You're lying! Father Reuben is coming to speak to our father tomorrow. I'm going to be his wife.'

Nto laughed, making the heat rush to Mama Agnes's dark face. 'You know, sister, you may be good with the books in the class, but where life is concerned, you are just stupid. Father Reuben cannot wed you even if he wanted.'

'Yes, he can,' Mama Agnes spat back. 'And he will! He loves me. Yebo, he's a priest, but he loves me and he's going to leave the Church for me and—'

'Oh? Is that what he said?'

Mama Agnes glared at her sister, who forged ahead, 'Besides, you know he's a Shona, you know Father will die before he gives any of us to a Shona. So, you had better stop dreaming. And you had better not have done what I saw you doing with him.'

The next morning, Mama Agnes heard the whispers between her mama and her sister in the kitchen, about the suitor who was coming all the way from Bulawayo, the City of Kings, to discuss lobola with her father.

Mama and Nto were in the corner of the kitchen hut, folded over a wide, reed sieve, almost flat like a tray, which they held between them, each gripping an edge, shake shaking it from side to side. Dried kernels of maize rattled in the sieve, a cloud of husks billowing in the morning light. She watched, Mama Agnes, out of the corner of her eye, as the debris that was too heavy to float slipped through the holes of the sieve, into the bucket squatting beneath. A separation of the things that were to be kept from those that would be discarded. Her mama's limbs were sturdy and a deep, glistening brown, the soles of her feet and the cheeks of her palms toughened from a lifetime of use. Her movements were quick and efficient, her buttocks big but firm, contained in every movement. Nto, on the other hand, kept teetering this way and that with the sieve, her skinny arms jostling awkwardly with the air. Nto, as her mama liked to say, was going to make an embarrassing wife one day. She had neither buttocks nor poise, unlike Mama Agnes who, her mama liked to say, had buttocks but lacked poise. But better one than none.

Mama stopped sieving and said, brightly, 'Hmmm, and uyazi, we have a very important person coming to visit us at the end of this week…'

'A man from the city!' said Nto.

'A man from the city,' repeated mama.

Mama Agnes's face remained impassive, for she could feel them watching her now; she continued to frown at the cracks on the mud floor, as though there was something interesting to be contemplated there. But her heart was galloping, trying to drag her with it, and she almost tumbled to the ground.

'Hmmm! I wonder who is the lucky girl he has come for?'

They giggled, mama and Nto, their laughter at once wise and girlish. Something rattled inside of Mama Agnes, and she couldn't help it; she grabbed the bucket of discarded things and made a dash for it.

She fled to the well. She knew how much the possibility of a wedding meant to the family; it would be a fresh start, which would cement their determination to forget the past. But who could ever forget? She asked herself, plunging her face into the mouth of the well, staring into its murky depths. She wondered just how bottomless its bottom was? How long before one could hit the dark, mysterious liquid with a splash? If the water would suck you to a deep dark down where you could never be found? If the sensation of liquid ballooning your lungs hurt?

She screamed into the well. But there weren't rippling echoes, only a bottomless-bottom timbre to her voice.

She had to tell Father Reuben to make his approach before this dreaded suitor made himself known. She dropped her pail and ran, cutting across her father's homestead and sprinting along the path to the priests' compound. When she arrived, out of breath, she asked one of the priests where Father Reuben was.

'He's gone.'

Her heart attempted to leap out of her chest. 'Gone where?'

'Don't you know? He has finished his apprenticeship with our congregation. He has gone back to his district. He left before the cry of the first rooster, so he could catch the bus to Bulawayo.'

Mama Agnes fell into an indeterminable illness. Because she could not *see* it, did not understand how a heart could be *broken* (like an arm or a leg or even a nose), but felt, somewhere inside, a pain of spiritual depths that was strangely almost *physical* (because a heart could be black, and sag heavy, but it had no bone, and therefore could not *snap*), she simply claimed she had a headache and then a stomach ache, and spent the rest of the week in bed. When my surrogate father arrived five days later, she rejected him, refusing to be impressed by his yellow Peugeot 504, which farted into her father's homestead laden with all sorts of town goodies. She snubbed the multicoloured dresses and shiny stilettos, eyed the assortment of sweet, cloying perfumes with a feigned nonchalance. She had resolved that she did, after all, want to see the better world, and Massachusetts sounded like a good place to complete her studies. There were all her black brothers and sisters over there, those slaves or once slaves. She would join them, and forge her path in the great United States of America.

'Why will you not have him?' her mother demanded.

'He's too old.'

'He is wealthy, he can look after you.'

'He's ugly.'

'Beauty never mattered in a man.'

'What shall I call him – grandpa?'

'He's not *that* old. Besides, you know your father will never stand for this.'

'I don't care what anyone says, I don't want him. And what kind of name is Abednego?'

'Abednego is a biblical name, it means "servant of Nebo", and Nebo was the Babylonian god of wisdom. He's a man of wisdom, my child, he will be good for you.'

'Well, they should have named him Reuben or something.'

When her form four results came, she discovered, to her dismay, that she hadn't done as well as she'd expected. She did not even have a single distinction in Maths, Integrated Science or English, the Important Subjects that were the professed favourites of any self-respecting, forward-thinking pupil. Though in truth, she liked Ndebele the most. It was a singsong language suffused with subtle wisdoms. But too heavy. Not light enough, like English, to carry one on the wings of progress all the way to Massachusetts. The Catholic Church scholarship was awarded to another pupil, and Massachusetts came to lodge itself as another confusing ache in her heart. She turned from the mirror of her life to find that this large, clumsy man – with the yellow face and a prominent lower lip drooping beneath a caterpillar moustache – was the only option she had left.

We were both startled by the sound of the gate squeaking; it was eerily loud. And then my surrogate father's red Peugeot 405 farted into the yard. Dammit! Abednego, why does he have such bad timing? Just when we were getting along really well, my Mama Agnes and I.

'Goodnight,' Mama Agnes said curtly, gathering herself and slinking out of Bukhosi's room before I could say anything.

No matter, we managed to pass huge hurdles. She even let me sleep in the boy's bed! I have Abednego to thank for all of this. If he hadn't... No, that's no way to think at all. But still, it's just, I've been wanting so long to connect with my Mama Agnes and now—

I heard him come in, staggering down the passage that leads from the back door to the sitting room. Where was he coming from, anyway? He paused by Bukhosi's door; I could hear his laboured breathing. I held my breath. I feared he would come in. I didn't want him to find me there, in the boy's room – he would surely kick me out. He stood by the boy's door for what felt like forever. And then, he shambled on, and I could hear him stumbling into Mama Agnes's bedroom. His voice reached me, a dull, mumbling, slurred speech; had he been drinking? I sat up and listened; would he beat her again? I would readily comfort her. But all I heard was grunting, and the sound of clothes being slipped off, and then, the next moment, raspy snoring.

I lay back in bed. I didn't want him to hurt Mama Agnes again. Of course not. I just wanted, I just wished... I had enjoyed our talk, that's all. It had felt so good to be there for her and have her open up to me.

I found I couldn't sleep. I lay in bed for a long time, thinking of what had transpired. I thought of Mama Agnes and how she must have felt meeting my surrogate father. She was sixteen then and he was, what, thirty-three? I can see how to a girl of sixteen he would have seemed incredibly old.

I can imagine her dragging herself reluctantly to her father's hut to meet my surrogate father on the fated day. Her mama flanking her on her left, Nto on her right. Dressed in the white, frilly dress she is wearing in the wedding photo hanging on the sitting room wall next to the portrait of baby Bukhosi. Her hair having been fried with a hot comb to get it to stand in those thin, curled rolls, like half-fisted hands. She looks so frightened in that photo.

My surrogate father would not have gone to meet her alone; he would have needed someone, a male relative, to accompany him; someone like Uncle Lungile.

Was it really so easy for him to move on from my Thandi, just like that? I feel as though I shan't ever be able to move on from her, as though I can never love again. But perhaps it was the family that pressured him to remarry, to try and rebuild what he had lost.

I can see Mama Agnes blinking at my surrogate father through the haze of smoke spiralling from a dying fire in the middle of the hut. No longer is he the rural boy that my inamorata had to polish into a man of the city! No longer is he shy and inarticulate and naïve!

'Do you know either of these men?' her father asks, feigning a frown.

And she, Mama Agnes, she's as bashful as a rural girl could be... To her this suitor is a large and yellow city man with a huge nose and a lower lip that sags as though from a mouthful of secrets—

'*Do you know any of these men?*' Her father's voice cracks, as though something hot has been placed on his vocal cords.

Mama Agnes nods, shakes her head, nods, shakes her head, nods, shakes her head...

Gasp!

'What is this?' demands Uncle Lungile. 'What, what is the meaning of this? We are the proud Mlambo clan, and this boy here is a virile young man, a freedom fighter, a hero who fought for his country. Any woman would be lucky to have him. We won't stand for this!'

Mama Agnes grimaces. I, too, would grimace, were I her! Boy? *Boy* is her brother Trymore, with his firm (remaining) limbs, why, not even Father Reuben can be called a boy but rather a *young man*. But this funny, yellow man who looks not at her but *through* her, with eyes big and brown and woeful, why, he's almost like her *father*... She scrambles to her feet and flees. She heads for the kraals, where she crouches behind one of the wooden posts and peers at her father's hut, just like my surrogate father used to do when trying to listen to that brother read the bible to his own surrogate father.

I can see Mama Agnes's father unbuckling his belt as he limps out into the late afternoon, his eyes rotating wildly in their sockets. There is her mama, right behind him. She sees Mama Agnes first, and shuffles ahead of her father, whose cracked voice bellows for her to come to him.

'I'll teach you a lesson, what do you, what is, what...?'

'Please, my king my life my love, let me talk to the girl,' her mama pleads.

Mama Agnes glares at her father, and at my surrogate father who has emerged, and now stands by the entrance of the hut, staring at her, quiet, unmoving.

'My daughter, please, Agnes, Agnes—' She turns to her mama, who cups her face and slaps her cheeks gently. 'What are you doing, why are you doing this, why are you embarrassing your father like this, why are you? Listen, listen to me. I was fourteen when I married your father, yes fourteen, and he was not much younger than this man who has come for you – listen, are you listening? – he was about twice my age, and I was so afraid of him, the first day in his compound I cried, yes I cried, but look at me, look how happy I am, how good our life, do you hear me, are you listening? You are no longer a child, Agnes, and this day was always coming, listen, are you listening?'

And though she wants to cry, Mama Agnes, something hard and hot has lodged itself in her chest, clogging her tears. 'I don't want to go,' she mumbles. 'I don't want to leave you and Nto and Trymore and Father and… Please don't make me go.'

'I know, I know,' her mama says, and begins, suddenly, to cry, a long, loud wail that frightens Mama Agnes. 'I know. But it's the way things are meant to be…'

Behind her mama, her father is being solicitous, murmuring apologies to my Uncle Lungile, who is hissing about being greatly offended. Behind them stands my surrogate father, arms folded, his gaze still fixed on Mama Agnes.

'Come,' yells my uncle, trying to yank him by the arm. 'We will not stand for this. We are the proud Mlambo clan. Come! We are leaving.'

'No,' he replies. 'No, Uncle! It is you who dragged me all the way here. Did you not say, my boy, the family needs your seed, we need to replace what you lost? Did you not say, my boy, I have found you a wife, she is a blot-out-sun, just you wait and see. So. We shall finish this. And look at her! Isn't she an Angela Davis?'

And so it was that Mama Agnes was wedded to Abednego, who must have demanded that she respectfully call him 'Baba', like I always hear her refer to him. And then she found herself, Mama Agnes, several months later, in that two-bedroomed house in Entumbane, the house meant for my Thandi.

THE PRAYER MEETING

Mama Agnes crept into Bukhosi's room early this morning and shook me awake, hissing at me to get up and go back to my pygmy room.

'Why?' I said, rather petulantly, although I knew why. But I wanted her to stand up for me. Would she have kicked me out like that had I been Bukhosi, even if my surrogate father hadn't wanted him there?

'Camun,' she said. 'Get up. Camun, chop chop.'

Her voice was cold. She averted her eyes while I slipped out of bed, picked up my shirt and slinked past her without another word. She couldn't have humiliated me more if she had tried! I have been sitting here since, cross-legged, on my put-me-up bed in my pygmy room, clickety-clacking away on my MacBook, trying to fight the urge to go to her, and beg her to talk to me, to show me some of the tenderness of last night, the same tenderness with which she talks about Bukhosi, softening her consonants, her voice taking on a husky timbre. I yearn to see this from her, for me, to be as we were last night, just the two of us, without that drunkard coming between us. My Mama Agnes. But I dare not go to her today; she won't tell me anything with my surrogate father there. I want to talk to her about that concentration camp, Bhalagwe. I want to bear some of her burden and share in her past. I want to know what it was like for her – and what it must have been like for my real mother, too. I have been doing some calculations: Mama Agnes said last night the Men in the Red Berets first came to her village in Kezi in '84; Uncle Fani said it was '83 when they first came to Tshipisane Village – it would have been around January, for I was born in that Gehenna in October. So, Mama Agnes and my mama probably never met, although their experiences would have been one and the same. My mama. My Zodwa Nsele Khathini. My most gracious Virgin Mary. To thee I come, before thee I stand, sinful and sorrowful.

I heard Mama Agnes, when I crept in to use the loo, telling my surrogate father that the Reverend Pastor is coming this evening to pray for Bukhosi, and that the Ladies of the Church will be accompanying him. My surrogate father wanted to know why they had to come *here* and my surrogate mother replied – I imagine pointing to her face – that as she can't go to the Reverend Pastor at the moment, the Reverend Pastor is coming to her. This shut him up. But a mere beating won't shut Mama Agnes up – she is determined to go on interceding for Bukhosi. Why couldn't she intercede for me with my surrogate father this morning, instead of kicking me out of the boy's room like that?

Still, I can't sulk. She's under a lot of stress at the moment; what kind of son would I be were I to abandon her at this time when she needs me most? Which is why I have made myself available this evening at the prayer meeting led by the Reverend Pastor. There has been a lot of hustle and bustle in preparation for his arrival. I don't know why Mama Agnes is so excited – you'd think we were hosting Jesus himself – busy putting up fresh curtains, polishing the floor, adorning the sofas in her special covers; she even went next door to ask MaNdlovu for some of her scented candles.

At the appointed hour, with a knock on the door and a procession of neighbours, we gather in the Mlambo living room: myself, Mama Agnes, the Reverend Pastor, the Ladies of the Church and all of the Mlambos' neighbours and friends who have come to pray for Bukhosi. My surrogate father, as to be expected, has slinked off on his lonely late-night searches. Doesn't Mama Agnes wonder where he goes to? Does she know? I doubt it; she's probably just relieved that he is out of the house. I look around at the congregation and marvel at how everyone has pooled together in a mass effort to find Bukhosi. He is loved. I wonder if there is anyone who would care today if I went missing.

I can't see Mama Agnes and I suddenly feel panicked, but then I spot her, turned away from me, away from the frisky bulb light, and hovering instead in the murkiest of shadows, right by the Reverend Pastor's crotch. For she's on her knees, her pillowy frame gathered in ruffled becomingness, in a floral, green veldt-coloured dress, which matches the doek on her head. Her divine countenance bob-bobs next to the Reverend Pastor's trousers, which, because Canali suits are made to measure, bulge rather obscenely in the shape of a banana lying flat against his right thigh. He keeps bringing her face dangerously close to his banana, rattling Satan out of her head with his huge paw and shouting, 'Can I get a Halleluuuujah!'

The neighbours give him a 'Halleluuuujah!'

'Can I get an Aamen!'

'Hameni!'

He's a famous man, the Reverend Pastor, scandalously famous. For the past months, he's been making the front news of the independent papers, which has been happening more frequently what with the presidential elections next year. He's been writing sermonic articles in which he pleads with the current government to step down, to leave the job of running a country to better-suited scoundrels, even praying, in one article, for God to intervene, to send a flood, to send a plague, to send the UN troops, to send America to invade us like they did Iraq and Afghanistan! To show who is God!

But he shan't get a Hallelujah out of me, and certainly not an Amen. I'm sitting on the floor in the shadows, opposite this spectacle, wedged between Bukhosi's sofa and the small, narrow bookcase. My face is tactfully angled away from the light; it is not to the light that I turn, not the shackles of that arresting light that I seek tonight, but the shadows.

As any discerning soul will have already guessed, Reverend Pastor Reuben is that same Father Reuben who took Mama Agnes's virginity all those years ago when she was but a lassie. I spent the afternoon online doing due diligence on him, this man from my Mama Agnes's youth who is back in her life playing the role of Father. The things I found out about him! He was kicked out of the Catholic order several years ago after it emerged that he had long since been submerged in sin, plugging his joy stick into many a female outlet and spasming with electric bliss. His proclivity had been for the married woman; he may have even blessed a man's house or two with child. But then, having since repented, he started his own church, Blessed Anointings, after the charismatic Pentecostal fashion, and made it his business to preach not only about the sins of the government but also those of the Catholic Church, which, he now claims, has always been a little too concerned with matters of this world rather than the next.

I'm reminded of the story Mama Agnes likes to tell of how she came to be reunited with the Reverend Pastor, that fortuitous meeting that in her telling has always seemed innocuous, nothing more than a spiritual guiding to a good church c/o the Holy Ghost. But now, knowing what I know about their hi-story… I can see her stumbling into him five years ago, in 2002, fluttering on a City Council bin, full-figured and photoshopped, advertising a revival at his Blessed Anointings, the lower half of his body obscured by a growing mound of rubbish congregated around the receptacle, a devoted nunnery of flies swarming him. She wasted no time, my Mama Agnes, in detaching herself from the mundane rituals of the dogmatic Catholics. She had no trouble severing her ties to that Church of her childhood, to St Rose of Lima, to St Barbasymas, to St Mary of Egypt, and all those other countless saints who populate the archives of the Catholic Church, to be dredged up dutifully for worshipful-genuflecting on holidays and mass ceremonies. She had no problem at all, Mama Agnes, in making the charismatic Blessed Anointings her new home.

I feel a little pang as I watch her struggling up from her kneeling position by the Reverend Pastor's crotch. She takes her place demurely next to him, her motherly countenance now haloed by the bulb light, enriching, despite her bruises, her walnut skin. Last night, I believed, stupidly, that it was thanks to my own powers of persuasion that Mama Agnes shared her youthful dalliance with me. But now, seeing them together, she gazing at him reverently, he beaming smugly at the room, I realize it's probably *this*, his Fatherly presence in her life, and not the special moment I thought we were having last night, that made her give in so easily to my entreaties to share her hi-story – of all the things she could have told me about her past, she chose to tell me about *him*.

And there he is moving away from her, with barely even an ounce of the attention I lavished on her yesterday evening. Her gaze lingers after him as he makes his way magnanimously through his congregants, smiling, shaking hands, mouthing 'thank you' to whatever praises his besotted sheep are singing him. What use is all this hi-story I learned about them last night, of what use is it to my Mlambo Family Chronicles, to my redemptive project, to me? Mccm. That's a part of Mama Agnes's hi-story I shall have to blot out – this man, like that other brother, must not be allowed to taint our family hi-story. What the hell is he even doing here, out of the pages of the past, in Mama Agnes's present?

I can't help but glower at the man – at his back, for the Ladies of the Church have monopolized him. They usher him to the cobalt kitchen table where they heap for him a plate of coleslaw beetroot samp fried-rice mashed-potatoes potato-salad grilled-chicken and beef-stew. Trust a sombre gathering to produce abracadabra delectable delights that you cannot find anywhere on the gaping shelves of OK and Shoprite and Spar and Meikles! The food is a mountain and he climbs it as surely as Abraham, shovelling spoonful after spoonful into his cavernous mouth. I glare at him, shake my head and scowl. I mustn't let these pangs distract me from my larger project. I musn't let him derail us.

Mama Agnes has now made her way to my side of the room; she's standing in front of Bukhosi's sofa, seemingly oblivious to me crouching between the sofa and the bookcase. She's busy staring at the boy's sofa as if he were seated there. I get up, so she can see me.

'Can I get you anything?' I say, placing my hand on her shoulder. 'Are you all right?'

'I keep going back to that Sunday when he disappeared,' she sighs. 'The last time I saw him, he was standing by the kitchen sink, drinking a glass of water. I remember his head was tilted back, his Adam's apple bobbing as he swallowed. And I remember watching him and thinking how much he had grown! Very soon, he'd start to grow a beard. He was becoming a man, my nanaza, bantu! But what was he wearing?' She blinks at the sofa. 'What was he wearing? What…?' She begins to sniffle.

'Do you think he's really in South Africa?' she says suddenly. 'My vision from the Holy Ghost the other day. I haven't seen any more but… Do you think he's in Jozi? Is it a girl, is that it?'

'Yes,' I say, without really thinking through what it is I'm saying.

She turns and clutches my arm. 'Did he tell you that? What did he say?'

I'm just on the verge of correcting myself when I notice that her eyes are as round as coins, her body suddenly stiff. Such beautiful intensity! Is this what a mother's love feels like? I frown, as though trying to remember. 'He mentioned something like that to me, about a girl in Jozi, but I don't really know any more than that.' I look across the room, at the Reverend Pastor, who is now helping himself to a second helping. How does he manage to shovel down so much food? 'But if the Holy Ghost showed you the vision, and the Reverend Pastor says it's true, then it must be so.'

Mama Agnes is practically gleaming. It's a powerful intoxicant, hope. 'And he'll come back,' I continue, confidently. 'I'm sure of it, Ma, there's no need for all this worrying. I have faith in the Holy Ghost. And the Reverend Pastor.'

'Praise be to God!'

'You look tired, Ma. Would you like me to get you some food? We can go and sit on the stoep by the back door, away from all this noise.'

'Yes, I'm so exhausted, it's been a long day. Wait, let me quickly go and say goodbye to the Reverend Pastor, I'll be right back.'

She didn't come back, Mama Agnes. She went to talk to the Reverend Pastor and remained by his side for the rest of the evening. She must have told him what I had said to her, about the boy and the Holy Ghost and his own supposed powers, for he looked up while she was whispering something in his ear, his eyes searching the room until they rested on me, whereupon he raised a hand and flashed me a smile. I nodded and bared my teeth back.

It wasn't until this morning that I managed to get Mama Agnes by herself. We cleaned up the wreckage from last night's prayer meeting in companionable silence, at least until Abednego trudged into the house, an old sheaf of my Bukhosi posters clamped under his arm. He claimed to have been searching all night, but I suspect he just wanted to avoid the prayer meeting. He's a real piece of work, that one. To think I was beginning to look up to him as a father! These days the man wants to act like he doesn't know me. Heh. Mama Agnes gushingly told him not to worry, the boy is in South Africa. The Holy Ghost came to her, plus I confirmed it, Bukhosi mentioned it to me, about some girl over there.

I smiled sheepishly when she said this, looking at me almost in the same way she devoured the Reverend Pastor with her eyes last night.

'Why didn't you say something sooner?' my surrogate father snapped at me.

'Ah, he said it in passing, nje, I wouldn't have made the connection had Ma not mentioned Johannesburg last night…'

He eyed me with suspicion, and then his whole body suddenly deflated. 'Really?' he said, looking at Mama Agnes. 'The boy's alive?' He swallowed a sob, and his eyes became wet. And then he turned around and stumbled back out the front door.

We sat side by side on the back stoep like we intended to last night, Mama A and I, with our cups of tea and a breakfast of fatcooks. Our legs were touching and I could feel every shudder of her plump, motherly figure as she talked and chuckled and swallowed her tea. Her mood was buoyant and I found it was easy to cajole her back to her story – indeed, hope is as powerful an intoxicant as my Johnnie! I sighed wistfully and said I remembered only too well the kind of first love that could send me chasing after a girl to Jozi – and at that moment it really did feel as though I was remembering it, this first love, this best friend's sister, for I was suffused with giddy bliss. 'But,' I added philosophically, gazing at the sky dreamily, 'first loves are quickly forgotten. Look how far you and Baba have come since this Father Reuben of yours.' (And not for a moment did I betray that I knew that Father Reuben was the same man who warmed our seats and tried my patience only last night.)

She sort of snorted, but seemed to catch herself. 'It's not that easy, you know. With Baba and I, it was an arranged marriage. It takes a long time to get to know someone, to learn to love them.'

She admitted to thinking of Father Reuben every day at first and often afterwards in her new home with my surrogate father, that nest built for my Thandi, so far away and so far removed from her beloved rural home in Kezi. How squashed the city houses were! Side by side like corn in a field, back to front, everything sideways, so that she could hear the dirty laundry from next door flitting in the wind as if in her own house; gudu gudu gudu, from the horny couple next door; the woman on the other side with such a foul mouth, her voice clambering on top of her husband's, even though Mama Agnes could always guess what was to follow, the muted thuds of his fists and then the sharp register of her screams.

'But city houses are so ugly!' she exclaimed to my surrogate father one evening, as she served him his supper.

It had been weeks of fiddling with things, the three-plate stove that was not as scary as it looked; the cold white thing that, strangely, had a very hot back, and which if you placed your ear to it you could hear the food inside humming and sighing; the buttons on the walls of every room, which if you pushed made the sun shine from the glass balls attached to the ceiling, and which if you pushed up-down up-down made the little suns blink on-off on-off, until the little suns blew out, making my surrogate father blow up; the hard, black floor made from cement that you didn't smear with cow dung like the mud huts back in Kezi, but with a slimy, black polish called Sunbeam; the bed that was too soft and made your back hurt but which was good because that was what town people slept on.

'But city houses are so *ugly*!' she said again.

My surrogate father at last looked up from a page of *The Chronicle* spread across his lap, startled. 'They are not… *ugly*. They're sophisticated. Something you wouldn't know anything about. Don't ever call my house ugly again.'

'But… no *space*… everything so *close*… everyone owns so *little*…'

'You think those clumsy mud huts you grew up in are better? Heh?'

'Well, yes.'

'Then you are truly stupid, and I have made a terrible mistake. Did I make a bad investment, marrying you? I bring you from the bhundu to the heart of civilization, to a place with real substance, like lights and cars and radios and things like that, and instead of being grateful, you insult me. The world is moving on, little gal. Shape up or ship out.'

And so, she began to think of the haphazard landscape before her as 'sophisticated'. The township houses were 'intimate'. It was all part of the sophistication. Shape up or ship out. She wrote long, sprawling letters to Nto, describing everything around her, the foul-mouthed woman next door – who Mama Agnes saw one morning wandering in her yard and who said in reply to Mama Agnes's greeting, 'You don't want to be plucking the chicken out of the cooking pot now, child,' like someone possessed, either by spirits or sadness – the Zupco buses that ferried the people into a big town that just never ended: the noise; how the people greeted you by name as you walked down the township streets, just like in Kezi, but how, unlike Kezi, they didn't really know you and did not themselves seem to want to be really known; how polished Bulawayo city centre was! Buildings that were as bright as diamonds. Tall structures that were called skyscrapers – because they touched the sky, you see, and if you went up all the floors you could see the soles of God's feet – ugly cars that were said to be beautiful only because they cost so much, women who wore perms in their hair, painted their lips red, puffed cigarettes like men and danced to Nina Simone – as though Massachusetts-America was a reality you could pluck from the air and inhabit, like someone called Alice who went to a place called Wonderland through a rabbit hole.

'I'm coming to the city, you'll see!' Nto wrote back. 'I'm going to be that woman smoking cigarettes like a man and wearing perms in her hair!'

It was not such a bad thing, Mama Agnes began to think, to be under my surrogate father for life. He had brought her from the bhundu to the heart of civilization, to a place with real substance, like lights and cars and radios and things like that. She was grateful. Bulawayo was such a sparkling place. Like Massachusetts-America. At least, for a while, before the beatings started, she was able to forget Father Reuben's betrayal and she was able to forget what it had been like to be a thirteen-year-old Matopo girl in '84 shuffling in a 5 Brigade pungwe.

FIRE ON THE MOUNTAIN

I messed up.

At the mention of the 5 Brigade, I couldn't resist sticking my fat finger in the hole of hi-story and wiggling it around, asking Mama Agnes what it was like at Bhalagwe. She clammed up immediately, her body stiffening, and I had no idea how to open her back up again. I suddenly wanted to hug her. There was something tight and painful in my chest. I wanted to lay my head on her lap. I have no idea what came over me! I had to bite my tongue and swallow back tears. I dared not touch her. Instead, I back-tracked, and tried to guide her once again to the happier memories of her married life. But my questions came out clumsy and desperate, and I could feel her slipping away. She got up abruptly, though she hadn't finished her tea, and said she had chores to do. And that was that; though she's still nice to me, smiling politely at my wack jokes, she refuses to be seduced into telling me about the good old days.

I shouldn't have brought up Bhalagwe! But it's the place where our hi-stories cross, Mama Agnes and I, though she doesn't know it. Just like how, unwittingly, my surrogate father and I crossed paths via that Black Jesus. Perhaps I went too far with my surrogate father. He seems to have come a little unstuck of late.

I'll be gentle with my Mama A. Though I must get her to tell me about Bhalagwe, that place where I was born, where my mama died, where Black Jesus did his business. If only I could conquer that Gehenna in these pages! For a man cannot shape his own life while still under the thumb of History. History has been known to consume men whole, to make out of them its playthings. No, I shan't be History's plaything! I need to know Mama Agnes's hi-story. I need to know what Bhalagwe was like.

The decision to follow my surrogate father to wherever he goes every night in search of the boy was not one I took lightly. But what else could I do? My charms have failed to work on my Mama A. Her coolness, the way she smiles politely, almost tenderly, whenever I speak to her, though she remains clamped up, is much worse than if she were angry with me. At least then, I would know I matter enough to stir some visceral feeling in her. No, the only two men able to rouse her passions are my surrogate father and that Reverend Pastor. And yes, yes, the boy!

I have no access to the Reverend Pastor or the boy, but I certainly have access to Abednego. And didn't Mama Agnes tell me her hi-story only after the beating from my surrogate father? All I planned to do was to recreate the conditions that made her open up in the first place. I intended to shake the hornet's nest just a little, nje. I would make sure my Mama Agnes didn't get stung… and if she *did* happen to get stung, well, I would be there, wouldn't I, to nurse her wounds?

Oh, but what kind of person are you, Zamani! What does this make me? To knowingly put my Mama Agnes in the path of danger. But it is not I who is the cause! It's that man! He's the wife beater! And I… I am only here to protect Mama Agnes! What are a few necessary pains in service to the bigger project of freedom, my freedom from the past – and also Mama Agnes's? Can there be freedom without sacrifice? Our own liberation war the state is always shoving down our throats is, after all, about the sacrifice necessary for freedom. And I would ensure Mama Agnes endured only the minimum needed to get the wheels of her hi story, our hi-story, going.

And so, there I was yesterday evening, hiding in the boot of my surrogate father's car, sighing with relief when I heard him finally pipe his usual 'bye bye, going to look for Bukhosi' as he drove off. I was lying on my side, with my legs folded to my chest, one hand in my pocket, clutching the ubuvimbo.

(Oh, but what I saw! What he told me!)

It was a bumpy, uncomfortable ride, only about half an hour, although it felt much longer, what with the car diving into potholes every few metres and Mama Agnes's bootleg olive oil rolling around wildly, pummelling my poor flesh. At some point, it began to feel as though the air was thinning, and just as I was about to bang against the roof of the boot and beg my surrogate father to let me out, we came to a stop. The car groaned as he alighted. My chest began to heave at the sound of his footsteps, getting nearer and nearer to the boot, but then they stopped, and a door squeaked open. I sighed. I could hear him patting the back seat, and then the door slammed and his footsteps began to recede.

Tentatively, I unclasped the lock, pushed open the boot and sat up. We weren't in the town brothel district like I had suspected (I certainly hadn't bought his story of looking for the boy every night). In fact, we weren't in town at all, but in some sort of field. I could see lights in the distance. It was uncannily quiet, the

November moon peach-coloured and bruised, splashing its light on rows and rows of hillocks. Only once I had climbed out did I realize that we were, in fact, in a graveyard! We were in Athlone Cemetery, in Northend. What in our ancestors' name was my surrogate father doing here?

I swivelled around, swinging my head this way and that, trying to locate Abednego. There – I saw him by the bopping beam of his flashlight, forging deeper into the land of the dead. I was afraid I would lose sight of him, and so I scampered after him, stumbling over small graves, surprisingly small, the graves of children, I realized; so many of them; how could so many of our nation's children be dying? My temples began to throb as I stomped after my surrogate father, tracing him by his beam, my heart lumping my throat, for I felt at any moment that a spoko would surely rise from one of the graves, a boy spoko, and spook me to death.

Finally, he halted by one of the graves, beaming his torch on the tombstone. And then he did the strangest thing: he plopped himself in front of it, the torch shining on the headstone. He seemed to be contemplating what was on there. I hesitated; I was not sure whether I should reveal myself. I had wanted to speak to him, to bring out a little more of that hi-story of his that made him such a volatile life-partner for Mama Agnes, but this, now, this was too creepy. I was about to slink back to the car, where I intended to climb back into the boot, when I heard sniffling. My surrogate father was crying! I felt a rush of tenderness and then, all of a sudden, a swell of guilt. What the hell was I doing! What was all this hornet-shaking business? What had I done to him and what was I trying to do to Mama Agnes?

'You!' he cried, making me jump. He had spotted me! 'What are you doing here? What do you want? How did you get here?'

I should have been asking what *he* was doing there – there was obviously no boy to be found. But this would have only antagonized him further. 'I was worried about you,' I said, helpfully. 'You go out every night and… what is this? What are you doing here?'

'I see you,' he spat, suddenly vicious now. 'Don't think I don't see what you are doing, trying to get yourself in with Aggie. Always Ma this, Ma that. Are you giving her the thing? Where is it?'

I slipped my hand in my pocket to feel for the ubuvimbo; there, its plastic packet was cold against my fingers. 'Of course not. I've only been a shoulder for the poor woman to cry on.' He was jealous of my budding relationship with Mama Agnes, I knew, afraid she would begin to love me. 'She's a mess, all thanks to you. And look at you, mani! Sitting in the middle of the cemetery at night, busy crying.' I made as if to turn around. 'I think I will have to call Mama Agnes. Maybe she can talk some sense into you.'

The response to the threat was immediate; he grabbed my hand. 'No,' he said. 'Please.'

So, he was up to no good, a no good he didn't want Mama Agnes to know about! A warmth spread across my chest. I appraised him, clutching my hand, looking up at me, his frightened eyes caught in the beam of his torch. 'Tell me what you are doing here,' I said.

Sighing, he released my hand, his face withering, his eyes dropping to the ground. 'Nothing.'

'You've been coming here for weeks now. Surely, it's not nothing.'

His body seemed to deflate. He swung the beam towards the headstone. I was able to make out the engraving.

ENNIS GRETA THORNTON
Born 15/06/40
Died 27/03/83

MOTHER AND WIFE. DEARLY MISSED. LOVE YOU FOREVER.
LOVING HUSBAND AND SON

I was stunned. 'But why are you here? Why have you come to Mrs Thornton's grave?'

'I don't know.'

'What do you mean, you don't know?'

He sighed. 'I just… I used to dream of building a life with Thandi, uyazi. I could see us, with our children, going on family outings to the Matopos. Coming home to her every day, it would have been enough for me.' He cupped his head.

I crouched beside him. I raised my hand to rub his back, but thought better of it. I was groping about for something useful to say. 'But it's not your fault, what happened.' I swallowed hard, conscious of the Red Album under my pillow at home. 'It's that man, Black Jesus.'

'Don't you dare say that name!' he snapped.

'I'm sorry. I didn't mean to upset you, what I'm trying to say is, there isn't anything you could have done.'

'I should have fought the Red Berets, I should have—'

'You couldn't have done anything.'

He slumped his shoulders. 'I haven't thought about Thandi in years. Aggie and I haven't had such a bad life. She managed to give me back what I had lost, but now, it's like it's happening all over again and I'm wondering if I'm being punished for what I did.'

'What did you do?'

I was leaning forward now. But he only shook his head and continued sighing.

'I'm a man, Zamani. You're a man. You know what it's like.'

'Yes,' I said, nodding in what I hoped exuded just the right manly temperament. 'I'm a man. I know what it's like. I understand what you're going through,' and then I added, 'only as a man can.'

'We fix things…'

'Yes, we fix things.'

'That's what we men do.'

'That's what us men do.'

'When something is broken, we fix it.'

'We are fixers.'

'I don't know how to just sit and do nothing. But I can't fix anything, I don't know how to find my son, how to make everything all right again. I've tried to ask Mama Thornton's spirit to forgive me, maybe that's why I can't find my son, because she hasn't forgiven me! All I've been doing in my life is running, just running all the time. I wish I could go back and fix things.'

I dared grip his shoulder. 'But what did you do?'

He shrugged it off. We stayed in silence for several moments. I had retrieved the packet of ubuvimbo from my trouser pocket. He caught the glint of the plastic packet in the moonlight, and sat up.

'What's that?'

He knew what it was. He leaned forward, grabbing my finger before I had fully immersed it in the brown root powder and sucking on it urgently. His hands were trembling. More. He wanted more. I fed him just another finger-laced dose, warning him that too much was dangerous.

We sat in silence for a few minutes. I waited till I felt his body slacken next to mine, till I could hear the grinding of his teeth, till the drug had loosened his tongue. 'So,' I said, trying to sound casual. 'What did you do, Father? Why have you come to Mrs Thornton's grave?' He didn't even mind, when he was under the euphoria of the ubuvimbo, my calling him Father!

He stared at the tombstone. 'Mama Thornton,' he said.

He began to sob, loudly, openly.

'Father—'

'Help me,' he said.

'Father, what did you do?'

He sniffled. 'Give me more of the thing.'

'Father, you have to tell me what's going on or else how can I help—'

'I ran, all right? I ran!'

'You ran?'

'I ran.'

He ran.

Through the thicket of a wilderness that seemed like it would never end because it felt like it was inside him. Wire breaking the skin on his arm; he tried to swat the pain away. He was in a familiar place that brought him to a childhood memory involving a giant watermelon; but he was panting and everything stayed just out of reach. Suddenly, he was before a shadow, which morphed into a house, with yellow streams of light coming from the windows. He banged on the door.

'Farmer Thornton!' he yelled. 'Farmer Thornton!'

Silence.

'Farmer Thornton, please, I know you're in there! It's me, Abed!'

There is Fire on the Mountain, Farmer Thornton! A big blaze melting my future away, sir, won't you come and run run run

He could hear the scuffle of feet.

'Please, Farmer Thornton! You have to help me save my boy! You have to help save the hut! It's... the children, they...! Thandi! She's, the baby, they... and... and... and...'

'I'm sorry,' came a woman's voice. 'You have to leave.'

He could hear the hiss of urgent, hushed voices, shuffling feet, a thud, a tussle.

'Please, you have to help me!'

Surely you can save my family, Farmer Thornton? Surely you can put out the Fire on the Mountain and and and

'Wait, son!' Farmer Thornton's voice yelled through the door. 'I'm coming!'

'Go away!' came the woman's voice. Mrs Thornton. 'If they find you here, they'll kill us all. Go away!'

'Please!'

'I said foetsek!'

'Open up, please! My family—'

Silence, except for the croaks of a man weeping.

He turned and fled. Back to his homestead in the adjoining Tribal Trust Lands. He saw it from afar as he ran, first the smoke from the burning hut, rising to the sky, and then the flames, now dying. The hut was a roofless, gaping ruin, the walls half-standing. His eyes fell on Thandi sprawled in the dirt, her abdomen now a black mass of flies. He let out a howl. A stray dog was sniffing the small body of his unborn child.

'Fuseki! Get away from there, mani, fuseki!'

He picked up a stone and threw it at the dog, which scampered off but did not run away altogether.

He fell to his knees between them, Thandi and his baby. Put his arm around her, upsetting the flies, which swirled in a buzzing black murmuration. Wrapped a hand around his baby, careful not to press too hard, shuddering at the cold, mushy feel of it. He shut his eyes. He touched them. Felt them. Remembered them. He hummed the folksongs of his childhood. He wailed.

He didn't know for how long he stayed there, prostrated

between them. Baying. Humming. He was losing his mind. He wanted to die.

It was when the shadows of the vultures circling in the sky above flickered over him that he finally got up. He picked up the foetus; it was covered in ants. He brushed them off. Its delicate, half-formed flesh was now purple. It no longer looked like a foetus, like a baby, like anything. But it was his baby. It was his. He said this over and over as he placed it on top of Thandi. As he tried to put her arms around it. It was his. They were *his*. His family. What was happening?

He carried them to the front of the homestead. There he lay them down, beneath the mopane tree. He removed his shirt and spread it over them. Then he turned and began to dig a grave, in the shadiest part of the tree, where his Baba used to love to sit. He had meant it to be a relatively shallow grave; but he found he couldn't stop digging. He worked steadily, through the rest of the afternoon into the early evening, until the grave had almost swallowed him. Then, he lifted himself out of the hole. Trudged to the now smouldering hut. He moved through the rubble slowly, looking for any sign of recognition, anything; but there was nothing left except charred little skeletons and dismantled bones. Which one was his Bukhosi? He felt he would know when he came across his bones. He threaded his way through the rubble, and then again, and again, waiting for a sign. And then, finally, he gathered all the bones and little skeletons he could find, gathered them all in his arms and carried them back to the grave.

The farmer had refused to help him save his family. How could the old man and his swine-wife refuse to help him?

He lay Thandi and his child beside the little bones and the charred skeletons in the mouth of the grave. He lifted the shirt and gazed at them. My Thandi. He couldn't bear to look at her face. Her features were contracted as they had been when the scythe sliced into her. He shifted the baby in the crook of her arm.

He went to work, flinging shovelfuls of soil into the grave, swinging his arms steadily, without pause, until he was drenched. His heart was the loudest thing he could hear. He focused on it; it kept his mind from fleeing.

He did not stop or take a rest, not until he had covered the grave. Then, he climbed on top of the mound, and lay down, hugging himself, though he did not go to sleep; he stared at the stars and the smouldering hut and thought of that Farmer Thornton and how he had refused to help him.

The sun was angled right above his head when he slinked back into the Thornton Farm the following day, staggering beneath the oppressive weight of the heat and the buzz of green-bomber flies around his stiff and bloodied clothes. The farmhouse was as quiet as death; he couldn't hear voices coming from anywhere, not inside the house, not in the yard. Farmer Thornton's truck was not in the driveway, and those of the farmhands who hadn't already fled the massacres, he knew, were probably out in the fields. He would make himself at home in the house, then. Eat whatever there was to eat, take what there was to take, break what he couldn't; teach that farmer a proper lesson. He broke a window at the back, near the toolshed, and scuttled in, oblivious to the jagged glass slicing at his skin.

He found Mrs Thornton in a floral dress and a Farrah Fawcett flip, angled over an ironing board in the kitchen. A rotating fan was whrr-whhring in the corner. The grainy tones of a BBC presenter blasted from a car radio on a shelf above the sink, next to a bottle of pickled mangoes. A tangle of wires twirled from the radio and into the car battery beside it.

He hit Mrs Thornton across the head with the stove iron – blacker than Black Jesus, with a rusty copper handle – and watched as she crumpled to the floor. Her forehead blistered with an uncivilized bruise. He settled down to wait for the farmer, and decided to help himself to the tray of Beef Wellington steaming atop the coal oven. He wolfed all of it down, found he was still hungry, and swallowed a jug of milk sitting on the windowsill. He gagged when a frog slushed into his mouth along with the last gulp of milk, no doubt dropped into the jug by Mrs Thornton to keep the milk from spoiling.

He chomped one of the frog's legs off as he spat it out. It flapped clumsily in a puddle of milk, and gave up after a while, its abdomen ballooning and collapsing in irregular beats.

He settled down next to the unconscious Mrs Thornton, watched the wheezing frog and waited.

As the minutes ticked and the hours tocked in that old Thornton Farmhouse with its floors that creaked as though under the weight of phantoms, rage gave way to retribution; what better way to punish a man than to take away the thing that he loved the most?

She had tanned freckled skin, Mrs Thornton. Delicate, with a growing red gash where he'd hit her with the stove iron. His hand hovered above her head, and then plunged into her thicket of fine, reddish hair. She had such thin lips. Faintly red. Or pink. What did her lips taste like?

He placed his palm on her breast. It was soft. It fitted easily in his hand. He could feel the beat of her heart underneath. He moved his palm further up and cupped her delicate throat. She had a mole just beneath her chin. He rubbed it playfully. He angled himself above her. Such a thin nose. A forehead free of worry. Brown dots from the savannah sun on her cheeks. A sharp jaw. Such angular features. He traced her face with his fingers. Patted her Farrah Fawcett flip.

Swallowed a sickly-sweet lump back down his throat.

He lifted her skirts, peeling back the pleats and then the skirt's petticoat and then yet another layer of petticoat beneath, and bunched them around her waist. Caressed her dimpled, doughy thighs. Spread her legs, and pulled her panties, moist where they hugged her, to the side. Sucked his breath at the sight of the orange, glistening tufts of pubic hair. He was already swollen as he unbuttoned his overalls. He thrust into her. The violence seemed to jolt her awake. He watched intently as her eyes popped open, the shock blistering when she looked up to find him heaving atop her. Deeper he thrust, clamping her thin lips with his palm; deeper he dug, but there was no solace to be excavated. Only shame. He wouldn't let shame win. He looked up. There was a chequered kitchen towel hanging by the stove. He reached out, gyrating still, and grabbed it with one hand. Thrust deeper and faster. He was wheezing as he wrung the towel taut around shame's ivory throat.

How delicate was its skin! How easily it bruised. How fragile, like a china doll.

She died as he climaxed, her eyes untamed like the savannah.

Panting, he got up.

He saw the boy standing by the kitchen door, in a pair of muddy shorts, a beach ball pressed to his chest. He was staring right at him, no more than six or seven, his flaxen hair so much like Farmer Thornton's, his face a piece of streaked porcelain.

He was about his Bukhosi's age.

He hesitated.

Then he turned and fled, his limp, wet penis slapping against his thighs as he ran.

THE OUTING

I have been thinking about my surrogate grandpapa's blog post, the one that went viral, about how he found his Ennis lying on the floor one day in the '80s, during the time of the Gukurahundi Genocide, having been raped and strangled by the dissidents. O surrogate grandpapa! How can you ever forget that day when you fell to your knees next to your Ennis's body and buried your face in her prolific hair blazing scarlet in the late afternoon sun? Even me, I cannot forget it! I cannot get my surrogate father's confessions out of my mind!

He didn't know for how long he knelt, Farmer Thornton, my surrogate grandpapa, cradling his Ennis, weeping, whispering *I'm sorry I love you*. On the shelf above the sink, the car radio, with its wires entangled like an electric hazard, was spitting static. The milk jug, which she'd placed on the windowsill that morning, now lay on its side on the floor. The frog was burping next to it, having splattered itself across a tile with its legs stretched out on either side. One of its legs was missing. He caught sight of it on the other side of the jug, near the stove, overrun by a regiment of ants. It was only when he straightened up from her body that he noticed that her legs were spreadeagled, that her chartreuse taffeta skirt was bunched up around her waist, that her cream cotton panties were torn, and that the hairs of her pubis, glaring apricot in the sun, were caked with a white discharge. He clamped his hand over his mouth.

'Papa.'

He whipped around, to find Sonny Boy seated by the door stoep, his face streaked, his bare chest muddy, a beach ball lolling between his feet. How long had he been seated there? How much had he seen?

'Come, my boy.'

They buried her in the north-west corner of the farm, where the pumpkin patch ended, next to the remains of my surrogate great-grandpapa, Captain William Thornton Junior, and also the body of my surrogate great-great-grandpapa, William Thornton Senior, and the memorial for the first Sonny Boy. Later, when the War Veterans came, in that millennial year 2000, to take his farm away from him, my surrogate grandpa was forced to exhume all of them, his grandpapa and his papa and his first Sonny Boy and his Ennis, and move them to Athlone Cemetery in Bulawayo.

But at that time the farm was still his, and he felt safe burying his Ennis there, on the land of his forebears. The farming community came out to show its support, everyone, including Mrs Willoughby who, after several glasses of Gordon's, put on her patois accent, garnered from a decade or so in Kingston with her first husband, the then British Commissioner, and began to throw stones at the black workers who had come to say goodbye to their madam, yelling, 'Bomboclats! Ye rassholes done stick punani madam when masser 'way! Ye gon burn in hell! Pussyclaats! Ye shall burn at the stake! What fuckery dis be? Raas!'

'Leave them be, Mrs Willoughby,' said my surrogate grandpapa. 'They've done nothing wrong. They are good boys. Honest, hardworking girls. They were not here when it happened.'

'Wah di rass? So, what Bumborass done dis abomination?'

My surrogate grandpapa hesitated. 'I don't know,' he said, finally. 'I have no idea.'

O, but you must have suspected, surrogate grandpapa, deep down, you must have known!

'It's the dissidents!' said old Richardson.

'Yes! It's the dissidents! They've been attacking the farms everywhere, all over Matabeleland!'

'The munts are hiding them in their huts!'

'Have you seen those President's boys, what's their name? The 5 Brigade. They've been teaching the munts a lesson!'

'Serves them right! That's what you get for harbouring terrs.'

'Let them burn themselves to death. That's all commies know how to do. And a black commie's twice as dumb and ten times as worse.'

He would repeat a milder version of these sentiments to the reporter from *The Chronicle* who came down a few days later to research an article on the recent spates of dissident attacks on the white farms, which made the front page.

It was the dissidents who'd done unspeakable things to his Ennis and then killed her! No, no, he had no idea who it could be, how could he know? No, he hadn't noticed any suspicious activity. *No*, no suspicious persons had visited the farm before the attack! Just those President's boys causing quite a racket in the neighbourhood. They were much welcome in the community, the President's boys! Doing a fine job of protecting the peace-loving citizens of Matabeleland and smoking out the dissidents! All the farmer wanted to do was to farm, to toil quietly on his land and provide food for the nation… No, no, he was happy with the new President, he was doing a fine job, especially with the dissidents, they, the farming community, were hundred per cent behind the government of the day, yes, yes, very good job.

The car ride from the cemetery three nights ago was a difficult one. We drove home in silence, this time with me in the front seat beside Abednego, though after what I had just heard, I really wouldn't have minded climbing into the boot.

'Zamani,' he kept saying. 'Zamani, I'm sorry.'

That was all he could say. I opened my mouth several times, but I, too, could find nothing to say. He could apologize to me as much as he wants, but forgiveness is not mine to give. Only Mrs Thornton can do that. Like it's only within Bukhosi's gift to forgive me; and it's only within my gift to forgive Zacchaeus for letching after my Thandi. But are there some things that happen in life to make other things, which once seemed unforgivable, forgivable? Does my surrogate father's grief and suffering make forgiveable what he did to Mrs Thornton? Has what happened to my Thandi – dammit – has what happened to my Thandi not made my Uncle Zacchaeus's vices forgivable? Because I know how my Thandi's death must have hurt him so! How he must have wept! How it drove him to near madness! Did he not, in the mid-'80s, right after her death, begin to scribble anti-establishment tracts that cut the government to the quick? Incisive, precise pieces that were so unlike his former, literary, wispy self.

Question marks everywhere: he was reported as having been seen on Bulawayo's Herbert Chitepo Street, outside the High Court, on the day of the signing of the Unity Accord in 1987, that marriage covenant between His Most Excellent Excellency Robert Gabriel Mugabe who, nerding it out at the signing ceremony with his oversize glasses and a cheesy smile, had dissolved the

Prime Ministership and assumed the all-encompassing role of President – Hail Bushollini! – and ol' fatso boy Joshua Mqabuko kaNyongolo Nkomo who, once fat with joy and now fatter with sorrow, looked absolutely miserable, his chin flopping over his shirt collar, those small, laughing eyes that my Thandi used to love no longer laughing, although his smile was still measured and his chubby, handsome face contemplative. They sat side by side, the two Eminences, one lean, one fat, pomp and grief, and with a tacky signature here and a snazzy signature there, signed the past into oblivion as though it had never existed – ushering in forever-lasting peace between their two nationalist parties, ZANU (PF) and (PF) ZAPU.

Was he not consumed by anguish and also guilt, my Uncle Zacchaeus, as he stood on the front steps of the High Court building? To know that, as Thandi lay dying, he was busy entertaining unsaintly reveries of her, pumping his man pump in the shadows of the Sheldonian at Oxford, while pretending to admire the theatre building, to take in the neoclassical tower rising from the roof of its poly-sided rear, to study the ornate filigree of the Corinthian capitals playing artsy games with light and shadow.

I forgive you for lusting after my Thandi, Uncle Zacchaeus! I forgive you!

And can Abednego ever forgive Black Jesus? As Dumo used to say, one can't just exist passively in the twenty-first century. One has to be, actively, an ethical citizen of our global village, seeing in others the mirror of what he sees in himself – humanity – and in himself what he presupposes to be in others – inhumanity. This was one of his sweetest sermons! The loftiest of his speeches, designed to elevate! And yet he, himself, despite admitting that our current oppressors, too, had been, also, once upon a time, victims of oppression under the fascist state of Rhodesia, from which they had learned well and whose lessons they were now applying full force in the jingoistic state of Zimbabwe, in spite of being able to realize all of this, he could not bring himself to recognize Black Jesus's humanity.

'There's nothing human about that man!' he exclaimed, tears streaming down his face.

And I don't blame him! I don't blame him for being unable to transcend this, and yet whenever I look in the mirror and see this face of mine which is as black as a velvet night, with my kissable lips and my finely sloping cheekbones, I can't help but think what this, then, makes me.

And finally, I thought to myself as the car bumped along back home, Abednego crying and murmuring softly beside me, would Mama Agnes forgive me? I had sought to stir up the hornet's nest just enough to send her running to my protective embrace and talking to my sympathetic ears, but as I looked over at my surrogate father, grinding his teeth as he stared out the windscreen, I worried that where I had hoped he might sting, he might actually be ready to kill.

It happened this morning. So soon! I woke up to the sound of shouting outside my pygmy room, voices clambering over one another, one angry, the other conciliatory. My surrogate father and Mama Agnes were arguing outside the house, Mama Agnes clutching a suitcase. She was leaving for South Africa to go and look for Bukhosi! My surrogate father was accusing her of trying to leave him. She kept asking, 'Why would I do that, heh? Tell me, why would I leave you, after all these years?' But it was no use; he kept yelling that she wasn't going anywhere, the spit flying from his mouth into her face, making her grimace.

I turned away, not wanting to witness what I knew was coming. *Just don't kill her,* I prayed. *Don't kill her.* I put my fingers in my ears, clenched my eyes, and waited.

When I emerged from my room, ten minutes later, I found the suitcase broken open, clothes strewn across the yard. Abednego was nowhere to be seen. Mama Agnes was slumped against the wall, her mouth bleeding. But she was alive! Thank God. I gathered her in my arms and helped her into the house.

She remembers his first beating as though it were yesterday. It poured out of her in sobs. I sat with her, rubbing her back, taking in the smell of her, cooing little encouragements as she told me about the first outing they went to, at the Sun Hotel, which had just been renovated to the Bulawayo Rainbow Hotel. She thought the lobby was gaudy, awash as it was in gold rills of light pouring from dangerous-looking contraptions that dangled from the ceiling, but Abednego insisted it looked ornate, a reflection of the patrons who frequented the place, he said, where you could perhaps spot a minister or two, if you were lucky, because it was that type of establishment, a place for real men with *sta-tuuss qu-oo.*

She was aggrieved by such unashamed displays of wealth, Mama Agnes, while her mama and her father and her one-armed brother Trymore and her sister Nto withered under a pitiless drought back in Kezi. It was no secret that this drought had been caused by the wandering ghosts of the dead from the terrible time right after our independence, ghosts which had risen from their mass graves in search of their true resting grounds.

The dress, too, aggrieved her; it was a pink, frivolous thing, which cinched her waist and ballooned out in useless layers of satin that made her legs itch. She would have enjoyed it, she really would have; but the thought of her family becoming pinched like sucked oranges back over there in Kezi made my surrogate father's kindness feel like an affront.

Her precarious, pointy shoes made it impossible to walk, so she sort of slid across the slippery floors of the Rainbow Hotel lobby, like the teenagers she'd seen outside the town flats rolling on shoes with wheels. The real challenge, however, presented itself when it was time to eat. Seated in the hotel restaurant, and blinded by the country's gold reserves spilling from the ceiling contraptions, she stared at the cutlery and found herself assaulted by a familiar panic.

She began to cry.

The flood burst through the dam of her lashes, surged down her cheeks, gathering the caked-on make-up and unacknowledged memories in its wake, and carried this flotsam to the bleached tablecloth.

Once the torrent began, it would not stop, and not even Abednego's hisses, not even the pain of his hairy fingers pinching the skin of her arm, not even the concerned waiter's polished enquiries delivered singsong in the Queen's finest English, could curb it. But Abednego had already ordered, and proclaimed, rather too brightly, that the evening would go on, no doubt determined to enjoy the exorbitant outing he had used the greater part of a month's salary on, although visibly shrinking in his seat, no doubt trying to hide from the real men with *sta-tuuss qu-oo* and the Ministers. He forced her to eat the steak – half done, peppered, with sour-sweet sauce and a sprinkle of parsley on top – even though she exclaimed through her tears, 'But look, it's not properly cooked!', gagging at the sight of the semi-raw texture of the interior, the slough of blood. He slapped her hands when she picked up the piece of steak and tried to eat with her fingers.

'Just do as I do, you've already embarrassed me enough, all this crying, always crying fornogoodreason… Now, pay attention, you start from the forks nearest to the plate like this, and you work your way out – no, now how would that blunt knife be able to cut the meat? You use that one there with the teeth, yes that's right – no mani, you hold the knife with your left and the fork with your right – I don't know why the knife was placed on the right and the fork on the left, the waiter must have made a mistake – right, now you hold the fork like this, see, and you stab, yes *stab*… You will swallow that damn meat or I will shove it down your throat I swear – eish, will you *stop* with the crying, mani, kanti what's wrong with you?'

And swallow she did, retching, aghast at civilized society's endorsement of such rawism. She was certain, as they drove back home, the radio turned to loud no doubt to drown out her whimpering, that she was in for a tongue lashing; and so she was surprised when my surrogate father slipped quietly into bed, and thought that perhaps her tears had frightened him. She'd try to explain, wouldn't she, that it wasn't her fault, that she didn't know what was happening, that it just happened, anytime like so, like something refusing to be caged, snarling and threatening to devour her, and no matter what she did it just came out, just came out like so, and now she didn't know what to do… But when she slid under the covers next to him, he descended upon her in a fury, his grip too firm, his fingers between her legs calculated to hurt, his plunge into her ripping apart yet more dams. The louder she cried, the harder he pounded; his teeth dug into her neck, the spanking of her buttocks turned into a wallop, and his moans were animalistic in her ears. She clamped a hand over her mouth, damming her snivels, the flesh between her legs raw.

THE BOX

I clutched my Mama A's hand, trembling from the thrill of having her talking to me again. She looked so delicate then, my mama, her anguished face open, hiding nothing, and I wanted nothing more than to be there for her, to guide her through that Gehenna, if only so we could conquer it together! But I was afraid to ask about Bhalagwe, it felt too soon, and instead cooed: Was it after this outing at the Rainbow Hotel that she began to despise my surrogate father?

She had never questioned his love for her, nor hers for him, for, as everyone well knew, husbands loved their wives and wives had to find ingratiating ways of loving their husbands. She believed he loved her, in his own way. He was remorseful for these intermittent beatings, she was sure, though she never understood their source, such was their arbitrariness; had she known what triggered them she would have at least tried to abate them. And though he never acknowledged them or said out loud that he was sorry, he showed his remorse, and his love, by bringing her gifts, like the box he came lugging home one cold June day whose contents, once he had plugged it in and hit the switch, transformed her world into a Carrollian Wonderland.

He came home a few days later, from the Butnam Rubber Factory where he worked as floor manager, in one of his moods. At first, she mistook his twitching eyes for anger, but it was the alcohol, she soon realized. The alcohol accentuated the tiny red veins in the whites of his eyes, and made his eyeballs swell out of their sockets, so that even when he was laughing, he looked like a man perpetually aghast. Anger, on the other hand – good, clean, sober anger – narrowed his eyes into slits.

'Why?' he bellowed, slamming a paw against the bedroom wall. 'Is the house not cleaned?'

She stared at his nose; the thing was busy quivering-quavering as though at any moment it would leap out of his face and lobby on his behalf.

'I said. Why. Is this house dirty, when I have a wife who spends the whole day at home?'

'The box,' she mumbled, staring at the floor.

'What?' He cocked his ear and brought his face close to hers, so that she was forced to look at him.

She pointed vaguely in the direction of the living room. 'That box you brought last week. It has people who talk and move all day long.'

That paw, with its open palm and its fingers wide apart, shuddered with the threat of a slap. She shut her eyes. Waited for it, waited for it… She could feel his body shaking. But there was no sting on her cheek. When she opened her eyes, his wide face was arched away from her, his shoulders shaking, his mouth wide open, though no sound ushered from his lips.

She smiled uncertainly. Was it funny that she hadn't cleaned the house? He wouldn't beat her? Wouldn't return her home and disgrace her mother with accusations of having brought up a lazy daughter?

'So, you mean to tell me that you have done nothing the whole day but watch TV? All day long?'

She chuckled, gaining her confidence. 'The people in the box, they would not stop talking and moving.'

He shook his head. 'You, my wife... Goodness. All right. You want me to treat you like a child? I'll treat you like a child. I suppose I'll have to lock up the TV every morning before I leave. You are a nincompoop.'

She smiled when he said 'nincompoop' in English. Nincompoop, she had never heard that word before, she liked the sound of it, it sounded so, so, so romantic, the way he said it softly, with tickles in his eyes, the same way he called her 'sweetie-licious' or 'baby-luscious' or 'long-lasting-chapis'.

She practised that word carefully – 'nin-kho-m-phoop' – so that, the following evening, as he licked her neck and panted 'My strawberry-yoghurt' in her ear, she throatily whispered back, 'My nin-kho-m-phoop,' and locked herself in the toilet when he slapped her, cursing – 'Disrespectful! How dare...!' – where she scrunched up into as small a ball as she could manage, just like she had seen the black woman from America in the box do, and cried tears she was sure would never cease.

She managed to convince him to keep the box in the living room – 'I will clean, Baba, I promise' – where she watched, animated, as the people went about their lives over-there-yonder in Massachusetts-America: *Cheers*, *The Cosby Show*, *Growing Pains*, *Diff'rent Strokes*, and a nunu called Alf. Though she always made sure to pretend not to know the goings-on of the box when Abednego was home, in case he accused her of liking it too much and threatened to lock it up again. He was a jealous man, this husband of hers, and anything she seemed to pay more attention to than him, he took away. But as soon as the Peugeot 504 reversed out of the yard every morning, she lunged for the remote control, only switching off her beloved box when she saw the car headlights turning into the yard in the evening.

'How was your day?'

'Oh, all right, Baba, I scrubbed the curtains, did some spring cleaning in the bedroom, and read the paper.'

'You don't seem interested in the TV these days, how come?'

'Ah, those people in the box are boring. I prefer to read… eh, Baba?'

'Hmm?'

'I saw an advert in *The Chronicle*, a teachers' college in a place called Hillside. All you need is basic O-level and I… I was thinking of having something to do…'

'Huh-uh. You want to be getting big ideas now. I want you to stay at home and look after the house. The answer is no.'

She didn't want the disappointment to show, and so she tried to swallow it. But it refused to go past her throat, remaining lodged there like a ball of isitshwala that had stayed too long on the stove until it became dry and hard as a dwala. It scratched her throat, so that her words became sullen, bloated her face, so that her cheeks swelled. She cut out the advert in the paper and tucked it beneath her pillow. Oh, how she wanted to go to teaching college! How she longed to perm her hair, stand in front of a class, and scribble with chalk on a blackboard. She would be good at it, she knew. She was better than this. She had almost gone to Massachusetts. And now!

'It's all about approach,' MaSibanda, the foul-mouthed woman from next door, told her.

They were leaning against the sagging fence that divided their homes, as township women are wont to do as they go about their outdoor morning chores, brooms-in-hand, the soil whipped about by a violent August wind around their feet. MaSibanda was busy picking her teeth with a stick of grass. Mama Agnes watched her, wide-eyed, animated by her lack of concern, the wild thicket on her head, her torn, see-through nightdress showing her torn, see-through panties.

'How do I do this... approach?' she asked.

'Heh! Little gal! Didn't your aunties talk to you when you became a young woman?'

She covered her eyes.

'When he's about to arrive, you take a long bath. Are you listening? A nice, hot bath. You scent yourself with some nice perfume, the one you know he likes. Then, when he gets in, you take his bag. Are you listening? You greet him sweetly, ever so sweetly. You take off his shoes. You pour warm water into a dish. You wash his feet, nicely, and as you do so, you ask him about his day. Tell him what a big man he is! Eh? And then, you cook him his favourite meal. After he has finished eating, when he wants to sleep,' and here MaSibanda's voice became husky, 'you begin to roll and roll on the bed, like you can't sleep. You mustn't wear anything to bed, are you listening?'

Mama Agnes giggled.

'What is it?' asked MaSibanda, chuckling. 'Is he not your husband? Grow up, little gal, you are somebody's wife now. Now, what was I saying? Ah yes, you roll and roll, like you are half asleep. At that moment when he begins panting, when you feel his hands searching you up and down like they have lost control, you just say, casually, how you wish for this and this and this. Just whisper it in his ear, nicely, slowly, sweetly.'

The woman leaned back and crossed her arms.

'And then what?' asked Mama Agnes.

'And then you wait.'

'Ah! Whatifhedoesnthearmewhatifheforgetshowwilliknow hehasheardme?'

'Believe me, he has heard you. You just do all I have told you, and you'll be telling me very soon that you are off to teaching college.'

'Oprah says we must have a talking relationship. That we must be open with one another, and discuss things freely.'

'Who is Oprah?'

'A woman in the box. She's from America.'

'Heh, so now you want to listen to a white woman from America over me?'

'She's black. With this nice wavy hair that you don't have to put perm in to make curly. Black women in Massachusetts-America are very pretty. They are a *sophistication*.'

'This is not America, little gal. Heh! All right. Choose who you will listen to – Oprah or me. What does America know about our customs?'

And so, Mama Agnes spent the day practising how she would make her approach to my surrogate father:

'I wish to go to teaching college...'

Too vague?

'I wish to go to Hillside Teachers' College...'

Too direct?

'Oh Baba, you are such a great man, so wonderful and IwishtogotoHillsideTeachersCollege...'

And so it was that at the end of that week – 12 August 1988, a muggy Friday which she would always remember, for she was certain that was when her life began its path towards Enlightenment, Mama Agnes took a long, hot bath, scented with a perfume called Illusion lent her by MaSibanda.

Exactly two weeks to the letter, just after supper, as my

surrogate father sipped a glass of iced water and perused *The Chronicle*, he said, casually, 'I think it would be good for you if I enrolled you at a teaching college, what do you think?'

To which she, trying to swallow her excitement, asked, 'You really think so, lovely husband-of-mine?'

'Yes, I think it would be good if I did that for you. You have good O-level. And me, I am a progressive man. Would you like it if I did that for you?'

'Oh, you are so smart. So handsome. You know best. Anything you want, lovely husband-of-mine...'

The following January, Mama Agnes enrolled at the teaching college, despite the fact that Abednego had changed his mind over his lapse into progressiveness – Mama Agnes was pregnant. 'It's not as if I'm moving to another town,' she said. 'I would commute and be home every day. Plus, we can hire a maid to help me out with the baby. That's what working women in the city do.'

'I will not have my child raised by a stranger. You are its mother, you are here, what's the problem?'

But it was too late for him to object; permission once received was never going to be relinquished, and by this point, Mama Agnes had become wily in the ways of manipulating her husband. She instead enrolled under the Long Distance option of the college, knowing this small act of defiance would go unpunished while she was carrying his child. In fact, during her pregnancy was the most excited she would ever see him throughout the years of their marriage. His severe glare softened, and he became playful, silly even, taking her to the disco at the beerhall, where he persuaded her to dance, though she didn't know how to move to the simanje-manje city music, and would just stand, stiff, staring wide-eyed at him.

He began to take an interest in her past, asking her to tell him stories from her childhood, about her father, her mother, her sister, her brothers. Where had she been during the liberation war? Had she taken part in any radical activity? She wished she had, for he seemed disappointed by her answers, about hiding from the guerillas, for she had been just a child during the war and had been petrified of them, of the fighting and the bombing, which she associated with the unusually tizzy sound of her mama's voice cracking through her sleep and ordering her to run for the bush.

My surrogate father took to doing things which at first unnerved my Mama Agnes; he insisted on rubbing her belly with coconut oil, even going so far as rubbing her feet when they swelled. He brought home a stack of books on parenting. He even tried to cook for her – a disaster over which they laughed – and took to bringing her Fanta and pastries and calling her 'chicken-pie'.

We were interrupted, Mama Agnes and I, by that yenta MaNdlovu. No doubt she heard the fight from next door between my Mama Agnes and Abednego this morning, and was now here to gather dirt on our family under the pretext of 'seeing if there's any news about the boy'. Of course, there was no news. Instead, that scandalmonger's meddling broke the spell between me and my Mama Agnes. She jumped up when the woman walked in, as though we had been doing something wrong. No longer did her head seek my chest; no longer did she grip my shirt as she remembered my surrogate father's beatings; no longer was she pliant to my murmurs of 'It's OK, Mama Agnes, your Zamani is here… what happened next?' Instead, she leapt into that gossiper's arms, as though into an old friend's, and broke into hysterics. And then she turned to me, quietening down, and asked me to leave them alone. I smiled what I hoped was a calm smile, for I was seething, and offered to make them tea.

'Aww, yes, I want tea,' that MaNdlovu said before Mama Agnes could decline. 'What a pleasant young man, you are lucky, NakaBukhosi, to have such a helpful lodger. Put three sugars in mine, do you have sugar? It's been so long since I last tasted sugar, uyazi. Where do you get yours, NakaBukhosi?'

(How I yearn to hear Mama Agnes called 'NakaZamani'!)

I made them Tanganda tea, with a squeeze of lemon for Mama Agnes and one teaspoon of sugar for that MaNdlovu, though I told her I had stirred in three. I also made myself a cup, and sat by the cobalt kitchen table in front of the TV stand, pretending to read an old *O Magazine* while listening intently to their conversation. I was happy to hear that although my Mama Agnes told MaNdlovu about the beating this morning, she didn't reveal anything about Abednego's history. Such secrets are for family only. But I was alarmed to hear her tell MaNdlovu that she planned to go to South Africa no matter what. She even repeated what I told her last week at the prayer meeting, that the boy had told me he wanted to go to South Africa after some girl. Meaning the Holy Ghost's visions were right, her boy was in Johannesburg! She wondered out loud if he was all right, why he had left, why he didn't call. MaNdlovu squeezed her hand and proclaimed that the Holy Ghost did not lie, and look, it had sent a confirmation of the boy's whereabouts through me, its emissary. Mama Agnes *had* to go to South Africa; she should run away in the middle of the night, while her man was asleep, if she had to.

It was all I could do not to yell at that busybody to shuttup. Mama Agnes was encouraged by her support, and seemed to be seriously considering running off to South Africa. One of these days, we'll wake up to find her gone!

How to get her to see that she doesn't need the boy? That I, Zamani, am worth two Bukhosis, three, even? I couldn't wait for that MaNdlovu to leave, but she spent the whole day at our house and drank six teas, only heading off when it was already getting dark, after which I couldn't convince Mama Agnes to let me stay a while. She had had a long day, she said. I lingered, hoping she would, after the bond we shared since my surrogate father's outburst, invite me to spend the night in the main house again. But she just stared at me, raising her eyebrows expectantly, and repeated, 'Goodnight', forcing me to repeat, 'Goodnight', in return and shamble back to my lodgings.

We couldn't even find some alone time this morning. My surrogate father had slinked back to the house in the night, and was now trying to slink back into Mama Agnes's heart by trying to cook her porridge with some new luxury-brand mealie-meal. The man has no shy. If you are going to make a woman a reconciliatory breakfast, let it be a full English breakfast, with the requisite toast and baked beans and crispy bacon and fried sausages and eggs sunny-side up and lightly seared tomato slices. It would be even more heroic were you to get hold of these ingredients at such a time of food shortages as this; it would be an accomplishment deserving rendition in these family chronicles, a feat so Homeric in these prosaic times that its telling would merit a whole chapter: Love in the Time of Inanition. But there was no English breakfast to be had from the man, and thus no Iliadic posturing to triumphant love in these pages. Instead, after watching a sombre Mama Agnes spooning his burnt porridge, with me having planted myself in the sitting room like a guard dog, the man finally gathered himself and slipped away, 'To look for Bukhosi,' he announced, eyeing Mama Agnes hopefully. She didn't even look at him, instead turning her pummelled face to the wall.

I must thank him for his discomfiting presence this morning! For my Mama A seemed to relax visibly as soon as he was gone, and was even pliable to my enquiries about her time enrolled in the Long Distance programme of the Hillside Teachers' College (I, clearing my throat noisily, that word, 'Bhalagwe', stuck in there – but it felt too soon! Softly, softly – I am only now beginning to gain her trust).

She glowed as she told me how it was at the college library, where she went often to get supplementary texts for her course, that she rediscovered her love of books. She began to find every excuse to go there, lugging her pregnancy at every opportunity to spend time among the seemingly infinite titles. There was a delicious thrill in walking along the stacks, in perusing the pages and pages of knowledge, in partaking across space and time in age-long conversations, in being privy to written secrets willing to be shared. She would always associate the musty smell of paper with this feeling of freedom; would always prefer old books to new; would always lean in involuntarily to sniff a page. Amidst these dust-latticed volumes, yoghurt-smeared paperbacks and vulgar-graffitied Mills and Boons, she watered her bibliophilia, and cultivated and fed it. She began to dream of another self which had once been a blooming aficionada – before the detours of Bhalagwe and Father Reuben – en route to eminence all the way in Massachusetts-America.

Her Enlightenment began, naturally, with Alice Walker. She found her lying behind a row of books at the library, dusty and neglected. It was the picture of the grey farmhouse on the torn cover that drew her attention.

'The. Color. Purple,' she mouthed. 'What a strange title. By Alice. Walker. Walker. Alice. Color Purple.'

Whatever did that mean?

She was never sure why she took the book – although later, after having read it, after having cried over it and read it again and cried some more – flinching beneath Mr Johnson's boot, weeping with Celie, palms fisted over her eyes – she claimed to have been drawn to it by some inexplicable force.

For one, she had never thought America could have any place that could be called 'rural'.

'Rural Georgia,' she read out loud.

Whatever did that mean? Was it rural like Kezi? Mud thatch huts? Or dapperwood double-storeys, like the picture on the cover? Did they have cows? A Catholic church with devastatingly handsome priests?

She cried for Celie, especially when she was made to marry Mr Johnson. She yearned to be as brazen as Sofia, 'large and spunky' so she would grow the courage to stand up to her Harpo – losing herself in daydreams that ended with her towering over my surrogate father, his steel-buckled belt in her hand.

She: 'Will you ever do it again?'

He: 'No no, never!'

Whhoop!

'I say, will you ever do it again?'

'No no please, never never *never*!'

Whhoop Whhoop Whhoop!

'Stupid, ugly old man! Now, go and make me some dinner, I's so hungry I can't see straight!'

'Right away! *Right away!*'

She began to see Celie in herself, so that she could no longer bear to look in the mirror, at her bright eyes and her bouncy breasts, those things that she once thought made her special. For nobody cared. Who dared to care about the big black ugly sorrows of the big black beautiful woman? Not the fellas, no.

Neither the Masser nor the Missus. Nobody.

'Eh? And what's wrong with you?' asked my surrogate father. 'Why is your face looking so long, like any moment it will fall off?'

'The world is purple all round.'

'What?'

'The world is full of Mr Johnsons.'

'Bring me my supper, I don't know what nonsense you're babbling about. I'm so hungry I can hardly see straight.'

'Git it your-sef.'

'What?'

'I said, *git it your-sef.* I'm darn tired got an assignment to do an' this baby of yours been kicking me all day.'

She knew he wouldn't hit her, not while she was round and large and shiny with what he kept insisting was a boy.

'And what if it's a girl?'

'It's a boy. I'm telling you. Anything this huge has to be. I know what I'm talking about, ah ah. My Bukhosi is going to make all the girls cry and grow up to be a big man one day. Better it not be a girl, you are sure everything is OK with you, woman? You'd better be able to bear me sons.'

She looked up at him then, eyes blazing, and saw, for the first time, how he exuded not an aura but, rather, a mephitic haze. He couldn't even speak English right. He was more than just a fearsome fool. He was also a *nin-kho-m-phoop.* She brought home from the college library Stevenson's Mid-Level Biology text, and slapped it onto his lap, before plopping triumphantly next to him.

'Page two-zero-three,' she said, and began to speak verrry slowly. 'Gal: XX khro-ma-sum. Boy: XY khro-ma-sum. Woman: me. Me carry XX khro-ma-sum. Man: you. You carry XY khro-ma-sum. Me give X khro-ma-sum. You give X khro-ma-sum or Y khro-ma-sum. Who makes the boy baby or the gal baby: you. OK.

YOU. Not me. So. If we are having gal babies, it's because *you* can't make boy babies.'

She noted, and it seemed to me with a little glee, how my surrogate father's jaw trembled, how he clenched his fists until his knuckles shone, but how he restrained himself from beating her, his eyes blinking at her large belly.

'Well,' he stuttered. 'I'm sure it's a boy. He'll grow up to be a big man one day. An engineer.'

'There'll be no growing he'll do with you working me like a slave all day. Been on my feet the whole day. They is swollen, see?'

'Stop talking like that.'

'Like what?'

'Like you're a character out of *Roots*. What are you doing to your lips? Stretching them like that? You think you're in America now, is that it?'

'I is do nothing.'

'Stoppit. I'm warning you. It's this television, isn't it? I think I should take it away.'

'You can take away my song, but you can't take away my spirit…'

'Why are you talking like that?'

'… Mr Johnson.'

'I'm going out. What has got into you? Leave me supper.'

'Slaving away in this purple-all-round world. Purple, purple like a… like a eggplant… like a… like a field of purple flowers amidst a golden meadow speeding away from the barn of doom…'

Purple-veined like the stillborn tot she squeezed out one evening in May of '89 under the dazed lights of Mater Dei Hospital. She didn't tell me this herself, Mama Agnes, glazing over it and only saying my surrogate father turned, inexplicably it seemed, from a doting father-to-be back to a wife beater. I had to let my surrogate father suck on an ubuvimbo-laced finger to get him to tell me what happened; Mama Agnes gave birth to a stillborn baby. I noticed, with alarm, how he announced this with little compassion, and even disinterest, if not a bit of malice. He may as well have been telling me something mundane, like the latest hike in our over-hyperinflation, which unofficial estimates peg at sixty-six thousand and something per cent. I don't know what that means, but the other day I had to use a whole ten-million-dollar bill on a loaf of bread.

'The baby was dead,' my surrogate father told me, licking my finger. I let him run his tongue all over it even when there was no longer anything there. When I raised an eyebrow, he said, 'Still-born. It was born dead.'

When he shuffled into the Mater Dei, he said, eyes as shiny as Tsholotsho diamonds, and peeked into the blanket, which he'd chosen himself, a navy blue throw-over with patterns of Super Mario stitched on, parting the tiny legs for a telling glimpse, the light died swiftly in his eyes.

'All of that, and for nothing,' he said, peering at my trousers, where I had pocketed the ubuvimbo. 'Do you know how expensive a private hospital is? All of that waiting, I had even planned a party, told friends, everything… all of that… and she brought me a dead baby.'

How my Mama Agnes must have wept!

'She killed him,' my surrogate father said to me, matter-of-factly. 'She was trying to kill me. She wanted to take my Bukhosi away from me.' He motioned to my trousers with his eyes. 'I want some more.'

For saying that about my Mama Agnes, I denied him another finger.

APRIL BABY

This morning, my surrogate father received a phone call from the police station to go to the morgue at Mpilo Hospital and identify a body.

When he told us this, gripping his Samsung to his ear still, I just stood there, in the sitting room, licking my lips, a little electric jolt shooting up and down my spine. Mama Agnes, who was sitting on her sofa, grabbed my hand, lifting herself up into my arms, her fists gripping at my shirt.

'Oh, Ma,' I said, rubbing her back, daring to rest my head on her shoulder.

I glanced up to find my surrogate father watching me, and quickly looked away. I tried to hush her, to assure her that everything would be fine.

We piled into my surrogate father's car, and honked our way through the crowded roads. Mama Agnes fiddled nervously with her phone. So, the boy is dead! I said to myself over and over as we eased into the car park outside the red-brick walls of Mpilo Hospital, its white window frames and trimmed gardens belying the death that awaited us inside. I didn't know how to feel about this. All I kept thinking was, what did I do, Zamani, what did you do?

That Mpilo Hospital where the boy had been born. He was squeezed out on 18 April 1990, Bukhosi, beneath the winking lights of Mpilo, this public institution that wore proud its government endorsement like a crown, tactfully near that Barbourfields Stadium where the cavorting crowds had, on that 18th day of April 1990, celebrated the nation's tenth anniversary. Seventy-nine hours of labour in the accompaniment of song and dance booming from the stadium nearby as the nation lifted high the banner of freedom, and then he slithered out, so wondrously adorned, cascading like a river, flowing free, proclaiming victory in a beseeching little wail.

The nation's baby that had been reincarnated, once again, on the nation's birth day, was now, again, dead! I thought, with growing bitterness, how Karma really was exhibiting some extreme bitchiness.

The Reverend Pastor met us outside the hospital doors; Mama Agnes must have texted him en route. She moaned when she saw him, and burst into tears again. The Reverend Pastor declared with a flourish of his hand that nothing could happen that had not yet been first ordained by God, that all things worked together for the good, and everything would be all right. It was all I could do not to sneak in a 'Hallelujah!'

My surrogate father just nodded to the Reverend Pastor's proclamations. Our eyes met again. I parted my lips, and then closed them again. He pursed his and looked away. He was breathing heavily.

I averted my eyes as we entered the building with the sign 'Mortuary' hanging lopsided on the front. It was Mama Agnes and I who led the way, Mama Agnes sniffling into my shirt. Behind us, my surrogate father and the Reverend Pastor followed. I gripped Mama Agnes and shuffled her along. Bop bop bop went her head, bop bop bop. The morgue assistant led us into the musky room, past rows and rows of covered trolleys, several toes or a leg or a dangling arm peeping from beneath some of the sheets.

The assistant lifted a sheet and beckoned us for a closer look. Mama Agnes stumbled, but I held her, and though my own legs were threatening to give way, I leaned forward, steeling my face, and peered beneath the sheet.

'It's not him!' I exclaimed, now flinging the whole sheet off the naked corpse. It was a ghastly sight to behold, the body of a boy yes, so small, the thin limbs attenuated by rigor mortis, with lips almost like Bukhosi's, the same plump pout the colour of wet soil. But the front teeth were tiny and not oversize, like Bukhosi's, the jaw was firm and not slack, and the ears flared out like a pair of satellite dishes, unlike Bukhosi's that sat flat against the sides of his head.

'It's not him!' Mama Agnes repeated. 'It's not my boy! It's not him!'

She began to laugh, slapping my chest, and then cry. I was about to put my arms around her when the Reverend Pastor muscled me aside, pulling Mama Agnes to *his* chest, letting her sob into his Canali lapels. I glared at him, and was about to cut between them when I saw my surrogate father standing alone, tears streaming down his sodden face, tremors assaulting his body. I went over to him. He let me embrace him. I hugged him, hugged him like I sometimes used to do for Uncle Fani.

And now, here I am, in the Mlambo living room, contemplating the miracle that is life, leafing through the Tiffany-blue baby album that usually sits on the bookshelf between the *Edgars Club* and *O* magazines. Above me is the framed photo of baby Bukhosi with his face cupped in a bonnet strung around his chubby chin appraising the living room. Behold those emerald baby eyes beholding the living room with shimmering virtue! Yes, the boy, although he has Mama Agnes's walnut complexion, inherited the emerald eyes of his true patrilineage, the Thornton Family Line. It was only thanks to the inverted teardrop nostrils, which belong undeniably to my surrogate father and are also a family feature of his biological clan the Thorntons, that Mama Agnes was not kicked out of her marital home under the charge of attempting to pass off another man's offspring as her husband's.

It overbrims with life, the baby album, it holds in its pages the measure of seventeen years of living. Behold, impilo lesikhathi – la vita e i tempi! There is baby Bukhosi on the first page at just three weeks, his tiny, walnut face peeping from a Super Mario blanket, his emerald eyes ashimmer, his mouth pinched around Mama Agnes's teat. He clinches that teat for dear life. Only an apocalyptic happening can separate him from the teat. Beware the enemy who dares to tear him away from his beloved teat!

These opening pages show the little prince in a series of varying poses, from that three weeks to twenty months or so, suckling on various substitutes for the beloved teat, which, for one reason or another, has been denied him, and denial of which is clearly not going down well; a frown in one snapshot while moulding the tiny lips around a little fist; a snarl in another while trying to stuff the foot of a teddy bear into the tiny mouth; an alarmed Mama Agnes in yet another, bent over, trying to brush soil out of the clenched hand being worried at by the greedy little gob. And then a tranquil snap of the little prince, at nine months old, in which he sits on the floor suckling on a dummy.

Next is a family of photos from twenty months or so to around three years in which we are presented with Bukhosi the philosopher of the human condition, helping us to realize the limits of our (im)mortality, our minds and dreams whose wildness is imprisoned in our bodies that bring us back to earth with every defecation. There is little Bukhosi lying atop a soiled nappy, having been betrayed by his little body; there again, crouching in a baby dish with his index finger prodding his anal orifice, looking up into the camera with a delighted grin; crouching in the same baby dish still, now smelling the index finger, now sucking on it, now smearing baby faeces on the walls of the baby dish; there, in a different snapshot, squatting on a potty, staring perplexed at the camera; squatting on the potty still, now crying.

Here is Bukhosi the three-to-six-year-old, standing on his parents' bed smiling into the camera, naked, one hand wrapped around his tiny phallus; now staring pensively at that phallus, now wagging it, now frowning; there, in another photo, stumbling in the backyard in our father's brown boots; in another snapshot, clinging to Mama Agnes's dress with his face pressed into her navel, as though hiding, perhaps from that other man our father, or just the camera.

Bukhosi the youngster-teenager; a face flattened against the living room window, with the tongue pressed to the pane, whorling circles of spit; now seated on one of the chocolate-coloured tables at Haefelis, stuffing pizza into his mouth; now standing outside Spar Supermarket, eyes closed, head tipped back, a bottle of Fanta, which he grips rather possessively with both hands, tilted to the lips.

There's a strange photo, tucked at the back of the baby album, of him at six or seven years old, suckling on Mama Agnes's breast, a sleepy jewel eye eyeing the camera. It's the only photo of its kind, belonging neither to the teat, phallic or Fanta guzzling years. Also, in many of the photos, it's Mama Agnes, and not my surrogate father, who is with him in the frame; it is she who hugs him, touches him, leans towards him, anchors him. But, as the years progress, he's more often alone in the photos. There's something precarious in the way he fills a frame; it is here that he reminds me, although I'm not sure why, of my Uncle Fani, and also of my surrogate father the day he told me about Black Jesus.

It feels as though the threat of disappearance had always been there from the very beginning.

Poof!

Abracadabra!

But this wispiness did not stop his parents from letting him spoil; by the time I met him earlier this year, he was skinny only thanks to the six-plus years of food shortages and runaway inflation that continue to plague the country.

During those early years of his childhood, as Mama Agnes told me after Abednego slammed her into the wall for trying to leave for South Africa, my surrogate father became, once again, affectionate with her, loving even. He stopped beating her, and instead would take her out to the drive-in on Fridays, where he let her choose what to watch, and even agreed to let her see *Honey, I Blew Up the Kid* twice, and where they'd sit in the back seat of his Peugeot 504 sharing a box of popcorn and sipping Coke from the same straw, he silently groping her, she perfectly still.

One day, while writhing to music blaring from the TV, her face scrunched up, her eyes closed, flinging her mfushwa hair from side to side and blaring along with Tina Turner, *What's love got to do, got to do with it*, she opened her eyes to find him standing there, leaning against the door, his jacket slung over his briefcase. She stumbled. But he was smiling.

'You shouldn't play the TV so loud,' he said. 'This is the city, not a growth point dhindindi.'

She lowered the volume.

'Did you used to go often?'

'Go where?'

'To the growth point dhindindi.'

'Ah! Never.'

'Then where did you learn to dance like that?'

I can picture her giggling, blushing. 'Tell me,' my surrogate father would have purred. 'You know how to dance. I don't know how to dance. Teach me. I want to learn.'

Later that night, as Mama Agnes told me – and I can imagine her ensconced in the nook of his arm, enjoying the scent of him, his soft snores purring in her ear – she watched him and thought, contentedly, how he had become somebody she could love.

'Zamani, bra – what's that? What's bra?'

'It means "brother", Ma,' I said, beaming.

'... bra, long time. Sorry I haven't writn – written? What kind of spelling is this? – written earlier. I just had two – to? – get away. I'm in Jozi working on a few things. I'm fine, crashing double-u – what's "w"?'

'That's short for "with", Ma,' I said, and offered to read the rest of the message for her and my surrogate father:

Im fine, crashing w some friends, looking 4 a job. Zim sucks, tshomi, n im trying my luck here. Things r betta here, bra, w 20 rand I can afford 2 buy myself a 2 piecer from KFC. They have KFC here, bra! Tell ma im comng hme soon, engaworry, I'm cool, I just had 2 get away 4rm that house uyazi, im tired of that man always beating me. U r the only one I can talk 2. Thanks 4 being

always there 4 me. U r the bro I always wished I had. Will write u soon. Will let u knw which bus I'll be coming on.
Later, bra.
Khosi.

I haven't felt such energy in our house since the boy went missing! Such electricity! My Mama Agnes was ecstatic, trying unsuccessfully to lift me off the ground, kissing my surrogate father on the forehead, which elicited a strained smile, though he remained seated by the kitchen table, cupping his cheek and staring at the message. It was because of what the boy had said in his message, I knew – that he had left because of him. I was hoping Mama Agnes would be the one to note this particular line in the message, but she was too excited, and only sang praises to the Holy Ghost.

And so, when we found ourselves alone in the kitchen, my surrogate father brooding still at the kitchen table in the sitting room, I tapped Mama Agnes on the shoulder and hissed, 'Ma.'

'Yes, mfanami?' she said rather loudly.

'I'm worried, Ma. About—' I nodded towards the sitting room. 'He's been violent with you lately and now to learn that it's because of him that Bukhosi ran away…'

Her face darkened, her hand pausing midway through stirring the soup she was cooking for supper; we were expecting the Reverend Pastor for evening prayers.

'I don't think you should be alone with him,' I continued. 'But don't you worry. I'm here for you. I'm not going anywhere. I won't let him do anything to you and the boy. Not any more. Not while I'm here.'

▪

It came to me as I lay awake last night in my pygmy room, worried sick that I'd wake up one of these days to find her gone – and if she goes, how will I ever conquer that Gehenna, Bhalagwe? A few days ago, the day after the scare at the morgue, I found a brochure with the schedule of the Greyhound bus to Jozi in her handbag, some dates and times circled in pen. I figured the best way to stop her from going after the boy was to get the boy to come to her. But how to get him to come without coming? It was only as the sky began to pale outside my window this morning, that crisp, delicious morning breeze fanning the smells of the township into my lodgings, that it came to me: Facebook. Bukhosi and I opened Facebook accounts a few months ago, though we had never used them. But we'd heard Facebook was the new craze among young people over there in America, much cooler than MySpace. Now, finally, I would put this Facebook to use. I got up, spurred on by a fresh burst of energy, and set to work creating a fake account in Bukhosi's name. I even used the profile picture that's on his original account, the one I took the Sunday before he went missing, at the Rainbow Cinema where we had gone to watch *Spider-Man 3*. And then I sent myself a message from this fake account.

When I showed Mama Agnes the message this morning, she raised her hands and shouted, 'Praise the Lord!' She beckoned my surrogate father, and together they huddled around my MacBook on the cobalt kitchen table.

It was all too easy, really, and would have been perfect, had she not told the Reverend Pastor about Bukhosi's Facebook message when he came for prayers this evening. He dared, that Reverend Pastor, to question me; he demanded to see the message, he scrunched up that chubby face of his as he read it, squinting, scowling, I don't know what the hell he was doing to his face. As though this was not enough, as though he meant to not only question me but outdo me, he declared:

'I can get my IT guys to trace it and get an accurate location of the boy.'

He could get his IT guys to do what, get his IT guys to – who the hell had asked for his help? And who were these IT guys?

I could feel the sweat beads forming on my forehead. 'Is it necessary?' I said. 'After all, Bukhosi is coming home, he says so, in the message, that he'll let me know.'

The man flashed me those Colgate teeth. 'Still, it won't hurt,' he said. And then, like those perfectly timed TV pastors with their Hallelujah shows, he turned to Mama Agnes, furrowing his brow in just the right way. 'I want to do all I can to help.'

Mama Agnes gazed at him reverently. The bastard! Did he think he could mooch off my hard work? I had to swallow my rage, though. I had to smile and nod in agreement as she kept nudging me and saying, her eyes blazing at the man, 'Isn't he great, Zamani? Glory be to God. Isn't he amazing? Hallelujah.'

I had to beg leave from the evening prayers, and stumbled away before Mama Agnes could see the tears I was trying so desperately to blink back, ignoring her offer to take a plate of that scrumptious meal she had prepared. I was hyperventilating by the time I got to my pygmy room. I rummaged through my things, flinging everything aside until I found the Red Album. I stared at it, trying to control my breathing. I felt its weight and ran my hands across the cover, which was made of tough, red plastic. I opened it. I leafed through it, kissing the pictures, sniffing them, wetting their plastic pockets with my tears. I gazed into those brown eyes floating in their super-white sclerae. The irises glimmered darkly, the pupils opaque. That Reverend Pastor! How I wished to thrash him, to smash his face and wipe away that smug smile he always shines on Mama Agnes. I would punch him, bash him, bloody his stupid Canali suit. I would squish him like the fly that he is. Who the hell did he think he was? I would – I saw myself then, glaring into my eyes in the Red Album, the lamp next to my little put-me-up bed arresting my profile, my wet, velvet cheeks glittering like a starry night sky. My eyes shimmered darkly, too, but it seemed with… fright. I was dismayed to see fright so naked there, and I could not bear it, I quickly closed the Red Album, shutting myself away.

I hugged my album, hugged it and thought of that Reverend Pastor. It was in this way that I finally fell asleep.

THE COMMISSION OF INQUIRY

I was hoping that Reverend Pastor would forget about his nonsense from last night, but the man is persistent, he was back in our yard early this morning to collect my laptop. I heard him outside my pygmy room talking to Mama Agnes and my surrogate father, urging them to wake me up so he could 'get down to business'. It was Mama Agnes who came for me; I pretended to be asleep, but it was no use; her knocks got progressively louder and more urgent, until I had no choice but to call out sleepily, 'Mama Agnes, is that you? What's happened?'

She tried the door, but I had bolted it. 'I'm not dressed,' I said, although I was in my pyjamas. But even this could only stall her; she insisted that I come out, that the Reverend Pastor was here and needed my computer. Those were her words, 'needed my computer'. Needed what? If the man was so desperate for a computer he should have got his own!

I took my time dressing, making sure to slide my Mac underneath my sheets, next to my Red Album, before finally stepping out. They were congregated right outside my door, my surrogate father's arms folded across his chest, Mama Agnes looking up expectantly, a smile spreading on her face, the Reverend Pastor grinning stupidly behind her.

'Eh, where is it?' he said, stepping forward, his hands stretched out. Even at that hour, he was prim and proper in a Canali suit. Did he have a wardrobe of them or what?

'This is unnecessary,' I said, turning to Mama Agnes. 'If we want to know where the boy is, all we have to do is ask him. I have already sent him a Facebook message.'

'My way will be the faster,' buzzed the fly. He just would not stop bzz-bzz-bzzing! He squared his shoulders. 'It will take only a few hours to determine the boy's location. My guys are already waiting – they will do the job and have your computer back to you by this afternoon.'

'Yes,' said Mama Agnes.

'Stop your nonsense, boy,' said my surrogate father. 'Give us the thing, mani. Camun.' And he beckoned for my laptop.

My precious Mac! Inherited from Dumo, back when he still considered himself my mentor and was only too happy to help me find my purpose. A real, mean machine, was my MacBook, a 2003 model, with a 13-inch screen I took care to wipe down regularly; a beauty, and damn expensive, too.

'No,' I said, because I had run out of persuasive things to say.

'Ah!' cried Mama Agnes, and I felt a pang, then, in my chest.

'Heyi, wena, we don't have time for your nonsense, just give it here, where is it?'

And with that, my surrogate father tried to push past me into my lodgings. Once again, he was bent on humiliating me, this time in front of other people. I stepped in his way, stopping him in his tracks.

'You know this is the reason Bukhosi ran away in the first place, right? You are bullying the boy, again. Why not simply ask him where he is? That's what I've done, and I'm going to wait for his reply, like a normal person. He will tell us where he is. It's as simple as that!'

'Do you know how serious this is?' buzzed the fly.

'What you are proposing is illegal,' I said. I didn't know whether it was illegal or not, but it certainly sounded so. 'How exactly are you going to use a privileged conversation online to find out where Bukhosi is? It is illegal. Illegal!'

I was quite shrill by this time, and feeling rather nauseous, and was on the verge of swatting the fly. I spun around to storm back into my pygmy room, but so blinding was my rage that I tripped on the step and was sent sprawling.

'Are you all right—'

I got up swiftly and, without turning around, slammed the door and bolted it shut. My poor toe was throbbing. I limped to my little put-me-up bed, sat down and took deep breaths. I heard them talking in hushed tones, but luckily, they dared not come knocking on my door again. Eventually, they left. I should have handled things better. I shouldn't have been hostile to the Reverend Pastor, not in front of Mama Agnes. But I had lost myself, if only for a moment. I had felt quite ill and it was as if… It would win me no favour, I knew. Mama Agnes would not let the matter of the laptop go. I set about writing my fake Bukhosi a message at once, asking him where he was – I had thought of that idea off the cuff earlier when the Reverend Pastor questioned me – and waited for two hours before scripting his reply.

It was late morning by then. I unbolted myself from my lodgings and limped into the house, calling Mama Agnes. I found her in the sitting room, beating the sofa cushions against each other, the mukwa oil cloth on her shoulder. She looked up when I walked in, giving me a strained smile.

'I have heard back from Bukhosi!' I announced.

This got her attention. She dropped her cushions, grabbing my Nokia from my hand. 'What is he saying, where is he, did he tell you where he is?'

'Yes, Ma. Just like I told you he would! He says he is staying in Berea with some friends, as you can see.'

'Berea,' she muttered, scrolling down the Facebook message. 'What would he be doing in Berea, is this where this girl lives? He could go to my sister Nto in Kempton Park, at least then we'll know where he is…'

'I don't know if he's with any girl,' I said. 'He just says he's with some friends.'

'Which friends are these? And he didn't give an address! Isn't Berea right next to that dingy neighbourhood, what's it called…' Her eyes widened. 'Hillbrow!'

This wasn't at all the reaction I had expected. I had thought she would be ecstatic, just like the day before when she read the first message.

'He says he's fine,' I tried again. 'Look, Ma, we should be happy, the boy, he's willing to talk to me—'

'You should have just given the Reverend Pastor your computer. We would have his exact address, the Reverend Pastor said—'

'The Reverend Pastor and I want the same thing,' I said in a conciliatory tone, even managing a smile. 'You can see just how worried he is—'

'The man of God can't even sleep—'

'Amen, Ma. I just think it's best if we use what we already have, see Bukhosi is already talking to me, he trusts me. We don't want to do anything that will scare him into running away from us again. Do we?'

'Oh no, no no no, Thixo, God, no.'

'Then let us do this the boy's way. Let him talk to me. Give me a chance to speak to him, I know how to handle him, Ma. Trust me.'

She nodded slowly. 'Maybe if I gave you Nto's number,' she said, her eyes lightening. 'Yes, let me give you Nto's South Africa number, tell Bukhosi to call her, I would feel better hearing from her that he's all right!'

I tried to keep smiling. 'That's a wonderful idea, Ma,' I said, because really, what else could I say? 'Yes, give me Aunt Nto's number. I'm sure Bukhosi will be happy to have it.'

I attended the Sunday service at Blessed Anointings with Mama Agnes today. I have only accompanied her there one other time, the Sunday after Bukhosi disappeared, when we went all over the city putting up missing posters of the boy, but I need to figure out this Reverend Pastor and so I'm going to keep him in my sights until I do. I can see that he's still not satisfied with this laptop business. Mama Agnes gave me Aunt Nto's phone number earlier this week, and she has been pestering me since. She's in touch with Nto who hasn't, of course, heard from the boy. She keeps asking me what the boy has said, and I've so far told her that he hasn't replied, but not to worry, he'll respond soon. I realize she won't let this business with Aunt Nto go, and that Reverend Pastor is fuelling her, because each time she asks after the boy she begins with, 'The Reverend Pastor thinks…'

I have to get him off my back. I can't just sit here and do nothing, like a hare meekly offering himself to a lion! Surely, there must be something I can do. That Reverend Nobody thinks he's the man of this house; he's not the man of the house here, my surrogate father is. No, in fact, I, Zamani, shall be the man of the Mlambo house, the son who protects the family!

As soon as the service was over, the Reverend Pastor gave me the slip. He and Mama Agnes bolted for his car. I followed, and asked to go with them to wherever it is that they were going. Mama Agnes looked flustered, but the Reverend Pastor leaned over and peered at me through the front passenger window of his Mercedes, and said a firm 'no'; they were going to a special place by the Mguza River to collect holy water, he said, and only anointed prophets and their subjects were allowed there. I should go home, he said, before pressing a button on his car door, winding up Mama Agnes's window and speeding away.

I took a khombi home, but I haven't been able to sit still, to watch TV, nothing. Instead, I consulted my Red Album, flipping the pages and asking it, 'What would you do?' It helped, talking to my Red Album; in it is everything I abhor, and yet everything as well I yearn for, a father, *my* father, *my* mother, to be somebody's son. Strong family roots in which to build my legacy. Being reminded of this helped to calm me, and I was able to think clearly for the first time in days. I've been feeling terrible, panicking, shrinking from my surrogate parents, all because I haven't been focusing on my redemptive chronicles. Ever since I started gleaning from my surrogate parents their hi-stories, and from this the seeds for my own new hi-story, I have felt myself progress. I have felt an inner change. I am becoming a new person, imbibing fresh stories, a new way of seeing and being, casting away the burdensome identity Uncle Fani thrust upon me on his deathbed. I am beginning, finally, to see the light.

When Mama Agnes came home this evening from her outing with her Reverend Pastor, she found me in the kitchen chopping some onions for a mince stew I was making.

'And then?' she said, surprised, for she had never seen me cook.

'I have the best news, Ma,' I said, leaning over and kissing her on the cheek – something I'd never done. 'I finally heard back from Bukhosi.'

'Oh? Let me see!'

I whipped out my Nokia ceremoniously, and showed her Bukhosi's Facebook message. He apologized for having been so quiet, he had gone down to Durban with his friends to see the beach. He would definitely get in touch with Aunt Nto. He missed me terribly, and wished I were there with him. He also missed Ma, especially her cooking – here Mama Agnes beamed – and not to worry, he would call her soon, he just needed some space, that was all, he loved her and missed her, and he was glad to hear I was there for her; that's what brothers did! He would write soon, and he would be home for Christmas.

Mama Agnes took hold of my hand and began dancing with me in the kitchen. I tried to twirl her around, but there wasn't enough space, and, laughing, ended up shimmying with her in a bum-jive.

'Let me call the Reverend Pastor,' she said, retrieving her Motorola from her handbag. I pried it from her hand and held it high above her head, looking down at her with mock sternness. 'Ah ah ah. Tonight, I want you here with me, to celebrate this good news. See, I am even cooking for you.' She laughed, and I could tell she was flattered that I had gone to the trouble of cooking for her. She started making plans for Christmas, what she would cook for Bukhosi, where she would look for the ingredients, despite the fact that Christmas was still a month away.

It's not lost on me that I was doing the very thing I had scorned my surrogate father for doing, winning back my Mama A through the softness of her stomach. Only, unlike my surrogate father, like a true Mthwakazi warrior I had hunted for the ingredients in this our foodless jungle, and now, I cooked up quite a Sahara storm for my Mama Agnes, refusing her offers of help, telling her she needed someone to spoil her for once, and who better, as Bukhosi had written in his message, than someone he considered his brother.

'I'm sure if Bukhosi was here, he would do the exact same thing for you, Ma.'

She laughed sceptically, pleasing me no end.

We sat by the cobalt kitchen table, just us two – I had slipped my surrogate father a baggie of ubuvimbo and suggested he go and look for the boy. The food tasted better than I had expected! We dug into platefuls of spaghetti, with a rich mince stew and potato salad, washed down with Mazoe Orange Crush. Nothing but the best for Mama Agnes – and nothing but the best if I am ever to get her to talk to me about the camp.

I imagined us sitting together, me as her son, her as my mama, opening up to me about the terrible things that Black Jesus did at that camp. I vowing to avenge her, kissing her cheeks, wiping away her tears, she beaming at me, her son, her protector, assuring me I was nothing like that man, that she loved me, my particular navy blue skin, my pouting lips, my refined cheekbones. She loved all of me, my mama, I was Bukhosi and she was Mama Agnes. It made my heart giddy, imagining this. I gazed dreamily at her.

'Ma,' I said, giving her a sober gaze. 'Ma. We can no longer deny what Father is capable of. I know it's hard, but, it's obvious his violence is what drove my little brother away.'

Mama Agnes looked embarrassed. She averted her eyes. 'He's not that bad—'

'No, Ma, uh-huh,' I said firmly, shaking my head. 'You can't keep making excuses for him. He's becoming increasingly unpredictable. This business of always disappearing to God knows where at night, the secretiveness. I won't sleep well tonight, knowing you are all alone here with him.'

She looked frightened then, Mama Agnes. 'Do you really think—' she began anxiously.

'I'll start on the dishes, Ma,' I said, getting up abruptly, as though I, too, were getting anxious and eager to change the subject.

She protested, as I suspected she would, helping me to clear the table and insisting that she do the dishes, after all the cooking I had done for her, shuwa. I made a show of demurring, finally relenting and agreeing to let her help. We did the dishes side by side, in the semi-darkness, with flickering candles for light, for the electricity had gone again. I soaped the dishes and she rinsed, placing them in the rack. I tried to stretch those moments, savouring each time our hands brushed as we passed a dish between us, basking in the happiness of mundane domestic tasks. What son would not delight in spending such quality time with his mother? Bukhosi, that's who!

Afterwards, when it had become clear that bed was the next order of business, I said casually, stifling a yawn, that I probably needed an extra blanket as Bukhosi's room got cold at night. There was a pause. Then Mama Agnes said all right, she had just the right blanket, nice and warm, and disappeared into her bedroom, appearing in Bukhosi's room a moment later with a duvet, one of her old ones, for I could smell her sweet perfume on it. By then, I had comfortably lodged myself in the boy's bed, thinking how I could get used to this.

She made quite a fuss, Mama A, covering me with her duvet, and patting around in the dark to make sure I was properly tucked in, asking if I was OK.

'I'm not feeling well,' I lied. 'I think I ate too much.'

'Eh, I saw you eating as if for a whole soccer team, bantu!'

I chuckled. 'Stay with me a while, Ma,' I said, patting the space on the bed beside me. 'I don't want our nice evening to end so soon.' I meant it.

I could hear from her voice that she was smiling. 'Just for a few minutes.'

She perched beside me. I sat up on the boy's bed, and groped about for her hand. It was warm, and her palms were soft, so motherly; she rubbed her hands religiously with Vaseline, and when she couldn't find Vaseline in the shops, with precious drops of the oil we use for cooking.

This was it. It was now or never. 'Ma,' I ventured, massaging her hands. 'I was hoping you wouldn't bite my head off if I asked you about Bhalagwe.' When she tensed I quickly added, 'I would never disrespect you like that but… I need to know.'

She snatched her hand away, and though I couldn't see her because it was dark, I could picture her walnut face discolouring. 'You should know better than to ask.' She took several deep breaths.

And now I played my trump card. If I expected Mama Agnes to share something that left her so vulnerable with me, I would have to be vulnerable with her, too. I lowered my voice. 'I'm sorry, Ma, it's just that… my mother, she, she died at Bhalagwe. She was there around the same time as you and I thought maybe you might know her…'

It was she, this time, who grabbed hold of my hand. 'You poor child! I had no idea—'

'That's why I was hoping that maybe if you were to tell me about it, Ma…'

Finally, she pulled away. She sat pensively on the edge of the boy's bed, her face partially caught in the pale strip of moonlight slanting through the window behind me. Her brow was furrowed. I stared at her and waited, massaging her hand. For a long time, she said nothing. She moistened her lips. She rocked herself to and fro. She looked at me. Looked away.

'That's something I can't talk about,' she said, finally. 'I just… I can't go back there. I can't.'

'Maybe if you tried, Ma!' I said, and then, softening my words, 'I just need to know what type of place it was for… you know… my mama.'

She seemed to consider this. 'I can't, Zamani,' she said again. 'I can't go back there.'

I nodded in the dark, trying to swallow my disappointment.

'But I can tell you about the Commission of Inquiry.'

I remembered the year the Commission of Inquiry came. It was in '96. I was thirteen at the time. The news that there was a Commission of Inquiry into what had happened in the '80s spread across Bulawayo in urgent, hushed whispers. Because one could never be sure, heh? There were ears everywhere, busy itch-itching, itch-itching…

Word on the street was that the Commission was taking testimonies. There were powerful men and women behind the whole thing, white priests all the way from Italy. The Pope himself was rumoured to have flown into the country, flapping about in his red and white robes that twirled about him like a dress, on a secret mission to meet all devoted Catholics from Matabeleland and heal them with the touch of his hand. They would even get to kiss the holy ring! But Catholics only. The Pope's power would not work on any of the devil-worshipping fools who served other denominations.

Word was, they would be taking the government to court. Oh yes! They would put the President on the stand, like a normal person. They would parade his crimes for all the world to see, and afterwards, they would throw him into Chikurubi Maximum Security Prison and throw away the key. Oh yes! Him and and and Black Jesus and The Crocodile and General Bae and the Others…

Word was, the white priests were lawyers too, and they would get *com-pen-sa-tion* for the victims of the… unmentionable era. Oh yes! All you had to do was to go to your village and give your testimony. Oh yes.

I am pretty sure that my Uncle Fani went to see the Commission of Inquiry People, at least, I remember him mentioning it, although when I asked him what a Commission of Inquiry was, he just gave me a sad, mysterious grin. I have calculated the days, and when the Commission of Inquiry People came, it was round about the time that Uncle Fani really took his drinking to new heights. I zoom in with sepia-tinted lens to see myself reading in horror and awe as Simon speaks to the pig's head in *Lord of the Flies* in this very living room, which did not contain its pretty maroon sofas and its bright cobalt kitchen table back then, boasting nothing but three Formica chairs. I am frowning with affected concentration at the pages. I suspect he's just come in from seeing the Commission of Inquiry People, Uncle Fani. He's busy sniffling on the chair beside me. He's a grown man, for goodness' sake! What the hell is he crying for?

His sniffles gather momentum and break into sobs. I've never heard him cry like this before; cry so freely, as though he were dying. Anybody who has ever heard the anguished, naked sobs of a man knows what a frightening sound it is.

'Zamani…'

I pretend not to hear and instead raise my voice to read from *Lord of the Flies*: 'Fancy thinking the Beast was something you could hunt and kill!…'

'Zamani!'

'You knew, didn't you? I'm part of you?'

'... Zamani...'

'I'M THE REASON WHY IT'S NO GO? WHY THINGS ARE WHAT THEY ARE?'

He gives up, thankfully, my uncle, gives up trying to beckon me to his lap so he can cling to me like I'm his mama. But that's a fatal mistake, *my* mistake, for that's when he really takes to the bottle like a newborn to the teat. Perhaps, if I'd once more lent him my bony, thirteen-year-old chest to cry on...!

Mama Agnes went to see the Commission of Inquiry People. She woke up as though it were a workday like any other and left for her rural home Kezi without telling my surrogate father where it was she was going. It was a pleasant April morning in which a brilliant sun dazzled the sky.

In the khombi from Bulawayo to Kezi, she sat amidst passengers who were squashed like a rural laity being carted off to a rally. The air was hot and sticky, and rose only to condense and settle on the passengers in sweaty, oppressive mists. Mama Agnes felt faint; she crinkled her nose against the mingling odours of boiled eggs and fried chicken. She felt otherworldly, watching the hawkers patrolling the sides of the road at every stop, mostly women and girls, and young men with the oiliest skin, their armpits dripping wet. They scrambled for the khombi as it rumbled to a halt, almost falling over one another in a bid to offer their wares to the open windows. Mabhanzi, Korn Kurl chips, Marie Biscuits, fizzy drinks, bananas and oranges. Maize that was not quite ripe, sizzling on a stake, and freshly plucked cane, the stalks sticky with sap.

She watched the hawkers as they punched and elbowed, their voices both crude and saccharine as they yelled obscenities at one another while attempting to coax the passengers into purchase. She wondered about their lives, which villages they were from, whether the Commission of Inquiry People had passed through their hamlets. If they'd been eager to speak, or whether the warnings of shrill mothers had long ago muted their voices. Why they were over here, instead of over there.

Trymore was waiting for her at the Sisters' Office at Tshelanye Mission Hospital. He hugged her for a long time, with his one good, strong hand, and when he finally pulled away, she saw that his eyes were wet. But he was smiling. She, too, smiled.

He had on their father's only suit, with the empty sleeve pinned to the shoulder with a thorn.

He told her that their mother had refused to come. Mama Agnes hadn't expected that she would. Trymore's hand was trembling as he showed her the photo of Mwangi and Promise. They startled her, her dead brothers' faces, in a way she'd never thought after so long they would. It had been torn halfway down the middle, so that the bit with herself and Trymore and Nto shoving their faces into the frame at the last moment was missing.

Promise had his head thrown back, in playful arrogance, so that his gums showed. It came alive, his laugh, and, standing in the middle of Tshipisane village square, amidst a crowd that was rapidly growing, Mama Agnes could hear her brother's guffaw. Next to him, Mwangi's look was more pensive, as though the camera had caught him in the middle of a thought. His forehead had a slight furrow, harrowed by a gash where Nkani the donkey'd kicked him one afternoon in their father's fields as he attempted to bully her into driving the plough. How they'd laughed at him as he made his way back home with the blood dripping from his forehead! But later, he became the centre of their envy, didn't he? After their father said he'd marry well, and have many cows, for women loved the scars of a man, they told stories of valour, which was doubly rewarded by the ancestors.

'He was always Father's favourite,' Trymore said, as though reading her thoughts. 'He was never the same man afterwards, Father.'

Trymore thrust a crumpled sheaf of papers into her hands, and left her to go and sit beneath a mopane tree, where a cluster of men was sharing a calabash. She was reluctant even as she straightened the papers, for she already knew what they were: a confessional about Bhalagwe.

Though I begged Mama Agnes to share the contents of the letter with me, she wouldn't. She couldn't, she said. I implored, but to no avail. All she told me was that after reading the letter, she carefully squared off the pages and handed it back to Trymore, sniffling as her brother was called in to testify.

She spoke at length about the chap who interviewed her, how exhausted he looked, avoiding her gaze as he addressed her in a crisp, accounting tone. His curt questions hurt her. She'd spent nights tossing and turning, willing herself to remember, desiring to forget, promising to go, swearing to retreat. She sat on the wooden chair in that classroom at Tshipisane, walls sullied by graffiti and bits of plastic fluttering from the windows where the panes ought to have been. Glanced furtively at the other two desks that had been arranged next to them. The voices of the occupants were too loud, the space too public for their harrowing, private confessions.

When she opened her mouth and began her speech, rehearsed and re-rehearsed and re-re-rehearsed weeks and days and hours before – 'My name is Agnes Ndiweni-Mlambo I lived in Kezi I am here to give testimony on Gukurahundi my family—'

'I don't need to know your name,' the chap said.

'Sorry?'

'I only need to state whether you are male or female. For your own protection, you see.'

'But. You said it was safe. You said we were going to be safe, that the government said it's OK, that we can speak freely—'

'We are just being careful.'

'All right. All right all right. I am a female. One night my family was—'

'When?'

'What?'

'Do you know the date of the incident in question?'

She stared at him. 'I don't know.'

'Could you give me an estimate, please?'

'I don't know.'

The chap rubbed his temples and sighed. 'Madam, I cannot do my job if you don't co-operate.'

Co-operate?

'1984. I think it was 1984.'

He picked up his pen and resumed scribbling. 'Which month?'

'November,' she lied, because he was clearly expecting an answer.

'All right. Please tell me what happened. Stick only to the very essential information.'

What was essential information? she wondered. Should she skip the part where she woke up to the screams coming from outside her hut, the thudding of feet, her mama screaming *get up get up get up! Get up mani lina lifuna ukufa yini do you want to die leave everything and run leave everything and run!* Should she tell this young man how she clutched her breasts as she ran, because they seemed like the most important thing to protect, cushioning as they were her heart, begging to be let out, pounding so hard her chest hurt? Was this essential information? Should she just move on to the part where they were rounded up in the village school?

'How many were rounded up at the school?' he asked.

She blinked at him.

'Madam?'

'Sixty-two,' she said, randomly.

Scribble scribble scribble. Every so often a long, drawn-out sigh. Never looking up to meet her gaze.

She decided, then, that she would not tell him anything of value. Anything that was *valuable to her.* He didn't deserve it. Had not earned the right to such intimacies. She regretted having come. Now, she'd been forced to remember things she'd worked so hard to forget, until they'd come to resemble a movie, someone else's life that couldn't possibly have any resemblance to hers, the brand-new, born-again Mama Agnes. Yes, *she had been happy.* Hadn't she been happy? Hadn't it been easier to *pretend nothing had ever ever ever ever…* Easier to ignore the dreams, the palpitations, the ghosts of Promise and Mwangi which, for a long time after Bhalagwe, took to following her around? Until she met Father Reuben, whose presence managed to soothe her, so that whenever she was with him, the ghosts of her brothers would leave her alone. Now, she'd been forced to remember all of it and more; the daily deaths at the camp, from starvation or torture or murder; the random shootings, so that you didn't know if you'd survive any given day; the daily chore of digging graves; being made to watch, one time, a detainee, a woman who Mama Agnes knew well, a respected village elder who just the month before had delivered lovely cloth made from African print to Mama Agnes's mama and asked her to make a dress for her daughter's wedding, this woman who was singled out by the Men in the Red Berets and made to prostrate her rump for a donkey to mount.

She stopped abruptly here, my Mama Agnes; she was struggling to breathe. I squeezed her hand.

'What happened next, Ma?' I hissed. 'What happened at Bhalagwe?'

But that word, Bhalagwe, was like a swear word – I shouldn't have said it! I should have just said, 'What happened over there?' – for at the mention of it, she seemed to jerk out of a trance and, wiping her tears, which were streaming silently down her lovely cheeks, reiterated that she did not share with the Commission People anything that was of value to her.

Later, after the interrogation by the brusque chap, as she strolled aimlessly about the village square, waiting for Trymore to finish his interview, she happened upon a familiar sheaf of papers fluttering in a crumpled pile by a bin behind one of the classrooms. Trymore's shaky, painstaking writing was legible on the sheets.

Afterwards, when the Commission People had packed up and left, Trymore walked her back to the tarred road where she was to catch a khombi back to Bulawayo.

'They said they could not speak for too long,' he said. The cheer in his voice was bilious. 'So many people to document, more people than they had thought would come. But I gave them the letter. They promised to read it. Promised to get back to me. Promised to get us money from the government, as *com-pen-sa-tion*. Promised to help with Promise and Mwangi. So, you see? Everything's going to be all right.'

'Yes,' she lied. 'Everything's going to be all right.'

After a while, he said, 'How much do you think it will be, sister? This *com-pen-sa-tion*? How much do you think the government would have to pay us to make us forget? How much do you think can make everything right?'

She stared at him then, sadly.

The promised compensation would never come.

As the khombi rumbled into the yonder, she turned for one last look, to find Trymore waving vigorously with his good arm, the pinned sleeve of their father's jacket flapping in the wind.

It was raining by the time the khombi arrived back in Bulawayo. She was glad for the rain. It masked her tears. Her inability to forget the things she had now worked so hard to remember.

And how could she ever forget, Mama Agnes, that afternoon a year later when Trymore called her from the Sisters' Office at Tshelanye Mission Hospital, his voice shaking as he told her he was going to see if Promise and Mwangi were among the skulls, femurs, humeri and other body parts that were being retrieved from Antelope Mine.

'Perhaps at last, we can give our brothers a decent burial, sister!'

She'd told him, hadn't she? To rein in his excitement, not to let it run so free so fast? Because she'd known, even as she begged leave from her teaching duties and boarded the Shu Shine bus to Antelope Mine, that they'd do something like that, those people from the government, murder hope with a few words penned on a flimsy piece of paper.

They were already in full swing by the time she arrived at Antelope Mine, the government people, looking solemn as they stood in front of the cameras, frying in the Matopo sun. They proclaimed the remains to be from the liberation era of the '70s. *Brave men and women who fought heroically for the freedom that every Zimbabwean now enjoyed*, they piped. They mopped their brows and showed their teeth to the cameras. Behind them stood withered maize stalks. Mama Agnes squinted at the crowd and tried to pick out Trymore among the clusters of frazzled villagers. Children took turns to run into the sights of the cameras, pull down their underpants and wiggle their bottoms. She didn't see Trymore until later, after the scuffle, which started when she – realizing that the day was orangeing and the craniums, mandibles, clavicles, scapulae, sternums, humeri, ribs, iliums, sacrums, pubises, radii, ulnas, carpals, metacarpals, phalanges, ischiums, femurs, patellae, tibias, fibulae, tarsals and metatarsals of her brothers were not going to be retrieved – shouted, 'That's where you threw them.'

Before long, the crowd was chanting, '*That's where you threw them, that's where you threw them*,' accusatory fingers aimed like pistols at Antelope Mine. Their fragile voices growing louder, carried on the wings of the wind, flapping in the faces of the government people.

But when a truckload of soldiers arrived, Mama Agnes turned and ran, hitching her dress up her thighs, just like she had when the Men in the Red Berets had come to Kezi. All around her, the villagers scattered like dissidents. They ran, even the old people, whose flesh swayed like heavy buckets and weighed them down as though they were carrying the burden of a whole nation.

And once aflutter, nothing could settle flippity-floppity hearts. Not even a report in the *Daily News* that the coins found among the skeletal remains dated from the early '80s, after independence, during the time of the unmentionable era, and not the '70s, as the government claimed. Afterwards, there was a shuffle of excitement from the people from the Lawyers for Human Rights, and the journalists from Amnesty International, who came and went clickety-click with their cameras, asking questions nobody wanted to answer. But it all died down, eventually, just like it always did. Just like it had the year before, when the Commission of Inquiry People had come to the villages with their bags of nugatory promises.

The remains, of course, were never seen again. Loaded onto a military truck, they chugged into the yonder and went poof! *Hard to tell* exactly *how far back the remains dated*, the people from the government stuttered, as they wet the cameras with their smiles. *Difficult, what without forensic experts and the tampering of the specimens by the police, who had good intentions, rest assured... Rest assured, somebody will look into it...* When Mama Agnes finally reunited with Trymore, at Tshelanye Mission Hospital after the scuffle, she fell into his good arm and wept. She shut her eyes and imagined him on the thirteen kilometre trek to Antelope Mine to confront the government people.

'Leave it alone,' she begged him. 'Please, enough, won't you just leave it alone?'

'How can I leave it alone? They came, those people from the Commission of Inquiry, did they not come, and awaken sleeping dogs, and tell us they would put them to rest? Did they not say, "Tell us what happened, we will help you, we will make the pain go away"? They went away, and they never came back, but the dogs they woke up in me won't stop barking.'

BHALAGWE

What Mama Agnes told me yesterday, about her experience with the Commission of Inquiry People, and that bit she slipped in unwittingly about Bhalagwe, the daily deaths, having to dig graves, the starvation, that woman and what they made her do with a donkey… I haven't been able to stop thinking about it.

I tried to catch her this morning to see if I could tease out a little more of her knotty hi-story, but she left early, bustling around the neighbourhood in preparation for another prayer meeting tonight. I even tried rummaging through her things in her bedroom, going through the tchotchkes on top of her wardrobe, thinking maybe I would find something about Trymore's confessional, to no avail. When that didn't work, I sought out my surrogate father, perhaps to play a game of draughts for old time's sake, but he apparently didn't come home last night – no doubt parked up in that cemetery of his, maybe enjoying the last of the baggie of ubuvimbo I gave him. It's just been me, pacing around in my pygmy room, nothing to do, nowehere to go. Mani, a *donkey*.

Company finally came this afternoon, when MaNdlovu brought some Formica chairs from next door, to help with the seating, for the house gets full every evening, these days, thanks to our superstar, the Reverend Pastor. He keeps asking about Bukhosi, wanting to read every Facebook message, pestering me about when the boy is coming back, saying his IT guys are still on standby, ready to help. It seems each time I make progress with Mama Agnes, calming her with a message from the boy, the man undoes my work with his incessant meddling, making her anxious all over again.

What is it about him? What is it about him that makes people want to get close to him, to lap up every word coming from his mouth? I remember Mama Agnes telling me proudly, as though this was somehow her own accomplishment, that Blessed Anointings gets so full, attracting new sheep all the time, that they have to hold three services on Sunday and lunchtime prayers every weekday. I can almost admire the man's powers. He seems impenetrable, standing up high on the pedestal his congregants have put him on, preaching down to the rest of us people, nje. But he's only human, like all of us; I bet if you removed that haloed suit of his and took away his title and his glittering King James bible, he would become disappointingly ordinary. That's why he's always dressed to the nines, as though he's on camera. I mustn't get caught up in his costume, in the aura he tries to hide behind. He's not God, after all. He's just a man, and so he must have his weaknesses, like the rest of us.

He arrives for the evening prayers with a flourish, his Ladies of the Church in train, having brought their yummy-smelling Tupperware bowls and skaftins, overbrimming with all the things that can't be found on the supermarket shelves these days. They look enterprising, these women, even as they proclaim, 'God is good!' in answer to questions from the likes of MaNdlovu about where they got the rice or the mealie-meal or the pork ribs or the chicken or the peanut butter. They are gleaming, plump and round and healthy despite the times. I imagine some of them are cross-border traders, going weekly to neighbouring South Africa and Botswana to shop for groceries, coming back here to sell it at exorbitant prices in their secret little spaza shops in their backyards, or even from their car boots – I've seen such enterprises lined up along Lobengula Street, one person standing by the half-open boot hissing their wares to passers-by, the other behind the wheel, on the ready in case the police show up.

Mama Agnes greets the Reverend Pastor, curtseying and rubbing her hands demurely, before helping the Ladies of the Church set up their food on the cobalt table, which has been moved out into the front yard, where my surrogate father's car would be were he present. All over the house, and spilling out onto the strip of yard outside, friends, neighbours and relatives have come to show solidarity with the family. They quickly become the Reverend Pastor's captive audience. His high notes are hitting their peak on this day, Monday 26 November, almost two months since our Bukhosi disappeared. He stands in front of the TV, modulating his preaching voice, which has given the Mlambo home the disco flavour of his Blessed Anointings church, looking like God himself in that white Canali suit. I'm trying not to listen, I don't want to give the man my time like that, no. It's Bhalagwe I can't get out of my mind.

I can see them huddled together, Mama Agnes and my mama, in one of the round asbestos holding sheds at Bhalagwe. I can feel their fright. They are sitting side by side. There's hardly any space to move, no way of stretching their legs. Everyone is quiet, save for the incessant sniffles, and the occasional wail, which begins as a low, long moan, rising like the crest of a wave, before it comes crashing down into silence again.

Today, the Reverend Pastor's sermon is about the Israelites and their time in Egypt. I'm trying hard not to listen, but dammit I can hear every word, so commanding is his voice, booming over us like an indictment. He swings the King James high above his head, his voice expanding into a hululu, though I'm not sure if this is meant to be a lamentation or a rejoicing.

'And therefore, the Egyptians did set over the Israelites taskmasters to afflict them with their burdens…'

'Hallelujah!' screams the captive audience.

Hallelujah, how they were afflicted, Mama Agnes and my mama, sitting side by side in that small space, my mamas past and future, bearing the torment of that place with the fortitude of dignified women; but no, no dignity for two teenage girls with only hillocks for breasts; only wide-eyed fear.

'And the Egyptians made the children of Israel serve with rigour…'

'Hameni!'

With rigour they cried, my mama and Mama Agnes, in that 12 × 6 asbestos holding shed; first, their feet touched, toes curling towards one another for comfort, and then a brush of the arms, a clasp of the hands; then sniffling, out of sync, wailing in unison.

'They made their lives bitter with hard bondage, in mortar and in brick, and in all manner of service in the field; all their service, wherein they made them serve, was with rigour…'

With rigour they made Mama Agnes dig grave after grave, day after day; with rigour my mama lay beneath Black Jesus, and also my many fathers the Men in the Red Berets; with rigour she screamed and squirmed and kicked; with rigour they thrust, with rigour they laughed. There was rigour everywhere, in every light breeze, in every grain of sand, in every blade of grass; rigour in the Bhalagwe hills walling in the concentration camp from the south; rigour in the Zamanyone hill demarcating the territory along the western edge; rigour in the crashing waters of the Antelope Dam in the east. With rigour Bhalagwe breathed, with rigour it pulsed.

'... but the people thrived, and waxed very mighty...'

'Praise Jesusi!'

And he made the detainees sing praises to his name, Black Jesus; they broke out in song, in worship they thrust; into the dark pits of Antelope Mine they were cast.

'And there went a man of the house of Levi, and took to wife a daughter of Levi. And the woman conceived, and bare a son; and when she saw him that he was a goodly child, she hid him three months...'

And there I was conceived, I, the bastard seed of the fatherland! But no, I reject all such association, I am fully repented, with the motherland I staunchly stand! Rather I be the casualty offspring of nationhood! Yes, I see her clearly in my vision, Mama Agnes. She nursed my mama through her pregnancy, gave her her measly portions of mealie-meal, which was fed to the detainees every second day, allotted her her daily half-a-cup ration of water. She was my second mama, or else I would never have seen the light of day in that Gehenna.

'And when she could no longer hide him, she took for him an ark of bulrushes, and daubed it with slime and with pitch, and put the child therein; and she laid it in the flags by the river's brink...'

'Jehovah Jireh!'

Yes, it was a Jehovah Jireh miracle that stuffed me into my uncle's backpack. I see her, Mama Agnes, angled between my mama's legs, easing me out into the world, on that fated day in '83. Oh, but why is it so dark? It's a dark world into which I come; I'm greeted by a night sky in which the moon has absconded its duties. They're behind the asbestos holding shed, Mama Agnes and my mama. Oo oO hoots an owl from a mopane tree nearby, swivelling its big head. Hearing this signal, my Uncle Fani slithers out of the bushes, backpack in hand. Mama Agnes cuts the umbilical cord, and hands me over to my uncle. Oo oO hoots the owl; ngwaa ngwaa wails baby Zamani.

Sshh! hisses my uncle, sshh sshh sshh!

But I don't sshh; it's as though I'm summoning the noose, summoning my many fathers to come and find me, and hand me over to the fate they intend for me, down the pits of Antelope Mine, where all newborn babies are thrown.

Let me see him, says my mama, let me hold him.

I can feel her grip; she holds me, raises me to her face. Her lips are moist on my forehead. See how I quieten down, see, I'm suddenly still. But he must go, my Uncle Fani; my many fathers are coming. Gently, he pries me from my mama's arms and places me inside his backpack. Off he slinks into the night.

'… And the child grew, and she brought him unto Pharaoh's daughter, and he became her son. And she called him Moses… And it came to pass in those days, when Moses was grown, that he went out unto his brethren, and looked on their burdens…'

But I've failed to live up to this lore, haven't I failed? For he confessed on his deathbed, Uncle Fani, and me, what did I do? I fled the burning bush! Fled like a namby-pamby.

She dieth behind that asbestos shed, mama, draweth her last breath on Mama Agnes's lap. And when the Egyptians, those Men in the Red Berets, findeth them, they doth slappeth Mama Agnes and spake, why have ye done this thing, and saved the man-child alive?

And she replieth, Mama Agnes, because the mother was lively, and delivered the man-child ere I come in unto her.

And thus I was saved. And thus my mama died.

Dammit, a dread creeps up on me, I can feel it. It enshrouds me, oh stop, please stop, but it won't stop, the Holy Ghost, it pounces on me, and all at once I'm spasming under its spell. I'm falling, falling, falling – it's the longest fall of my life. I come crashing down, and the floor comes crashing up; we meet each other halfway. The ground punches me in the back of my head. The world becomes a blur.

'Hallelujah!' cries the Reverend Pastor.

'Hallelujah!'

THE INVASION

After my assault by the Holy Ghost, the Reverend Pastor, asking if I was saved, proclaimed it was a sign that the Spirit was beckoning me to his church. My poor heart was trying to take flight in my chest, and my toes were tingling… was this what transcendence felt like? Was this my overcoming? Had I finally conquered that Gehenna? Mama Agnes clucked over me, getting me a glass of water, bringing me a plate of the scrumptious food brought by the Ladies of the Church, insisting on feeding me, which I enjoyed thoroughly. And though I was feeling better by this time, I pretended to faint all over again, following which she insisted that I spend the night in Bukhosi's room. She and the Reverend Pastor helped me onto my feet. I could walk perfectly well by myself, but I leaned heavily on the Reverend Pastor who, loving as he does to play the role of Father, rose to the occasion, calling me 'son' as he gripped me firmly around my waist, to which Mama Agnes said, 'Are you all right, mfanami?' (Did I enjoy having the man call me 'son'? I don't know. I felt a twinge of pleasure, that's for sure. But it's nothing compared to the thrill I have felt when my surrogate father has called me son.)

I must thank the Reverend Pastor for unwittingly bringing me and Mama Agnes closer together, for, instead of driving him home again like she did the other day – he hadn't brought his car – she elected instead to stay with me. The Reverend Pastor had to ask for a lift from one of the Ladies of the Church. Even better, when my surrogate father finally crawled home, Mama Agnes didn't hide me from him! He paused by the boy's bedroom door upon arrival, appraising me through slit-eyes. My Mama A told him in firm tones that I had been overcome by the Holy Ghost and, quite unused to its power, had fallen sick, and she was not about to leave me to die in my pygmy room. I played my part well, blinking weakly at my surrogate father, even going so far as to mumble the gibberish I have heard my Mama Agnes spout whenever she's speaking the language of the Holy Ghost, what she calls 'speaking in tongues'. My surrogate father watched me coldly. And then, he opened his mouth and began to laugh, harder and harder until he was bent double, barely able to breathe. Mama Agnes and I both reached for one another's hands at the same time. 'He's crazy,' she whispered. He lurched down the passage, still howling with laughter as we heard the front door squeak open and then slam shut, gone again into the night.

I told her I feared for Bukhosi's safety if – *when* – he came back home, and Mama Agnes, looking worried, admitted she had seen my surrogate father like that only once before. She told me about an incident that happened in November 2000, when my surrogate father came home in a jittery mood and again unleashed his belt on her. It seemed to come out of nowhere, she said, in the midst of a relatively tranquil family life. 'It turned out,' she said with a world-weary sigh, 'that it was just after he finally found out that the white farmer was his father.'

My whole body tensed – I was being let into family secrets! Of course, I had already guessed my surrogate father's patrilineage from his stories, but to hear it confirmed by my own dear Mama Agnes!

'Of course, everyone already knew,' Mama Agnes continued. 'We all knew that white farmer was his father. Everybody in the family knows, his whole village knows, I myself was told by his own mother. Heh! And can he pretend not to have known? Mccm. He knew! Deep down, he always knew. Just look at his yellow skin! He was just in denial, nje, coming here to perform for me, beating me, am I the one who said that white man should be his father?'

'How did he find out?' I asked, deflated to learn that I was probably the last to know this particular family secret. 'How did he find out that Farmer Thornton was his father?'

Here she curled her lower lip. 'He had got wind that the War Veterans were going to invade the white man's farm, and he decided he wanted it for himself. Baba's family had lived on part of the farm, before the whites came to this part of the world and kicked them off the land. So, he felt it was rightfully his, and he wanted to stake his claim before anyone else did.' She began to cackle, Mama Agnes. I had never seen her this way. 'Had he faced the truth earlier, he would have known that he had zero right to that farm. Helping the War Veterans kick his own father off the farm and then trying to claim it as his own! Ha.'

Black Jesus's continued rise to prominence must have stoked my surrogate father's anger and led him to answer the call to invade that Thornton Farm. This call followed years of disappeared dreams and disappeared monies – for like any country overbrimming with the abundance of platinum and diamonds and such like, we were vulnerable to plunder from all and sundry (especially our own, like our Minister of Mines the Hon. Mvelaphi Mpofu, once upon a time The Rebel in a Césaire play in a long-ago life). And in the early 2000s, with the birth of a new opposition party, with a robust urban following that threatened to topple from power our fossilized leaders, our government, under the one true leading party of the nation, began to crack down on our TV viewing and the whole of our cultural life. Gone from our screens was the fatty diet of American movies and TV shows that every urban kid gorged on! No more Friday night sitcoms! No more *Oprah* for poor Mama Agnes! They were all banished from our screens, the heroes and superheroes, stars and superstars, everything that our Minister of Propaganda deemed the world-wide domination and glorification of Western egotism.

Next, following an alarming defeat in the Constitutional Referendum that had been put to a vote to The People, said defeat of the ruling party which bolstered the opposition, our government declared a War on Terror, with us zombie, TV-watching urbanites as the recognized threats, and called upon the ruralites to action-pack the white-owned farms and take back the land By Any Means Necessary.

I can imagine my surrogate father eagerly answering this call after learning that the Thornton Farm was one of the farms the War Veterans intended to take back By Any Means Necessary. I can see how he would want to stake his claim, especially since deep down he knew that Farmer Thornton was his father. The state of things in our country, especially after 2000, when our government started controlling every facet of our lives, including what part of our history to remember and what part to forget, is proof that it's not what's true that matters, but what you can make true. He, Abednego, was only living out this reality. Had he managed to lay claim to the farm in Baba's name, this, then, would have become his official history, this and not his Thornton patrilineage; he would have had concrete proof that he was Baba's son, via the act of publicly reclaiming Baba's ancestral land, the kind of proof that could be officialized and concretized through inscription, through official lease deeds and other such documentation.

My surrogate father, like me, was only trying to reinvent himself.

I can picture him lurching into the Thornton Farm at the back of one of those government-sponsored War Veterans trucks, catching his breath as the farm comes into view, set on the brae of the Dongamuzi Mountain, the bushveld scrambling up its incline, its igneous blades ruffled by a doting breeze, just like all those years ago he told me about when he first brought my Thandi to his village.

There would have been a ZBC TV crew to film the whole thing. Who hasn't seen those angry War Veterans and self-proclaimed War Veterans on TV ringed around the white farms? Who hasn't seen them banging on the doors of the white farmhouses?

'We are taking over this farm!'

'Get out, you colonial imperialist!'

'Get off our land!'

'Get out or we will burn this whole place down!'

'Get out or we will set fire to your crops!'

'Get out or we will set fire to your house!'

My surrogate father would have been shouting the loudest, because of course he had something to prove, to everyone but especially to himself.

'But how did he find out that the farmer was his father?' I asked Mama Agnes.

'Was there anything to find out?' she replied. 'Eh. Apparently, he found his mother there, at the farm. He had helped to kick down the door, and found his own mother behind it. Yes, she was living with the white man. Her thing with him had been going on for years – over ten years, in fact. The story is that after the white man's wife died – raped and murdered by some monster, poor thing – she began to take on with him. Heh! Imagine, the scandal of it! Busy over there in the big house! Me, I say good for her, she was moving up in the world and she didn't care who said what. But you know, Abed says he didn't know, or didn't want to know, because he never went to his village, you know, he has never even taken me there, he refuses to go, so I don't even know what he was doing there busy invading the white man's farm. She's the one who told him, when he tried to take the farm, that he was stealing from his own father. Heh! Where have you ever heard of such a thing?'

I imagine my surrogate father pushed back when his mother tried to tell him that the farmer was his father. I can see them in the lounge, him and Farmer Thornton, my surrogate grandpa. I can hear the War Veterans and self-proclaimed War Veterans already running through the arteries of the house, chasing down the house staff, staking claims to rooms, claiming valuables. But this confrontation would have happened alone. My surrogate grandpa seated in the gloom, on a deep, padded chair in the corner by the unlit fireplace, surrounded by his memorabilia, photos of his Sonny Boy First Generation standing proud and tall next to the Honourable Prime Minister of former Rhodesia, Ian Smith, in the uniform of Deputy Commander of the Independent Company Rhodesia Regiment, showing all of his teeth to the camera. On his lap is one of my surrogate grandma's Kango cups. My surrogate father sees the Kango cup, squints at its chipped, yellow enamel body, and recognizes it as belonging to his mother. He starts, at the sight of the farmer with his mother's Kango, the farmer he last saw some two decades ago, when he was here last and did what he did and vowed never to come back. Would this be a moment of compunction? Would he look involuntarily out the window, his stomach lurching at the memory of what he did to Mrs Thornton in this very house? Would he be pulled towards his Baba's homestead, desire to see how the mopane tree where he had buried my inamorata and the charred bones and his baby was doing? Would this moment, with the Kango on the farmer's lap, the sound of his mama's footsteps hurrying down the stairs leading into the lounge, the thud-thud of her feet calling him back to his childhood, the farmer thrashing his brother meanwhile giving him a wedge of watermelon, knowing it's his mother even before he turns around; would this be the moment of deepest regret? Asking himself why he had come back? Unwilling to face hi-story. Unable. Having run for so long from it all. For he's a man who has always run, my surrogate father, that's the one constant in his past; that's what he knows how to do best.

My surrogate grandpa raises his eyes, their once vivacious emerald now filmy and moist. They settle on my surrogate father. He parts his old-man lips to reveal a loose set of dentures.

'My son,' he croaks.

My surrogate father jumps, as though he's just heard a shot fired.

'My son!' he repeats, his voice stronger this time.

Winces as though he's been shot.

'My son!' comes the answering voice of his mother, stepping into the lounge as if it were her house.

Watching her come down the stairs as though she were the madam of the house, a madam and not a mistress, would have made my surrogate father nauseous. He would have finally admitted to himself, then, what he had always known. He would have acknowledged, perhaps for the first time, his teardrop nostrils replicated on the farmer's face, his second Bukhosi's emerald eyes swimming in that watery film. I can imagine the anguish he felt; I too have lived through the dread of the glint of recognition.

Of having to stare into a face and be faced with the truth of your own face.

'Mama!' he says, pushing her away as she tries to embrace him. 'Ma? What is this, what is going on, what is happening?'

'You've always known,' she says, looking at him in a way that makes him want to bury his head in the soil. 'You knew. Your yellow skin—'

'I got it from my Indian great-great-great-great-grandma who had white blood…'

'My son!' croaks my surrogate grandpa.

'I'm not your boy, you hear, this is not Rhodesia any more, we're in Zimbabwe now, this is Zimbabwe!'

'… my son…'

'You crazy old fool! I'm not—'

'He's your blood, my son.'

After Mama Agnes had left, switching the light out after her, I ducked under the covers of Bukhosi's bed and went online on my Nokia to reread a post I've brushed over before on the farmer's blog, about 'a new flame' he rediscovered after the war, 'the love that dared not speak its name finally being able to speak proudly in this new Zimbabwe', his 'grief at the loss of his Ennis soothed by the gain of this other'. I hadn't paid much attention to it then, assuming he had fallen in love with some other white woman after Mrs Thornton's brutal murder. But now, having heard that my surrogate grandma had moved in with the farmer…!

I wish I had the juicy details of that amorous affair. I have only these oblique references on the farmer's blog. I imagine they met at a spot that had not been named but had been arrived at through a tacit understanding, as is the way of rural encounters. Would it have been the same spot where they used to meet all those years ago while my surrogate-surrogate grandfather was away in the Second World War fighting for King George VI? The perfect place to rekindle old memories! My surrogate grandma wouldn't have looked the farmer in the eye, no, that was not how rural women behaved. She would have angled her gaze deliberately away from his, perhaps somewhere just above his head, enough to keep track of his movements without having to look him straight in the eye. Was he taken by her attire? She wouldn't have worn the usual rural clothes to meet up with a man she wished to impress, no, none of those long, shapeless skirts that flow all the way down to the ankles, with nothing exciting to show off, neither shapely behind nor curvaceous hip. She would have met up with him in something that flattered her figure, like a knee-length, African print dress, even taking care to oil her hair and tie it back, instead of wearing a doek, which wouldn't at all have been becoming. I imagine her Vaselined face glistening like a mature gingerbread baked to perfection, and as my surrogate grandpa beheld her he silently asked his Ennis to forgive him.

She would have needed some convincing before finally accompanying him to his farm. Rural women aren't forward like these town ones whom you can proposition and lay with on the same day without even knowing their names. No, she would have played it coy, protesting even as she finally climbed into his truck.

And what about my surrogate grandpa? He would have eventually invited her to move in with him. But she wouldn't have done it immediately, no, even though the land around her had been watered by the blood of her husband; mulched by the bones of her grandchild. She would have moved out of Baba's homestead gradually, bit by bit, first taking this and then that, leaving a dress at the farm, and then maybe a cup, some plates, and before long, a whole suitcase. This would have pleased my surrogate grandpa, to have his amour living with him, to be able to live with her freely in a new Zimbabwe, although I'm sure village gobs gabbed, as village gobs are wont to do. And then, perhaps, once in a while, he would visit Mrs Thornton and his first Sonny Boy and his forebears at the bottom of his fields and prattle on about the days of yesteryear, when this country was still theirs. And afterwards, he'd sit with my surrogate grandma in his lounge in the dark enjoying her company and they would talk about their future in this new country that now belonged to her and her people, that perhaps belonged to him too, that, perhaps, could belong to them both.

Farmer Thornton, though he mentions neither my surrogate father nor his mother by name, writes bitterly, on his blog, about being kicked off his land in his beloved Zimbabwe. He professes, at the same time, to have loved Rhodesia. To have loved what it stood for. At least then they had had a place they could call home, he writes. Before the munts came and destroyed everything they had worked so hard to build! They just woke up one day in 1980 and it was all gone. It didn't go to the marauding veterans who evicted them that grim day in 2000, oh no, but to a fat-cat minister who added the farm to his personal collection of three others. Three! And *they* were the ones accused of greed? They weren't allowed to cry, weren't allowed to grieve for their home, to at least say goodbye. Go back to Britain, they said! What did he have in Britain? Living now as he was in a council flat in Yorkshire with his Sonny Boy, who was reduced to working the till at Marks & Spencer? *He was not British!* Everything he had was back in his beloved Zimbabwe! Everything, his life, his hard work; the munts had stolen everything from him! (O surrogate grandpapa! How I wish you would stop calling us munts! You did, after all, fall in love with one of us!)

THE REVEREND PASTOR

It has been seven dreadful days, during which I had to record events by hand in an A4 exercise book, in my ugly handwriting that brings back terrifying memories of my grade one teacher, Mrs Moyo, who used to rap me on my knuckles with a ruler whenever I didn't shape the letters of the alphabet correctly or, worse, got my English spelling wrong, yelling all the while that I was a savage, did I want to be associated with the savages, heh, who couldn't write properly? Was I a human being or was I a savage? Human being, I would answer timidly, my voice shaking, to which she would say no, I was a savage, because look at the nonsense I was writing! I have been reduced to such crudities, this scribbling by hand, having to be insulted by my own handwriting, without the delight of beholding my neat Times New Roman 12-point font on the sleek screen of my Mac, the most pleasing evidence of my progress in the world, far away from the triggering memories of my grade one class. All of this because that Reverend Nobody forcibly took away my laptop seven days ago and gave it to his IT guys.

I have got my laptop back, thankfully, and now I can continue, with the help of my handwritten notes, recording my chronicles and inscribing everything I have missed. But I shouldn't skip the order of things; I shall relate events as they happened, as I have scribbled them these past six days in my exercise book.

It all started the morning after my assault by the Holy Ghost. I woke up quite auspiciously to a bright Tuesday sun shining all over my face, my Mama A leaning over me, swinging open the window to let in some air.

'Each time I come in here, it's just,' she said. 'It's like I'm going to see him, lying in bed as you are now…' She sighed and tried to brighten up. 'And how are you feeling this morning? Better?'

'My head hurts,' I lied.

'Oh, you nanaza! Why don't you lie down a little longer? Maybe I should call the Reverend Pastor to come and pray for you…'

'No, no, no, I mean…' I put on a smile. 'I think I'll be fine after a few more hours' sleep.'

'All right!' (She did call the Reverend Pastor, though…) 'Are you hungry, would you like something to eat?'

'Yes,' I said. 'I miss your scrambled eggs, Ma, the ones you cook with milk and margarine. That and toast.'

'Bukhosi's favourite!'

Yes, I knew.

'Really, Ma?' I said, laughing. 'I didn't know!'

She paused by the door, surveying the boy's pile of dirty clothes beneath the posters of Beyoncé and Kanye West. Then she bent and picked up a lime-green sports shirt, ruffling the Nike tick on the left breast as she brought the shirt to her nose. She closed her eyes and inhaled. 'He loved this shirt,' she said. 'He was always wearing it! Sometimes without even having it washed, can you imagine?'

'Everything is going to be all right, Ma. He's going to come back to us by Christmas. He just needs some time away from Father. You know how sons can be at a certain age.'

Later that morning, having had my fill of Mama Agnes's fluffy scrambled eggs and perfectly toasted toast, I woke up reluctantly to go back to my pygmy room. As I left, I bent, picked up the lime sports shirt lying atop the pile of dirty clothes, scrunched it up and stuffed it into my trousers.

I had just stashed it among my own clothes when the Reverend Pastor arrived. Things started amicably enough. I came out to greet him, and Mama Agnes found us chatting outside my pygmy room, the Reverend Pastor talking me through a brochure from his church that explained how to answer the call of the Holy Ghost. I indulged him, and would have been happy to continue indulging him had he not started talking about Bukhosi. He began by asking, casually enough, whether the boy had finally called Aunt Nto. When Mama Agnes said he hadn't, the Reverend Pastor turned to me, eyebrows raised, and then asked for the boy's South African phone number, whipping out his BlackBerry, ready to punch the keys.

'I don't have it,' I said weakly, already sensing what was to come.

The man looked up at me sharply. 'What do you mean, you don't have it?'

I tried to shrug like it was nothing. 'We communicate through Facebook.' And then, because he was still looking at me in a funny way, 'It's a young people's thing, you wouldn't understand.'

'All right, give me his friends' phone numbers, then.'

'What?'

'His friends. You told Mama Agnes Bukhosi is staying with friends in South Africa.'

'He's the one who told me he's staying with friends,' I said evenly.

'OK. What's their number, we can call them right now.'

'I don't have their number.'

By now, Mama Agnes had sort of moved away from me, and was standing quite still, beside the Reverend Pastor, looking from one to the other as we spoke.

The Reverend Pastor slapped his forehead. 'OK, let me get this straight. You don't have Bukhosi's phone number, or any of the numbers of the friends he is staying with.'

'That's right,' I said, my face beginning to break open in what I hoped was an encouraging smile, the kind that didn't say, 'Phew!', but rather said, 'Finally, you are catching on!'

'OK, give me the address of where he's staying, I'll get someone to go and check on him.'

'I don't have an address,' I muttered, my smile disappearing.

The man shook his head. 'That's it, give me your laptop.'

'What?'

'Something's not right here. The boy hasn't bothered to get in touch with Aunt Nto and the family is worried sick, his mother here can't even sleep. Boys dzangu will have the address in no time, and we'll be able to get someone to check on him.'

I turned away from the fly, to address Mama Agnes. 'Do you want the boy to disappear again—'

'Iwe, why don't you want to hand over your laptop?' he buzzed before she could answer. 'We're all on the same team here, finding the boy is top priority. I'm not interested in anything on your computer except locating the boy, whatever you have in there is safe. Now, hand it over, mhani, I have people waiting for me at church.'

'I really don't think—'

The man swatted me out of the way, like *I* was a fly, and barged into my lodgings. I stormed in after him, trying to block him from going through my things, yelling that his bullying tactics would scare the boy away, the boy was communicating to the family through me, the boy trusted me, the boy was all right, this was illegal, would he put my laptop down, put it down—

He pushed me to one side and stepped out of my pygmy room, one hand clutching my Mac. I followed him out, shouting still, but no longer daring to try and wrangle my machine from him, already sensing that it would be of no use. He was taller and bulkier than I and had already manhandled me without any problem. He spoke to me as though speaking to an irrational child, assuring me in soothing tones that I would have my laptop back by the end of the day. Then he placed his free hand on Mama Agnes's shoulder, reassured her everything would be all right, he would locate Bukhosi in no time, and with that, turned and walked away. I watched him climb into his Mercedes Benz, at which point I began shouting at him to take my laptop – even though he had already taken it – he should take it, take it and let us see, take it!

When I spun around, practically in tears now, I found Mama Agnes gaping at me. I cannot describe the look on her face. I have never seen that look before, not even when she told me about my surrogate father's most despicable acts. I knew, then, that if I didn't get rid of this Reverend Nobody, and fast, my days with the Mlambos, my dreams of becoming their son, my whole project of self-reinvention and thus the felicitious future I was trying to shape for myself, away from the shackles of the past, would all come to a painful, disastrous, irreparable end.

As soon as he left, I logged onto Facebook via my Nokia and deleted all of the boy's fake messages. Believing the problem solved, I concentrated on the bigger issue of how I would rid myself of our holy man. I consulted my Red Album, leafing through the photos, staring into those beguiling eyes. The longer I stared, the more an intense rage bubbled in me. But I was not a killer, no. I may have had fantasies of squishing the fly, but I doubted that when push came to shove, I would have the stomach for it. Killing the fly would only destroy my project of reinvention in another more subtle way; it would confirm to me the very thing I was trying most to avoid, that I was like Black Jesus, that I could not escape my patrilineage, and all the work I had so far done to fashion myself into somebody else, somebody new, somebody better that the Mlambos could love, that I could live with, would be nullified. I was not about to cut off my foot and give over my whole body to gangrene.

I needed an elegant solution.

I set about writing down, by hand, begrudgingly, what I knew about the Reverend Pastor, trying to remember if there was any crucial titbit about him I may have missed. I hadn't paid him any mind the first time I met him. He hadn't seemed important to our lives then. I should have paid attention! It was the Sunday after Bukhosi disappeared, when I accompanied Mama Agnes to the Blessed Anointings morning service, tacking up missing posters of the boy along the way.

HAVE YOU SEEN THIS BOY?

BELOVED SON MISSING.

We tacked him onto street photos, around the City Council bins, on the walls of the *Chronicle* offices, on top of the life-size cutout of the commie-thwacking Rambo displayed outside the Vine Cinema, and on the windows of the Columbia Night Club, glinting at us in all its pure-liberal strobe-lit glory. We tacked him on the walls of the Buscod Supermarket, where I paused to savour the aroma of blooma bread coming from inside. My tummy began to groan. Blooma bread is the most tasteless tasting bread I have ever tasted, with no yeast no sugar no cooking oil no butter nothing, and sometimes only a little salt, but at that moment, I would have sold my soul to the devil for just one bite. But alas, the devil was off that day, he had gone to church to sing Hallelujah with the other angels. My eyes followed the rod of sunlight slithering through the restless crowd blocking the entrance of the supermarket. I looked up and saw Mama Agnes glaring at me, and quickly turned and followed her into the Marion Court Building next door. Off we clattered, up the steps, to Blessed Anointings on the second floor.

The service was already in full swing when we arrived; Formica chairs faced the makeshift stage, and a banner that read 'PRAIZE JESUS HAMENI HALLELUJAH' was draped across the exposed beams of the ceiling above the altar.

Mama Agnes made us waddle all the way to the third row, which would afford her a privileged view of the Reverend Pastor.

'*Glory glory!*' she screeched, in tandem with the choir, clinging to the faces of Bukhosi. *Glory glory* we sang, and the House of the Lord tromboned, the angels came down and gave us a Hallelujah, we gave them an Amen, but they weren't satisfied and trilled Haaaalleeeeluuuujah, and we were electrified and cheeped Haaaaaaameni bo God is Goooooood, and that was good, and we were good, and all was good, and the good Reverend Pastor galloped down the centre aisle and gambolled onto the makeshift stage. We clapped Hallelujah and he bowed Amen.

He tinkered with his laptop, balanced on the podium, and cleared his throat:

'*Boom boom*, is that the sound of a soul tripping?' He cupped his ear. 'A piece of heart sticking onto a piece of paper? A bit of thought left over to dry on a page? You wander the corridors of your mind like a vagabond on Robert Mugabe Way, two cheeks smacking the truth from your buttocks, that truth running like the lies from your mouth, your heart implodes and thought explodes—'

'Bukhosi!' yelled Mama Agnes.

'*Boom boom!*'

'*Boom boom* your back sags because your heart has so much to carry, tuck in a loaf a half pint and a bag of sugar, add some flimsy bearer's cheques to that mess why don't you, all borrowed from that old woman from next door, who wipes from her brow the sweat of her children yes them, them nurses them nannies them bum-wipers yes them, them pounding the pounds in the UK yes them, there is so much to carry there is too much to carry, so much so that you forget what you are carrying, so much so that you forget what you shouldn't be carrying, and now you carry everything and forget where you are going.'

'Bukhosi—'

'*Boom boom!*'

'*Boom boom* you stand in queues all day waiting for something to happen, in the end you forget what it is you are waiting for, listen as you say, *Oh oh oh look at what Mugabe has done*, and then you are laughing like Mugabe is the funniest man, listen as you say:

'*Yo hayi ah shuwa look at the price of everything going up all the time how are we gonna survive how are we gonna survive hayi ah shuwa sesidiniwe we are tired*

'*At least the opposition can do us better*

'*The opposition is a puppet of the West you woman you don't be stupid Zimbabwe shall never be a colony again*

'*Well we suffered then we are suffering now*

'*Not to worry we have our angel Robert Gabriel*

'"*Blair keep your England and let me keep my Zimbabwe.*".'

'BUKHOSI—'

'Boom boom!'

'Boom boom you laugh at yourself at the irony of your suffering, garbled sounds escaping from mangled throats, thus the chaos from without has been taken, ripped apart and sewn back together, uglier now than it was before, tattering already at the seams. But the chaos within ferments and if someone were to ask you would not be able to explain why, all you know is that something rots from within. Something rots within because the things of this world rot within, I say something rots within because the things of this world rot within, I say the things of this world rot, I say give me a Ha-le-llluuuu-jaaaaah-Amen!'

'Hallelujah-Amen!'

'I can't hear you!'

'Hallelujah-Amen!'

'Jesus can't hear you!'

'Hallelujah-AMEN!'

'Yessus!!! Jesu-Christu-amen.'

'BUKHOSI!'

The Reverend Pastor's sermon was interrupted by a truck that had pulled up outside Buscod Supermarket next door, its back laden with mealie-meal and sugar and cooking oil. I joined those who were watching the commotion below from the windows; a manic crowd was descending upon the truck. I shilly-shallied, but only for a moment, casting Mama Agnes a sheepish smile as I gathered my belongings and followed the sinners who were already shuffling out.

For all my shoving and elbowing in that crowd, I didn't manage to get any blooma bread or mealie-meal or sugar or cooking oil, although I did earn myself plenty of bruises. When I went back into the church, Mama Agnes had already disappeared with the Reverend Pastor, probably off to the Mguza River to collect holy water. Collecting holy water by the river… By the river they first lay. (She, recounting their tryst all those years ago by the Mpopoma River with such amorousness, eyes aglitter, bosom aflutter, forgetting conveniently how the man had taken advantage of her, how instead of renouncing his priesthood and marrying her, he had left her crying a river.) Would my Mama Agnes dare to…? She would never… Would she?

I admit I was a little angry with Mama Agnes, angry at myself but angry at her too, for falling for the Reverend Pastor's charms, for being someone he could so easily turn against me, even after the work we had both done to build the foundations of our budding relationship. The idea of her having such a weakness thrilled me, for it would be something I could hold over her, she who was holier than thou. But more than delighted, it would make me sad, because then our relationship would not be built on love, as I had been trying so hard to do, to win her over and gain her affection; it would be predicated on fear. How far could that take me?

Anyway, all of this was speculation at this point, and I really was grasping at straws, but one thing was evident, from what Mama Agnes had told me about the Reverend Pastor and from the reasons he had been excommunicated from the Catholic order: the man had a weakness for the skirt. Such a defect, starting all the way back from his youth, surpassing even his love for God during his days as a priest, was surely chronic.

I hoped.

The pattern was there, wasn't it?

It was so easy that I was almost disappointed in him. A nemesis is only valued as a nemesis if they are our equal; and it was hard to consider the Reverend Pastor an equal when, after only seven days, I wandered into his office at Blessed Anointings to find him between Sister Gertrude's legs, Sister Gertrude who was spreadeagled across his desk like a chicken offering itself for the plucking. (Ha! The man's affliction is more serious than I thought. He needs a dose of the marathon prayers he is always performing for his congregants. He he he!) At first, they didn't see me, so engrossed were they in their ardour. I retrieved my Nokia from my pocket, angled it at them and began to take photos. By this point, Sister Gertrude must have clocked me, because she began to moan theatrically, like a brothel-queen, quite unbecoming for a Sister, but very good for the camera. The Reverend Pastor, taking her moans for encouragement, thrust between her legs with renewed vigour.

I couldn't help it; I started laughing.

His head snapped up. Yes, I wanted him to see me. I wanted him to see that I had seen him. He leapt off Sister Gertrude, bumping into the chair behind him, his hands covering his rod of iron. Sister Gertrude groped to pull him back to her. 'Deliver me, Pastor… Deliver me!' She was earning her money.

I smiled. 'Say "cheese."'

I snapped another shot of them both, his hands raised, like someone had shouted, 'Freeze!', Sister Gertrude squashing her breasts to her bosom. I winked at him. And then I spun on my heel and walked out the door, leaving it ajar. I could hear him calling after me.

'Zamani! Wai – Zamani!'

It felt so good to hear someone call my name with such yearning.

■

I found it quite ironic when I walked into town six days ago that it was I who was now seeking out a brothel, an indictment for which I had only been too willing to crucify my surrogate father some weeks before when I had suspected him of such slutty business. The place was as dingy as a brothel can get, squashed between a night club and a bar, on Fourteenth Avenue. It was narrow, and surprisingly packed for a Wednesday night, with a bar to the right, and a string of chairs without tables to the left, and a narrow walkway in between. The lighting was poor. The air was rancid, thick with all sorts of odours; the creamy smells of pudenda, of coitus, of used rubber.

The moment I entered, I was accosted by several women, each murmuring what they could do for me, demanding that I do things to them, throwing out prices like market dealers. I tried to extricate myself, murmuring that I was unavailable, to which they protested. I squinted at them to see if any one of them was what I was looking for. I felt a hand grab my property, then, quite possessively, at that, and, upon finding me limp and unexcited, it began to rub me, slowly at first and then, finding me not only unexcited but unexcitable, with vigorous professionalism. Oh, the poor strumpet! If only she knew that nothing short of a handsome maturity would do it for me, nothing but the umber face and lilting voice of my inamorata-turned-succubus as I had imagined her during my surrogate father's telling! Nothing else could excite me, not her pair of voluptuous breasts, the nipples hard against her see-through blouse; not the supple curve of her youthful hips; her alluring eyes flutter-fluttering, her ruby lips parted, the tip of her tongue visible. Not for me, not for me, no one but my Thandi would do for me!

It was in this way that I met Sister Gertrude, or Getty, as she introduced herself to me, rubbing my property and then, when it became evident that I was immune to her charms, quite aggressively, with impressive determination. It was this that made me pick her. Lifting her hand from my groin, I pulled her away from her brothel-sisters, and asked her where we could go to be alone. This seemed to please her, and she led me away triumphantly, pulling me by my belt, swinging her hips in exaggerated movements, no doubt a victory walk for her sisters, but also for my benefit; a worthy show, I admit, but totally wasted on me.

She took us to one of the brothel's back rooms, which had just enough space for a single bed and a chair. I asked her to switch on the light, to which she obliged, murmuring, 'Oh, you are one of those who likes to see, heh.'

Under the bulb light, I could see that she was older than she had first seemed in the dim lighting up front, probably closer to thirty than twenty. Good; I would need experience on my side, I thought, that and charm, and determination, and prowess. She had so far exhibited the first three. She began to slip out of her see-through blouse and belt-skirt, her smile coquettish, her eyes no longer alluring now but quite calculating as she took me in, sitting not on the bed, but the chair.

'What would you want?' she asked, dropping the coquettish voice.

'I'd like to get down to some real business,' I replied, pulling out a thick wad of notes.

He had to be stopped, you see. First, Mama Agnes told my surrogate father about my altercation with the Reverend Pastor. The man stormed into my pygmy room on Wednesday morning, yelling at me to get up and get out. He had been watching me, he said, he had known all along something was up, and now he knew what it was. I didn't want the family to know where Bukhosi was because I was helping him with this girl of his he had run off to. Was she pregnant, was that it? I had to stop listening to the boy, stop protecting him and listen to *him*, Abednego! He was the parent, he had a right to know where his son was. I wanted to deprive him of the chance to make things right with the boy, didn't I?

I knew Mama Agnes could hear him from inside the house, and I hoped she would come out and defend me. But she didn't, and that was when I knew the Reverend Pastor was finally getting to her.

My first instinct was to give my surrogate father some ubuvimbo. I hissed at him to lower his voice, ready to retrieve the root powder, but this only made him yell louder, and I was afraid to give it to him right there, what with him acting out and Mama Agnes in the house. I yelled, for Mama Agnes's benefit, that I was hurt (which I was, his acrimony hurt me very much, especially the way he was kicking me out like I was a dog. Did I mean absolutely nothing to him? We'd been through so much together. He was only speaking out of anger, I know that, he was angry, and he was hurt, but so was I!). I was hurt by his words, I shouted, especially after all I had done to convince the boy to come back. It had been his fault that the boy had left in the first place, and now he was taking out his failings on me.

This didn't deter him, but only made him angrier. He began to fling my clothes out of the pygmy room, shouting that I was a menace and I would leave his house if he had to drag me out himself.

'All right, I'll leave,' I hissed, so Mama A wouldn't hear us. 'But not before I tell Ma what you did to Mrs Thornton. Yes, I'm going to tell Ma, and I'm going to tell Farmer Thornton, and I'm going to tell everybody. I'm going to tell Bukhosi, too. Yes, I'll write to him and tell him.'

The man froze. I could see him practically shrinking. I hated it, having to do that to him. I was surprised to feel these things! Yes, I had grown to care for him, in spite of myself, in spite of everything he was and had done, and I didn't want to see him hurt. These were frightening emotions, threatening to overwhelm me, I didn't know what to do with them, but I could sense their minatory power, how they could derail my carefully calibrated plans.

He dropped the boy's Nike shirt, which he was holding, ready to fling out with the rest of my things, and shambled out of my pygmy room, suddenly an old, crumpled man. I watched him go, watched him trudge into the house and disappear in there, not even bothering to shut the door. I stood there for a while, my chest heaving. Finally, I gathered my things, which were flapping about in the backyard where he had flung them, and put them back in my pygmy room.

I went to see the Reverend Pastor later that afternoon, after his lunchtime service, to find out how far he was with his machinations, and was happy to learn that his IT guys had had a glitch while trying to retrieve the FB messages; they couldn't seem to find them, he said, eyeing me with suspicion, at least that's what I thought it was. I was sick with worry, feeling at any moment as though I would throw up. I began to shout, my voice cracking, asking him what kind of amateurs these IT guys of his were, it had already been a day and still I hadn't got my laptop back, and I wanted it, it was mine. None of my shouting helped; the fly simply would not give the laptop back, declaring that he would discover the boy's location. The more I shouted, the more obstinate he became, and I realized that he, like my surrogate father and perhaps now my Mama Agnes, believed I knew where the boy was but didn't want to give up his location.

With each passing day, I felt the Reverend Pastor and his IT guys closing in on me on one end, and the acrimony of my surrogate family pushing me away on the other. I couldn't sleep, feeling quite ill, and couldn't bring myself to face my surrogate father but especially Mama Agnes. And so, I badgered poor Sister Gertrude, resorting to pleas and threats, anything I thought could make her work faster.

It was three days ago, on Saturday evening, that I received a text from her telling me that she had finally had a meeting with the Reverend Pastor, and she had 'made progress'; she would be seeing him again at his offices on Monday after the evening service.

It was the perfect honey trap for a man with a weakness for sweetness. I was right to trust the man's hi-story with women. Did that Reverend Nobody really think he could take me on? Did he really think he could come out as the hero in all of this, mooching off my hard work, destroying my relations with my surrogate family?

BOOK THREE

UNCLE FANI'S HOUSE

I feel myself changing, undergoing hydrolysis – for the body is but a land mass steeped in seventy per cent water – darkening as I come into contact with hi-story's iron particles, cleaving my being from the present to form new bonds with the past. Perhaps I shall succeed in saying of the past, 'Thus I willed it.' Perhaps it is yet to do a number on me, denying me the pleasure of becoming a self-made man, one who has transcended hi-story and got hold of the present, and is thus able to rule the future.

I've been trying to understand why I find myself here today, as the man that I am, a man wrestling with that fiction of many versions, hi-story. It is through hi-story's shadow that we conquer the past, this past in which nothing can live but from which everything springs.

When I returned from my travels abroad earlier this year, in February, I found the country living in hi-story. Everywhere, odes to the past were being composed, sung, recited; here, the past lived more vividly than the present, for there was no future that could be seen, no future to be imagined. Each time somebody important, like Uncle Zacchaeus, tried to talk about the future, they quickly became part of the past, in this way encouraging us to always look back.

I, too, feeling this strong pull of the past when I returned home, went in search of mine; first to Tshipisane, the village where my mama and my family come from, with the hope, quite an illogical hope, now that I look back – like Trymore – of finding their remains so as to give them a proper burial. I was refused access to enter Antelope Mine by a pudgy, self-important guard, where I had hoped to uncover what had once been Bhalagwe. The landscape was dry and unyielding, scattered with several markings of mass graves, in the form of rushes placed over an area or branches boxing in a piece of the ground. None of the graves were labelled, and it was only thanks to the locals that I was able to identify them for what they were. Whenever I mentioned that word, Gukurahundi, though, I was met with shakes and fears, trembling, blubbering, and advised to leave the area immediately.

This one word, *Gukurahundi*, you only have to say it slowly, in order to understand its weight:

Gu – that's a hard g, like *go* – and I can imagine her, my mama, as she went, bundled into the back of a truck as a teenage girl with those, like Mama Agnes, from neighbouring villages, my Uncle Fani by her side, my Cousin Khohlwa with them, bundled by the Men in the Red Berets, with Black Jesus leading the charge.

Ku – a hard k, like *Kool-Aid* – and the truck took flight into the night, swallowed whole by the darkness, headed for that death camp Bhalagwe, near Antelope Mine fifty-six kilometres north-east of Bulawayo. In the back, my mama sat huddled in the arms of another young girl, bouncing rickety-kickety-bounce as the truck lurched across dirt roads.

Ra – a rumble, like *run* – and the Men in the Red Berets watched, laughing, as the villagers leapt off the truck once it eased to a halt at Bhalagwe, leapt and ran, running for their lives, running to God knows where, for they were trapped from all sides, there was nowhere to flee.

Hu – a huff, like *human* – and he called my mama, Black Jesus, called her into his bunker, where he made her take off her clothes and appraised her supple, teenage body, her small breasts, big nipples, tiny waist and wide hips, the jet-black curls of her pubis. My mama stared at the floor and tried to cover her nakedness.

Ndi – a tender n, pronounced with the tongue tapping against the soft inner palate of the mouth, followed by a hard d, like *ndy, handy* – he ordered her to lie down and took her on the hard, cold cement floor. Afterwards, the Men in the Red Berets had a go too; they, my many fathers who later tried to smother my provinciality. At night, she would clutch her growing belly, my mama, clutch it and cry.

I, of course, have no way of verifying any of this. It is only through many-an-afternoon spent sniffing about in the National Archives, many-an-evening hunched over my MacBook reading this and that article online, many-a-morning flap-flapping through newspapers at *The Chronicle* in mid-town Bulawayo, many-a-sleepless-night at Dumo's sunny flat in London, and perhaps the evidence of a mirror reflecting the telltale features of my face back to me, that I have been able to get but a blur of what hi-story hides in the shadows.

Gukurahundi: the early rain that washes away the chaff before the spring shoots. They washed her away, my mama, threw her body in one of the many mass graves. She was the chaff and I am the spring shoots.

▪

So.

I returned to Bulawayo, the same city I had fled five years before, after Uncle Fani's death. I had forgotten just how gorgeous the city is! I walked for hours on end, feeling at once surreal and substantial, enjoying the wide thoroughfares, the sense of breadth and the flamboyant trees gracing the sides of the roads, how the buildings did not block out the glare of the sun. I had forgotten what it was like. Blackness pulsated around me, so unconsciously going about the business of living; men about Dumo's age looking quite frumpy with their bellies hanging over their trousers, the women looking deliberately motherly in their modest floral dresses and retro perms, the young people cosmopolitan in their jeans and tank tops and NYC caps worn slanting to the side. Something was bursting inside me as I threaded through the crowds, brushing against a mélange of umber, tawny, walnut, coffee, caramel, hickory and carob hued skins teeming in the never-ending queues outside CABS bank on the corner of Jason Moyo and Seventh, stretching all the way around the block to intersect with a rowdy queue outside the Baker's Inn at the corner of Jason Moyo and Eighth. Such noise! A cacophony of babbling, laughing, arguing and animated shouting that made me chuckle.

And there, diagonally across from the corner of Eighth and Fife, was that haunt of my teens, Haddon & Sly, outside which we boys would hang out after school, waiting to accost the girls from Townsend High as they alighted in the City Hall Square across the road. The H & S was still pasted on the off-white building in cerulean blue; it was reminiscent of the British high street shops I had spent the past five years wandering among in London, and, like many of Bulawayo's Victorian buildings, gave the city a historic Sussexy-feel, leaving no question about its colonial past.

The past was an overpowering presence, too present and not past, as it should have been, cannibalizing our present, mutating our future.

It was when I alighted from the khombi in Luveve 5 that the nostalgia hit me proper. I dragged my feet wistfully in the dust, past the colourful houses with their satellite dishes angled on their roofs like fascinator headpieces, huddled together as though for comfort. You would think nostalgia is a beautiful thing, but not for me, no. I had never felt such emptiness! Such anguish! It was as though my whole childhood had been a lie; I, myself, was a walking lie.

It shocked me to realize how much things had changed, inside me but also outside; I gaped at the potholes gaping in the streets; at the daylight all shimmery-slippery, rippling across the varooming metal bumper to bumper in the fuel queues.

I wanted to weep.

It was in this state that I found the Mlambos living in my Uncle Fani's house. It was thanks to Uncle Zacchaeus that the Mlambos were able to buy my Uncle Fani's house. Dear Uncle Zacchaeus! After his death in the mysterious car accident in 2003, his inheritance, as per his will, went to my surrogate father, mostly in the dismaying form of boxes upon boxes of books, but also, thankfully, in the way of a sizable chunk of money. And thus, the Mlambos were able to sell my Thandi's house in Entumbane and buy my Uncle Fani's bigger house in Luveve Township.

(RIP, Uncle Zacchaeus, RIP! But if it so happens that the other side does, indeed, exist, and that you are over there having the time of your life with my inamorata, then may you fry and cry, you lucky letch, may you fry and cry!)

I was surprised to find signs of life upon arrival at my Uncle Fani's house. I had fled without putting his affairs in order, leaving unattended the house in Luveve while I worked as a geriatric caregiver in London. (I had skedaddled to the place where it all began, to our former colonizer and present patron, Le Monsieur Boss Lady – God Save the Queen! It was during that time when the population curve of the Land of Her Majesty had got mountain-steep. Her snooty British offspring were not willing to wipe and swathe the wrinkled buttocks of their progenitors, and thus the floodgates of the nursing profession had been yanked open. Our former colonizer welcomed her former colonial subjects, beseeching them, beseeching us, to once again labour towards her glory. I filled in some application forms and before I knew it I was on a plane on my way to do a sponsored six-month training course towards geriatric care, and I even had free student lodgings and a stipend.)

Still, I expected to find things as I had left them. Instead, there were people living in my uncle's house. I stood for a few minutes on the street, evaluating it. It looked nicer than I remembered, I'll admit that. It had a new coat of yellow paint, and somebody had gone to the trouble of planting some peach and yellow flowers in the front. There was a 'room for rent' cardboard sign fastened to the gate. The gate no longer creaked; somebody had bothered to oil it. The yard had been swept clean. I made my way to the back, edging along a narrow corridor, for a pygmy room had been built opposite the house in huge, grey blocks, quite ugly; the proposed lodgings, I rightly guessed.

I didn't knock but pushed open the back door, which creaked still, and stepped inside. The cement floors shined in a way they had never shined during my years of living there, so much so that I could make out the outline of my body. The smell of Cobra polish mingled with the residual aroma of beef stew. There were pretty, motherly things in the kitchen; pots and pans lined up along one wall, hanging from a rack. A white kitchen cupboard with blue finishings stood against the wall to my left; dish and cup sets, stacked one atop the other, were visible through the glass-fronted cupboard doors. The door leading to the sitting room stood ajar. The first thing that caught my eye when I stepped into the sitting room was not the brand-new, sparkling cobalt kitchen table vying so desperately for my attention. It wasn't even the bottles of cooking oil stacked in the corner, to my right, behind the TV stand, with a measuring cup and varied smaller bottles, clear evidence of a black market operation. No. It was the framed portrait of baby Bukhosi hanging above his sofa to my left, next to the bookcase, his emerald eyes gazing at me, frightened, imploring me, pleading with me.

I was still standing there, studying the portrait, resisting its entreaties to move closer, to caress the glossed-up cover, to perhaps plant a kiss on those glossy baby cheeks, when I heard a shriek behind me, and turned to see Mama Agnes. She was standing by the back door, her bags of groceries scattered at her feet.

'Who are you?' she cried. 'What do you want?'

'Who are *you*,' I said, 'and what are you doing in my uncle's house?'

A look of comprehension darted across her face, quick as a street thief, before she put on a blank stare, no longer frightened this time, but rather deliberately recalcitrant. 'This is our house,' she said. 'We bought it from the previous owner, fair and square. Please leave.'

I did not want to leave. I was so drawn to the baby portrait. And there were such pretty, motherly things everywhere. And this was my Uncle Fani's house. But I was not about to physically attack this lady who reminded me so much of a mother, and here I wish I could say *my* mother, if only I'd had the chance to know her, my life would have been different! I may have had no mother growing up, but Uncle Fani did his best to raise me proper, and I never forget my manners around mothers. So, I walked over to Mama Agnes, who was still standing by the back door, picked up her groceries, walked her to the kitchen, placed them on the floor next to the fridge, offered to unpack them for her, she shook her head, and then I said sorry for having walked in like that, unannounced, and I was looking for a place to rent and had seen the sign on the gate.

'We are no longer renting,' Mama Agnes said, eyeing me through slit-eyes.

'Please,' I said.

'We already have somebody,' she said.

'I'll pay you six months in advance,' I said, and pulled out a wad from my pockets. 'In pounds,' I added, counting the bills carefully for her to see.

She looked at the pounds, then looked at me, looked down at the pounds, looked up at me. 'My husband used to be a soldier,' she said. 'So, I won't tolerate any trouble.'

'I'm a good boy, madam,' I said, taking her hand.

Finally, she smiled. 'All right, all right. It's the room at the back, you saw it coming in? It's small, but we've made it as comfortable as possible, and for what we're charging, it's really cheap cheap.'

I am now ashamed to say that in spite of all my smiling, I went straight to the Luveve Housing Office the next day to report the theft and/or illegal sale of my Uncle Fani's house. But there seemed to be no record of the initial sale of the property to my Uncle Fani, only a record of sale to one Abednego Mlambo by a Mr Edward Msimangu, registered owner. I knew Old Edward, he'd lived on our street and had since, after selling a house that did not belong to him, skipped the country to Australia.

'We need at least a title deed,' said the man who served me. 'That or a birth certificate at least, to start somewhere.'

I had neither of these things. Uncle Fani, ever since the concentration camp, ever since Black Jesus, had been, like many of Gukurahundi's victims, unable to get a new birth certificate. I suspect the man knew this, that there was no title deed and no record of an identity document, and that's why Old Edward had managed to sell a house that didn't belong to him, probably with forged papers or even a bribe. Such were the new times in the House of Stone.

Declaring the matter not over, I returned to my new pygmy lodgings, which were rather sparsely furnished, with a little put-me-up bed and a lamp, and a plug extension running in from the house and looping through the small window that faces the gate and looks out onto the street, where on many-a-day, and sometimes during the early evening, while clickety-clacking away on my MacBook, recording for posterity the chronicles of my Mlambo family, I have had the pleasure of glimpsing children playing Catch on the street. In a way, although I have not yet and probably, like my surrogate grandpapa, shan't be able to reclaim the land on which I found myself – whether by hook or by crook – I can say I am somewhat glad things turned out the way they did, otherwise, I would never have come to know the Mlambos and love them as I have, and they never would have come to know me and – in their own ways – love me as they have, taking me in as their surrogate son and enveloping me in a family warmth the thought of which just makes me all mushy inside.

Mama Agnes invited me to join them for supper on my first night, that and the following nights, and then, realizing the impracticality of expecting me to cook in that pygmy room that did not even have a gas cooker, she began charging me for meals, as well as washing my clothes, which I was only too happy to pay for, money being only a vulgar estimation of the immeasurable, motherly love she was showering on me. On that first evening, I met my surrogate father, and also Bukhosi. Bukhosi, whose emerald eyes swam like precious stones in his face, staring out into the world with a beguiling fragility. I could already feel, though, as he walked into the sitting room and, without so much as a greeting, ordered me to move, I was sitting in *his* chair, that air of entitlement he carried about him. It was an entitlement to love, to Mama Agnes and Abednego's love, I could tell by the way he ladled the beef stew from the warming bowl in the centre of the table without first waiting for his elders, by how he complained to Mama Agnes that the stew tasted 'bland'. Tasted bland! It was the most delicious beef stew I had ever had the good fortune to taste, and I made it a point to say so to Mama Agnes, who, although she smiled and said thank you, seemed fazed by the boy's complaint. He had an appetite to match his father's, hampered only by the food shortages. Mama Agnes had to keep standing up to attend to the steady stream of customers who arrived to purchase the cooking oil and, it turned out, also rice measured and sold per cup, which she kept stashed in her room.

They were a perfect little family, the Mlambos. Mother, father and son. I admit, I did not know the devastating secrets that roiled beneath the surface then, but what family doesn't have secrets? All that matters is that they were together in my Uncle Fani's house, making it warm in a way it had never been when I was growing up. And they looked so happy! So complete as a family.

It was on the fourth night, I think, while seated at the dinner table, having rice and beans, with no cooking oil, for a disciplined and enterprising Mama Agnes said we had run out of the family portion for the week, and she had no intention of dipping into her side business, that a fidgety Bukhosi, perhaps high on the fizzy drinks I saw him gulping down so often, said, 'Baba. What was Gukurahundi? What happened during Gukurahundi?'

It seemed this was not his first time asking that, for he was on his feet before he had finished his questions. Our father winced with each mention of that word. He got up, tried to upset the cobalt kitchen table, couldn't upset it because the portly maroon sofas were in the way, lunged around the table, grabbed the boy, who was trying to escape on the other side but couldn't fit his oversize rump in the space between the wall and the table, dragged his flabby behind, laid him face down on one of the sofas, pulled down his trousers, unbuckled his own belt and proceeded to thrash his buttocks proper. The boy writhed and screamed. Mama Agnes, too, tried to shout, attempting to grab hold of the belt while ducking the lashes. Finally, whether overcome by or exhausted into common sense, our father dropped the belt.

'How many times have I told you I don't want to hear that word mentioned in my house?' he said. 'Stop talking nonsense about things you know nothing about!'

The boy sniffled in response.

'Heyi, wena, I'm talking to you! Do you hear me?'

Again, the boy refused to answer.

Panting, our father stumbled out of the house and into the night.

'My nanaza,' murmured Mama Agnes, over and over again, trying to kiss the boy's face, which he kept snatching out of reach of her pouted lips.

I got up, went to the bathroom, filled a bucket with water, which was warm, for the Mlambos, having moved from Entumbane to Luveve, had moved up in the world, and to celebrate this rise in middle-class-hood had not only acquired the cobalt kitchen table and the kitchen cupboard, but also installed a small boiler, which is useful especially whenever the water goes, which is less often than the electricity but is, nevertheless, very much a nuisance, and returned to the sitting room with the bucket and a cloth. There, I knelt and pressed the wet cloth to the boy's bruised buttocks. He grunted each time, but did not raise his head. I admit I felt tender towards him. But what had just happened had also shown me the dynamics of the family. Perhaps the first seeds of opportunity were already beginning to sprout. I understood, very clearly, one thing: the boy, who absorbed all the heat of Mama Agnes and my surrogate father's love, leaving me out in the cold, was the key to gaining the family's affection.

I slept fitfully that night, dreaming of those frightened, imploring, pleading emerald baby eyes that haunted the Mlambo living room, wanting so badly to take in a world that did not want to be seen, only looked at.

It was from Bukhosi that I learned that our father was a reformed alcoholic. The height of his drinking, from what the boy told me, coincided with the time that he invaded the Thornton Farm and the resurgence of his beatings which Mama Agnes told me about. I'm not certain if it was finding out that his true father is a white man or being disowned by his own mother afterwards that drove him deeper into dipsomania. My surrogate grandma, who is living out her octogenarian days back in my surrogate-surrogate grand-dada's homestead, refuses to speak to my surrogate father to this day still; as far as I know, after my surrogate grandpa was kicked off the farm thanks to him and his War Vet comrades, she said something to the fact of 'you are dead to me' and has lived the past seven years as though, indeed, he is dead to her.

By the time I met my surrogate father in 2007, he was a reformed wife beater and a recovering alcoholic. His infamy still ran far and wild, though, and during my first weeks as a lodger with the Mlambos I heard many entertaining stories about his public drunken performances.

'I'm so sorry you have to hear such stories,' Bukhosi said when I asked him about our father. 'He wasn't always a bad man! He could be very kind to us. I promise! How I wish it were you, Zamani, who is my father!'

If only he knew my joy! Not at this awkward projection of fatherhood, for I am only twenty-four and he had at that time just turned seventeen, but rather at his hero worship. I didn't reply immediately, assessing him, trying to think of the best thing to say.

'I'm here for you,' I said, finally. 'Anytime you need anything. And I know your father isn't that bad. In fact, I think you should keep asking him about Gukurahundi. He wants to open up.'

'But he keeps beating me!'

'He just doesn't know how to talk about it. And you, as his son, should help him do it. Trust me, he'll thank you for it.'

Though I learned that my surrogate father had overcome his violent ways, it was plain to see that the boy and his constant probing about Gukurahundi was a trigger. I was truly pleased for Abednego for managing to quell his abusive tendencies. He reminded me of my Uncle Fani, without the tears, the sleepless nights and the drinking sprees. He rejuvenated my faith in the redeeming power of family, in the possibility of transcendence. At the same time, I couldn't help but see, in his periodic outbursts with the boy over Gukurahundi, the glint of opportunity, and I admit I actively stoked those flames.

I began to spend more and more time with Bukhosi. I did enjoy our time together. He was sensitive and pliant, and looked up to me as no one else had. I could sense a similar disquiet in him, which I later attributed to our father's determination that he be an engineer, for though he was over-passionate, making for a feverish Mthwakazi disciple, he was very weak in matters of rational and mathematical thinking, particularly where Newton and his theories were concerned. It was a mutual feeling of confusion and exclusion that attracted him to me, or I to him, what's it matter, we were two elements with opposing charges brought together through a magnetism of vision and purpose. Both of us fumbling about in an unmoored present, untethered, without knowledge of a robust family hi-story in which to cultivate our roots.

But it's not my fault that he went missing! It's Dumo's fault! His and the boy's! I was never the instigator here, only the catalyst! And yet, every photo of the boy fills me with guilt. His pictures are plastered everywhere, on the walls of the High Tek Intanet Café by the shops, and also outside the Bakery and Spar Supermarket, and also the community hall down the road. Even in the city centre he's there, on the streetlights, on the shop walls, on the City Council bins where he competes for attention with posters of the Reverend Pastor's advertisement for his Christmas revival at Blessed Anointings. I can't bear to look at those posters of Bukhosi! I can see his photo in my mind still. Black and white is that printed face, yes, just a picture, but his lips assault me with the memory of their nostalgic, fleshy plumpness, brown and moist like dewy soil. They hover in the air, suspended from the rest of the black and white printed image, and part to reveal two front teeth, the one on the left chipped. And now, they are guffawing, a voluble aaaha ha ha ha that tapers off into a tormenting chuckle, klklkl klklkl klklkl, spattering spit in its wake.

HELP ME

The Reverend Pastor called around yesterday morning, as I knew he would have to, holding my laptop out like a holy relic. He made a show of handing my Mac back to me, patting me on the back and apologizing profusely – he had been wrong, he said, his IT guys hadn't been able to find anything that could help them with the boy. On reflection, he believed that I, Zamani, had been right all along. I had only been trying to help the family.

It's wonderful how the aims of blackmail never have to be stated; how those being blackmailed intuitively know what it is that the blackmailer wants. I didn't have to go to the Reverend Pastor after catching him at his prayer session with Sister Gertrude, because I knew he would come to me. I didn't have to tell him what I wanted from him, because I knew he would already know. I wonder if his IT guys really did fail to find out anything about Bukhosi's Facebook messages? They did, after all, have a whole week to try, even without the boy's messages. But who the hell cares? I can send that Reverend Nobody's life crashing down with the click of a button, and it's enough for now that he knows this.

Finally, I can breathe! Yoh.

Today, Mama Agnes invited me to have breakfast with her and my surrogate father, something she hasn't done since the Reverend Pastor started making a noise about his IT guys. It felt so wonderful, to be able to bask in her presence once again! We sat out on the back stoep, her and I side by side, slurping our tea, which was creamy with Chimombe milk, and biting into chunks of warm, fresh Baker's Inn bread layered with margarine, gifts from the Reverend Pastor. My surrogate father was hunched over on an upturned beer crate, opposite us, sitting right in the sun's glare, nibbling at his bread and barely touching his tea. His skin was like paper – he's almost become a ghost.

She asked me, Mama Agnes, if I had heard from the boy. I said I hadn't, but that I was sure I would hear from him soon. My surrogate father began to say something, and then seemed to change his mind, shutting his mouth without making a sound.

Looking pointedly at him, I said I would write to the boy again.

'Yes, we need to prepare for his coming,' said Mama Agnes. 'Christmas is just a few weeks away. Ask him when he's arriving, hantsho?'

The problem is, I can't keep the boy 'away in South Africa' forever. I don't know if I should tell my surrogate family that's he just not coming back. But that will force Mama Agnes to try and leave us, again. Perhaps I can offer to be the one to go to South Africa and look for the boy? I don't really want to go. These past few days with the Mlambos have been my happiest in I don't remember how long. I haven't even felt compelled to pick up my Red Album. And when I looked at myself in the mirror this morning, I noticed the shadow of a paunch; under my Mama A's care, I'm beginning to fill out.

In the end, I decided it's better if the boy says he's coming for Christmas. If he says he's never coming back now, he'll rob me of a happy holiday with my new family. Just like he robbed me of my filial relationship with Dumo.

I couldn't stop grinning this afternoon when Mama Agnes kissed me on the cheek after I showed her the Facebook message from the boy saying he was coming home, he would arrive on Christmas Day. She did it like it was the most normal thing for her to do. I took the opportunity to cup her cheeks then, my Mama, and she let me, she didn't pull away. My heart was loud in my ears. I took a moment to take in her face, up close, the December light enriching her walnut skin, softening the bruises where my surrogate father hit her. I dared to press my nose against hers, her petite nose with its concave, hyperbolic triangulation, flared with prosaic sensibilities. I trembled at the sight of her lips, their nostalgic, fleshy plumpness reminding me of Bukhosi. I pulled away then, the image of the boy spoiling the moment. When I looked up, she was smiling.

'Thank you,' she said, 'for bringing our Bukhosi back to us.'

I brought my palm to my face, to the place, still moist, where she had kissed my finely sloping cheek.

It was always me taking the boy places, him taking the places meant for me. I did take him to see Dumo. It was during the first of Dumo's cell meetings, where the first of the future cell group leaders of the Mthwakazi Movement had been summoned. The meeting was held in a mottled house in Mzilikazi, that township named after King Lobengula's father, the ferocious King Mzilikazi ka Khumalo, on a Sunday afternoon in mid-August, two months before the Mthwakazi rally where Bukhosi and

Dumo disappeared. The house was situated right across from the Barbourfields Stadium, and as we walked up its crooked path, picking a delicate way across cracked tiles, weaving through an untidy queue that had coiled into itself on the street outside the house to fill empty containers at the mouth of the trickle where a pipe had burst, the cheers of the soccer spectators swelled over us like revolutionary chants. Dumo stood stiffly by the entrance, dressed in a grey suit and a powder blue shirt. He hugged me and shook Bukhosi's hand.

He had put up a life-size, black and white photo of Queen Lozikeyi on one of the walls. The Queen appraised us haughtily from her position on the ground in front of a beehive hut, her legs folded beneath her, her hands clasped on her lap, her small, pretty face angled, unsmiling, at the camera. The crown of her head was coiled in beads, and a pair of buckhorns dangled from a necklace. Her midriff was bare, and a cowskin kilt was secured around her waist. I bowed before her, making sure to avoid her bare midriff, lest my prying eyes be met with a disapproving queenly gaze, avoiding also her magnificent bosom that could no doubt feed a whole nation, and which Bukhosi, who was staring with open interest, if not a little insolence, for she was the Queen, I'm sure would have loved to suckle on, what with his perennial yearning for the motherly teat.

It was on that day that Dumo taught the boy how to recite the Queen's totems. He had tried to teach me too, impressing upon me their ceremonial importance, how they kept the past alive and relevant to the future by officiating the present. There was immense power in ceremonies, he had said to me, they helped build community and fostered among a people a sense of purpose. Still, it took me a while to learn the Queen's totems, and at times I still forgot one or two – because I wasn't a rigorous enough revolutionaire, Dumo always chastised. Perhaps that's why he expressed such excessive joy when the boy, hearing him say the totems only once, began to recite them, leaping from side to side, his hand curled around an imaginary spear which he raised solemnly to the Queen:

'Queen Lozikeyi, daughter of the Dlodlo clan. Mother of mothers, your copper skin is an aesthete's dream! Materfamilias! Mpangazitha! How do I tell of the mocha of your eyes? Mbanjwa! How do I trace the crescent of your cheeks? Mabango! Mtingi! How to fill the generosity of your nostrils? Bangile! Bringer of Rain! How to taste the sassy plumpness of your lips? Mthiyane! Mathabela!'

He recited the Queen's totems over and over, even going down, at one point, on bended knee before the glossy life-size photo. Dumo raised his eyebrows at me. I admit, I was pleased with the boy then, quite naïve to the fact that he had already begun to usurp from me Dumo's affections.

The meeting proper started soon afterwards. And there, crammed in the sitting room with the furniture, were eleven occupants, four men, including myself and Bukhosi, and seven women, some of whom could well pass for men, our shoulders hunched like thieves on the prowl – for what else was this talk of secession, if not, like government ministers at the country's coffers, an impolite way of stealing pieces of a nation? We were huddled like a soccer team, ready to wage war over our little turf. And as the roars of the regiments in the Barbourfields Stadium peaked, Dumo, who kept pat-patting his 'fro, and whose Mandela parting glistened with Vaseline, like a slice of sun shining upon the long walk to freedom, cleared his throat and began:

'Em, first I must begin with, what is uMthwakazi? What is it that we stand for?' And here he shook a fist. 'We are peacefully but firmly advocating for the emancipation of the Mthwakazians from the oppression and the colonial rule of the Republic of Zimbabwe!'

'Amandla!' we boomed.

'To create a democratic state of uMthwakazi, with the capital uMhlahlandlela, where our people will live in peace and harmony with all tribes!'

'Power to the People!'

'The rewriting of our Mthwakazian history and the restoration of Mthwakazi pride!'

'Amandla bo!'

'Power to the People!'

Spurred on by the chants of the gathering, Dumo's voice became a current of smouldering lava. 'The Mthwakazian state shall be based on internationally recognized democratic principles, and shall be a beacon and source of pride for Africa. We shall adopt the precepts as stated in the Universal Declaration of Human Rights, the United Nations Convention against Torture, the principles of the Rome Statute, the Convention on the Prevention and Punishment of the Crime of Genocide, the International Convention on the Elimination of All Forms of Racial Discrimination, the International Covenant on Civil and Political Rights, the International Covenant on Economic, Social and Cultural Rights, and the Declaration on the Elimination of All Forms of Intolerance and of Discrimination Based on Religion or Belief.'

'Hawu hawu!'

'We are saying that we are against the shutting up of what happened to us via that Unity Accord Agreement of '87. What was that? We are not even allowed, after Gukurahundi, to acknowledge our dead, to build shrines in their honour, to search for their bones in the mass graves. How do we bring peace to our dead, how do we restore our self-confidence as a people? Nonsense, boMtshana, nonsense! These colonial borders are artificial. The white man didn't understand what he was doing. They should have grouped us with South Africa, at least. Not this nonsense. Now, we want the land Mzilikazi occupied here. We want self-determination!'

'Amandla!'

'We are vehemently asking and peacefully demanding for a secession from the Republic of Zimbabwe, to form a peaceful Mthwakazian Republic, where our people can thrive in peace.'

Somebody in the group laughed. 'Aliphuphi nje. Are you stupid or-o what? We all know that will never happen. They will never give you a piece of Zimbabwe.'

The chorus ebbed, and ten pairs of eyes turned towards the chap who had spoken. He was tall, and incredibly dark, with a wide face and a flat nose. His Ndebele was hesitant, with inflections in all the wrong places.

'And why not?' said Dumo. 'South Sudan is busy trying to break away from the rest of Sudan. Eritrea managed it in 1993. Heh? You've got to wake up, boMtshana, ah ah! We've got to think. Already, we have offices in the UK. And we are planning on opening something in South Africa.'

'UK? Are you drunk? You mean to tell me you're heading a movement from the UK?'

'It's not safe here, Mtshana, ah ah. You know how it is. Unlike the Opposition Party, we don't have the backing of the West, don't have friends in high places. Everything is grassroots, uyabo. But come with me two months from now, we're organizing a meeting at Stanley Hall, the first Sunday of October. Come, I'll introduce you to some interesting people. The revolution is real, Mtshana! The revolution will be televised!'

'You delusional fool,' the man said, this time in English. 'You are all fools, all of you. Fools!'

Dumo seemed to contemplate the fellow for a minute. 'And who are you, Doubting Thomas?' he said, finally. 'Why did you come here? I don't seem to remember seeing you in these parts before. We have not shared a drink, you and I, like brothers.'

The man started. The crowd had formed a fist around him.

Dumo began to spit compulsively. 'I said, who are you?'

I grabbed the chap by the scruff of his collar.

'Who are you?' I asked.

'Who are you?' chorused the crowd.

Who are you? Bukhosi echoed.

'Are you a Mthwakazian?'

'Are you a Mthwakazian?'

Are you a Mthwakazian?

'Speak up!'

'Who are you?'

'Where are you from?'

'Look at his ID, he's a Shona! Spy!'

'Spy!'

'Spy!'

Spy!

I thrust the first kick. Boots, sandals, sneakers, mocs, bucks, captoes, plimsolls and loafers in various stages of ageing rammed into the stranger. Outside, the uproar at the Barbourfields Stadium swelled, momentarily drowning the fracas in the house.

'Help me,' croaked the stranger.

I stopped, breathless. There had been something exhilarating in throwing the first punch, in kicking the first kick. Too exhilarating. I had not, before this, considered myself a man of action, a man of violence. I had also never seen Dumo so worked up before.

The boy was staring, open-mouthed. I yanked at his arm, dragging him through the scrum, away from the stranger. Together, we slipped out.

I took long, rapid steps, so that the boy was obliged to stumble after me, struggling to control his irregular breathing. I felt afraid.

What kind of country would our Mthwakazi be? Would we continue the legacy of violence? Could we imagine into being the country as a Manifestation of Love? What kind of country would that be? It was at this point, as I walked and thought the thoughts I thought, Bukhosi wheezing beside me, that I wondered what my own contribution to our hi-story had been, would be, could be. That struggle between the fallible ambition of man to lean towards immortality and the fleshly evidence of his certain mortality; that tormenting battle with his consciousness, which is able to live vicariously at any point in time, which dreams, loves, hopes, and aspires to the immortal, but is always brought down to earth by his flesh, this container in which he has been contained, and which will inevitably return to the earth to rot. Too much dreaming, and he begins to forget his fallibility and, believing himself to be infallible, he commits horrendous acts of ambition which amount to crimes against humanity; too much dying, and he begins to forget the sacredness of life, the beauty of dreaming, to live in fear and be paralysed by this fear.

What had we become, Dumo and I?

The following morning, Bukhosi confessed to me that he had slept fitfully, his slumber punctured by dreams of a pair of bloodied lips that kept croaking, *Help me.*

I, too, began to have dreams that unsettled my sleep; visions

I called them, so vivid were they, of mortified morticians beholding in their morgues corpses in various states of anime; from bellied men with orgasmic grins to emaciated women wearing varied synonyms of mirth, to malnutritioned children blissed with laughter, their distended tummies swollen evidence of death's irony.

There cropped up in my dream those killed by the puzzling infinitude of arithmetic, so that it seemed no matter how much it ballooned, there was to be no end to our over-hyperinflation, to the electricity and telephone bills that came with more and more zeros added each time, inciting a tubby Reserve Bank Governor to enter the stage of my dream with a flourish, wearing a red cape and a top hat and, while tapping his short, fat fingers against his huge belly, lambast those demonic Western Powers who were to blame for each and every one of the nation's calamities. Behind this invective, the Governor slash-slashed the imperialist zeros from the national currency. So that, instead of carrying one hundred quintillion dollars, the people of the House of Stone emerged from boa constrictor bank queues fingering flimsy blue notes bearing the tender of only one hundred trillion Zimbabwe dollars. But this was of little comfort; what was the arithmetic limit, they asked themselves? None, apparently, came the whispers. They were yet to surpass the nonillions, the octodecillions and the novemvigintillions. Such looming mathematical torture proved too much – the prospect of standing at shop tills trying to work out quindecillion change from quattuorvigintillion bank notes was more than the spirit could bear – and some dropped dead right then and there, on the pavements outside the banks. (What kind of Einstein offspring was the Frank-Einstein nation trying to birth? Children who could differentiate a quintillion from a trillion before they had even turned three?)

They became more vivid, my dreams; I beheld The People pounding on the doors of the Presidential Palace. In the sky, vultures were circling. It seemed as though the near-death of their morality had strengthened their will to live. And not just to merely exist, no; but rather to live with desperation at the helm of things, carolling an ode to life.

The People in my dream began to run. But they were not fleeing, no; just running, carrying balloons and throwing confetti all over the place, and babbling in many languages, in Ndebele and English and Shona and Karanga and Venda and Nguni and all of the languages of the world. Before us, in the middle of the City Hall Square, a great golden monument had been erected; a towering isosceles triangle, on whose apex reared a magnificent bull, glinting in the sun. People knelt by the base and placed flowers and wreaths and letters and all sorts of trinkets. Along the gleaming sides of the triangle were names, thousands of names, of our dead, etched all the way up to the apex. I elbowed my way through the crowds to the monument, and there, shoulder height, was etched the name: *Zodwa Nsele Khathini: Bhalagwe,'83*.

I fell to my knees and broke out in song.

FORBIDDEN FRUITS

Christmas is two weeks away. Christmas is two weeks away and decorations have sprung up all over town and in the stores where there are discounts and seasonal goodies; in the townships old knick-knacks have been dusted and tinkling little bells fastened to the gates and plastic Christmas trees put up in living room corners and everyone is happy happy joy joy.

Everybody, that is, except for my surrogate family. Early this morning, I woke up to a terrific din and I knew immediately that my surrogate father was up to his violent shenanigans again. I ran into the house and this time I told myself that I would kill him for laying hands on Mama Agnes. But MaNdlovu, our nosy neighbour, had already beaten me to it, not the killing of my surrogate father, but the scene of the crime, where she had managed to insert herself between them and was clinging to my surrogate father, who was trying to reach Mama Agnes cowering behind her. Upon seeing me, Mama Agnes made a dash for it, rushing past me and out of the living room, sobbing, to the bathroom where we heard the click of the lock. The pipes shuddered, there was a splash, and then running water drowned her sobs.

MaNdlovu left soon afterwards, no doubt to spread the news of what has happened, not of the beating itself, which isn't so scandalous around these parts, but the reason for the beating, which is super scandalous, and so will soon be known all over the township and beyond.

For, today Mama Agnes and the Reverend Pastor made the papers. Their picture is splashed on the front page of *The Chronicle*, beneath my artful work of Sister Gertrude and the Reverend Pastor.

Yes, I informed on the bastard! He really thought I would be satisfied with just the return of my laptop? He, who had sought to usurp me from my Mama Agnes's affections, to dislodge me from the bosom of my own (surrogate) family? I had flicked through my Red Album while wondering what to do, and I found the answer written in the returning stare of Black Jesus: *show no mercy.*

I had gone to an internet café, set up an anonymous email account and simply sent the pictures of him and Sister Gertrude to our nation's informer hotline. The best way to take care of your enemy is by handing him over to his enemy, and this loudmouth Reverend Pastor has earned himself some serious enemies in high places with his weekly tantrums in the independent papers. And now, they're doing to him what they did to that other outspoken critic of the government, the Roman Catholic Archbishop of Bulawayo, earlier this year, in a video of him fucking some woman that was all over the eight o'clock news.

It was Mama Agnes's picture with the Reverend Pastor, second in a string of photos of the man with various other women, that robbed me of the pleasure I would have derived from my artisanship. Their picture, Mama Agnes and the Reverend Pastor, on its own, without the surrounding innuendo, is innocent enough; it's a zoom-lens shot of them sitting cross-legged in a patch of wild grass by a river, the Mguza River where they go to collect holy water, I'm guessing. An indecipherable book, which looks like the Reverend Pastor's King James bible, is lying face down on the grass between them. It is all innocent enough, until you look back at my damning photo featuring Sister Gertrude, and then read the caption:

ANTI-MUGABE PASTOR ENSNARED IN SEX SCANDALS

Look again at the picture. What do you see? No longer Mama Agnes and the Reverend Pastor, but a man and a woman, seated by that secluded Mguza River where they can get on with their holy business without interruption. And between them is a black, ominous book, on which the article helpfully speculates: what sort of diary-of-terrorist-fondling-and-political-frolicking is the little black book? The pastor is a buttock-kissing British puppet parading as a man of God, the article goes on to say, who was thrown out of the Catholic order a few years ago for just this kind of devilish behaviour. A hypocrite, a hyena dressed as an impala, a Judas of Judases. A cockroach, an informer, a virus. A Traitor of the Struggle. And is the fool not married, busy as he is frolicking with half his congregation? And frolicking with his congregation he is, for beneath this scathing attack, accompanying the photos, in a neat row like a grocery list, are the names of those Ladies of the Church, the Reverend Pastor's impressive concubinage who have been each of them supplicating at different times and locations to the Reverend Pastor's phallus. And right there, at the top of the list, for, like any serious list listing important things, it goes in alphabetical order, is Mama Agnes's name.

(My Mama A! Of course, I wanted to end the Reverend Pastor, swat him like the pesky fly that he is, but I never imagined that Mama Agnes would be collateral!)

We are doing a poll, ends the article. Which of these women do you think has been a flattering Hagar, and which a bashful

Bilhah? Email your suggestions, and tell us why! The results shall be published next week in our Monday edition. Merry Christmas!

If you look at the photo closely, having read this front page article, which is mostly pictures and grocery list and very little in the way of substance, you begin to notice new elements, such as the apparent tension between the Reverend Pastor and my Mama Agnes, so obviously sexual, leaping in rays so refined they appear in the photograph as strange, atomic sparks. This tension, understated and implied, suddenly makes my own photographic work, which I thought artful only a few moments ago, seem kitsch.

See how she leans back in the photo, my Mama Agnes, one hand stretched out behind her to support her slanting position, so that her breasts perk up at the Reverend Pastor. See how her floral dress is riding up her thighs. And the Reverend Pastor, why is he leaning forward like that? They are in tandem, Mama Agnes and the Reverend Pastor, they are in sync, they share a point of view, stand as one at the standpoint, perceive with the same perspective, posit from the same position, look out with the same outlook.

I felt a sudden pang of tenderness for them both, even for that Reverend Pastor; I smiled at the idea that, beneath the cover of Blessed Anointings, they could rehash the tryst of their youth, no longer Agnes and Reuben, girl and Father, but a woman and a man, freely, nje.

The woman swayed her hips like Hagar.

The man touched her like Abram.

She fluttered her eyes like Bilhah.

He kissed her like Jacob.

They began to talk about love.

'What does Corinthians say?' began the man.

'It says that… "These three remain: faith, hope and love. But the greatest of these is love"…'

'What sayeth it of love?'

'That… "If I speak in the tongues of men or of angels, but do not have love, I am only a resounding gong or a clanging cymbal. If I have the gift of prophecy and can fathom all mysteries and all knowledge, and if I have a faith that can move mountains, but do not have love, I am nothing. If I give all I possess to the poor and give over my body to hardship that I may boast, but do not have love, I gain nothing"…'

'That's right. And you, woman, are full of so much love.

I compare you
to a mare among Pharaoh's chariots.
Your cheeks are lovely with ornaments
your neck with strings of jewels.

'—no no no, listen to me, there's no need to be shy, look at me, look up, look at me—

Behold, you are beautiful;
behold, you are beautiful;
your eyes are doves.

'So, you see, it is not faith that will carry you, but love…'

'Oh, but I have no love…'

'Oh, but you do…'

'Oh, but I feel so unloved…'

'And yet you are so loving…'

The man's lips, balmy like an august morn, kindled the woman in a spiritual rousing. She tasted his tongue, probing her small mouth *yes?* Her tongue probing *yes!* back. Man hands gripped her buttocks. The man squeezed her, clutched her, tasted her. The woman moaned; she could feel his body trembling. She pressed into him and quivered. Rubbed herself against his manhood. Hardened years of lust bulged the corona; swollen rivers of ardour ruptured the lips. Flooded the glans; bedewed the vulva. A lick, a shudder. A plunge, a moan.

How she wanted to sing:

Let him kiss me with the kisses of his mouth!
For your love is better than wine;
your anointing oils are fragrant;
your name is oil poured out;
therefore virgins love you.
Draw me after you; let us run.

The sweetness of it!

I am very dark, but lovely,
Tell me, you whom my soul loves
where you pasture your flock,
where you make it lie down at noon;
for why should I be like one who veils herself
beside the flocks of your companions?

Divinely saccharine.

My beloved is to me a sachet of myrrh
that lies between my breasts.
My beloved is to me a cluster of henna blossoms
in the vineyards of Engedi.
Behold, you are beautiful, my beloved, truly delightful.

Like all things forbidden.

Sugar flowed, crystalline in its pleasure. Delight ejaculated across her thighs. The smell of spittle and kisses. Sweat and perfume. And the odour of love. Tangy. Sweeter than the Apple that was plucked from the Tree.

BLACK JESUS

Mama Agnes locked herself in the bathroom and refused to come out. She kept the taps running all morning, as though this would dissolve the front news picture of her and the Reverend Pastor, wasting water the municipal didn't have, just so we wouldn't hear her sobs, even though her crying was so loud we couldn't help but hear her anyway. My surrogate father disappeared into the bedroom they shared and reappeared with a knobkerrie. It had a shiny handle, the same walnut colour as Mama Agnes's skin, and a lumpy head the size of a man's fist. He swung it in the air, hwa hwa hwa, like a stick-fighter practising his moves. Then he rapped on the bathroom door and demanded that she come out. When she didn't respond, he banged on the door, threatening to break it down.

'Promise me you'll be reasonable,' she said.

'I will show you reason, very much,' he said. 'You and that pastor of yours!'

'I'm a God-fearing woman!' she cried.

'Clearly you are afraid of the wrong god. Today, I'm going to teach you what fear is.'

Again, he banged on the door, demanding that she come out; again, she refused, her entreaties drowned partially by the running water. I stood in the passage, trying to plead on Mama Agnes's behalf, each time my surrogate father throwing eyes at me like I was a fly bugging his ear.

Finally, the door unlatched and Mama Agnes came out, quickly ducking behind me. She gripped my arms. Her grasp was firm, her grasp was motherly; it made my muscles spasm.

My surrogate father swung his knobkerrie, its lumpy head fisting me full in the chest, for Mama Agnes was busy swivelling my upper body this way and that, using me as a shield. My chest heaved, but I stood my ground.

'This mess started when our nanaza went missing!' Mama Agnes cried. 'Where is our boy, Abednego, heh? You drove him away! And what have you been doing to bring him back? What, exactly? Because the Reverend Pastor has done plenty, every day he has been praying, he has shown up for me every time—'

My surrogate father lunged at us, tried to swing the knobkerrie past my head, missed and struck my temple. I staggered and tried to blink back the tears. I could feel my legs folding, but I did not fall, I held firm, held firm for Mama Agnes. I could no longer see properly; shapes were dancing before my eyes and everything refused to remain still.

'It only happened once!' cried Mama Agnes.

'Liar!' roared my surrogate father.

'Twice!'

'Hey, wena—!'

There was a woosh before my eyes, and I imagine he must have been raising his knobkerrie.

'Mrs Thornton!' I cried, staggering about, my hands swinging from side to side.

This must have stopped him in his tracks, for I could no longer hear the hwa-hwa sound of a swinging knobkerrie.

'We don't want another Mrs Thornton!'

I could hear my surrogate father breathing heavily. Then the tread of his feet on the cement floor reached my ears, getting lighter and lighter, in the direction of the sitting room.

Mama Agnes helped me back to my pygmy room, all the while murmuring how she was sorry. There she made me lie down on my mattress, on my back, and pressed a warm cloth to my temple. I was suddenly ashamed that she should be in my humble lodgings. I had never felt such shame in her presence before, and it confused me, making my head throb even more violently. I wished I had something nice to offer her, like a cup of Tanganda tea with a slice of lemon. She cupped my face, murmuring how so very sorry she was, she was sorry for everything. Her hands were soft and warm on my cheeks. I tried to lie absolutely still. I could smell her perfume, a soothing, fruity fragrance. Sorry, she kept saying over and over, rubbing a thumb over my pronounced cheekbone, tracing its elegant arc. Something warm spread across my chest. Sorry, she said, so sorry. But it was I who was sorry! Had I not inadvertently informed on her by informing on that wanton Reverend Pastor?

'It is I who is sorry!' I said.

'Oh, mfanami, you have nothing to be sorry for! It's just Baba sometimes, he gets a little angry, and then you see…'

She lifted her warm hands from my cheeks then, and I imagined she was making a gesture of despair, throwing her hands in the air. I wished she'd cup my cheeks again! No one had ever caressed my face like that before. Was that maybe what my mama Zodwa Nsele Khathini's hands felt like?

▪

Desperate to save my Mama Agnes from the wrath of my surrogate father and to save my surrogate father from himself, I intercepted him that evening just as he was coming out of the house, to slink off on one of his nocturnal escapades to Mrs Thornton's grave, I thought.

'I was coming to see you,' he said.

'Oh!' I said. It would be easy, then, to neuter him with a dose of ubuvimbo; to talk him down from his anger; to cajole him down from his high horse.

But for the first time, he wasn't interested in ubuvimbo. I could see his lips trembling as I dangled my ubuvimbo-laced finger in front of him. And yet, instead of lunging for it as he usually did, he stared at it for a long time, and then slowly shifted his eyes to mine.

'I got this, today,' he said, slapping a piece of paper onto my lap. 'From the IT people.'

I picked it up and pretended to study it. So, that Reverend Pastor had got the findings from his IT guys after all! And this was his pathetic revenge. Well, rot in hell, you quack.

'Oh?' I said, as though I couldn't decipher the report. 'Have they found the boy?'

'You know they haven't! You know they haven't because that Face-what account is yours and not Bukhosi's! It was in your computer!'

'What?' I said. I held my surrogate father's stare. I wished it was Mama Agnes, and not he, whom the IT guys had contacted. I could have easily dealt with Mama Agnes; it would have been easy to use her recent shame against her.

I held out my ubuvimbo-laced finger to Abednego. 'Here,' I said, 'this will make you feel better.'

But he whacked my finger aside. 'Where is my son?' he said.

'I don't know,' I said. 'Why are you looking at me like that?'

'I'm going to the police. You are going to tell them where my son is. And if you don't, I'm going to kill you. I'm going to kill you with my bare hands!'

I grabbed his arm. He tried to yank it away, but I held on to him, pulling him down. 'Wait,' I said. 'You have it all wrong, the IT guys are lying, why would I—'

He punched me in the face.

'Father—'

'Stop calling me that! How many times must I tell you to stop calling me that! I'm not your father, bakithi!'

'But you're the one who said I'm your son.'

'When? When did I ever say that?'

'That day, when you came to my room and said I was your son—'

'I have never said such a thing. I don't remember ever saying that to you, and I wouldn't, because you are *not my son*.'

'But Father—'

'You are never going to be my son.'

'Father—'

'I'm not your father and you are not my son!'

We both froze. My chest hurt. My head hurt. My eyes. Everywhere it hurt. I was hurting everywhere.

I started laughing.

'Why are you laughing?'

After everything we'd been through!

'Heyi, wena, what's so funny?'

He still preferred that brat to me!

'Why are you laughing?'

I'm the one who had coaxed him out of his shell, helped him to get to know himself. I have even kept all his secrets! I haven't even told Mama Agnes what he did to Mrs Thornton!

'Stop looking at me like that!'

Would he be able to live with that?

'You have no idea, do you?' I said. I admit I could not help myself; he had hurt me badly.

'I want you out of here, do you hear me, I'm taking you to the police, and I want you—'

'I'm not going anywhere.'

'Heyi, wena mfana, who do you think you—'

'Come closer, Father, come. Come and have a look. Come, see.'

I fumbled about until I felt the hard plastic of my Red Album beneath my covers. I pulled it out. I caressed it, I kissed it, all the while watching him. And then I opened it.

He began to whimper. His eyes ran across the pages as I flipped them. He began to back away, but I grabbed his arm.

He looked up at me. 'What is, what's wrong with, what are you doing with, what's this?'

'Look,' I said. 'Really look. Don't you see? Can't you see what's been right under your nose, all this time?'

Still, he couldn't make the connection. In spite of our matching inky skin, in spite of our noble cheekbones, I admit mine more refined than his; in spite of our lips, so distinct, so unmistakable, he just couldn't make the connection.

'I know you are not my father, Abednego. I only thought, I only wanted—' I shook my head. 'Never mind. *This* is my father,' I said, finally.

He just sat there, rooted to the spot, his eyes moving from the album to me and back. I thrust my face towards him, so he could have a better look.

He began to shake his head. 'No. No no no…'

'Yes. Yes yes *yes*…'

There, I had said it. I had done what he has failed to do all along, what I have been running away from. I had claimed my patrilineage.

'No,' Abednego whimpered. 'You are lying. No! You don't even look alike!'

'What do you mean—?' The bastard! He sought to destabilize me, I knew, to get me to question myself. But I wouldn't give him the satisfaction. I recovered my poise. 'This man is my father. I'm his son. Take a good look, because each time you see me, I want you to understand that you are seeing *him*.'

I don't have the words to describe what I saw on his face. It crumpled, it just! It fell apart. I admit I had not expected this. I don't know what I expected; how could I have known that my confession, this shame I have been hiding for so long, would be the ultimate weapon? Better than any Bell's or Johnnie or even the ubuvimbo.

'I don't know where your boy is,' I said to him, bringing my face close to his. And though it hurt me how he cowered away, though I yearned for him to cup my face, though I longed to kiss his, it was better than the disgust with which he had beheld me a few moments before as he tried to chase me away. Fear is better than rejection. 'But I can help find him. These IT people are lying to you.' I paused, to let this sink in. 'How can you trust anything coming from that Reverend Pastor? After he has been eating your wife for you, all this time?' This hurt him, I saw. 'How can you even be sure the boy is really yours? With a wife who can't be trusted like that?' I leaned even closer to him. I could feel his breath warm and stale on my face. 'And if you go to the police with these lies, I'm going to tell Mama Agnes what you did to Mrs Thornton.' This didn't seem to elicit the reaction I had expected. 'I'm going to write to Farmer Thornton and tell him,' I went on. 'I'll plaster you all over Facebook.' Still, nothing. 'I'll call my father. My father, Black Jesus, he'll come for you. And this time, he'll finish you.' This, finally, had the desired effect! The man collapsed into my arms, his eyes opened wide, staring into my face. I held him, I cooed to him, I rubbed his chest. I bent and kissed him, on the lips.

'It was you!' he whimpered, trying to turn his lips away from mine. 'I thought I had imagined it, that day on my couch with the booze, the, the Johnnie Walker, when you, you, and then you, and you made me, and you called me father and you kissed me, and – it was you! Spawn of Satan! I didn't imagine it! I, I didn't...'

'Sshh,' I said.

'I didn't... I didn't... I, I, I...!'

He began to sob. I hugged him. I rocked him. I tried to sing him the folksongs of his childhood. 'It's all right, Father. Everything is going to be just fine. I'm here for you. Come now, Father, stoppit, hush now, it's OK...'

CHRISTMAS DAY

There is no use denying it; I am truly my father's son.

I have tried to escape it, to change it, to run away from it. It's a relief, I admit, to acknowledge my parentage! At the same time, it dredges up painful things in me. A part of me hates my father. While another part is transfixed. He is, after all, my father! His blood, his genes, his penchants, they all run in me! What does this mean? I can never forget what he did to my mother. And then, I cannot deny the yearning in me for love, his love, a love that only a father can give!

Who can escape his patrilineage? Father has tried to escape his own white ancestors, and look where he has ended up. Even in his denial, his patrilineage has followed him, imprinting itself through his teardrop nostrils, leaking through his blood into Bukhosi's emerald eyes.

What delight to know your roots! To be firmly rooted. To look into a face and see in it something of your own. To notice a familiar tic. To come into knowing of your father, of yourself.

It's because of me that the boy disappeared. It is I, I made it happen. I feel so much pressure off my chest, finally admitting this!

Having a perfectly nice family of his own, he still saw fit to push me out of my filial relationship with Dumo. I, who had already lost everything, losing not only my past, but also my Uncle Fani, who had tethered me, at least, to a semblance of a present; losing in the process, also, all illusion of substantial family roots in which to build a respectable future.

It is I who found Dumo, while we were in London. I who befriended him at the Ó Dubhghaill Pub where he worked as a bartender – what he insisted I call a mixologist, one of the last enduring art forms of our epoch. Such were his airs, a hollow fastidiousness that presented itself in his neatly pressed shirts and equally prim trousers, above which was a face losing its battle with age even though it looked like it was soaked religiously in Olay's exfoliating cream.

I was his first disciple, sitting with him in his one-bedroom flat in London listening to his dream of a Mthwakazi Republic, trying to shape its vision. With what symbols would we garnish its governing bodies? What hi-stories would it tell? Sketching drawing scribbling thinking during those days that stretched into night and then day again without our noticing. Papering the walls were hand-drawn and printed maps of various parts of Zimbabwe, fluttering goldenrod and mustard yellow in the breezy January light streaming through the windows. Spread out across the floor before us were clandestine pictures that he, Dumo, had got from God knows where, of Pumula Mission and Mbamba Concentration Camp in Tsholotsho and Lupane where my surrogate father comes from and also the Bezha area and Bhalagwe Concentration Camp in Matopo and Kezi where Mama Agnes and my mama Zodwa Nsele Khathini come from. In these pictures were the hi-stories that had been excluded from the national symbols but had instead symbolized themselves as scars on whipped backs crippled arms blinded eyes women lying sprawled in the grass with their skirts pulled up children in unnatural positions lying as though asleep. The many dried wreaths of maize stalks spread across numerous mass graves.

It was I who helped him draft the proposals for our movement, I who helped him get funding, I who listened to his wild theories about our future. I had even seen him naked (literally; he would ask me to accompany him during the winter months to his favourite spot in a wooded area just a few kilometres outside London, where we would strip, right down until we were just as we had come into this world, our little tushes trembling in the chaffing cold, and we would fling ourselves into the snow).

I I I! I who brought Bukhosi to him, so he could find the answers his own father couldn't give him. How was I to know they would start seeing each other outside of our tripartite meetings? That the boy, overbrimming with juvenile passions, would take to Dumo like a fanatic? It's clear to me that it was this that Dumo had wanted all along; someone in thrall to him, malleable to his ideas, not someone like me, who questioned him, and who pushed for our Mthwakazi idea to be a new era in the lives of our people, rather than a repetition of the old.

The match lit when I, in true Ironist fashion, asked Dumo what he thought he was doing when he accepted money from a neoliberal outfit based overseas, and which it was evident would, once it came to collect all those promises of mining rights and business contracts and what-not, derail our plans for a socially democratic Mthwakazi Republic. He laughed, Dumo, that deriding laugh he had taken on especially with me of late, and told me to stop being stupid, there was a time for ideology and a time for practicality, and he had to make things work under imperfect conditions, kind of like when they first taught you at school that 1 – 2 = it can't, and then later they told you that no, actually, it can!

'Why are you always mocking me?' I said, feeling, I admit, rather petulant.

'I wouldn't be bothering with you if I didn't see something in you, boy,' he said. 'If I didn't care for you. But you keep on fighting me, all the time it's this and that, I mean, when will you take action? Can't you see the value in what we're doing? All right? Because poking holes in our plans and all of that, it's just so easy, boy. The hardest thing is to act! When are you going to open yourself up to the possibilities before us?'

'I am open.'

He cackled. 'You, open? You are as tight-fisted as our ATM machines, these days. Won't even spit out just one hundred-million-dollar note. My God! Allow yourself to be vulnerable, for once. Do this Mthwakazi thing with me!'

'But wait a minute—'

'Stop with that! This is your problem, Zamani, all your what-is-truth and oh-Dumo-you-sound-like-our-politicians and your wait-a-minutes! I've tried to teach you, boy. You can't even be bothered to learn the Queen's totems properly. You were the closest thing that I've had to a son, but I've had enough!'

He thought of me as his son? Although I had been the one, ever since our meeting in London, to put effort into cultivating our relationship, trying to get close to him and gain his affection, it hadn't dawned on me that he could adopt me as his son, that anyone could adopt me as their son!

'Lord knows I've tried with you. But you're like a wall! Everything keeps bouncing back. Even the young boy, Bukhosi, agrees with me that at times it feels as though you aren't in this thing hundred per cent.'

'You've been talking about me with the boy?'

'Look, why don't you take some lessons from him? The boy's heart burns with a hot flame! His passions surpass even mine. He'll go far, that one.'

'I believe in the movement!' I cried to him. 'I believe in you!'

He looked at me sadly, did Dumo, and clapped a hand on my shoulder. 'The trouble is, Zamani – I don't know if I believe in *you* any more. I need people who take after me. People who will learn from me. Look at your Bukhosi.' And then he turned his back on me. 'I'm tired of your endless what-whats. Hayi ah.'

Those words were a scythe through the heart. The boy was pushing me out, and Dumo was letting him! Evidently, they had been meeting without me, and discussing me, making plans for the movement that involved just them two. After everything I had done for Dumo! Meanwhile, back at home, the boy was becoming more and more of a brat, openly insolent to our father, criticizing Mama Agnes's cooking, refusing to help around the house.

Didn't he know what he had?

It would be only a matter of time, I realized, before I would be left out in the cold, unbonded from Dumo, without any support system, no Uncle Fani tears to wipe, nothing, only a hollowness that had been growing and would continue to grow, a negation of the self, of *my* self; a walking lie.

But what could I do? I was quite aware of the fact that no matter how many times I proved myself, whatever acts of service I did for Dumo, I would never again be granted a seat in the inner circle. He had metaphorically and literally turned his back on me. Never get to bask in his erudition, never luxuriate in his heady speeches, in the seductive force of his ideas. And more precious than that was the sense of identity he had given me as his protégé. He had even called me his son. In the most beautiful way, that casual, everyday way a father claims his own, without even giving it thought, because it's such an inherent part of him.

This is what Bukhosi was stealing from me. And Dumo was letting him.

At the Mthwakazi rally, the boy wore one of Dumo's blue propaganda shirts that read: *Mthwakazi – A Better Tomorrow!* His smiling face printed beneath the caption. I had thought to wear that shirt, in spite of the vulgarity of having Dumo's face on it, like some cult leader. But when I saw the boy wearing it, owning it, Dumo slapping him on the back, calling him 'mfanami' ('It looks good on you, mfanami!'), I couldn't bring myself to do it.

I admit I did, before the start of the rally, slink off to the gents to cry. It had wrenched my heart, seeing them together like that.

We were expecting a moderate crowd, because it was supposed to be a secret rally, formally lodged as a pre-Christmas holiday gathering. In spite of this, the gathering was a thousand-fold strong! Word had reached our people, and they came from Bulawayo's nooks and crannies, even all the way from Victoria Falls and Gwanda. By eleven in the morning, Stanley Hall was bursting!

The early October spring was purple with promise. Through the windows of the hall, I could see the flame-lilies raging, sunflowers sashaying, and the jacarandas had come out in full bloom and were busy sprinkling their confetti. Next to me, Bukhosi stood with his hands folded across his chest, uncharacteristically still, although his eyes kept darting about, every so often resting on me, and then looking away, and then coming back to me. At first, I pretended not to notice, until I couldn't take it any more and turned to him, snapping, 'What?'

He shook his head and mumbled that it was nothing. I flashed him a grim smile. He tried to smile back, but couldn't do it, and in the end, he had to look away.

The crowd cheered as Dumo lumbered onto the stage. Bukhosi broke out of his quietude, cupped his mouth and whistled at the stage. He slapped my shoulder. Chuckled. Bum-jived my little tush. I tried to smile, but I was trembling. My legs were trembling. My hands were trembling. My heart, everything... I was a shamble of shivers. But Dumo's voice was strong. He was warming up the crowd when the sound reached us, a low keening, swelling slowly, like a drone, rising in pitch. Police sirens.

The crowd dissolved into chaos, mothers and daughters running with their hands clutching their breasts, fathers and sons thrusting desperately through the air. I turned to run. But Bukhosi grabbed my hand. He wouldn't let go, even as I tried to shake him off. He clung to me, threatening to drag me down with him. I had to lug him along as I ran.

I could smell it as we ran, The Revolution, stinking up the air like *Notes of a Native Son*, the notes clear and smooth and liquid black, like the last keys of *Epthalia* pumping to the dither of a dying heart.

Shrill in the air, ever so shrill.

And it wasn't the smell of the sewer that reached my nostrils, no. It was something altogether more familiar, like my own shadow; the reek of sweat – so much like fear that I almost didn't recognize the difference – good old Bulawayo sweat, like the musty scent of summer; somewhere the ntswiiii of a chicken bus, the shudder of feet; I could feel it, that pulse of a city-on-the-run.

Sweet and heady and oh-so-bloody.

Because what's a revolution without a little blood?

Securing my own family was just that, a revolution with a little blood – Bukhosi's blood.

I ran, I who had sold my life to Dumo's dreams – fleeing the one who had dreamed this life I was living and made me live it. Nothing but a scribble of cloud in a clean sky, cold blue like the heart of a slave, icy where the embers once burned. My heart tried to leap out of my chest, wanting to soar, to find a ray of sun and lie stunned like a dew of hope. My face straight as death, dead as solemnity. Shimmering like a chimera between vinous puffs of wild chocolate, that cocoa-coloured wet dream dripping unfettered from the glands of the imagination.

Through the screaming crowd we ran, the boy and I, and across the road to a brambly bush growing out of the fence of McKeurtan Primary School. There we sidled into a shallow pit I had dug earlier, before the start of the rally, beneath the brush, sufficiently hidden from view.

Because it was I who had informed on Dumo.

It was I who had called our nation's toll-free number and told them about the rally.

It was I who got rid of the boy.

I informed on the movement so as to punish them both. And yes, I beckoned Bukhosi to safety – only because I wanted to make sure he ended up with the wargs and orcs, as I had intended. He was panting like a dog and his skin was slithery with sweat. Busy grinning stupidly at me. I saw my chance when a pair of black boots galumphed past our brambly bush. I squeezed the boy's hand to still his heart; his breathing was spookily loud. His grin widened as he nodded, trying to quieten down, gulping air through his open mouth. I winked at him and smiled. My smile evaporated as I grabbed him by his slithery arm and pressed my hand to the small of his back. I shoved him, hard. He stumbled out of our hiding place, hitting the ground with his shoulder, skidding right into the policeman's boots.

He looked up and looked at me. His eyes were wild. They were the last thing I saw. Those emerald eyes of his glinting with surprise. And then the policeman pulled out his baton and went to work on him. *Di di* thud thud punch punch, like that. His eyes never left me. I cringed and looked away briefly, catching sight of the wide-eyed pupils of McKeurtan Primary School standing along the school fence to my right, watching the policeman beating up the boy, clinging to the fence like shrubs, their shirts a summer viridescent, their jerseys a spring verdant. They began to cry.

I'm no monster; I didn't enjoy witnessing the policeman beating him like that. I would have stopped it, if I could. All I had wanted was for them to take him away, clean and fast, with no fuss. I hadn't known they would brutalize him before my eyes, like that. And he, he could have sold me out. He could have cried out to the policeman or pointed at me or something. But he didn't. He just kept staring at me. The policeman grabbed his bloodied arms and dragged him to a police van parked outside Stanley Hall across the road, like he was a sack of mealie-meal. Like he was nothing.

I stared at the police van across the street, glimpsing the boy, who was still looking at me, his emerald eyes a fierce, sparkling green, and next to him Dumo, whose face was a congealed mass of blood. Just a glimpse, and then the police van slammed shut and swallowed them and they were gone.

Everyone has been glum, and Christmas Day has been sombre even though the ZESA people wished us a Merry Christmas by not taking away the electricity and Mother performed her black market magic and got us a leg of lamb to roast, complete with carrots, spinach, celery, beetroot, cucumbers, tomatoes, butternut, gem squash, cauliflower, potatoes, sweet potatoes and garlic paste, which she whipped up into a most delicious stew along with some salads, boiled squash, mashed butternut and potatoes baked in butter, garnished with a dollop of fresh cream and a sprig of parsley on top. It's all for Bukhosi, she keeps saying, peering out the window, wondering what time he will arrive.

'And then?' she asked this morning when Father walked into the kitchen, saw me, groaned, turned around and shuffled back into the sitting room.

I leaned in, speaking out of the corner of my mouth. 'I think it's because of the talk I gave him a few nights ago, Ma. I told him I won't let him beat you, not when I'm around. I don't care what it is you've done. Even this thing with the Reverend Pastor, it's not your fault, I told him. If he had been taking care of his business like he should have…'

She blushed, Mother, and lowered her eyes.

'He tried to chase me away,' I said, shaking my head.

'What?' she looked up at me.

'Yes, Ma! He wants to remain here with you, by himself, so he can do whatever he wants to you. He knows that as long as I'm around, I won't let him lay a finger on you. Do you need help with those veges, Ma?'

She handed me the knife, and then froze. Looked me up and down. Stared at my lime sports shirt with the Nike tick on the left breast. 'Where did you get that shirt?'

I looked down innocently at my shirt, and then looked back up innocently at Mother. 'Why, this old thing, Ma?'

'Bukhosi. That's Bukhosi's shirt.'

'Oh? He also has a shirt like this? This is mine. I've always had it. I love it so, it's my favourite.'

She frowned. Looked long and hard at my lovely shirt, then shook her head as if shaking away a dream before handing me the knife and motioning to the cucumbers, mumbling, 'Thin slices, I want really thin slices.'

For Christmas, we cooked a meal large enough to feed a multitude. She had meant it to be for our lunch, but when four p.m. chimed and still there was no sign of Bukhosi, Father complained that he was starving. We were in the sitting room, seated at the cobalt kitchen table, the lamb roast laid out on a tray in the centre, surrounded by the dishes of baked potatoes, mashed butternut, boiled squash, stew, spinach-and-tomato salad in a dash of olive oil, cauliflower-and-carrot salad in fresh cream, and sliced cucumbers sprinkled with black pepper. Mother had put out her best cutlery, even allowing us to use her squat, crystal glasses to drink water.

I quickly piped up that Bukhosi could eat when he arrived and we would get the pleasure of his company all the same. Father looked up at me sharply, then. He announced, suddenly, that he wasn't hungry.

'But you just said you were starving,' Mother said.

He mumbled something about wanting to lie down and eating later, getting up as he did so.

I suggested that he ought to sit and eat with us. We didn't want Mother's efforts to go to waste, did we? It would be better to eat as a family.

'I *insist*,' I added when he seemed to hesitate.

Sighing, he sat down, and asked for the water jug.

I handed him the jug, which he seemed to accept reluctantly.

Mother went over to the wall, stood on my brother Bukhosi's sofa, unhooked his baby portrait from the wall, got down, came back to the table and placed it on the empty seat before his plate.

Father watched her but said nothing. We closed our eyes to say grace. Mother asked the Good Lord to bless this meal, asked him to bless our Bukhosi, wished our Bukhosi a Merry Christmas, asked the Lord to look after our Bukhosi and bring him back safe and sound, told the Lord she loved her husband dearly and that she hoped the Lord made sure her husband knew this, then said a loud Amen. When we opened our eyes, Father was glaring at her.

She said, 'Please will you cut the lamb for us, Baba?'

'Why don't you ask the pastor to do it for you.'

Mother blushed, then got up and picked up the knife. I got halfway up out of my chair.

'Let me do it, Mama.'

'Sit down,' said Father.

I sat down. We watched, silent, as Mother carved the lamb roast, which was tender and didn't take much effort. Father allowed her to dish for him lamb roast and boiled squash and mashed butternut and baked potatoes and stew and spinach-and-tomato salad and cauliflower-and-carrot salad but shook his head no to the sliced cucumbers.

'Are you sure?' she said. 'They taste really good. I put a little bit of chilli, I know how much you like it.'

'Are you sure it is I who likes chilli and not the pastor,' said Father.

Mother put the dish down. Her hands touched the lamb rack, then the potato tray, then the spinach-and-tomato salad bowl, and then, patting her weave in an absent-minded fashion, she finally took her seat next to Father, and began to nibble on her food. I ate heartily, smacking my lips hmmm hmmm every now and then, complimenting Mother on her delectable dishes; but it was no use, they both ignored me, Mother staring at her plate, Father glaring at Mother, neither of them eating their food.

To waste such scrumptious food during these foodless times in this nation ought to be a punishable offence.

After the disastrous lunch, with much of the food still remaining on the table, in criminal heaps despite my best efforts to demolish it, I decided to show Mother and Father the Christmas present I had got them. I asked them to remain seated, rushed to my pygmy room and returned with a framed portrait, of myself, slightly bigger than Bukhosi's enlarged baby portrait. I had it retouched and framed at the Kodak shop in town a few days ago. It took a long time for me to get just the right photo. I tried all the poses for the cameraman at Kodak, tried putting a hand on my waist, tried to stand tall, tried a sitting position, tried smiling, tried frowning, tried to wear no expression at all; but it was no use, for all my photogenic properties, none of the pictures had that imposing quality that my father has in his photos. And so, finally, I photoshopped a snapshot of me smiling what I hoped was an overpowering smile onto a photo of my father, the one where he looks super regal in his navy blue Air Commander's uniform. Now, that's a photo!

I held it up to Mother and Father, beaming. Father was gaping at the photo. Mother smiled politely, cocking her head. 'I didn't know you wanted to be a soldier,' she said. 'Where did you get that uniform from?'

I shrugged. 'Oh, I borrowed it from... my friend,' I said, baring my teeth at Father, who now sat slumped on his chair by the table, agape, hand frozen, crystal glass in mid-air. 'He was very happy to lend it to me. I told him it was a gift for you both, and that I wanted to look my best. He says to say hello. You hear that, Father? Our friend says hello.'

Father moaned.

Mother frowned at him. 'Are you all right?' When he didn't

respond, she sighed sadly; no doubt she thought he was ignoring her because of her shenanigans with that Reverend Pastor. She turned back to me, raising an eyebrow at the portrait. 'It looks… good. Thank you. I'm sorry we didn't think of getting you anything, what with everything that's been happening…'

'Your cooking is present enough, Ma!' I said, turning around to face the sofas. I pretended to look around the room, as though searching for the perfect spot for the portrait. And then, I made my way to the boy's sofa, climbed it, and fastened my portrait to the nail on the wall, in the space where his had been.

'What are you doing?' cried Mother.

'I thought it would sit perfectly here,' I said, twisting my neck to give her an innocent look, my hands still holding the portrait. She had stood up.

'That's where Bukhosi's photo sits,' she said, no longer smiling.

'Oh, I can always take it down when he returns,' I said. 'I'm sure he won't mind.'

Before either of them could interfere, I whipped out my Nokia, frowned at the screen for several moments, and then said, 'Oh, look! A message from Bukhosi.'

Mother's face lit up. 'What does it say?'

I turned to Father, smiling. I got down from the boy's sofa and opened the Facebook message. I read out loud:

Hey, bra! I hope all is good! How's ma? I won't be coming any more, at least not til maybe next year! I got a job n im working over the Xmas break. I need more time away. Tell Baba I'm working thru all the stuff he did 2 me, I just need time away to sort thru the trauma he caused me n forgive him properly. N u can use my room while I'm away. In fact, we can share,

I'd love nothing more than to be around my big bro! Love u, bra!
Will holla soonest.
Xx
Khosi

Mother's smile evaporated. 'So, he's not on his way already?'

I cluck-clucked sympathetically. 'It seems not. I'm sorry, Ma. At least, he's keeping in touch! He says he'll come after the Christmas break. That's something to look forward to.'

But she didn't smile. She sighed, slid to her chair and cupped her head. Father, too, shut his eyes, bowed his head into his hands and sighed. Mother blinked at him, and then looked at me with her eyebrows raised.

I shook my head with what I hoped was the right measure of confusion, walked over to Father and nudged his shoulder. He looked up.

'Isn't it good news, Father? The boy is willing to forgive you. He understands the power of forgiveness. Isn't that great?'

But he was looking beyond me at the wall. I followed his stare, to my portrait.

It has just the perfect pictographic ambiguity, just like that picture, *My Wife and My Mother-in-law*, by W. E. Hill, where one moment, you see a young belle with her face turned away, and the next moment, you see an old woman with a hooked nose, all in the same photo. I can see how to Father I look, in that portrait, dressed as I am in that august Air Commander's uniform, like a revitalized, younger, handsomer version of my father, Black Jesus, and then, to someone like Mother, I look just like me, Zamani.

I turned away from the portrait, back to Father, whose eyes, now shimmering, were glued to it. 'Isn't my photo great? Don't I look handsome in it?'

He whimpered.

I turned to Mother, whose eyes, too, I was annoyed to see, were glistening. 'I'm sure my little bro will write to us soon with the exact date of his arrival,' I said. 'I'll write and ask him. He wouldn't want us to have a sad Christmas. Let's not spoil what should be a happy day. Now,' I beamed at them both, Mother and Father. 'When shall I move in?'

ACKNOWLEDGEMENTS

Special thanks to Samantha Shea who, by the sheer force of her belief in this work, made magic happen. I am grateful to Maria Guarnaschelli for her encouragement. A very special thank you to the wonderful James Roxburgh for his heroic editing, and to Ashley Patrick for her brilliant editorial eye. It has been magical – ngiyabonga! Thank you to everyone at Georges Borchardt, Atlantic Books and W. W. Norton for welcoming this book and its author.

I am greatly indebted to the Iowa Writers' Workshop for the support it gave this young writer from Zimbabwe, making the years I spent there some of the most crucial to this work. Thank you to Connie Brothers, Deb West, Jan Zenisek and Kelly Smith. Many thanks to Lan Samantha Chang, T. Geronimo Johnson, Charles D'Ambrosio and Bennett Sims for the care you showed *House of Stone*. To NoViolet Bulawayo, Garth Greenwell, Nyuol Lueth Tong, Marcus Burke and Jamel Brinkley; thank you for going above and beyond. Thank you to those who have accompanied me on this journey, including but not limited to Nana Nkweti, Okwiri Oduor, Nicholas Richards, Dini Parayitam, Avro Chakraborty,

Heidi Kaloustian, Christa Fraser, Bongani Ncube Zikhali, Kwandi Ncube, Nothando Moyo, Sinokuthaba Moyo, Mabel Mnensa, Micah Stack, Alexia Arthurs, and David Wystan Owen. Work on this novel was supported by a Maytag Fellowship, a Teaching Writing Fellowship and a Rydson Award from the Iowa Writers' Workshop; many thanks to the University of Iowa, and Laura and Marlyn Rydson, for their generosity. My work was also supported by the Kimmel Harding Nelson Center for the Arts, an Inprint Fondren Foundation/Michael and Nina Zilkha Fellowship, and a Rockefeller Foundation Bellagio Arts and Literary Arts Residency; thank you.

I am indebted to my mother, Thenjiwe Dube-Moyo, my sister, Nobubelo Moyo, and my family back home, who have been supportive throughout the writing of *House of Stone*. Thank you to Mama Burke, Xandria Burke and Ayana Burke for your love and support. And to the beautiful people of my homeland, Zimbabwe, you full of abundant hope you, you tender people you, this was all about you, all about us, all about everything.

Ngiyabonga!

Houston, Texas
February 2018